DOZEN DATES

BY MEGAN CRAWFORD

Dozen Dates

Megan Crawford

Text copyright © 2025 Megan Crawford

No part of this book may be reproduced in any form or by any electronic or mechanical means, including information storage and retrieval systems, without permission in writing from the author. The only exception is by a reviewer, who may quote short excerpts in a review.

Without in any way limiting the author's exclusive rights under copyright, any use of this publication to "train" generative artificial intelligence (AI), including but not limited to large language models (LLM), to generate text is expressly prohibited. The author reserves all rights to license uses of this work for generative AI training and development of LLM.

This book is a work of fiction. Names, characters, places and incidents either are products of author's imagination or are used fictitiously. Any resemblance to actual persons, living or dead, or events is entirely coincidental.

Megan Crawford

Cover design and formatting by Laolan Art

*To anyone who has ever felt broken.
I see all the beautiful pieces that make you whole.*

Note from Author

If you prefer to enjoy Dozen Dates without the open door spicy scenes, please avoid the following pages:

🌶 107 - 113
🌶 134 - 137
🌶 326 - 330

Trigger Warning

There are subjects discussed in this book that may be upsetting to some readers. For a complete list that includes some spoilers, please visit my website at: www.megancrawfordwrites.com.

Brianna's Menu of Men

Name	Nickname	Location
Derrik	Mr. Rental Car Guy	Dallas
Griffin	Mr. GQ	New York City
Preston	Marina Man	San Diego
Kevin	Scuba Steve	Hawaii
Trent	Mr. Gym Guy	San Antonio

Chapter 1

Dallas

Chris is going to kill me.

My flight to San Antonio is canceled, just like that. I scan the gate area at Dallas Love Field, hoping to share a *misery loves company* look with others nearby. An older man stomps toward the ticket counter, and the gate agents brace for impact.

A young woman melts into her boyfriend's arms, her forehead tucked under his chin like they're posing on the cover of a romance novel.

Gross.

But I can't look away—they're dressed like they raided a Hawaiian gift shop. He's in a button-down, she's in a floor-length sundress, both covered in the same white hibiscus print, as if they coordinated their outfits for a luau.

If my eye roll was audible, it would shatter every window in Terminal B. Dramatic? Maybe.

I direct my attention to the real problem. *How am I supposed to get to the finalist meeting that starts in a few hours?*

Sure, I've had flights canceled before—comes with the territory when you live out of a suitcase twenty-five weeks a year.

Usually, it's no big deal because I'm a responsible adult who flies out the night before. But I haven't been home in weeks, and I couldn't miss Sara's birthday party. The woman rarely gets five minutes to herself since their baby arrived, let alone an entire evening where she's the center of attention.

Passengers scatter like ants whose hill just got kicked, everyone scrambling to execute Plan B. The departure board flickers with cancellations, a digital cemetery of travel dreams.

I open my airline app to find I've been auto-rescheduled to a flight that leaves in three and a half hours. I'm willing to be late for plenty of things. My sales executive's reputation and numbers aren't among them. He once had a woman pulled off his account because she was late to a client meeting.

Missing our finalist meeting in San Antonio isn't an option. Chris has busted his ass for six months to land this client, sweet-talking his way through initial pitches and playing up the data intelligence platform. But when they ask him about API integrations, he'll be about as useful as a screen door on a submarine. His charm and good looks only get him so far—and today, they won't get him far enough.

This leaves me with one viable option.

The route materializes on Google Maps: Dallas to San Antonio—four and a half hours of Texas asphalt separating me from professional survival. I know the route. Sara, Beck, and I have driven it countless times when life was simpler and deadlines were suggestions rather than ultimatums. Back then, the journey mattered as much as the destination. Today, the destination is everything, and the journey is just a few hours of controlled panic dressed up as a road trip.

The little blue line from one major Texas city to the other looks deceptively simple, like the app is mocking me. *Just drive here. Easy.*

Nothing about today is going to be easy.

Making the impossible look effortless? That's my specialty. Turning disasters into opportunities? My trademark. If I could salvage a failed integration rollout with the client's CEO breathing down my neck, I can sure as hell drive to San Antonio.

Every moving walkway falls victim to a power-walk worthy of the airport Olympics as wind catches my loosely curled hair, sending it flowing past my shoulders. My carry-on wheels protest with each sharp turn as I navigate the terminal, scanning for rental car signage.

Chaos has claimed the rental car area by the time I get there. Business travelers pace in zigzag patterns, phones pressed to their ears, voices raised in the universal language of travel frustration. I scan the lines, calculating wait times like I'm optimizing an algorithm.

There—Advanced Rental has the shortest queue. I quicken my steps to beat another traveler to the line, successfully claiming victory until my purse catches the rope barrier and I nearly yank the whole contraption down with me. Instant karma at its finest.

I sway from foot to foot, my patience thinning with each shift of my weight. The guy behind the counter moves with the urgency of a sloth giving a TED talk. The woman in front of me is having an animated phone conversation about wedding venues while her white garment bag drapes across her suitcase, and even the buzz of the airport crowd around me can't drown out her bridezilla vibes.

This is fine. Everything is fine.

I check my watch: 7:43 a.m. My meeting starts at one. I'll make it, assuming no traffic disasters, construction delays, or acts of God. In Texas. On a Monday.

Chris remains in the dark about the canceled flight. Lectures from him on punctuality and prioritizing work before parties can wait. I can hear him already: "Brianna, this is irresponsible behavior," like he's my dad. And he's younger than me. Sara is my best friend. She'll always be a priority.

"Welcome to Advanced Rental, what's the name on the reservation?"

My mental spiral is interrupted by the guy behind the counter. I step forward, glancing at his name badge.

"I don't have a reservation, but I desperately need a rental car." I give Xander my best I'm-in-pain look.

"I'm so sorry. Unless you have a reservation, we're completely out." His face crumples like he's equally hurt by the words coming out of his mouth.

"How are you out of rental cars?" Heat rushes to my cheeks, indignation replacing desperation.

"The Mary Kay convention is in town," he says, so matter of factly.

I blink. "So?"

"It's the biggest conference in the west. Twenty thousand people attend. It's a massive make-over . . . get it?" His eyes crinkle and his lips tug into a grin.

I stare, speechless. Why is this guy talking to me about Mary Kay? *Side note—I didn't even know that was still a thing. Good for them, though.*

The other rental car lines stretch on, each one mocking my sense of urgency. I can't cut my losses yet.

"Great. Glad to hear that. So, I have a meeting in five hours in San Antonio and I can't miss it. Do you have a truck? A Humvee? Passenger pigeon?"

Is it the passenger pigeon reference that makes the corner of Xander's mouth twitch?

Either way, the universe hears my desperation.

A tall drink of water in a rental company polo approaches from behind the counter—brown hair, blue eyes, the kind of small-town handsome that makes you forget why you're in a hurry—and he's holding a set of keys like they're the Holy Grail.

"If you wait about an hour, you can have this one," he says, dangling the keys from his middle finger.

My gaze lingers a little too long on his rough, well-worked hands, even as I tap my foot in a steady rhythm.

"Any chance we can speed that up timeline?"

I flash him my most devastating smile—the one that got me out of a speeding ticket in Los Angeles, and has served me well in conference rooms full of skeptical executives.

He studies my face, the mind behind those blue eyes doing some sort of quick calculation. He takes a step closer and I catch his scent—outdoorsy without trying. He leans over the counter, voice dropping to a near whisper.

"If you don't mind it dirty, I can give it to you in ten minutes."

Xander's head swivels toward his coworker with the speed of a continental drift, his eyes going wide. "Are we still talking about cars?"

His question hangs in the air, and I can feel his blue eyes on me, waiting to see how I'll play this. Game on.

"Normally, ten minutes would be disappointing. But I'm in a hurry, so give it to me dirty"—I pretend to only just notice the name tag—"Derrik."

Xander turns away from both of us to hide whatever expression just hijacked his face. He pretends to busy himself at the printer as Mr. Ten-Minute-Wonder's gaze lingers on me, his smile growing. He gives me a simple nod as if saying, *Well played.*

I can totally play along with these stupid flirting games. It's the rest of it that I steer clear of. It only comes with complication and hurt. Who the hell wants that?

After Xander walks me through all the terrifying reasons why I should buy every insurance option, roadside service, and whatever other add-ons they dream up, I sign my life away in the rental agreement. Now, I sit in a row of chairs near the exit, awaiting my keys.

Several hours down the road is our final sales meeting with Mercury and if we land this account, it opens doors to bigger clients and bigger bonuses. Chris needs me there. We're a dynamic duo, and today, we either seal the deal or watch months of work slip through our fingers.

Chris may be leading the charge, but I'm the one answering the nitty-gritty questions about systems, dashboards, and training. Gift or curse? Jury's still out. I can talk ROI with the C-suite one minute, then dive into APIs and firewalls with the tech team the next. Chris always smiles when I pull my bilingual act—executive and geek in one package. He claims he'd be lost without me. But we'd be lost without him, too.

I text him about the change from flying to driving, then stash my phone before he fires back a response. He's a control freak, and me becoming an unpredictable wild card on the day he closes this deal is his worst nightmare.

"Brianna? Your car is ready. Slot A-seventy-two." I lean back and take in the tall, muscular frame blocking my view.

He seems to have lost his brazenness now that we're not separated by the rental counter. Shame.

I catapult out of the chair, barely getting out a "Thank you," my gaze whipping back for one last look at those blue eyes before I speed-walk through the doors to the rental garage. I pull my suitcase around to push it in front of me—my preferred method—when the front wheel catches in a crack of the asphalt. A *snap* echoes against the uneven ground as the wheel breaks off, sending me stumbling forward.

So much for a smooth exit.

"Are you okay?" Derrik asks as he rushes over. "I'll get it," he says, and picks up my everything-but-the-kitchen-sink suitcase.

"Thank you . . . again." My sultry comebacks are long gone, just like my ego after that near spill.

I follow behind him, attention narrowing in on his shirt stretched across the broad span of his shoulders. After fumbling with the key fob, the trunk pops open, and Derrik slides my suitcase in as if it weighs nothing. He slams the trunk shut and turns to me, that smirk playing at his lips.

"Have a good trip," he says, running his fingers through his disheveled dark hair in a way that shouldn't be as attractive as it is, then strides away.

I'll miss those eyes, but I've got a meeting to get to.

As I barrel down the highway, my fleeting moment with Mr. Ten-Minute-Wonder fades in the rearview mirror—just like every other romantic interest.

I call Sara, needing her familiar voice to calm the chaos in my chest.

"Why aren't you thirty thousand feet in the air right now?" Sara asks, the cooing of baby Grady in the background.

I sink into the driver's seat with a heavy sigh. After setting my phone on speaker in the cup holder, I recount this morning's unexpected turn of events.

"Did you get his number?" Sara asks, chuckling.

"No. Are you crazy?"

"Are *you* crazy? He was basically propositioning you. You should've taken him in the back of your rental." Mimicking my voice she says, "Put your money where your mouth is, country boy."

"I don't sound like that."

"It doesn't matter. What matters is, a hot guy was clearly

into you and you let him slip through those pretty, manicured little fingers."

My eyes roll behind my sunglasses. Why are the married ones always so eager to set up their single friends?

"He could've been the one," Sara mocks.

"Can we move on from this?" My voice strains.

"Fine. How pissed is Chris right now?" Sara loves keeping up on my work drama now that she's a stay-at-home mom.

"He requested hourly updates . . . with mile markers." I groan.

"That guy is over the top. Is he single?"

"Sara. Stop. I have no interest in dating right now." *Or ever, really.*

"You deserve to have a good guy in your life." Her teasing gives way to genuine warmth.

"Traveling half the year doesn't leave much room for dating, Sara."

"True. I mean, how would you ever stay in contact while traveling? If only there were ways to communicate while you were away from home."

"Your sarcasm is noted."

"People fall in love every day, *Brianna*. You can, too."

Her words hit closer to home than I'd like to admit.

Relationships don't follow the same rules as business deals. There's no clear ROI, no predictable outcomes—just chaos disguised as romance. Like that couple at the airport with their matching Hawaiian outfits, probably about to discover vacation love doesn't survive real life and a joint checking account.

"Have you and Evan ever worn matching outfits?" I'm curious if this is a thing.

"Stop changing the subject." Sara's exasperation carries through the phone. "You need to give this the good ol' college try. You want a partner. I know you do. But you're not making any space for it. Not all guys are like Harrison—"

Sara goes breathless.

"Call him by his real name."

"Sorry. Not all guys are like Dirtbag."

Bitter pain twists in my stomach.

Sara's voice softens. "What if you just go out on a few dates? A little dare—twelve dates over the next three months."

Damn it. She knows I don't back down from challenges. In college I always took the dares. Making an ass of myself was safer than revealing secrets. Once, I had to frolic through Main Street in a bra shouting, "I'm so pretty." Sara still threatens me with the video.

"I love that you think my dating life is a game."

"That's not what I mean, and you know it. Twelve dates. CEOs, mechanics, teachers—it doesn't matter. No commitment. Just get back out there. Have fun."

I'm not sure whether it's the sun beating through the window or her dare that's making my face flush. I adjust the air conditioning vents, blowing cool air directly on me.

"What did they eat in here?"—I wipe crumbs off the middle console—"It's gross. Crumbs everywhere. I can't even imagine—" My attention diverts to the passenger side floor. "Is that a French fry?" I lean forward, lifting my sunglasses for a better look.

"Don't you dare eat it."

"I'm not going to eat it. Besides, everyone knows the French fry window of freshness is twenty minutes."

"You're ridiculous."

I smile in acknowledgement.

"Speaking of French fries, Beck sent me over her new recipe for air-fried sweet potatoes."

After years of friendship, Sara can spot my walls going up from a mile away.

"What blend did she use?"

"Elvis Parsley with a pinch of something my baby brain can't remember."

Beck creates these awesome herb blends and they sell like hot cakes at farmers' markets. She's very creative with the names: Father Thyme, Tarragon Alley, Say It Ain't Cilantro. I use Poultrygeist whenever I make chicken.

"Shoot! Grady just threw up on me. I gotta go. I want you to think about my dating challenge. Dozen dates in three months. It'll be good for you."

"Not happening."

Chapter 2

San Antonio

I'm nearly at the client's office, and in desperate need of a bathroom. I call Chris to give him a heads-up.

"Hey," I say, applying my soft pink lip gloss.

"Hey. You here?" His voice carries both annoyance and relief.

"Almost. Are you hooked up to the projector? Did you print paper copies of the presentation just in case?" If Chris and I have learned anything during our careers, it's that technology never works when you need it to.

"They brought their IT guy up. We're good. How far you out?"

"Fifteen minutes."

"You are cutting it close."

"Thanks, Captain Obvious. I know. I'm turning onto the city streets n—Oh! There's no line at La Panadería!" My attention diverts to the pastry shop on the right.

"Don't you dare stop for pastries." He knows me well. I would stop. Instead, I press harder on the gas pedal, silently promising myself I'll come back after we nail this presentation.

"We're going after the meeting. I need bedtime snacks," I declare. It's not often I get to overrule Chris, but pastry decisions are firmly in my jurisdiction.

He laughs and hangs up on me.

You would never believe we were polished professionals the way we talk to each other.

I clip the curb turning into the parking garage, front tire screeching. Several items tumble from my purse and are now scattered over the passenger-side floor. Fifteen minutes—that's all I've got to haul ass up to the eighth floor. I snatch my purse, ignoring the trail of random items now decorating my floorboard as a gift for my future self to sort out.

My heart is still pounding when I make it upstairs, expecting to walk into a room full of annoyed executives checking their watches. As my shoulder knocks into the door frame, I see the relief settle on Chris's face.

"They're running late," Chris says, as I flop into the chair next to him.

The meeting's over, and Chris delivered his pitch flawlessly, hitting Mercury with case studies about our AI software that basically stalks the internet, tracking what customers say and what competitors are up to.

"What did you think?" He presses the fancy digital display at the elevator bays. It directs us to take elevator six.

"We killed it." I follow him through the elevator's opening doors. "That case study about finding the leaked earnings article in *The Times*—they were hooked. Makes me wonder what skeletons they're hiding."

"I noticed that, too."

My stomach growls. "I was disappointed you didn't use the burger example."

"The Burger House one?"

"Yeah. Burger House beating its competitors to market with their own value meal? That's our software in action."

Chris has his phone in hand, already checking email. "They don't give a shit about burgers. They want to know the second their competition screws up publicly so they can flood the market with messaging about how much better they are."

"True," I say. He continues to scroll. "Still think I should've brought pastries."

He smirks. "You and your pastries." The elevator dings our arrival at the lobby. "One day you're going to close a million-dollar deal with that place."

"La Panadería is the greatest place in San Antonio." I gesture wildly. "Besides the historical treasures, obviously. And the line might not be long now."

Chris taps away on his phone as the doors open. With a quick tug at his arm to steer us around the foot traffic, I continue.

"I can't wait to sink my teeth into a chocolate concha. The soft Mexican bread with that sugary topping . . ." I mime squeezing bread with both hands.

"Please don't do that with your hands. There are professionals in this lobby."

"What? This?" I raise my arms higher, exaggerating the squeezing motion until Chris dies of embarrassment and speed-walks toward the exit.

He waits outside by a cement planter, the tree inside it a splash of green against the stark urban backdrop. It's early March, and San Antonio is showing off with blue skies and that perfect temperature that makes you forget summer will soon try to kill you.

"You can get the answer on the software program Gus asked you about, right?"

"Yup. I'll email him tonight. Just need to confirm with our tech guys."

I catch myself staring as he loosens his tie. Something about how carefully coordinated he looks makes me think of that couple in matching Hawaiian outfits at the airport this morning.

"Have you ever worn matching hibiscus outfits with a girlfriend?"

He blinks, the creases at the corners of his eyes deepening as if trying to figure out how I made that mental leap.

"No. That's dumb. My brother and his wife got matching outfits for Hawaii. He said there were at least ten other couples wearing the same print."

His answer earns a smile from me.

As we approach our cars he says, "I'll message you if I need anything."

"It's as if you expect me to be online tonight working. How rude!" We both laugh, knowing I most certainly will.

In the hotel parking garage, I kneel near the passenger seat to collect everything that spilled from my purse earlier, including a bottle opener that gets more use than I'd like to admit. Sweeping my hand under the passenger seat, I feel something that definitely isn't mine. I pull out what looks like a marina

ID badge with a faded photo and the name Preston Brookes. I study the blurry headshot for a moment before sliding it into my purse. Preston whoever-you-are probably wants this back.

The car beeps twice as I lock it, echoing through the hotel's garage as I make a beeline for the stairs to street level. I'll deal with my suitcase later. Right now, those soft, seashell-shaped conchas are calling me, and I need to get there before the shop closes for the afternoon.

My stride lightens as I cross the street and peer in the bakery windows.

La Panadería's glass door yields to my pull, the metal handle sun-warmed and smooth. Scents of espresso and sugar set me at ease as I bob-and-weave around customers to see how many conchas are left in the glass case. By this time in the afternoon, locals and tourists have scoffed up most of the sweet treats.

This place is my San Antonio happy place—authentic Mexican pastries and an espresso bar that rivals anything in Seattle. I glance longingly at the bistro tables with their oversized ceramic mugs, wishing I had time to sit and savor the atmosphere. But with an early closing time and hotel check-in still ahead of me, takeout it is. I order a decaf caramel latte and snag the last three chocolate conchas. I nearly float out of there with my pink pastry box. Sara would roll her eyes at my portion control.

I cross the street to The Elysian, the most beautiful boutique hotel I've stayed at. The moment I step through the doors, the lobby greets me with its custom scent of white tea and verbena. An elegant table anchors the center of the room, topped with a gigantic vase of fresh flowers.

"Welcome back, Miss Whitmore," Grace says from behind the marble check-in counter. "Room 1010 as usual?"

"Yes, please." I set my pastry box beside my latte, the familiar ritual calming my frazzled nerves from this morning.

"I see you have your usual snacks." She grins while sliding my key card across the counter.

"Creature of habit. Want one?" I'm always eager to share my pastry love with others.

"Oh, no, thank you." She pats her stomach. "Will you be needing restaurant recommendations? Javier is in a meeting, but—"

"I'm good. Thanks, though."

I grab my coffee and pastries and walk past the concierge desk to the elevators, my phone buzzing several times along the way. The first message displays on my home screen.

> Sara: I've taken the liberty of creating you a dating profile on Tinder.

"You did *what*—" The elevator dings, cutting off my outburst.

The doors crawl open and a man inside drags his gaze from the floor to meet mine. His smile stretches wide, showing a dimple on the left side. His hands are clasped low at his waist.

"Miss Whitmore, what a pleasure it is to see you." Javier walks toward me, grinning.

"The pleasure is always mine, Javier. How are you?"

"I'm well. Quick trip this time."

He's used to seeing me for extended stays—usually four or five nights when I'm working the San Antonio accounts.

"Yes, but you can't get rid of me that easily," I say.

"I would never want to." He pauses respectfully, his expression earnest and sincere before continuing. "Have a wonderful evening. And please let me know if I can help in any way."

His lean, athletic frame strides toward his desk until the elevator door blocks my view. Always so formal, that guy. His cologne lingers in the elevator—cool water, fresh and clean. I breathe it in before I can stop myself.

The elevator ride to the tenth floor gives me just enough time for my irritation about my luggage situation to resurface. By the time I stash my pastries and drag my suitcase to my room, I'm ready to have words with Sara.

"How mad are you right now?" Sara asks as I pace in front of the TV, holding my phone with a death grip.

"Oh, let's see. On a scale of one to ten . . . one hundred." Each word comes out clipped and precise. "Why would you do that? I said no. No means no."

"In most situations involving the male species, yes, it does. But you said you didn't have time, so I figured I'd help you out." Sara's soft tone usually gets her out of trouble. It did in college; it does with Evan. But not tonight.

"Sara. This is crossing the line, even for you." My finger stabs the air emphatically.

"B, I'm sorry, I'm just trying to help."

"Help? You created a dating profile without my permission. With my photos. My information. You completely disregarded my feelings like they don't matter." My voice goes up an octave.

"Of course they matter. But B, you haven't been on a date in years. Not since—"

"I don't need you shoving that in my face." My words slice through the air.

"But what about the goals we made after college?"

"Just because you have your perfect little family—" The sentence dies on my lips. I suck in a breath, knowing I can never take back what just came out of my mouth.

"Wow. Okay."

I rub my hand down my face. I officially went too far.

"I didn't mean it like that," I say, my voice full of regret. "It's been a stressful day."

"I know. And I'm sorry, B. I'm so, so sorry." A forceful sigh comes through the speaker before she continues. "But I'm not backing down on this. I saw who you were before him and I see who you are after him. When he left, he took your light. And you let it happen."

My eyes burn and I squeeze them shut.

Sara has used her corporate coaching tactics on me in the past when it comes to him. The whole *guide you to your own conclusions* approach that works so well in boardrooms. She throws a series of questions my way in hopes I will uncover the knowledge that she thinks I don't already know.

He broke me. There is nothing to uncover. The man broke my spirit, my soul, my confidence. He made me doubt my own judgement. He made me lose trust in myself. He wiped the slate of my future. A path paved out for the next sixty years, erased. No man has ever brought me to my knees like he did. Not *that way*, at least.

"He's been out of your life for years, and he still has power over you," she continues. "It breaks my heart."

A tear escapes and I pat it away. What I hate the most is knowing that people around me notice how he still affects me.

"I'm not asking you to find a husband. I'm asking you to go have fun. Explore new places. Have conversations that don't involve technology or dashboards."

"But I like talking about technology and dashboards."

Sara laughs. "You're such a nerd."

I twist my waves into a ponytail off my neck. "Can we move on from this for now? Because this conversation is exhausting and I have one more thing to share." Now that I've worn out the carpet from my pacing, I sink into the desk chair.

"*For now*, but make it quick. Grady's getting fussy and Evan is giving me the *please help* look."

"I found this guy's marina ID in my rental today."

"Like, he works at the marina?"

"No, he has a boat there. It says *Slip* 23 on it."

"What's his name? I'll do some investigative work when I feed Grady later."

"Preston Brookes."

I spend the next ten minutes recapping my travel nightmare while Sara alternates between sympathetic noises and laughing at my expense. Finally, she has to go—Grady's bath time. She's always been rigid about her routines. She even created our schedules in college too. I had weekly printouts of when we went to the gym, did homework, and had free time. I never followed them.

I grab the box of pastries and my lukewarm latte and open my laptop, ignoring the flashing instant message from Chris, and clicking on LinkedIn from my bookmarks. I click the search field, type Preston's name in, and sink my teeth into the concha.

Mmm . . . Sugary heaven.

"There he is." My eyes widen as I lean back. Of course he's attractive. Because this day needs one more complication.

I scroll through his profile, absorbing snippets of his career progression and endorsements. His work history reads like a greatest hits of tech companies—all director and vice president roles.

My mouse hovers over the *Message* button below his profile picture, but the flashing application on my desktop tray is like a strobe light in my face. If I don't respond soon, Chris will start calling.

Chapter 3

San Antonio

I blink away the dryness in my eyes as I close my laptop. The six o'clock news murmurs in the background. With flats on my feet and phone and room key in hand, I head to the hotel bar.

As the elevator doors open to the ground floor, the familiar scent of white tea and verbena wraps around me. Staring into the mirror across the hall, I tuck the unruly waves back into my ponytail before I exit, and force a smile I don't feel.

"Good Evening," the bartender calls, smiling as I approach. I eye the bar stool, clearly designed for a seven-foot giant. As in the past, it takes two tries and an undignified wiggle to climb up. When I finally settle, he's still watching me, amusement flickering across his face. "What can I get you?" He polishes a wine glass without looking away.

"I'll take your house cabernet." I set my phone on the live-edge wooden bar and return his smile. After today, the wine will be a welcome reprieve.

Leaning back, I feel the curved backrest pressing comfort into my spine. My eyes sweep the bar—couples everywhere. To my left, a man feeds his girlfriend olives from the charcuterie board between them. To my right, Grace checks in two women at the front desk, their body language intimate and familiar.

A woman appears beside me, tapping my shoulder. "Is someone sitting here?" She gestures to the empty stool.

"Nope. All yours."

"Thanks." She settles in and immediately turns to the woman who follows her. They order matching wines and fall into easy conversation, as if I've become invisible.

With desperate fingers, I unlock my phone, seeking distraction from the sea of coupled bliss surrounding me. My feed opens to a family photo posted by a friend from high school. I zoom in—identical smiling faces that match their identical shirts. I read the caption: *Family is Forever. Blessed to be a mom and wife.* Something heavy settles in my chest.

I tap on the three dots above the photo and snooze Candice for thirty days. *Enough of you, Candice.* The bartender slides a stemmed glass my way.

"Can I get you anything to eat?"

"I'll take the hummus plate." My voice sounds steady, even when it doesn't really feel that way.

At the end of the bar, the charcuterie woman lets out a soft giggle. The guy she's with leans in, arm draped over her chair, his mouth brushing her ear.

Looking elsewhere, I take another sip. The wine cuts sharp and bitter across my tongue.

It's not that I hate people who are happy. It's that I don't believe I can have that anymore. The realization sits heavy in my stomach. Growing up, I wanted the whole picture—marriage, kids, and sunburned mornings at soccer games. A life that felt settled and bright. I thought I had it. With Dirtbag. He was my home, my future, the father of children who would never exist.

Of course I want what Sara has, what that couple at the end of the bar has. But it feels as if someone tore it out of my hands and told me not to ask for it again. So why try? Why be let down? My throat grows tight. I stare at the swirling red in my glass, the thought of another disappointment, another person walking away.

The textured edge of the bar grounds me, keeping my tears at bay as my fingers trace its rough ridges.

I know I lost my light. *I lost everything*. The future we planned. The love I couldn't wait to give. All of it, scraped out of me like someone hollowing my chest with a dull spoon.

But what kills me the most is that Sara sees it. For years, I thought I was hiding the emptiness. That if I could fool everyone else, I could fool myself, too.

I hate knowing I'm different *because* of him. That he took more than just my hopes and dreams when he left. I hate that she's right.

The bartender slides the hummus plate toward me, and the charcuterie couple stumbles toward the elevator, arms tangled like they're afraid to let go. I grab my phone and open LinkedIn. At least I can end this shit show of a day with one good deed.

The next morning, I head to the lobby for breakfast. Today will be a new day. Javier is standing behind his concierge desk when our eyes meet.

"Good Morning, Miss Whitmore."

"Good Morning, Javier." His soft blue button-down shirt looks like it was tailored just for him.

"Will you be joining us for breakfast?" He extends his arm behind him.

"I can't pass up the infamous Elysian breakfast bar."

He quirks an eyebrow. "Infamous, I like it."

I follow him to the table closest to said breakfast bar.

"Will you have time to visit the Riverwalk before you head home?" he asks, motioning for me to take a seat in a wingback chair.

"Sadly, no. My flight is in four hours." I drop my laptop bag and purse onto the empty chair next to me. My broken suitcase is already stashed in the car.

He clasps his hands low in front of him.

"When you come back, allow me to make some recommendations for you and your colleagues. There's a new Italian restaurant with seating right on the river. It's excellent." He gestures a chef's kiss.

I smile. "Thank you, Javier. That sounds great."

He nods and steps back. "Enjoy your breakfast."

My eyes track him as he walks away. I thought Chris and I were formal when speaking with our clients, but Javier takes it to a whole other level.

The breakfast bar includes everything from tiny pastries to the usual eggs, bacon, and rosemary potatoes. I reach up for a white plate, still warm from the dishwasher. Elegant tongs wait in front of the gold-accented chafing dishes.

An employee replenishes the fruit basket at the far end while I lift the lid on the eggs. Real eggs—small miracle in a hotel breakfast buffet. I load up on the rosemary potatoes, figuring I'll need the fuel for my flight to NYC.

Rebellion strikes when I place the tongs back on the spoon rest. They snap open and catapult themselves off the table. *Shit.*

A backward glance confirms my good luck—no witnesses.

A new appreciation for wingback chairs blossoms in my mind as I squat down, my pencil skirt banding my legs together. The tongs have bounced halfway under the table.

I wobble as I stand, pinching my skirt in place, then hide the tongs behind the chafing dish before continuing down the table. If this is the start to my day, God help me. With my plate loaded, I find my table again and slide into the chair, trying to reset my morning.

Buttery flakes of pastry stick to my lip gloss as I bite into a croissant. Last night's conversation with Sara won't leave me. Her words echo as I stab at my scrambled eggs with unnecessary force. *He took your light.* My fork clatters against my plate.

She's right. I've been carrying him around like dead weight for years, letting his ghost influence my decisions. Every time I meet someone new, a voice whispers in my ear.

Remember how this ends? They'll discard you, just like he did.

I take a sip of coffee, the bitterness matching my mood. When did I become this person? When did I let someone who couldn't be bothered to show up for me when I needed him most still control whether I show up to my own life?

The dating app idea is ridiculous. Of course a *married* person suggests it. I can't. I just can't. You know why? Because it feels like a full-time job I didn't apply for. I'm supposed to clock in after work and swipe through a lineup of men holding dead fish, and I'm supposed to swoon? Absolutely not.

Sara will emphasize that 'it's just for fun.'

There's nothing fun about staring at my phone while some stranger says 'hey' and then disappears for three days. Or worse, they *don't* disappear. They just keep sending dry, boring responses like, 'wyd.' What do you mean, what am I doing? I'm *sitting here regretting ever matching with you.*

And then if I do agree to meet someone, it's a gamble. He

could be fine, or he could look nothing like his photos and talk about crypto for two hours while I'm stuck with a fourteen-dollar cocktail and no escape route. That's if he actually shows up. And how many guys do I have to meet before I actually find one worth my time?

Twelve dates with strangers sounds like twelve opportunities for awkwardness and disappointment.

I drink deeply and shut my eyes, my head rolling back as my tension finally breaks.

But maybe that's the point. Maybe it's the perfect catalyst to finally leave Dirtbag's dark cloud in the past.

My thumbs hover over my phone's keyboard. Am I really going to do this? Once I agree, there's no going back. No more excuses about being too busy or too tired or too anything. If all else fails, I can treat them like business meetings until this dating dare is over. I text Sara my decision.

> Me: All right. I'll do your stupid challenge. But I won't enjoy it.

> Sara: That's the spirit.

I already regret my decision. Dating apps are like breakfast buffets. You think the eggs and bacon are the best the buffet offers, but then you spot the waffle station down the line with all the toppings. Your eggs grow cold while you second-guess yourself, wondering why you chose them in the first place before abandoning them completely.

> Me: But it's going to be on my terms. I will meet these guys "in the wild."

> Sara: How about a compromise? In the wild and on the dating app.

Tossing my phone into my purse, I grab my coffee mug just as a gentle squeeze lands on my shoulder. Chris's handsome face appears above me.

"I can see your nose hairs from here," I say, squinting my eyes as if taking a deeper look.

He steps back, covering his nose. "Don't be jealous that your nose isn't as cute as mine."

He smirks and reaches for my laptop bag. I tip my head back, savoring the last sip of coffee, not tasting as bitter as it did a few minutes ago. A soft hum escapes my throat. I need to ask Javier where they get their coffee.

"Come on, Honker. Let's go." I stand up and bop Chris's nose with my fingertip, nudging past him toward the lobby.

We walk past Javier, who stands with a group of businessmen. His eyes are bright as he gestures to the group with sweeping motions.

"He's got T. rex arms," I murmur, nodding toward Javier.

"Ahh, yes. The dreaded T. rex syndrome. Thank God you were cured. It was painful to watch."

I level a look at him. "It wasn't *that* bad."

He rolls his eyes. "Your elbows were permanently pinned to your sides while your forearms flailed around, begging for more range of motion during presentations." He demonstrates, tucking his arms in at his waist and wiggling his hands until my laptop bag slides off his shoulder.

"My T. rex arms closed a lot of sales," I say, bumping his shoulder with mine.

I approach the check-in desk to hand over my room keys. Diane, the general manager, looks up from her computer.

"Checking out?" Her eyebrows lift, though her face stays blank.

"Yes, Room 1010." I smile, hoping to lead by example with

this whole being-nice concept she clearly missed during orientation.

I glance over my shoulder at Chris, who's a few feet back, on the phone.

"I'll finish checking out Miss Whitmore," Javier says to Diane as he steps behind the desk. "I believe Victor is looking for you."

The general manager silently stands. She turns her head toward Javier in a slow, mechanical way, as if joy is a foreign language she doesn't quite understand. Maybe some of his will wear off on her, but I'm not holding my breath.

Javier's attention shifts entirely to me, his eyes warm and focused, completely dismissing her presence. "I hope you enjoyed your stay."

"Wonderful, as always."

"I see you have an upcoming stay with us in a couple of weeks. We look forward to having you back."

"Thanks, Javier. Me too."

I turn away to cross the lobby, and my phone starts vibrating in my purse as I join Chris near the exit. It's an unknown number from Dallas.

"Hello?" I plug my right ear as Chris's voice echoes around me.

"Miss Whitmore? This is Derrik from Advanced Rental. I'm the one who gave you that . . . dirty car yesterday."

Mr. Ten-Minute-Wonder? I blink in disbelief.

"Hi, Derrik. Thank you again for doing that. You really saved me."

"No problem. I'm doing a courtesy call to make sure everything is going good with the vehicle."

Wait. Does he know about the marina ID? Did Preston call him looking for it? Is this a trap to get me to confess I found it?

"Yes. The car has been great." It might have some minor

scratches from when I clipped the curb yesterday, but nothing to disclose here.

"Great. So, uh—" My eyebrows scrunch as I wait for him to continue. "I feel bad about the dirty car."

Chris shoots me a look and gestures toward the doors. He reaches the exit first, holding the door open with one hand.

"I'd like to make it up to you," Mr. Ten-Minute-Wonder says, and then pauses. "With dinner."

My beige heels glue to the sidewalk. Chris continues to walk, oblivious to my abrupt stop.

"Dinner? As in a gift card?" One time I got a Raging Crab House gift card from the car dealership and it sat in my kitchen for months. Shellfish allergy.

He laughs into the phone. "No. I wanna take you out to dinner."

Chris turns around, noticing I'm several feet behind him. He throws both arms out in a 'what gives?' gesture.

"You want to take me out to dinner?" I should say no. This crosses every professional boundary I can think of. But Sara's voice echoes in my head about taking chances, and before I can stop myself, I'm saying, "You know what? Yes. Let's do it." My heels unglue, and I walk toward Chris, who's tapping his watch.

Chapter 4

New York

The classic yellow New York cab that Chris and I are in pulls up to The Eroquois hotel, it's chocolate-brown canopy jutting out over the entrance. Through the back passenger window, skyscrapers swallow the last of the daylight.

The thought of my upcoming date with Mr. Ten-Minute-Wonder feels as distant as these towering buildings. Sara will be thrilled that I already have a date lined up, proof that I'm taking this whole dating thing seriously. Too bad I'm only going through the motions.

Chris opens my passenger door, his dark peacoat eclipsing the brick building.

"Why do you always want to stay here?" I ask as he wrestles with my new, overpriced suitcase that I purchased at the airport. Do not get me wrong. The Eroquois is a beautiful, elegant, and timeless hotel. It sits in the heart of midtown Manhattan near Bryant Park, close to our client. But Chris racks up hotel points like stock dividends, and The Eroquois isn't part of his usual hotel chain.

"Because the name reminds me of Jamiroquai." He closes the trunk, smacking it twice and alerting the cabby to drive off.

"The English funk band from the nineties?" An amused smile tugs at my lips as I pull my coat tighter, fighting the chill.

"Yeah." His face shows zero embarrassment as he pulls open the main door.

I shake my head as I walk past him. The checkered floor of the lobby beckons just ahead, but my luggage wheels snag on the door frame, stopping me dead in my tracks.

Distracted by whatever's on his phone, as usual, Chris doesn't notice and crashes into my back. The cold coming off his coat sends a chill down my spine.

"Normal people pull their luggage behind them," he says, his voice dropped to a warm murmur against my ear. He steps closer, his chest brushing my shoulder as he reaches around me to give my bag a firm push, sending it rolling across the white and black marble floor. His cologne lingers as he pulls back with a playful smile before returning to his phone.

I catch up with my luggage and continue to push it out of spite. "Whoever said I was normal?"

"Welcome to The Eroquois!" The employee—who looks like he graduated from high school yesterday—beams with an enthusiastic smile.

Chris leans into the back of my neck and whispers, "Jamiraquoi." He can't stifle his laugh as he steps back. This guy. No wonder he's single.

"Checking in. Brianna Whitmore." I pull my wallet from my purse, grabbing my corporate card, which is nestled behind Marina Man's ID.

"Here are two complementary bottles of water for you and your husband," the employee says, still beaming.

"In her dreams," Chris mutters without looking up from his phone.

The smile slides right off the employee's face as his cheeks flush bright red.

"Please excuse my coworker," I say. "The universe hand-picked him to be my daily punishment."

"My apologies." He hands me my room key and one bottle of water.

I can't tell if he's apologizing for the husband mix-up or sympathizing with my daily punishment situation. Either way, I'll take it.

I wait across the lobby, inspecting the brochure rack and mentally checking off all the touristy places and restaurants I've been to. Traveling for work does have a few perks. I grab a brochure for Verge's BBQ. I love anything smoked—chicken, beef, potato, whiskey. Anything.

"Are you good for dinner?" Chris says as he rolls his luggage in behind me. "I'm going to meet up with Brett and the boys for drinks."

Ah, yes. Brett and the boys. I don't even know who *the boys* are. Chris has never mentioned any other names besides Brett. What I do know is they were in the same fraternity in college. Based on that fun fact alone, I'm glad I am never invited.

I turn, tapping my finger on the brochure. "Yep. I'm good."

"I'll text you if I need anything." He picks up the pace and heads down the hall toward his room.

I nod, pressing the elevator button.

My phone makes an unfamiliar noise—not a text or phone call. A notification.

Griffin Super Liked You!

"What the hell is a *Super Like*?" I mutter as I step into the elevator. It came from the dating app which I logged into earlier while we were waiting for the flight to take off. It's terrifying to see what Sara thinks is a "good" photo of me. I swapped out at least four photos before getting annoyed and closing the app all together.

I unlock my room, drop the room key and my phone on the dresser, and grab the remote to turn on the local news. I should probably deal with the notifications and unread texts on my phone. But first? Food. Smoky food.

I swipe open the food delivery app and scroll through Verge's menu. BBQ Nachos for an appetizer, the brisket dish with baked beans and their famous mac 'n' cheese for the main course. It's way more than I can eat in one sitting, but somehow it always disappears by check out. Delivery time is sixty minutes, which is surprisingly shorter than the last few times I ordered.

I flip over to LinkedIn—no new messages. I'm not sure if I'm relieved or disappointed. It's not like his ID is burning a hole in my pocket, but I'd like to close this loop and move on. I text Sara to say Preston still hasn't surfaced.

Next on deck is the dating app. I need to figure out what this *Super Like* nonsense is. I tap the tiny heart on the bottom menu. A congratulations screen appears with streamers and confetti: *Griffin Super Liked You.*

"Hello, Griffin," I say in my most seductive voice, then tap on his boyishly handsome face to view his profile. I built walls around my heart, not my vision.

My phone rings, Sara's name flashing on the screen. I mute the TV.

"Hey."

"Hey! How was your flight?"

"It was good. Chris slept the whole way while I added data to the presentation for tomorrow's meeting."

"Look at you, gettin' shit done . . . while I'm over here monitoring my child's diaper consumption trends." Sara pauses, then says, "I'm not complaining, I just miss spreadsheets."

I can't imagine the jump from Director of Finance to Director of Tummy-time. Her former life had been a blur of deadlines and conference calls. Now her days revolve around nap schedules, laundry cycles, and the unpredictable moods of a tiny human.

"I'm sure Chris is happy you're working hard on his clients," Sara adds.

I scoff. "Chris will be happy once we secure their renewal, which is coming up. We're still a little expensive." I drift over to the TV to grab the Wi-Fi info so I can get online later.

"So, nothing from Marina Man?" Sara's quick to shift the subject.

"Not yet. However, you'll be pleased to hear that I was *super liked* today." I dig through my suitcase for my llama pajamas, tossing aside wrinkled blouses. *Looks like we'll be doing some ironing later.*

"Super Liked?" Sara has been married for 12 years—to her college sweetheart. She's never had to endure the misery of dating apps.

"Yes. Apparently, if you pay more, you can super like someone and direct message them, even if they didn't swipe right on you."

I hang a blazer in the closet, attempting to beat out the wrinkles.

"Well, do you like what you see?"

I swipe through the five photos in his profile.

"He seems very worldly, based on these photos. He's forty, owns a group of hotels, and despises pineapple on pizza."

"He gets a green light for the pizza preference, but he's only forty and owns a group of hotels?" Sara doesn't do much to hide the disbelief in her tone.

"I mean, he's dressed like a *GQ* model posing in front of

beautiful landmarks all over Europe. And before you ask, no. They don't look AI-generated."

"I don't know, B."

"Need I remind you that this was *your* idea?"

I continue scrolling through his profile.

"Yeah, I know. What else does his profile say?"

"Not much. These dating sites give you stupid prompts to answer. Dating me is like . . . My weekends look like . . . My simple pleasures are . . . a favorite memory of mine is."

I scroll mindlessly up and down his profile, already over it.

"Are those really supposed to help you get to know the guy?"

"Don't be naïve. Dating apps are not about uncovering their favorite memory."

She laughs. "I know, I know. Any other matches?"

"None."

I grab my laptop and place it on the small wood desk.

"Give him a chance. You never know. And you're going out with rental-car guy when you get back home?"

"Yeah. Saturday night." My face slips into neutral.

"Your excitement is overwhelming."

I scoff into the phone so she hears it.

"He appears to be a man of few words in our text exchanges. It looks like the dirty car banter is the best he's got. It's been downhill from there." Emergency lights flash against the wall as a fire engine flies by like it's the universe warning me of what's to come. "He is taking me to my favorite restaurant, though."

"He's taking you to Casa de Sabor?" Sara's voice goes up an octave. "That's awesome. You love that place." She pauses. "Maybe he's just not a texter. Evan sucks at texting, too. It's only one data point. Besides, we're testing different models, right? You're meeting that objective."

I roll my eyes and turn back to my laptop.

"I'm surprised you don't have a spreadsheet for this."

"Who says I don't?" We both laugh. Of course she does.

Grady's cry ramps up in the background.

"Well, if you go out with Griffin while you're in New York, please enable the tracking app so I can find you if you go missing."

"There's a pleasant thought."

"It'll be fine. Happy swiping. Grady is getting fussy so I gotta go."

I end the call and look out at the city lights twinkling against the darkening sky. Even several stories up, the hum of Manhattan is constant—car horns, sirens, the distant rumble of the subway beneath the streets. Bryant Park spreads out below like an oasis of green in the concrete jungle, its tree-lined paths offering the only respite from the urban intensity surrounding it.

As I stare at Griffin's face, I begin to get cold feet. Is this what I should be spending my time on? Chasing men? I'm completely self-sufficient without one. Besides, I've been out of the game for years. My dating muscles have completely atrophied. And what about the dating lingo? Beck had to explain what breadcrumbing means as she described a girl she met last year.

This was never supposed to happen—me on a dating site. And look at me now. Scrolling Griffin's profile, reading about how dating him is like 'checking into a five-star hotel,' and how he watches sunrises over Santorini with champagne. At least there's no photo of him holding a fish.

But as I think about the matching hibiscus couple from The Elysian hotel bar, I'd be lying if I said I didn't crave that closeness. The easy affection that comes with having someone. I just don't know if I'm ready. Dating has become a foreign concept I've been running from.

I remember the goals Sara and I mapped out after college—wedding venues, which schools our kids would attend, how we'd juggle sports practices and carpool schedules. After Dirtbag, those dreams died along with everything else.

Well, here goes nothing.

> Me: Hi Griffin, thanks for the super like. I see from your photos that you like to travel. Where's your favorite place?

There's a green light next to his profile photo as I hit send. My heart does this weird flutter thing, but not from excited anticipation. More like dread. I flip to the "swiping" screen and scroll through several profiles as a distraction. Some of these guys' selfie game is seriously weak. Mirror shots in dirty bathrooms, the classic fish photos, and way too many gym selfies. Do women really swoon over shirtless photos? Those photos tell me their bare chest is the best they have to offer the relationship.

Next.

I notice a little number 1 pops up next to my messages icon.

> Griffin: Hi Brianna 😊 You have the kind of smile that would make a 12-hour flight feel like a walk around the block. Spain is my favorite. Are you a traveler too?

> Me: That's quite a line. Frequent flyer, I take it? I travel within the US, mostly.

Griffin: Guilty. ✈ Last month: Lisbon, Tokyo, and a quick stop in Patagonia. But I promise I'm not always on a plane. I'm grounded at the moment. Especially if there's a chance to get to know you.

Me: I could be a serial plant killer or allergic to international travel.

Griffin: I'll take my chances. Besides, if you were a plant killer, I'd just teach you how to keep succulents alive. And if you were allergic to travel, I'd bring the world to your doorstep.

Me: Is this your standard script or am I getting the deluxe version? Are you even real, buddy?

Griffin: At least I didn't start with "Did it hurt when you fell from heaven?" But just to prove I'm real:

He attaches a photo. Grinning in a wrinkled linen shirt, his curly hair a little windblown, holding a street taco in one hand and a napkin in the other that he wrote Hi Brianna on. It looks like he's near Times Square.

Me: So you're a taco enthusiast . . .

Griffin: Best taco I've ever had. But I think I'd have a better time if you were here. Lunch sometime?

Me: Maybe. Still deciding if you're charming or just collecting passport stamps and phone numbers.

Griffin: Fair. If it helps, you're the only one I'm messaging right now. I'm just hoping you'll say yes.

Chapter 5

New York

"You have a date?" Chris asks as we exit the client's building downtown.

"Yes, I do. And I don't appreciate the surprise in your voice." My forehead creases in a scowl.

He snorts. "Have fun, and don't get kidnapped." He swats my shoulder with his portfolio as he grins at me. "Will you be online later?"

Of course that's what he worries about.

"Yes, I will."

After dropping my laptop off at the hotel, I walk to Bryant Park to meet Griffin. He said he only has an hour. If he's a total dud, I know there's a hard stop.

The combination of the cool breeze and the warm sun makes my skin tingle as I approach the park. Or maybe that's my nerves.

New Yorkers have claimed every bistro table along the park's edge, proof that spring has finally arrived. I weave around dozens of them toward the fountain, our meeting point.

The fountain resembles an ancient copper goblet overflowing with delicious ale. People dodge the spray as a gust of wind blows through it. I spot a *GQ*-looking guy leaning against the wall of the fountain. His brown curly hair shines in the sunlight. His camel-colored, double-breasted coat looks like it costs more than my car payment. I press my fingers down my Costco puffer jacket. It was such a good deal, I couldn't pass it up. Now, I wish I did.

My heels click against the stone pavers. His head turns and our eyes lock, his smile spreads wide. Thank God he looks like his photos.

"Brianna, you look beautiful."

His sincerity catches me off guard. His hazel eyes sweep over me, slow and deliberate, like he's seeing something he wants to remember.

My skin warms under his attention. I'm not used to being looked at like this. Like I'm wanted. I guess it's been a while.

He grabs my hand but doesn't shake it. Instead, he gently drapes his other over top of mine. His hands are surprisingly warm considering it's fifty-five degrees today.

"Thanks, Griffin. Nice to meet you," I respond, feeling a bit exposed.

"Shall we?" He pushes off the fountain, sliding his hands back into his coat pockets. "I thought it'd be fun to walk through the local art." He nods to the far end of the park where large sculptures line the sidewalk.

"Sounds great."

Griffin's gaze follows me as we weave through the crowd. "I'm happy we could meet before you head back home."

"Me, too."

My attention catches on the wall of tourists blocking our path ahead. I pivot to dodge them when my heel betrays me, sending me into his arms. Perfect. I finally touch a man, and it's by accident.

"Easy there," he says, steadying us both. There's a hint of muscle under his coat—solid, but not sculpted. Like someone who works out when it's convenient.

"So sorry. I swear, I'm not the kind of woman who body-checks on the first date." I move to extract my wrist and pretend I didn't just launch myself into his personal space.

Griffin tucks his arm to trap my hand between his ribs and bicep. Pretty sure that move was intentional.

"I'm not opposed to it," he murmurs. "One more move like that and I'll start thinking you're falling for me." He winks.

I ignore his comment, and we walk in silence a few more feet until we reach the sculptures.

"These sculptures are inspired by eighteenth-century Ketharian art. Each artist was told to create something modern, but it must reflect the truest intentions from that era," he says.

I hadn't expected a personal art history lesson on this date.

"What type of art do you lean toward, Brianna?"

Shit. The only art I lean toward is my Instagram photos of strategically placed coffee and beer. "I haven't given art the appreciation it deserves in recent years. But Monet has been a favorite since high school. I love when you stand a few feet away, you see this beautiful scene of flowers and ponds. But up close, it's a jumbled mess of color."

I owe that save entirely to the movie Clueless.

Statue after statue, Griffin delivers elaborate analyses like he's studied them for years. Lady Sonterra, the matriarch who led her people to freedom. The symbolism of the clay pot's triangles. The eighteenth-century artistic vision. He studied art history in Rome, he tells me, hands clasped behind his back as he strolls from sculpture to sculpture.

It's impressive that he knows so much. It's also exhausting. There's been zero opportunity to actually get to know each other.

My aching feet are happy when we leave the final sculpture.

Griffin looks at me with a childish grin. "It's not a proper New York City experience without a hotdog. Care to join me for this local delicacy?"

A hotdog?

I hesitate, schooling my features into what I hope passes for consideration rather than bewilderment. "Um...."

This guy talks about art history for the last thirty minutes, looking like a *GQ* model, and then offers me street food? There are several grab and go restaurants nearby. I know because I've eaten at most of them.

"Sure." I force brightness into my voice, but it sounds hollow, even for me.

The cart's smell reaches us first—grilled onions that make my mouth water, undermining my disapproval. Steam curls up from the cooking surface, collecting under the dull yellow and red striped umbrella overhead.

"Two classic hotdogs." Griffin flashes a peace sign with his left hand. I smile behind him, but it's not an admiring one. This smile is pure disbelief wrapped in politeness.

The vendor's large hands push two foil-wrapped hotdogs across the cart's counter.

We find a park bench near the copper goblet fountain. Griffin unwraps his hotdog, the foil crinkling as he peels it back, releasing a wisp of steam.

"Where our story began." He grins at me.

I shift in my seat, suddenly aware of the cold bench beneath me.

When Griffin offers condiment packets, I attack the mundane task. Anything to dodge his flirtations. Naturally, the ketchup packet stages a rebellion, laughing at my first two attempts before nearly exploding across my white jacket.

"So, where is home for you?" I ask, taking my first bite. The hotdog bun, compressed by the vendor's large hands, is soggy from the steam.

"Tough question." He takes a bite and chews thoughtfully, his gaze drifting to the fountain. "Born in California. My parents traveled constantly so I went to boarding school in Boston. Been on-the-go ever since." He shrugs. "Hard to call anywhere home."

Something in his tone makes me look at him more closely. For all his confident art lectures, there's something almost wistful in the way he says it. I take another bite of my hotdog, using the moment to study his face. The core experiences that make someone who they are matter more to me than art history knowledge, but something in his posture—the way he's looking at the fountain instead of me—makes me decide to move on, for now.

"How did you get into owning hotels?"

I snatch a napkin as ketchup drips down my fingers.

"My parents are venture capitalists and invest in businesses as a hobby. They backed my first hotel, Vivante. Used those profits to buy two more." He shrugs like it's no big deal. "The rest is history."

I wipe the remaining ketchup from my fingers, giving myself time to process this casual mention of multiple hotels. Like acquiring them is as simple as weekend shopping.

"Tell me about them."

"Vivante has been a labor of love." He tilts his head just enough to catch my eye, one brow raised "It was run-down and completely neglected when I found it. The previous owner didn't appreciate its architecture or understand the old structure. He had no patience for its quirks, and refused to work with the very abnormalities that make it unique." His expression shifts.

"It just needed to be understood," he says, eyes tracking a couple as they stroll past. "It had been closed for almost a year before I got the keys. It just needed someone who knew how to enhance its existing beauty."

"I'm glad Vivante is well cared for now. Sounds like it found the right owner. What about your other two hotels?"

Griffin springs back on the bench, obviously excited to share more of his passion.

"I just retiled the pool and spa at Amore Albergo." He shakes his head, glancing up. "I know—riveting stuff. But I was able to source some Italian tile from the Monastero di Felice, a monastery from the 1600s. Only seven crates of original, intact tile exist in the world. I managed to get one of them." His chest puffs slightly as he nods.

"That's incredible. If there are only seven crates, I'm sure one must have cost a fortune."

He nods. "It did. But it's worth it. Those small details attract high-dollar clientele. It's stupid, if I'm being honest." He shrugs. "Guests want to brag about staying somewhere with sixteenth-century Italian tile. They want to one-up their pretentious friends. I had to buy high thread-count bed linen and I can't even tell the difference. But that's what they want."

I'm forming my next question when he slaps his hands on his knees.

"I've had such a lovely time with you, Brianna. I'm sorry I can't stay longer, but I need to get back for a meeting."

As he shifts to stand, I catch a glimpse of a designer label on his untucked shirt.

"Oh—" I blink, my half-formed question dying on my lips. "Of course. I understand." How can I fault a guy who works as much as I do?

I fumble with my crumpled foil and condiment packets, heat creeping up my neck as I take in the mess I've made.

He takes my hand—the sticky, ketchup-stained one—and lifts it to his lips for a kiss. It should be a sweet gesture, but all I can think of is the ketchup smell.

"I really enjoyed our time together," Griffin says.

"Yeah, me too."

"I'll text you later, sunshine."

Griffin's silhouette fades into the shadows, his coat billowing behind like a dark cape.

I'm still hungry.

I replay the date while waiting for my to-go order. Griffin left me with an empty stomach and an abrupt goodbye, but this chicken parm sub will fill the void—no designer labels or monastery tile stories required.

The date wasn't *bad*, really. His childhood sounded interesting. I can't imagine having parents who travel so much and ship you off to boarding school. My parents could barely handle me going out of state for college.

Still, going on a date with someone so different is intriguing. Me, trapped in corporate America, him jet-setting across Europe. The contrast appeals to me. But if I'm honest? His lifestyle is kind of intimidating.

What would it be like to travel like he does? My wardrobe would need some updating. The fanciest clothes I have are from the mall. His button-down shirt was Saint Laurent—I caught the fancy emblem stitched at the bottom. I glance down at my dress pants, already pilling on my inner thighs.

If I'm honest, the pilling on the inner thigh of my pants is due to the number of soft pretzels and beer I devour while traveling.

Maybe Sara's kick in the butt is what I need, but I'm still not sure I'm ready. The fact that my relationship with Dirtbag ended years ago makes this admission sting even more.

Well, one down. Eleven to go.

Back at the hotel, I turn on the news and dig through my suitcase for something comfortable. I may present myself as a business professional, but my llama-mama pajamas tell a different story.

I pull down the light beige diamond-paned quilt and sink into the bed's plushness. I stack four feather pillows behind me, soft and supportive against my spine.

A quick Facebook scroll reveals no one else I need to mute, so I flip over to LinkedIn. Three new messages wait in my inbox. Two are sales reps hunting for leads. The third one is from Marina Man. I sit up straighter.

Hi Brianna,
Thank you so much for reaching out. I can't tell you how grateful I am that you found my badge. It was going to cost $100 to replace it. A little outrageous if you ask me. I see you work at VerityLens. I did some consulting work for them a few years back. It's a great company! I recall their office is in Dallas? I'll be in Texas in 2 weeks for a bachelor party. Maybe we can find a central meeting location for late lunch as a thank you. You saved me a lot of hassle. Shoot me over some dates and I'll make it work.
Talk soon,
Preston Brookes

I stare at my phone screen. Shit. I wanted to mail the badge and be done with it. Now he wants lunch? No good deed goes unpunished.

And why would he want to meet up with a stranger? I could be a total bore, and then he'd be stuck making conversation until lunch was over.

But I guess since he's consulted for my company, he feels a connection. A business connection. He probably wants an update on his old project, or he's fishing for new consulting opportunities.

I leave my plush cocoon and crawl out of bed to check my work calendar for when I'll be back in Dallas.

Damn. I'm going to have to meet up with this guy. But do I have to? What if I lie? What if I say I'm out of town for the next six weeks? Then I can just stick it in the mail and be done with it. I tap my finger on the corner of the laptop, my lips pursed. But maybe . . .

This could count as date number two. My left eyebrow rises, and I feel like Jim Carey when he gets his brilliant idea in *How The Grinch Stole Christmas*.

Sara and I never talked about the rules of this dating challenge. But Preston is a good-looking guy and he's buying lunch. That seems like a date to me.

I declare this date number three and respond to him.

Hi Preston,
It's absolutely my pleasure. Late lunch sounds great. I'd love to hear about the consulting work you did for VerityLens, and curious what you're working on now.
I'll be in Dallas in two weeks - Wednesday, Thursday, and Friday are my best days. Anytime after 3pm works for me. However, I'm happy to adjust based on your schedule.

Feel free to text or call to finalize plans (cell # is below my signature.)
Brianna

A notification floats down from the top of my cell screen, letting me know Griffin texted me.

> Mr. GQ Griffin: Hey Beautiful. I had such a great time with you today. I'd love to see you again.

I side-eye myself in the mirror, glaring at my reflection like it's personally responsible for this mess. How? He travels. I travel. I don't know when I'll be back in New York.

> Me: I had a great time too. Unfortunately, I don't know when I'll be back in New York.

> Mr. GQ Griffin: Then I'll come to you. Just tell me when and where. Sweet dreams, Brianna.

What have I gotten myself into?

Last night's delayed flight brought me back home to Dallas exhausted and cranky. My phone won't stop buzzing between Chris, Sara, and my dates. Plus Lucas is finalizing my airport pick-up details for later this week. He labeled our chat "Cousins take over Oahu."

Fingers crossed this date with Derrik doesn't turn into a regret. His text messages are short and boring. He's either working or getting out of the shower after work or eating.

I fire off my last reply to Chris with the latest presentation for Mercury. He gets needy when he knows I'm about to go on vacation, and I've been very clear with him that I am not working while in Hawaii with my cousin. We both know the truth, though.

After glancing at the clock, the ceremonious closing of my laptop begins—slow and intentional, like closing the veto box on Big Brother—marking the end of my workday.

Time to shift gears—find a cute outfit for tonight's date with the car rental guy, begin packing my suitcase for my Hawaiian vacation in two days, and somehow pull it all together in two hours.

This closet is living proof I don't date. Nothing says *fun and flirty*. Everything screams *business meeting*. I feverishly sift through hanger after hanger, disappointed with each flick.

Black blazer. Gray slacks. Navy cardigan. More black blazers.

God, when did my wardrobe become so depressing? I yank a beige sweater off its hanger and hold it up. Beige. *Beige*. What was I thinking when I bought this?

I toss it aside and keep digging. There must be something—anything—that doesn't make me look like I'm heading to a quarterly review meeting. My hands move faster through the hangers, the metallic scraping growing more frantic with each disappointing option.

This is hopeless. I'm hopeless. How do other women make this look so easy? I know I've been out of the dating game for years—my body shudders at the realization—but it really shouldn't be this hard.

I take a step to reach the blouses in the back of my closet when my foot hits something solid. The instant stab of pain doesn't come from my foot.

I know what I've kicked before I even look down. The

white cardboard box sits there, unmarked, innocent-looking. But I can't look away.

My eyes fix on it like it's calling to me, and suddenly the closet feels smaller. The air thinner. Everything else—the hangers, the clothes, the chaos of my search—fades into nothingness. There's only the box and the weight of what's inside.

Opening that box will unleash emotions I've spent years burying. Pain that everyone else has moved on from, forgotten about. I can't face that flood alone, especially when I'll be the only one drowning in it.

With shaking hands, I twist my hair up in one jerky motion. My neck prickles with heat, but it has nothing to do with the temperature. It's coming from somewhere deeper, somewhere I've spent years trying to bury.

The room tilts. My knees give out and I sink to the closet floor, the carpet rough against my legs. My head drops forward, chin to chest, and I force myself to breathe. In through my nose. Out through my mouth. The way the therapist taught me. I reach for the box, grasping on to what I lost.

I don't know how long I sit there before the neighbor's dog starts barking outside my bedroom window. The sound cuts through my spiral, forcing me back to reality. I drag my gaze to the clock near my bed. Shit. I need to get ready.

Several breaths and only a few scattered tears later, I stand up and resume the outfit selection process—pretending I'm fine, like I always do. I settle on a pair of dark jeans from my casual Friday rotation and a geometric print blouse. Green Chucks. The gold-plated half-moon necklace feels right—not too flashy. I slide on my favorite bracelet that Sara gave me for Christmas and step in front of the mirror, hoping to give myself the final approval.

"Well, here we go. Fake it till ya make it, right?" The woman looking back doesn't look convinced.

Chapter 6

Dallas

As I pull up to Casa de Sabor restaurant, I send Derrik a quick text letting him know I've arrived. I take a deep breath and push everything else down. Tonight, I'm just a woman on a date. If all else fails, I'm a woman in a business meeting. I can handle a business meeting.

> Derrik: 5 minutes out.

As I wait, I scroll back to Preston's message and my pulse quickens. Three o'clock tomorrow. Downtown Dallas.

A dusty blue pickup truck pulls into the lot, and through the open passenger window, I catch a glimpse of crystal-clear blue eyes as the driver searches for a parking spot. The golden hour light catches in those eyes—the same light painting orange and pink streaks across the sky as the sun dips below the horizon. The days are stretching longer now, a welcome change after the endless winter.

I wipe my palms down my thighs and step out of my car. Derrik's truck is parked several spaces down. He's changing shirts—work polo off, clean polo on. I keep my distance, but can't help watching. His undershirt slides up a bit, showing off the contour of his lower back.

The wind presses his washed-out blue polo against his chest as he approaches, outlining those pecs I've been somewhat curious about.

"Hey." His greeting is about as enthusiastic as a grocery store clerk at midnight. He reaches back to double-lock his truck with two sharp beeps.

"Hey, Derrik." I glance around, wondering if I missed something.

We walk side by side in silence, the fading light making it impossible to read his expression. The restaurant building reflects the cultural crossroads that has shaped Texas's history, and I'm flooded with memories of when Sara and I came here . . . which is the only thing making me smile right now.

He opens the door, his rough hands making the handle look like a toy, and waves me in without making eye contact.

"Reservation for Derrik." He shakes his hands out as the hostess checks the clipboard and nods.

Is he *nervous?*

"Right this way," she says, leading us through the crowded restaurant with oversized menus in hand.

My eyes wander as we weave through tables, taking in the classic cowboy restaurant with its wood paneling and old brick fireplace that dominates the room. The crackling of the fire settles some of my tension.

We're seated in a small room with five tables, but should probably only fit four. Derrik immediately claims the chair facing the entrance.

"You been here before?" he asks.

"Yes. It's actually one of my favorite restaurants."

His face brightens with the first genuine smile I've seen tonight.

"Have you?" I steady my purse in the chair next to me.

"No, but Xander recommended it. He was the one at the desk that day."

Ah, yes. Mr. Mary Kay. Which reminds me I need to find a consultant.

We pick up our menus at the same time, creating a wall between us. The silence resumes.

I pretend to scan the menu, but I already know what I'm ordering. I always rotate between three dishes: chicken fajitas, chile relleno, or carne asada.

After what feels like an eternity, I set my menu down and wait, playing with the bracelet Sara gave me while I stare at the back of Derrik's menu. The server appears at our table.

"What can I get you to drink?"

"Spicy margarita on the rocks, extra salt." Because I'm starting to feel extra salty.

Derrik peeks over his menu. "I'll have a Dos Equis Ambar."

The server nods and steps away.

"What are you thinking?" I nod toward his menu.

"I usually get tacos or a burrito but I don't see them."

Because you can only order them at the bar.

"Want some suggestions?" I can't help myself, I explain the options like I'm pitching a client until the server returns with tortilla chips and salsa. She returns several minutes later with our drinks.

"Ready to order?"

"Yes," Derrik says, motioning for me to go first. At least he has manners.

"Carne asada." I hand my menu to the server.

Derrik grins. "Same for me."

He shrugs and we both laugh.

My fingers curl around the salt-rimmed glass and I take a sip.

"Smart man. You picked a winner."

At this point, the basket of chips is flirting harder than Derrik. If this goes badly, I can tell Sara that the only spice came from the salsa.

I'm reaching for the tortilla basket when something—or someone—slams into the back of my chair.

The impact jolts me forward. My fingers, already committed to their chip-grabbing mission, knock the basket skyward. Time slows as red and white tortilla chips arc through the air like confetti at the world's most awkward celebration.

Derrik's ocean blue eyes widen. A chip bounces off his forehead. Another lands in his beer with a tiny splash.

The basket crashes to the floor and chips scatter everywhere—one sticks to his shirt pocket like a crunchy boutonniere.

My hand flies to my mouth. The silence stretches.

Then Derrik grins. His grin becomes a chuckle. The chuckle explodes into full laughter.

His laughter unlocks something in me and I drop my head into my hands, my shoulders shaking.

"I am so sorry," I manage between gasps. "I swear, I'm not usually this dangerous around appetizers."

He plucks the chip from his pocket and holds it up like a trophy.

"You could've just asked if I wanted some," he says, laughing.

We corral as many chips as we can back into the basket until the server appears with a broom and a knowing smile. I peek over my shoulder to find an older gentleman seated behind me, unaware of the fiasco he caused.

"Well," Derrik says, settling back into his chair, "That's definitely going in my top three most memorable first dates."

He runs his fingers through his dark brown hair.

"Only top three?" I raise an eyebrow. "What could possibly beat flying tortilla chips?"

The next twenty minutes passes easily. We cover the usual first date territory: jobs, families, and hobbies. Family seems to be a big deal for him, with his parents still living in the house he grew up in. His grandma's just down the block, and they all gather for Sunday dinners. It seems he's not much of a traveler since he asks what New York is like. But he gets around Texas well enough—fishing on Lake Texoma, camping at Eisenhower and ATV'ing at Barnwell. By the time our entrees arrive, we've moved on to the topic of glamping. Derrik seems to think it's any type of camping with access to toilets or off-the-ground sleeping. I disagree.

The server appears with our food. I breathe in the spices and eye the shiny sauces overlaying the steak, the orangish-red rice, and black beans. Derrik nods in approval as we pick up our forks.

"Do you travel a lot for work?"

He takes a large gulp of his Dos Equis, but not from nerves this time. He's leaning back in his chair, shoulders loose and relaxed.

"I do." My fork hangs in the air. "I travel about twenty-six weeks out of the year."

His face looks like he just sucked a lemon.

"That's . . . a lot," he says carefully.

"Yeah, I know. It's not for everyone. I live out of a suitcase. I have no sense of home."

He raises his beer, the white square napkin sticking to the glass bottom.

"You enjoy that? Not having a home?"

"It gets old, believe me." I reach across the table, grab the napkin that clings to his beer glass, and place it back on the table. "It's not in my long-term plan. But I'm happy right now. I love what I do." Grabbing the salt shaker, I shake salt onto his napkin.

He stills, his glass resting on his bottom lip. I look up. My cheeks heat as I realize I've overstepped.

"What are you doing?" he asks, hesitant to put his beer down.

"It's a trick to keep your napkin from sticking to the bottom of your glass. You've never heard of this?"

He slowly places his beer onto the salted white napkin, then picks it up again. The napkin stays put on the table. His eyebrows raise.

"Where did you learn this?"

"College." I smile. "My parents are very proud."

I wink as I grab another chip from the basket.

"So, that's what happens in college." He tilts his head, grinning. "And here I thought it was all about studying."

The rest of dinner flows easily. We settle into a comfortable groove, ordering a second round of drinks and digging into our food without worrying about manners. Conversation moves effortlessly from topic to topic—how we grew up, favorite movies, and music. He talks about rebuilding the motors on his ATV, and the image of him leaning over the engine, his arms covered in grease is pretty damn hot. He apologizes again for the dirty car but never mentions Preston's marina ID.

The server appears with the check, placing it in the middle of the table. Derrik reaches for it without hesitation.

After paying the bill, I follow Derrik through the restaurant toward the exit. He opens the door for me, and we step into the cool night. I wrap my arms around myself as we walk side by side toward the parking lot, his easy chatter replaced by silence.

"This is me."

I slow my pace as I point toward my car, the sleek curves of the sedan reflecting the overhead parking lights.

"Thanks for coming to dinner. And sorry about the dirty car."

"Derrik, you saved me." I tilt my head, eyes wide with gratitude. "I had an important meeting in San Antonio, and thanks to you, I made it there."

His smile fades into an awkward nod. He shifts his weight, hands finding his pockets. The moment settles around us like an ill-fitting sweater.

"And sorry about the chips," I say, because apparently my brain thinks humor will save us from whatever this awkwardness is.

That gets a genuine laugh.

"Right. Well, I should let you get home." He takes a step toward his truck with careful politeness. "Drive safe, okay?"

"You too."

He gives me one last smile before heading to his truck.

My car's start button glows, waiting for my touch as Derrik's taillights disappear around the corner. Dinner was nice. Fun even, once our nerves settled. He's got all the ingredients of a great guy, but if Derrik even considered this a date, the recipe isn't working. We're just too different. He wants someone who'll be home for Sunday dinners, and I can't remember the last time I sat at my own kitchen table.

I step inside my dark, quiet condo, placing my keys on the kitchen island, and dropping my purse to the floor. The soft couch beckons, and soon my shoes are on the floor and I'm curled up against the padded arm with my legs tucked under me.

Checking my messages, I'm surprised to see texts from Mr. GQ and Marina Man.

> Mr. GQ Griffin: Hello Gorgeous. I miss that beautiful smile. I can't wait to see you again! I'm currently in Shanghai. I have an important dinner meeting with investors tonight. Wish me luck!

My face scrunches with each word of Griffin's text. We had one date and now he's sending me play-by-play updates like we're in some long-distance relationship. Too much, too fast, too intense.

Preston's message is the complete opposite—short, direct, business-like.

> Marina Man Preston: Hi Brianna. I'll be touching down in Dallas tomorrow around 1:30pm. I'll be at the Starlight Cafe at 3pm. Thanks again for going to the trouble. See you soon. Preston

Chapter 7

Dallas

I wake up with a lightness in my chest. Is it from sleeping in my own bed? Pay day? The sun streaming in through my windows? I don't analyze it. I let it carry me through selecting an outfit. My brown and black swirled pencil skirt that hugs my curves just right is the winner, paired with an off-white silk blouse with puffed sleeves and a neckline that straddles the line between professional and tempting. Cream pumps complete the look.

Work drags, though. I catch myself staring at the clock, willing the hours to pass. I'm caught up on all my work, and presentations for Chris are ready to go. I'm bored enough that I'm hoping Mr. GQ texts with another one of his trademark novels about my "ethereal beauty" or how I'm his "missing puzzle piece"—anything cheesy enough to give me a good laugh and remind me why I'm glad I dodged that bullet. Nothing comes through. Even Sara's been quiet since she took baby Grady for his shots today.

The office feels quiet without Chris, who's still in New York courting another potential client. No random pop-ins to his office, where I hold the unofficial record for turning "Do you have a minute?" into "Where did the last hour go?" I usually work from home when he travels, but the office is close to the restaurant where I'm meeting Preston.

When two o'clock rolls around, my laptop is already shut and packed away. I visit the bathroom for one last outfit and makeup check, reapplying my sticky lip gloss with tiny sparkles in it. I nod at my reflection, then stride out of the bathroom with a confidence I haven't felt in ages.

Parking is limited near the restaurant, but I snag a spot about a block away. My parallel parking skills are on point. If Sara is driving, she literally stops the car in the middle of the road so we can run around and switch seats whenever parallel parking is required. She doesn't even care about the honking cars behind us.

The humidity today makes my pencil skirt feel like shrink wrap. I slow my walk to avoid working up a sweat.

As I approach the café, I turn on the confidence—perfect posture and silky smooth movements as I reach for the door handle. I've watched enough romance movies to know the love interest is always inside, watching as she makes her entrance. Just don't tr—

"Oh, my God!"

My left pump hits the polished tile and slides forward like it's auditioning for the Ice Capades. My arms windmill frantically as my body lurches forward, nearly achieving an accidental split that would make my middle school gymnastics coach weep. My purse launches ahead of me like it's escaping disaster, dragging me a few more mortifying inches over the threshold.

The unmistakable sound of fabric ripping cuts through the air.

I recover by pulling my right leg into some kind of

desperate squat and bracing my hands above my knees until my legs remember they're supposed to work together.

That's when I see him. His hand reaching for my purse. Another hand extending toward me.

Mortification washes over me, making me want to wave him off—as if I could somehow rewind the last ten seconds and glide to a table like nothing happened.

Preston's outstretched hand finds mine as I'm still mentally cycling through what the actual fuck just happened to me. The large, sun-spotted hand lifts me to standing while another holds my purse out like a shield. I peer around it, hoping by some chance it's not him.

Kill me now.

He has that serious, concerned expression I've seen guys get when they witness a woman's dignity die in real time. I mean, I should be used to this feeling, but I'm not.

I slowly reach for my purse, wishing to erase the last fifteen seconds of my life, when he gently grabs my shoulders.

"Are you okay, miss?"

Oh, my God. He doesn't recognize me. Of course he doesn't. Because the polished and professional Implementation Manager from VerityLens he's meeting today would be able to handle walking through a damn door.

My brain spins with possibilities. I could leave right now and he'd never know I was the girl with his marina ID. I could fake a sudden illness and pretend this moment never happened. I could move to another city and start fresh.

"Thanks, Preston."

He tilts his head, recognition flickering across his face.

"Brianna?" The smile spreading across his handsome, weathered face is genuinely warm.

I look down and sigh. "Yes. My entrance is generally less . .

. chaotic." I force my eyes back up, bracing myself for the polite disgust or awkward pity I'm sure is waiting for me.

But there's none of that. Instead, I find something that looks like concern mixed with . . . is that intrigue?

"I'm used to women falling for me, but not literally," he quips.

My brows furrow as I look at my purse that he's still holding.

He quickly adds, "I'm kidding. Kidding. I'm trying to make you laugh and I'm an idiot."

I stare at his face for a moment—sun-kissed with freckles and the kind of sun-carved lines that come from squinting into ocean glare. His jaw has that rugged thing going on that I'm apparently weak for, based on how my breathing changes.

"Well, how's that for a first impression?" I recover enough to make a joke of myself, and he laughs, running his hand through his reddish-brown hair that falls perfectly on top.

"It's a first impression I'll never forget."

His smile makes me relax a little as we walk over to the table where he's been sitting. I'm still flustered, but I need to pull myself together. I reach around to assess the damage to my skirt, my fingers finding frayed fabric just above the intended vent. Great. The back of my pencil skirt just became a little more scandalous.

He quick-steps to my chair, pulling it out, and I begin to panic—not wanting him to see my newly extended skirt vent. Part of me wonders if he's being chivalrous or just trying to prevent another disaster. I drop into my seat, grabbing the sides of the chair and hopping the rest of the way to the table.

This is so embarrassing. I'm supposed to be a poised professional, and I just flew through the front door like some kind of human projectile. What is my issue with walking through doorways?

I take a final deep breath, give myself a small mental shake, and plaster a smile on my face while Preston studies the menu.

"So, how was your flight?"

Good thinking, B. Turn the attention to him.

"Uneventful, but good. I flew standby, which can be a pain, but it all worked out. How was yours?"

An evil grin spreads across his face, his left eyebrow raised.

"Oh, we've got jokes, huh?" At least he's entertained by my ongoing battle with forward motion. "My flight was spontaneous with a rough landing." I glare back at him and he laughs, crossing his arms over his chest while leaning back in his chair.

"What's on the agenda for the bachelor party tonight?"

"Oh, it's top secret. I can't say." He makes a zipping motion across his lips. "But it should be a good time. My friend is finally taking the plunge. It's just a small group of us. Three of our mutual friends from grade school and two of Jack's friends from who knows where."

"Should I have bail money ready and waiting?" The words slip out before I can stop them.

Wait—am I flirting? Is this what flirting feels like? I haven't done this in so long I almost forgot how fun it could be.

"With the trouble we might get in, I'll definitely keep you on standby."

He winks at me, picking up his menu again. I take a sharp breath and follow suit. I stare at the words without reading them, replaying our banter from the last few moments.

"You're smiling," he says, amusement in his voice.

I wink back.

"I was just thinking about how much you'd owe me for bailing you and your buddies out of jail."

"Ahh . . . the debt would be enormous." He nods, taking a sip of his water, eyes locked on mine. "But I'm pretty creative when it comes to repaying debts."

The server approaches our table, interrupting the flirty tension, and asks if we're ready to order. Preston motions for me to go first. Considering I have no idea what's on this menu, I scan desperately for the first words I can focus on.

"I'll take the French dip with the potato salad." I offer up my menu.

"I'll have the club sandwich." Preston hands his menu to the server and she leaves. He turns his attention back to me. "So, where did you find my marina ID?"

"Oh, yes!" I fumble through my wallet for his ID. "I kept it safe and sound." I reach across the table, and our fingers brush as he takes it from me. The contact lingers a beat longer than necessary.

"You're truly a lifesaver. I didn't want to pay to replace this flimsy piece of plastic." He shakes his head.

"That's ridiculous. I'm sure you pay enough to dock your boat there." I sip on my water that the server dropped off a few moments ago.

"Yeah, but it's so convenient. Easy to get to, easy parking. Some of the marinas require street parking, and it's a hassle to lug all your gear from three blocks away."

"*Mmm.*" I nod, scrunching my eyebrows as if I have any idea what that's like. "What type of boat do you have?"

"I have a thirty-foot Catalina cruising yacht. It's a 2007, but it's in great condition."

"I'm impressed you know how to sail. My best friend and I took sailing lessons in college, but we never did anything with it after that." I smile, thinking of Sara's aunt who insisted that if we marry a man who sails, we'd be set for life.

"I grew up sailing." His eyes light up. "My parents had a twelve-foot dinghy that I learned on, then in college I captained larger boats with the sailing club. I still have the dinghy. Bright red sails, white hull with a blue interior. My parents argued the bright colors were for safety, so they could keep eyes on me while on the water." He laughs, caught in a memory.

"What a fun way to spend your childhood." We study each other across the table as if we're trying to solve the same puzzle. The more he talks, the more I see how our pieces might fit together.

His phone buzzes against the table. We both glance down as he reaches for it.

"I need to take this, I'm so sorry," He swipes to answer without leaving his seat.

The ice clinks as I lift my water glass, and I focus on the condensation beading the sides instead of his voice. But his tone cuts through my attempted politeness—sharp, businesslike. Something about a report due next week.

The server sets down our sandwiches. Preston nods his thanks without breaking conversation.

"Get it done. We don't have time to mess around. A million dollars rides on this." He pauses, listening. "Fine. Handle it."

He ends the call and slides the phone into his pocket. "Sorry about that." His smile doesn't quite reach his eyes as he picks up half of his sandwich.

I shift in my seat, dipping my sandwich into the au jus gravy more times than required. The sharpness in his voice lingers. Was that normal Preston or work Preston?

Chris sounds exactly like that when he's closing a big deal. Intense, demanding. But five minutes later, he's back to laughing at my terrible jokes. Maybe that's all this was.

"So, you consulted with my company a few years back?"

"I did. Short-term project evaluating licensing costs for premium data. Sexy stuff." His right eyebrow quirks up. He takes a massive bite of his sandwich, and I watch in amazement as half of it disappears.

"Oh right, the paywall nightmare. We needed to figure out

which news outlets to pay for. It was like wanting to binge series on Netflix, Hulu, AppleTV and Max but you could only afford two of them." I pause, the sandwich hovering at my mouth. "Wait. Was it you who said paying for premium data from LinkedIn and Bloomberg Alerts would cost more than our company's worth and wouldn't provide the value our clients want?"

He tosses his hands up in front of him. "I just did the analysis. Your company chose which subscription-only news feeds and industry databases to purchase." His voice shifts, taking on an edge of pride. "But I did offer my recommendations and saved them from pouring half their budget into premium data they didn't need."

I recall Chris stalking around the office back then, brandishing Preston's presentation slide like evidence in a murder trial. 'We lost the Morrison account because we couldn't access one *Wall Street Journal* article,' he ranted.

"I never understood why we couldn't just scrape LinkedIn posts and call it a day."

"Sure, if you want lawsuits. Most of the good stuff isn't freely available. There are copyright issues, API limits, and closed platforms. Trust me. I did the math," he replies, taking another large bite.

I spin my fork, pointing it at him.

"Classic consultant move. Drop the bomb and vanish before the explosion."

"Hey, I gave them options: cut the scope, license smarter, or build a premium tier. There were paths." He spreads his hands. "Just not cheap ones."

"Fair enough." I take another bite, studying him. There's something appealing about his certainty—as though he knows exactly what he's worth and isn't apologizing for it. "So basically, you're expensive but effective."

"That's one way to put it."

He grins, and there's that warmth again, softening the edges of his arrogance.

The server appears beside our table. "Can I get you anything else?"

"Just the check, thanks," Preston says. His plate is practically empty while I've barely made a dent in my French dip.

"And a to-go box, please?" I call after the server. "So, when do tonight's festivities begin?"

He grins. "Kickoff is at five o'clock in Fort Worth. Steak dinner, bourbon, live music, and endless debauchery."

I quirk an eyebrow. "Yeah . . . I'll definitely have that bail money ready."

The server places the check and to-go container at the edge of the table.

"I got it." He pulls the check toward him with a dismissive flick of his wrist.

"Thank you," I say, before taking another bite of my sandwich and reaching for the food container.

Preston scribbles his signature across the receipt and slides it back to the edge of the table. He glances up at me with a smile. "Ready, Brianna?"

I nod as we stand and he gestures for me to go first.

As we walk toward the door, his hand finds the small of my back. The touch is light, guiding, and when we reach the crowded entrance, both his hands settle on my shoulders from behind.

He leans close. "Just in case," he says, his laugh warm against my neck.

Embarrassment should be my initial reaction, but instead I find myself leaning back into his touch.

"Thanks for hunting me down to return my ID," he says as we pause outside the café.

"No trouble at all. Thanks for lunch."

He opens his mouth, then pauses. Silence stretches between us as a breeze whips my hair across my face. He watches as I tuck the unruly strands behind my ear.

"I'd love to take you out on the boat sometime, if you're interested." His smile suggests he already knows what I'll say.

"That would be amazing! We have a client north of San Diego. I could probably swing down."

"Perfect. I'll text you after I recover from my boys' weekend and we can set a date." That confident smile again.

"That sounds great. And I'll keep the bail money on standby." I wink as he leans in for a hug, and I catch his cologne for the first time—something warm and expensive that makes me want to stay right here.

As he pulls back, his lips brush my ear, then find my cheek. I press closer, his lips soft against my skin.

"Talk soon." He squeezes my forearm as he steps back, turning to head in the opposite direction.

My eyes follow his retreating form, lingering on his broad shoulders before dropping to those well-cut black slacks.

I'm practically floating with each long stride around the block to my car. There's a lot to like about Preston—successful enough to have climbed the corporate ladder to VP roles, handsome and confident in a way that makes you do a double-take, and the way he handles business calls with that demanding tone shouldn't be as attractive as it is. Plus he gets my career, which is huge since most guys glaze over when I talk about work. And the sailboat doesn't hurt either. Maybe this dating challenge was a good idea.

I grab my phone, excited to text Sara the good news:

> Me: Mission complete. He asked me out on his sailboat in a few weeks!

A quick scroll through my remaining texts reveals one from Griffin. There's a photo attachment of a painting—a woman walking down a city street, umbrella in hand, her dress caught by the wind. Only her skin is painted in color. The rest is a gray-scale.

> Mr. GQ Griffin: I saw this painting and thought of you. It's timeless, romantic, and breathtaking. Hope you're having a great day!

Three weeks ago, I hadn't been on a date in years. Now I'm getting sailing invitations and being compared to a work of art in the same afternoon.

The only response Griffin gets is a quick smile emoji because I'm not sure what to say to that. Time to head home and finish packing for Hawaii.

Chapter 8

Hawaii

The walk to my gate is surprisingly smooth through DFW's 6 a.m. corridors. The airport feels different this early—less chaotic, more purposeful. I grab a caramel latte from the Starbucks counter, silently blessing whoever invented mobile ordering as the growing line of passengers debates their caffeine choices. The terminal windows show the first hints of sunrise stretching across the Texas sky, and this evening I'll be watching that same sun set over the Pacific with my cousin who's been through it all with me.

My phone has been buzzing nonstop since I got out of the ride share. As I settle at my gate, I scan through my messages.

> Marina Man Preston: We survived the night! No bail money needed. Let me know when you're in CA, we'll plan a boating trip!

> Mr. GQ Griffin: I was going to ask if I could visit you in Hawaii for a night but I'm dealing with an issue at one of my hotels. How was your flight?

> Lucas: Aloha cuz! Txt me when you land. I'll pick you up outside of baggage claim. Safe Flight!

> Sara: OMG. You landed another date with Marina Man?!?! CALL ME PLEASE.

I haven't heard from Derrik since our date. Was it the flying basket of chips that did him in?

Spotting an empty gate with no departing flights, I head to one of the vacant chairs. It's still early enough that Sara should be free before baby Grady's morning routine kicks in, so I give her a call.

"How was it?" Sara whispers.

"I think I'm experiencing symptoms of romantic interest."

"They're called feelings, B. Not a disease."

"I'm struggling to see the distinction."

Sara laughs softly. "Okay, but seriously . . . how did the date go?"

"It went well. He's handsome, successful, driven, and he understands the work I do."

"That's awesome, B!" Her voice is bright with barely contained excitement. "He asked you out on the boat?"

"Yep! But . . . I walked into the café and immediately tripped, splitting my skirt open."

"Wait, stop. I want those details next. But right now I need to know. Do you like him? Like, actually *like* him?"

My cheeks warm. "Maybe? It's too early to tell." Admitting that shocks even me.

"B! This is wonderful! I'm so happy!"

I fidget with the zipper on my purse. "Yeah."

"So, what about the other guys you're dating?"

"Well, Derrik was a one-time thing, Griffin is laying it on thick with the compliments and—"

Sara interrupts me. "Wait, who's Derrik?"

"Derrik works at Advanced Rental. Griffin is the one from New York who dresses like a *GQ* model."

"Okay, so Rental Car guy is out. Mr. GQ is clingy, and Marina Man is our front runner. This is awesome, B! Look at you doing the whole dating thing. I'm proud of you."

Sara's praise settles over me like my mom congratulating me on a perfect report card. I smile while watching a plane lift off from a distant runway.

Then our call is cut short when baby Grady's cries begin to wail from the baby monitor.

Lucas pulls up as I walk outside baggage claim into Hawaii's humid embrace. He jumps out of the driver's side, jogs around his rusty Ford truck, and drops the tailgate, reaching for my luggage.

"Welcome to Oahu!" He rolls my suitcases toward the truck's bed.

I follow, wiping the sweat that's already beading on my forehead.

"Thank you! I can't wait to knock back some mai tais."

He eyes my laptop bag with disapproval. "That better not be your work laptop. You said this wouldn't be a working vacation like last year." He wags a finger at me.

Guilt twists my stomach. He's right. I did say that. But Chris panics over nothing whenever I'm out of the office. Besides, how bad could it be having my laptop open on the shores of Waikiki Beach?

"It won't get in the way of our fun, cuz." I try to sound convincing.

We hop into the truck, the rusted passenger door creaking as I close it. The AC blasts my face, a welcome relief.

"What's on our agenda for the next few days?" I ask as Lucas loops around the airport toward the highway.

"I got a dive tomorrow with some of my buddies, and we'll be tailgating afterward. I figured you can enjoy the beach while we're sixty feet under, then we can do some grilling." He looks my way, and I can't believe how grown up he is.

"Sounds great." I stare out the window, admiring the scenery as we make our way to his apartment on the Army base.

Hard to believe my little cousin has been stationed here for two years already. Three years ago, he was just another college graduate with a Criminal Justice degree. Now he's serving in the Army, sending me underwater videos of turtles and sharks, diving shipwrecks like it's all in a day's work.

We drive for about thirty minutes before approaching the military base. As we pull up to the guard gate, several men in fatigues are checking IDs before waving cars through. Lucas catches my stare toward the guard station.

"Easy there, killer . . . they're too young for you." He grins as we drive up to the guard.

Lucas hands over his military ID, then shoots me the *stop staring* look. I throw my hands up and mouth, "What?"

"Thank you," the guard says, and Lucas takes his ID back. The gate opens ahead.

Once out of earshot, he looks at me again. "You're ridiculous."

I press my hand to my chest, feigning shock. "Who, me?"

He shakes his head as we drive deeper into the base,

cruising past a massive granite monument dedicated to fallen soldiers before turning into the townhome complex.

"I can't help that all men look good in uniform."

"Even the youngest ones . . ." he says, and I smack his arm as he pulls the truck into his driveway.

Wet air wraps around me as I step out of the truck, taking in the identical brown two-story homes surrounding us. Basic, no frills, no landscaping—just a few overgrown trees. Lucas grabs my luggage from the truck bed and hauls it inside as I follow.

"Can I get you a drink? Are you hungry?" He pushes my suitcases down the hall where the bedrooms are.

"Mai tai?" I smile, clasping my hands together. He should know this is my expectation. It's all I drank last year when I visited.

"Of course."

I follow him into the kitchen—small, with a short U-shaped counter separating it from the eating area. He reaches into the classic nineties-style cabinets and grabs a wine glass. They look like the same cabinets from his parent's house when we were growing up.

"Those cabinets have aged about as well as frosted tips and MC Hammer pants." I smirk, scrutinizing the cream cabinet with fake wood trim.

"Hammer pants was your generation, not mine." His eyes lift toward me as he pours from a Costco-sized jug of mai tai mix.

"Rude! Doesn't the Army teach you to respect your elders?"

He hands me the wine glass. I take a sip and let out a happy groan. Vacation has officially begun.

"Don't drink too much. We have supper with my buddies later at the on-base restaurant. It's a Friday night tradition."

"Will they be in uniform?" I ask in a low, seductive voice, waggling my eyebrows as I take another sip of this tropical treasure.

"Don't be gross." He tilts his head, smirking.

After catching up with Lucas and finishing two mai tais, I stumble to my room to freshen up before we leave for the restaurant. I'm too tired from traveling to put much, if any, effort into my appearance. I change into jean capris and a flowy off-the-shoulder top covered in tropical flowers, and a pair of flip flops.

The drive from Lucas's place to the restaurant takes four minutes, maybe.

"Is the faded paint part of the look?" I ask, pointing to what use to be solid red wooden beams at the entrance. Decades of storms have left their mark on the building's exterior. Lucas laughs while holding the door open.

The inside matches the outside—old and weathered. The walls look like aged wooden planks you'd find on a raggedy dock, with metal signs hung randomly throughout. Lucas slides past me and heads toward a six-top high table in the bar area. I sit across from him, taking in the ambiance. Ocean waves crash in the distance, steady and soothing as a lullaby.

"I'm going to grab us some drinks. What do you want?" He stands, pushing in his chair.

"*Mmm* . . . local IPA." He nods and turns for the bar.

Chris used to make fun of me when we traveled for work because I'd ask for the lightest beer they had. He called it "yellow water" and said I was a disgrace. To make it worse, he claimed our clients would judge my poor taste and it could hurt *his* sales. I gave in, and he created an "IPA ramp-up plan," like I was some work project. Over three months, I was assigned beers to drink, each one hoppier than the last.

I take out my phone to check in with Sara. She becomes a

mother hen when I travel, requesting proof of life texts as if she can't log into the tracking app and see exactly where I am. I notice another message from Mr. GQ. Nothing from Marina Man.

> Mr. GQ Griffin: Hey beautiful, thinking about you. When do I get to see that gorgeous face of yours again? Name the time and place. I'll come to you.

He wouldn't really get on a plane to come to me, would he? I respond, hoping this might be the out I need to get rid of this guy.

> Me: Hey Griffin! I don't have any NY trips coming up. I'll be stuck in San Antonio for the next few weeks.

There's no way he'd fly across the country for a girl he just met.

Lucas comes back and slides my beer in front of me before sitting down. As I take my first sip, there's a commotion from my left as four guys barrel into the bar area toward us. Two wear Army fatigues, the other two are in shorts and T-shirts. I shake hands with all of them, committing each name to memory as they shout them at me.

The next two hours blur together in a haze of military stories, cold beer, and easy laughter. Lucas's friends are exactly what I expect—loud, loyal, and completely comfortable roasting each other. I lose track of time listening to stories about training exercises gone wrong and weekend adventures around the island, and what they miss on the mainland. The sun sets while we're there, the pink sky giving way to stars.

Lucas notices my energy level drop after the third round of beers and whispers that we'll leave once our beer is done. I nod in agreement, resting my elbows on the table top and pick up my phone to check whether Mr. GQ responded. Of course he did. He doesn't know how to play hard to get.

> Mr. GQ Griffin: I will see you in San Antonio. Does that first Tuesday afternoon you're back sound good? I'll swing by your hotel around 5pm?

Wait. What? He's flying to San Antonio? To take me out? This guy must be rich. Or crazy. *What have I done?*

"All right, guys, we're going to take off. I've got an early dive tomorrow. Oh, speak of the devil." Lucas reaches his hand out to another guy walking in. He's older than the rest of Lucas's friends, maybe mid-thirties—around my age. He's wearing a black baseball cap that shadows his face until he turns toward me.

My breath catches.

He extends his hand, and I realize Lucas has been introducing me to his friend Kevin while I've been staring like an idiot.

"Nice to meet you, Brianna." His grip is firm and sure, the kind that makes you feel small in the best way.

"You, too."

I would be lying if I said I wasn't scanning his other hand for a wedding ring as he talks to the rest of the table.

His military training is evident in every line of his body— the way he stands, shoulders back with quiet, assured confidence. His chiseled jaw could cut glass, and when he removes his cap, dark hair falls just right across his forehead.

Now I'm sad we're leaving. I suddenly have all the energy in the world. But Lucas and I say our goodbyes anyway and head out.

"So, Kevin will be diving with you tomorrow?" I ask as we hop into the truck.

Lucas's head swivels toward me with theatrical slowness, I can practically hear his neck creak.

"You're ridiculous," he replies, shaking his head.

"What? I am simply fulfilling a quest that was placed upon me."

"A quest? A quest to get laid?"

"Well, that would be a bonus. But the quest is that I need to go out on a dozen dates within three months."

"Or what?"

"Or . . ." I pause. "Actually, I don't know. Sara and I never talked about what happens if I don't do it." I frown, feeling silly for not addressing this with her.

"Why do you need to go out on a dozen dates in three months?"

"Because Sara thinks I am afraid to get close to a man and I have walls up, and I've written off dating, and I work too much, blah blah blah."

"Oh, so you're damaged," he says, and then visually braces for impact.

"Screw off, Lucas! I am not damaged. Take that back!" I smack him hard in the stomach as he turns out of the parking lot.

"That's exactly what a damaged girl would say," he teases, giving me the side eye. But it's an insult to be called *damaged* by family. "Is it because of that dirtbag?"

It's like the air gets sucked out of the truck. My body goes rigid, every muscle locking in place. My breathing turns shallow and quick. Even after all this time, just his name—or the refusal to say it—rips something open inside me.

Anger floods my chest, hot and familiar. Not just at Lucas, but at *him*. At the way he still has this power over me, still makes my hands shake and my throat close up years later.

I dig deep for the energy to reply, my fists clenching.

"Sara says it is."

"Sara is probably right. Is he the last guy you dated?" He abandons any pretense of empathy.

"Yes."

I look down, wringing my hands like I'm trying to squeeze water from them.

Lucas sighs, hesitating. "He was an asshole. A selfish asshole. When you lost—" He stops, shaking his head. I sink deeper into the seat, my chest tightening.

Don't say it. Please don't say it.

"He shouldn't have left you because of it, B."

I turn toward the window. I can't relive it. The rejection. Being discarded like I was broken beyond repair.

"Yeah, and he took the cowardly option of cheating to get out." My voice cracks on the last word.

"I'm sorry, B." Lucas cuts the engine, his hands falling to his lap as he waits for me. I stare up at his townhouse. "There are things that aren't in your control. And they're not *all* assholes. I mean, most of them on this base are . . ." He offers a small smile, coaxing one from me. "My point is, you're too cool not to share your life with someone. You can't wait until menopause to start looking."

My head whips to him. His words slam into me like a physical blow.

"I'm so sorry. I didn't mean to—" Remorse pours over Lucas's face.

"It's fine."

I let my head fall back, the head rest absorbing the weight of everything I can't say.

Lucas reaches over and pats me on the knee. He was in

Dallas when I was with Dirtbag. He watched it all unfold—the excitement, the loss, the carnage of everything we built.

The memory hits like a sucker punch. *Him* standing in our kitchen, a box cradled in his arms, staring at me like everything was my fault. Three years together, a ring on my finger, wedding invitations already ordered.

Friends kept saying it wasn't about me, but when someone you're planning to marry decides they'd rather be anywhere else than building a life with you, it's impossible not to take it personally. The shame was almost worse than the heartbreak.

And the loneliness that followed was more than I could handle. More than anyone around me could understand.

The passenger door opens. Lucas stands there with a sad smile, ready to help me out.

"Mai tai?" he asks, his head tilted down, eyebrows raised.

I nod, wiping my tears.

Chapter 9

Hawaii

The sun beams through the white translucent curtains, waking me from a dream about Marina Man. I blink slowly until my eyes focus, looking around the room. Lucas's guest room barely fits a queen bed and one nightstand, yet somehow, he squeezed a chair into the left corner near the foot of the bed. My clothes from last night drape over it. Across the room, a wooden plank American flag takes up half the wall.

The floor creaks outside my door, and the smell of coffee fills my senses. I glance at the clock on the nightstand. Six thirty. I drag the covers away and roll to my side, my legs dangling off the bed. I stay there for a few moments, remembering last night's conversation. A drawn-out sigh leaves me as I push myself to stand.

I haven't talked about Dirtbag for a long time, until Sara cooked up her dating dare. I shoved that shit down deep so I don't have to feel it. But the truth is, it still hurts. And I didn't realize how much until recently.

Falling in love was always my north star. It was what I

wanted more than anything. More than my career, and I finally had it. I had a strong, successful, handsome man whom I loved more than I ever thought possible. We were picture perfect. We worked through arguments, supported each other, believed in each other. I had everything I wanted.

"Hey, B?" There are three light knocks at my door. I snap out of it, feeling hungover from the thoughts in my head.

"Yeah?" I walk the two steps to open the door. Lucas is standing in his scuba shorts and a plain brown T-shirt, holding a cup of coffee. Steam billows off the surface as he hands it to me.

"Thank you." I take a sip.

"Leave at seven?"

"I'll be ready." I smile, but I'm sure he knows it's forced. He hesitates but ends up walking back toward the kitchen.

Rummaging through my suitcase for appropriate beachwear, I settle on khaki shorts with pleating in the front and deep pockets, paired with an orange spaghetti strap top that fits in all the right places. A light long-sleeve button-up joins the pile in case I need a break from the sun, along with my laptop bag, reef-safe sunscreen, and a book. Flip-flops and my Texas Rangers baseball hat complete my look.

Lucas chuckles as I walk past the kitchen, only my left eyeball visible as I carry all my crap to the couch before dropping everything.

"Packing light, I see?" He smirks while unloading the dishwasher. I roll my eyes, pushing the stuff deeper onto the couch.

"Where are you diving today?"

"North Shore. Kevin heard the water is calm enough to dive. Well, for his standards, at least. Most scuba tours don't open for the season until next month. Haven't been out that way since last September, though, so I'm excited."

Kevin. I'd forgotten about that gorgeous specimen of a man

I met briefly last night. He might be just the right amount of distraction I need.

"How far is the rental car place from here?" I ask, placing my empty coffee mug into the sink.

"It's a mile away." I nod as he grabs my mug and places it upside down in the dishwasher he just emptied. "Almost ready?"

After a quick stop at the rental car agency—I need my own car since Lucas is working all week—I follow behind him to the beach. Like a cocoon, the car wraps itself around me in comfort. The radio crackles as I flip through stations, searching for island music to match the setting.

The landscape transforms as we drive toward North Shore —lush greenery everywhere, jagged green mountains rising breathtakingly in the distance. I crane my neck to see a massive Banyan tree, its ghostly trunk supported by dozens of root-pillars that spread like fingers into the earth.

I spot the iconic Haleiwa sign on our right, its white lettering and wave-riding surfer instantly recognizable. The bright colors make it irresistible to photographers and tourists.

Lucas's truck signals to make a left at the acai bowl shop, and I follow him to the beach entrance. As we enter the parking lot, beautiful monkey pod trees surround us with their expansive green canopies casting shadows across the ground.

I pull into the parking spot next to Lucas's truck, anticipation building for the beach ahead. Lucas reaches into the truck bed, pulling out a folding chair and his scuba gear. Stepping out of the car, I let the serene atmosphere wash over me. Waves crash rhythmically against the shore while palm trees sway overhead in the ocean mist. The colossal green mountains rise like ancient guardians in the distance, and every breath I take is perfumed with salt and possibility.

A couple of guys I don't recognize approach from my right.

One is wearing a full wetsuit; the other is in a two-piece wetsuit with baggy dive shorts like Lucas's. I didn't think his shorts were functional, but watching Lucas shove tools and gadgets into the large pockets proves me wrong.

No Kevin yet. Not that I'm watching for him.

Opening the back door of my rental reveals my scattered beach essentials. I toss the book, reef-safe sunscreen, hat, and wallet into my tote bag in one swift motion. The car gets locked and the door tested before I join Lucas and his dive buddies.

"Hey guys, this is my cousin, Brianna. B, this is August, Demi, and Hag."

I pause, mentally cataloging the names.

The guy in the full wetsuit speaks up, explaining while attaching the regulator to his air tank. "Hag is for Hagers, my last name. And Demi is for Demetri—nicknames we got in bootcamp. August is just . . . August."

August shrugs, lifting his hands in an *oh well* way before grabbing his fins off Lucas's truck.

"Got it, thanks," I say, giving a quick wave.

Out of the corner of my eye, a familiar black baseball cap bobs across the other side of the truck, the cab blocking my view of his face. My heart does a little skip as I wait, anticipation building like the moment before unwrapping presents on Christmas morning.

When Kevin finally steps into view, he's every bit as gorgeous as I remember, possibly even more devastating with the early morning sun casting shadows across his chiseled features. Tall and lean, but solid muscle. His dark brown hair is shaved close on the sides, and his deep blue T-shirt hugs the muscles in his chest and biceps perfectly.

He catches me staring and I awkwardly shout, "Hi!"

Lucas jumps, pausing mid-zip on his wetsuit to give me an *are you okay* look.

"Hey, Brianna." Kevin gives a devilish smile before turning back to his friends.

Oh, it's nice to see you, fine sir. Very nice.

If I stay here, I'll only embarrass myself more. I need to leave before I start drooling. And then Kevin lifts his shirt over his head.

Lean muscle ripples across his chest and shoulders, abs carved from years of military discipline. I can stay.

Definitely staying.

The rental car provides the perfect support as I lean against it, grabbing my dark sunglasses. Kevin's chest draws my attention again, and something long-dormant stirs to life inside me. Desire, yes, but something deeper. A craving I haven't experienced in years. Want. Raw, honest, breath-stealing want. I've almost forgotten what it's like to look at someone and experience that magnetic pull, that desperate need to touch and be touched. The intensity of it catches me off-guard, startling after so much time in emotional hibernation.

Wow, I really did shut everything down, because this hunger feels foreign.

Kevin slips his right arm into his wetsuit's sleeves, the material clinging to his frame. He jokes with August while zipping the front, and I find myself wondering what his hands would feel like roaming my body. I fidget with my beach towel, anticipation building as I wait for him to step out from behind the truck to see the full, gorgeous view.

"Brianna!" Lucas calls, snapping me back to reality. He laughs, and I know he caught me staring. "Do you want to go set up on the beach? We'll be over shortly."

My face flushes with embarrassment. Nothing like being busted by your cousin while ogling his friend.

"Absolutely. Do you want me to bring the cookout stuff too?" I point to the camping grill in the bed of his truck.

"No, we'll get that once we resurface. Just go and find a place past the grassy area."

Gathering my tote bag and chair, I head down the sidewalk alongside the guys assembling their tanks. *Don't look. Don't look. Don't look.*

As my feet sink from firm grass into soft sand, I'm reminded how hard it is to walk on the beach. Each step feels like I'm walking in place, so I kick off my flip-flops for better purchase. My heels plant firmly enough, but the effort to push forward and roll through to my toes turns each step into a mini workout.

Maybe I should've stayed on the grassy area. After a few more steps, I give up, dropping my tote bag and sinking into my unfolded chair. Sweat beads on my already sun-soaked skin.

The view never gets old—endless blue ocean, volcanic rock formations rising from the water, families scattered across the sand with their colorful umbrellas.

Lucas pauses beside me. "Hey, we should be down about an hour. Kevin gets bored after that."

I nod as Lucas walks toward the water—effortlessly, I might add—followed by the others.

"Not swimming?" Kevin asks as he passes by.

"Not today," I say, smiling.

He moves with confident strides toward the water, his athletic build evident beneath the neoprene. My gaze drifts down to his backside, and even the loose cargo dive shorts can't hide that view. A low hum escapes me as he and the others wade deeper into the water.

Not until their bobbing heads sink below the surface do I reach into my tote for my baseball hat and book. I press my back into the chair and slide down to ease the pressure on my tailbone, extending my legs with my feet buried in the sand. *Ahhhhh . . . This is the life.*

I make it through the first chapter of the romantic fantasy

before my eyes begin to feel heavy. They close for a few seconds at a time until I finally give in to relaxation. The book drops to my lap as I rest my head against the back of the chair. Waves wash up on shore, wind rustles through the palm trees towering above me, and faint voices drift from somewhere down the beach. It's enough of a lullaby that I succumb to the peace and drift off.

I feel movement on my right arm before any sound hits my ears. The sensation is constant, back and forth, and annoying. I groan as my body wakens.

"Brianna ... B ... " My eyes crack open and I lift my head, confused. The sun has disappeared, blocked by five dark figures in full scuba gear towering above me. "Damn, girl, you were out!" Lucas laughs and smacks my knee with his wet glove.

Salt-tinged air rushes into my lungs as I take a deep breath. The sun reappears as the rest of them move on. Lucas sees my dazed expression and chuckles.

"Stay here. We're going to change and set up the barbecue on the grass. Give me five minutes, then meet us up there."

He points behind me while unclipping his BC vest. I nod, still in a dreamy haze.

All I can think as they walk away is, *I hope my mouth wasn't hanging open when they found me.* How mortifying would that be?

I lounge for a few minutes, shaking off my grogginess before searching for my dropped book in the sand. I pack everything up and trudge toward the white folding table with Lucas's camping grill on top. Relief floods me when I step onto grass again. If Lucas witnesses how much I struggle walking, I'll never hear the end of it.

Hag and August carry coolers in the distance while Lucas approaches with several grocery bags.

My phone buzzes inside my tote and I squat, digging to the bottom for it. Three new messages.

> Sara: Hi! How's your trip going? You better not have that laptop open! 😉

> Mr. GQ Griffin: Good Afternoon, gorgeous. I'm ready to book my flight. Just want to confirm Tuesday works and I'll make it happen. 💚

> Marina Man Preston: Hey Brianna. I'm back in San Diego and thought of you yesterday when I went sailing. Looking forward to getting you out on the water! Let me know what day works for you once you're back from Hawaii. Take Care!

Overwhelm floods my mind. How does one go from not dating at all for years to juggling several at once? I run my hand through my hair in frustration, knocking my hat off in the process. After tousling my hair back to life, I toss my hat and phone into my tote. When I look up from my frazzled packing, I'm met with the most gorgeous brown eyes watching me with patient curiosity. Kevin. And judging by his amused expression, he's been there long enough to see my entire internal crisis play out.

Pushing my hands into my thighs, I stand, my gaze still locked on him.

Say something, Brianna, before this gets awkward.

"How was the dive?"

My hands slip behind my back and disappear into my khakis' pockets.

"It was good. We saw a bunch of turtles and cool fish," Kevin says, unwrapping the cheese slices.

"And I saw a shark!" August shouts from the other side of the table while handing Lucas a raw burger patty for the grill.

My eyes widen.

"Well, he *thinks* he saw a shark. But he was the only one who saw it, and we were all down there," Kevin shoots back. The rest of the guys break into laughter as August's face falls.

"I believe you, August," I say.

"Beer?" Hag asks, pointing to Kevin and then me. We both nod, and then a can comes flying toward Kevin's head. He catches it just above his chin.

"Yo! Watch it, Hag. You almost took off my face." Kevin reaches out, offering the beer to me.

"Believe me, it would be an improvement, buddy," Hag laughs, looking way too pleased with that comeback. He tosses another beer to Kevin, this one at chest level.

Kevin flips the tab, the beer making its *cshhhheee* sound. My attention follows the path of his hand, admiring his physique in the snug shirt before landing on his defined jawline as he sips.

"You okay with that beer?" Hag's voice cuts through my trance.

I glance down at the can in my grip. "Yeah, this is great."

Golden ales are probably better than IPAs for being in the blazing sun all day. At least, that's how I rationalize it.

Cshhhheee. I take my first sip. Cold and refreshing.

I wander over to Lucas, who is manning the grill. Ten burger patties sizzle in neat rows as he presses the spatula on them. Kevin and Demi finish putting their gear away while Hag and August sit in chairs a few feet away, Hag's hand deep in a bag of chips.

"Gimme some," August says, nodding his head at the bag. Hag reluctantly shares.

"You were really knocked out back there." Lucas looks up from the grill.

"Yeah, I didn't even realize I left." I laugh, taking another swig. "Was it a good dive?"

"It was." He pokes at the patties with the spatula. "Except for August becoming an air wolf down there, nearly running out by the time we breached the surface." He gives August the *you're in trouble* look.

"Oh, that's alarming." I look at August, who looks unbothered.

"It's not a big deal. All of us have dual regulators, so if he did run out, he'd just buddy up to one of our tanks," Lucas says.

Kevin and Demi approach the other side of Lucas and peer over at the burgers like hungry vultures.

"Have a seat, guys. I'll let you know when they're done. You too, B." Lucas shoos us away, and we comply like little children.

I move my chair next to August, while Kevin and Demi settle on Hag's far side.

"Demi, get your ass off the cooler? You're gonna break it. Go get your chair." Hag motions to the cooler that Demi is straddling.

"I forgot to grab it. It's too far to go back to the parking lot," Demi complains while standing briefly to grab another beer from inside it. "Convenience," he adds, holding out his beer.

"So, Brianna, how long are you on the island?" Kevin asks, his steady stare sending a quiet flutter through me.

"Till Wednesday."

"What else have you got planned?" He takes another swig.

"I'm not sure, actually." I look toward Lucas, who is tending to an out-of-control flame on the grill. He grabs the nearest water bottle and frantically drenches the left side of the grill.

"I've been here before, so I've seen all the classic touristy attractions. I'll probably repeat my favorites and relax on the beach."

I lift the can to my lips, emptying it.

"'Nother beer, Brianna?" Demi asks, pointing to my empty can. I nod.

"Are you taking off work while she's here, Lucas?" Kevin turns his head back toward the grill.

"Nah, I used too much time this year. She'll be flying solo when I'm at work," he responds, flipping the burgers. "Demi, get the cheese."

"Don't you work tonight?" August chimes in after wiping his chip-dusted hands on his shorts.

"Yeah, gotta leave at twelve. Brianna got a rental car, so she'll drive back herself," Lucas replies.

When the burgers are done, we all line up, waiting for Lucas to slide the juicy, cheese-dripping patties onto our buns. Then we wait again, this time to pile on our choice of toppings. The conversation subsides as we settle back into our chairs and take those first perfect bites.

Hag opens a second bag of chips and decides to share this time, offering to pour some onto our plates. I extend my legs, slipping my feet out of my flip-flops to wiggle my toes into the cool grass.

Something about this moment—the ocean's whisper behind us, cold beer cutting through the heat, Lucas and his friends' easy laughter—melts the tension I didn't realize I am carrying. I sink deeper into my chair and let their voices wash over me. Army stories flow into good-natured ribbing, each man taking his turn as target.

"Best dive story. Go!" August points at Lucas.

"I shit in my onesie at seventy feet." Lucas leans back with a satisfied grin.

"Why do you think I wear two-piece, numb nuts?" Hag shakes his head with fake pity.

"I drink Capri Suns on long dives." Kevin crosses his arms, completely at ease.

August chimes in. "That's not a story. You're just braggin'."

"Under the water?" I lean forward, elbows on my knees. "The kids' drink?"

"Yep." He wants me to take the bait.

I do. "How? I can barely keep it in the pouch on land."

Kevin ignores August muttering "That's what he said," and continues, "It acts as a one-way valve. The straw prevents water from going in as long as there's a good seal."

I nod, processing. His knowledge impresses me more than it should.

"Thank you for that PBS educational moment, Kev," Hag says, draining his fourth beer.

The stories continue—Crystal getting narcosis, someone's regulator failing at a hundred feet—and I'm horrified while the guys just nod and shove chips in their mouths like near-death is a regular Tuesday.

"Wow, your stories really inspire me to learn to scuba dive." Sarcasm drips from my voice as I push myself out of the chair to throw out my beer can. I feel Kevin's gaze follow me.

"All right, guys. Storytime has been fun, but I gotta go to work. B, you good to manage without me?" Lucas looks at me with that big brother concern.

"She'll be fine." Kevin's response is quick and sure. "We won't corrupt her—"

"Too much," August adds, and everyone laughs.

After Lucas leaves, we drag our chairs under a sprawling Monkey Pod tree. The afternoon passes in easy conversation and cold beer, the ocean breeze cutting through the heat as the sun moves overtop of us. I find myself stealing glances at Kevin whenever I can.

As our conversation fades, we collect the grill and scattered equipment, making our way back to the parking lot as the afternoon winds down around us.

We load the table and chairs into Hag's truck bed while August grabs the leftover chips and buns. Quick goodbyes all around, then Kevin and I continue alone toward my rental, our flip-flops slapping against the hot asphalt.

"I hope we didn't ruin your idea of diving too much." Kevin looks down at me as we walk shoulder to shoulder on the sidewalk.

"No, I learned a lot."

I'm hyperaware of every step bringing us closer to my rental car. Closer to goodbye. The late afternoon breeze carries the sound of waves lapping against the shore, and the distant voices of children echo off the bathhouse. I want to walk slower, ask him to tell me more dive stories, anything to stretch these last few minutes.

Kevin picks up on my reluctance and stops several feet from my car, his smile fading. I follow his gaze to the pavement, where shattered glass glints in the sunlight. Glass that wasn't there when we arrived.

My heart hammers against my ribs. The peaceful lapping of the tide suddenly feels too loud, the shrieking of kids' voices like nails on a chalkboard. I force myself forward on unsteady legs, glass shards crunching under my flip flops, hoping to see all windows intact on my rental.

But as I round the back of my car, my stomach drops. The passenger window is completely gone except for the jagged teeth of glass clinging to the frame, blue tinted fragments scattered across the back seat.

"Oh, my God." The words come out as barely a whisper. I

freeze three steps away, one hand flying to cover my mouth, the other reaching out as if I could somehow undo what I'm seeing.

"Shit." Kevin's voice cuts through my shock as he rushes past me.

He peers through the gaping window frame, then circles the car like he's surveying a crime scene while I stand paralyzed on the sidewalk, tourists walking by with beach bags and whispering under their breaths.

Chapter 10

Hawaii

Kevin turns to look at me, concern all over his face. "What did you have in your back seat?"

My mind feels like static. I scan my memory, retracing those first moments when I arrived at the beach, giddy with vacation excitement and the prospect of seeing Kevin again.

And then it hits me like a cold wave. My hands fly to my head, fingers digging into my scalp as I bend forward.

How much will this cost? Will the rental company blame me? How do I even report this in Hawaii? What if my insurance doesn't cover theft? Do I call local police or—

Embarrassment, regret, anger. It all crashes over me at once.

"That bad, huh?" Kevin asks, folding his arms across his chest.

My head rises slowly, and all I can see is my stupidity reflected in his sunglasses.

"My work laptop."

"Oooh. . ." He pulls off his baseball cap and runs his fingers through salt-tousled hair, the same gesture I found charming an hour ago now a physical manifestation of how badly I screwed this up.

"How could this happen?" My words come out sharper than I intend. "It's the middle of the day on a Saturday. The beach is packed with families and couples and—" I gesture wildly at the paradise around us, my voice rising. "How did no one see this? How did no one care enough to—"

My embarrassment is curdling into something hotter, more stabbing. I whip around to glare at the nearest beachgoers: A family walking to the parking lot with their cooler, kids shrieking with laughter as they run toward the bathhouse, tourists snapping selfies near the banyan trees, and suddenly they all look complicit. Like they watched it happen and did nothing.

"I'm sorry, Brianna," Kevin says, shifting his stance. "It happens a lot. They take advantage of the noise. The waves, the wind, the voices." His voice is so calm, almost clinical.

"If it happens so often, why doesn't anyone do anything about it?"

Kevin shrugs, a gesture that somehow manages to be both sympathetic and resigned. The defeat in his gesture makes me want to scream at him, at the tourists still laughing nearby, at this whole beautiful, treacherous place.

But even as the words form in my throat, I know I'm being ridiculous. I scoff, my head falling to the side as the fight drains out of me. I want to be mad at everyone else. I want someone to pay for this. But it's my own damn fault. I knew the risks. There are signs everywhere warning tourists not to leave valuables visible. I'm the one who has to pay for my decisions.

Kevin steps forward, gesturing to the car.

"Let's clean up what we can to make it safe to drive. We'll go back to my place and grab the shop vac to get the remaining glass. You can call the rental car company and have them swap out the cars, and then tomorrow you can work on getting a new work laptop."

My shoulders sink as I look back at the windowless back seat of my rental car. "Okay."

Kevin grabs a dried husk from beneath a nearby palm tree and uses it to scrape the glass off the back seat, the rigid casing protecting his hands.

I'm not sure what to do, so I stand here as he takes control of the situation with that automatic authority that must be from his Navy days. He doesn't ask permission or wait for direction, he just assesses the problem and handles it, moving with the kind of calm efficiency that comes from years of training. He checks the front seats to make sure they're free of glass, then meets me back on the sidewalk where I haven't moved.

"Best we can do right now. Follow me back to my place?"

I nod as words fail me. I unglue my flip-flops from the sidewalk and avoid looking at the windowless door as I get into the driver's seat.

Following behind Kevin's blue BMW, we head back toward the iconic Haleiwa sign. We drive through neighborhoods where older homes tell the story of the islands—weathered wooden houses with wide lanais, their tin roofs stained by decades of salt water and trade winds. Then we turn into a newer development that feels almost sterile by comparison, all matching mailboxes and fresh paint.

Pulling up against the curb in front of his house, he waits for the garage door to open. My grip tightens on the steering wheel, thoughts spinning. As his BMW disappears into the shadows of the garage, I let my head fall forward, my hands clenched tightly around the steering wheel. *This was such a great day. I was having so much fun. And I ruined it.* A sigh escapes me as I replay the day's highs and lows.

Tap tap tap.

My head lifts to find Kevin staring at me through the window.

"Pull into the driveway for me?" He motions turning the wheel with his hands, followed by a smile and a thumbs up.

I nod, forcing a smile. I would be lost without his help. Give me a hostile client or a crashed presentation, and I'm in my element. But a smashed car window in paradise? It's nice to have someone else taking the lead for once. I pull into the driveway as Kevin strides into the garage.

"Come on inside," he calls out, and I follow him through the garage into a small hallway that opens into the living room and kitchen area.

His kitchen looks like it stepped out of a home magazine—white walls, gray cabinetry, and a granite island stretching across the center with four bar stools lined up like soldiers who've never seen battle. Even the coffee pot seems positioned with intention. I scan for personal touches but find none, just clean lines and order.

"Have a seat." He motions to the square glass table beside the kitchen island. "Can I get you a drink?" He moves toward the double-door stainless steel fridge, each step smooth and unhurried.

I almost say no, but then remember the only water I have consumed is whatever was in the beer.

"Water?"

My gaze follows him as he moves around the kitchen. His T-shirt clings to his upper back, shoulder blades pressing against the fabric.

I search for my Advanced Rental email on my phone while Kevin pushes a glass to the water dispenser on the fridge. All day I've been hoping for exactly this—time alone with him, maybe even the courage to make a move. But the busted window killed the vibe, and now that I'm here, surrounded by this museum of perfection where everything sits in its designated place, I feel stiff and out of place. I'm too aware of my emotional messiness as I perch on the chair's edge, afraid that settling in might somehow leave a mark on his flawless world.

"I'm going to shop vac the rest of the glass while you call the rental car company." He pauses and then softens his tone. "They're used to this; it happens all the time. Just have them drop another car off here." From his stack of mail, he pulls out an unopened mortgage statement and slides it toward me. "Here's my address."

"Thank you, Kevin. You have been a huge help."

My hand grazes his forearm as he steps back. A spark flickers through me, cutting through the day's disappointment.

"It's what I do. I'll be in the driveway if you need me."

He disappears down the hallway.

His envelope balances between my fingers as I dial the rental car company, my left knee bouncing under the table. Dread creeps in as I think about the cost—financial and professional. My work laptop is in the hands of some thief, and I'll have to tell my boss it was stolen.

Twenty minutes later, I find myself leaning against the doorframe that leads into the garage, shamelessly admiring Kevin's ass as he bends over the shop vacuum. He steps out of the back seat and slams the car door.

I'm caught.

"Enjoying the view?" He smiles as he grabs the power cord and coils it around his thumb and elbow.

"You're the best." Warmth spreads through my chest—gratitude mixed with something I'm not ready to name.

He strides past me, locking eyes as he passes.

"Everything good with the rental?"

"Yeah. They will be here within ninety minutes to swap out the cars."

"Excellent." He lifts the shop vac onto the second shelf. "Dinner?"

I stumble over my words. "Will we be back in time?"

"I'm making dinner."

He steps closer, trapping me between his body and the doorframe, an inch of space between us. My heart hammers against my ribs as he leans in, his eyes locked on mine like he's reading my thoughts. His hand reaches to the wall beside my head, and my heart stutters.

I can smell his sunscreen and see the flecks of gold in his eyes. Every nerve ending is alert as he leans closer. I wonder if this is finally the moment when . . .

The mechanical grind of the garage opener motor shatters the silence.

The satisfied smirk on Kevin's face as he waves me inside tells me everything. He absolutely knew what he was doing. I look behind me to see the garage door button and let out a brief groan of frustration as I follow him down the hallway and into the kitchen. I prop myself onto a barstool at the kitchen island, patting my dewy forehead.

He leans across the granite, his dark eyes gleaming.

"Can I pour you some wine?"

"Yes. The bottle, please." Screw the water.

He lets out a quick laugh. "Let's start with a glass, killer." He stands and goes to the cabinet for a stemmed glass. "Red okay?" He pulls a bottle from the small wine fridge beneath the island.

"Perfect. Thank you. And thank you again for your help with the car situation."

He glances up while filling my glass. "It's not a problem at all. I'm sorry it happened." He pushes my glass toward me, then pours his own.

As the minutes tick by, he takes ownership of dinner like he took ownership of my rental car—intentional, focused, deliberate. We fall into easy conversation while he works, his voice mixing with the soft thud of the knife on the cutting board and the sizzle of something in the pan as he moves between the stove and counter with quiet efficiency.

"I hope you like fish?" His eyes lift to mine while he slices through carrots. He moves to the stove, adjusting the heat under a cast iron pan.

"I do, yeah. It's hard to get fresh fish in Dallas."

Palm trees outside his kitchen window sway in the evening breeze, deepening the shadows through the house. Kevin flips on the overhead pendant lights.

"How long have you been in this house?"

My question feels clumsy as soon as it leaves my mouth. Between his easy competence in the kitchen and the way he fills out that T-shirt, I feel as though I've forgotten how to form coherent sentences. It's like talking to hot men is a foreign language I can't remember anymore.

"Five years. When I got out of the Navy, my security clearance opened more opportunities here than on the mainland. And I didn't want to leave anyway."

"I can imagine. You are in paradise." My wine glass hovers at my lips.

Kevin looks out the sliding glass doors off the living room.

"Most of the time it is."

"So, when did you start diving?"

"In the Navy. I joined the dive team about a year in, and the rest is history." He chops the ends off the green beans. "We did some crazy shit. More than your average diver. We were trained for EOD work." He raises his eyebrows while tossing the green beans into a glass dish. "Explosive ordinance disposal."

"Under the water?"

"Fun stuff." He lifts the cast iron pan, the sauce sizzling as he spoons it over the fish.

I find myself studying his shoulders again, the way his lats flare like wings beneath his shirt—my favorite part of him.

"How long were you in the Navy?"

"Eight years. I probably would've been out in four if it wasn't for diving."

He grabs two square plates along with silverware and napkins, laying them out on the island.

"Have a seat at the table. I'll plate these and be right over." He reaches for the pan with a black oven mitt, swirling the juices around the cuts of fish a few more times.

The chair feels cool against the back of my legs. I run my fingers up and down the stem of my wine glass as Kevin strides over with our dinner.

"Here you go." A waft of lemony goodness drifts past my nose.

Kevin sets the square plate down in front of me, then pauses. His eyes narrow as he studies it. I follow his gaze, scanning for a rogue green bean or sauce splatter, but the food looks perfect.

He reaches over and rotates my plate with two fingers, aligning the corners with the table's edges. The adjustment is maybe half an inch, but now the plate sits in perfect harmony with the table's lines.

"There." He gives a small nod of satisfaction.

Witnessing his need for precision, an obsession that doesn't exist in my world, something wicked sparks in me. I nudge the right corner of my plate, deliberately misaligning it with the table's edge. I look up, poking the bear.

An annoyed groan erupts as he leans over and pushes the left side so the plate is square to the edge of the table once again.

"Are you trying to kill me?" he asks as he sits down across from me.

I wait to answer, moving my finger closer to the plate's corner, threatening to push it again.

"Don't you dare."

He points his fork at me, his mouth twitching as if he's trying not to smile. Not until he sees my finger retreat does he take his first bite.

I pick up my fork and follow suit.

The tuna is seared to perfection. It's cooked all the way through as I requested, and flakes like layers of pastry. I let out a quiet *"Mmm,"* taking the first bite. Kevin looks up with a pleased expression as he stabs at the green beans on his plate

"This is delicious. The lemon, butter, and whatever you used to season it." I cut into the fish for another bite, savoring the perfect balance of flavors.

"I'm glad you like it." He takes a sip of wine, eyes locked on mine over the rim of his glass.

I raise my fork for another bite, too absorbed in our silent staring match to pay attention to what I'm doing, and end up stabbing my lip. My bite of fish drops to the table. *Smooth.*

Kevin bursts out laughing, coughing on his bite while I drop my head in mortification. I'm a complete idiot. Why do I even try to be sexy?

"You know, a little to your right and you would've had it," he jokes. "Like this."

He opens his mouth wide as he demonstrates the proper technique.

"Do I really have to open up my mouth that wide?"

"You do with me." His brow lifts, playful and unbothered.

A nervous laugh slips out before I can stop it, and just like that, dinner becomes the last thing on my mind. I wasn't prepared for this—for how easily he can unravel me with words.

When was the last time someone made me this flustered?

We finish eating without any more innuendos, just stories that reveal pieces of Kevin. He talks about his Navy travels and near-death scuba dives, casually tossing out brush-with-death moments as if he's reading off a grocery list. He's either fearless or numb, and I can't tell which, but both are intoxicating.

As he describes managing his team through equipment failures and emergency rescues, I start to understand something about him. His years commanding a Navy crew clearly ingrained an automatic response to crisis. He doesn't think about taking charge when things go wrong, he just does it with instinctive efficiency. Taking control isn't a conscious decision for him, it's muscle memory.

And it's hot.

"Can I help clean up?"

I stand from the table as Kevin walks his plate to the sink.

"Nope, just relax." He heads to the kitchen and grabs a second bottle. "Another glass of wine?"

"Any more and I might not be able to drive home."

"Would that be a bad thing?" He grins over his shoulder at me, and the air shifts—subtle, but unmistakable.

His eyes stay on me, my silence stretching between us, heavy with meaning.

The doorbell rings, breaking through the tension like a cold splash of water.

Chapter 11

Hawaii

Kevin wipes his hands on a dish towel while I dig out my car keys and follow him to the door.

A young guy in his twenties stands at the door wearing the same gray work shirt Derrik wore when I met him at the Dallas airport.

"Hi, I'm with Advanced Rental, here to swap your vehicle."

"Here you go." I slip between Kevin and the door, my arm brushing against his solid chest as I hand over the keys. The space between us thrums with tension, even as the attendant swaps keys and hands me a new rental agreement. The mundane transaction feels surreal against the electricity crackling between me and this scuba diver.

"Keep both agreements with you," the man from the rental agency says. "The damage will be discussed when you drop the car off."

He steps back, signaling he's done.

I catch half his words. If he said I owed ten thousand dollars for the car, it wouldn't even register. Not with Kevin this close, energy pulsing between us like a quiet current. The anticipation has been building all day, coiling tighter with every glance, every harmless touch, until now it threatens to snap.

Kevin closes the door, and I follow him into the kitchen where I place my wine glass in the sink. I sense him behind me, the air between us charged.

When I turn around, I'm met with all that solid muscle barely contained by cotton, and when my gaze finally lifts to his, he's already watching me.

He braces both hands on the counter, trapping me against the sink, and heat spreads through my chest. The way he moves—confidently, deliberately—makes me wonder if this is how he commands everything. Does he take charge in the bedroom the same way he commanded his crew? The thought sends a thrill through me that I wasn't expecting.

I study the hunger in his stare as he leans in, and my breath catches. Those strong hands can navigate underwater depths and handle diving equipment with such precision, I wonder what they'd feel like exploring every inch of my body.

A part of me that I buried years ago claws its way to the surface, desperate and alive, and I realize what I've been starving myself of—what it feels like to be wanted, to want, to let go and open myself to something real. I shut it all out for so long, but now it's here and I don't want it to end.

Kevin's face inches closer, then stops. His jaw is tight, his breathing uneven. He hovers, close enough that I can feel the heat radiating off him, but he doesn't close the distance.

Then his lips brush mine—light, questioning, uncertain—and a spark flickers in that gentle touch.

I don't pull away. His lips linger, soft, as though he's testing the waters while my hands find his forearms, steadying myself and maybe him, too.

His eyes flicker open, searching mine, that obvious hunger. He bridges the gap between us once more, his lips meeting mine like a whispered promise. He deepens the kiss just enough to let me know he's completely present, patient, and wanting more.

His control surprises me. I expect him to be more aggressive, more demanding, but this restrained intensity might be even more dangerous. Is he holding back because he's a gentleman, or because when he finally lets go, it's going to be overwhelming?

My lips move against his in breathless bursts. Then something shifts. His restraint cracks, and his careful control gives way to pure need.

His arms wrap tightly around my back, pulling me flush against him while his tongue traces mine—urgent, demanding. His hips press into mine, and the weight of his arousal is undeniable and insistent.

A soft moan slips from me, releasing the pressure coiled beneath my skin, and he takes it as permission.

His hands slide to my waist, fingers searching for the break between fabric and skin. When he finds it, he pauses, just for a second, then traces the line of my hips with slow reverence. The careful way he touches me, as though he's memorizing every curve, makes me wonder if he approaches everything with this kind of focused attention.

His hands trace back up my sides, thumbs brushing my stomach until he reaches the edge of my bra. I suck in a breath and he pauses, still reading me, still giving me space to stop this.

I don't want it to stop.

I press my chest into his, giving him my answer without words, and his thumbs graze my bra, circling and teasing until my nipples tighten under the fabric. Another moan escapes before I can stop it, and he responds instantly, his hands shifting as his fingers curve to cup my breasts.

I want so badly to rip off this bra. Now.

He pulls me closer, the solid strength of his body against mine intoxicating. I can feel the power in his arms, the kind of strength that comes from years of physical training and discipline. What would it be like to have all that controlled power focused entirely on me? To have someone who's used to being in command surrender that control—or maybe not surrender it at all?

One hand slides down, hooking into the waistband of my shorts before he pauses, his forehead pressed to mine, breath shallow.

"Is this what you want?" he asks, his voice low, breathless.

God, yes.

I grab the hem of my tank top and lift it over my head, letting it drop to the floor. I lean back and his gaze drops to my breasts, perched in my pink balconette bra, and when his eyes meet mine again, they're dark with hunger.

He kisses me hard, and this time, we stop pretending we're not all in. He stumbles slightly, still kissing me, and I feel the shift as he pulls my back away from the countertop.

His lips break from mine, and the loss is instant, sharp. But then his hand finds mine, fingers interlocking as he leads me out of the kitchen and down the hall.

My body is a live wire, energy zip-lining through every vein.

His bedroom is dimly lit, masculine and clean, with a king-sized bed that dominates the space. The reality of what's about to happen hits me like a wave.

Kevin cradles my cheek as he takes several sure steps, backing me against the door until it slams shut, then crashes his lips into mine. Air escapes as his hard frame presses into me. The kiss is reckless and consuming. I'm too busy chasing the strokes of his tongue to recognize where his hands are traveling.

My entire body flares to life as he kisses a path down my

throat. He palms my waist, pulling me against his hard angles. My hands slide up his well-defined arms to his shoulders. My fingers fall into the valley between his collar bone and chest.

Then I reach down for his shorts and work the button and zipper until gravity takes them to the floor and I'm greeted with a pleasant surprise—nothing underneath. I glide my hand down past his belly button, and his jaw flexes. He groans as I squeeze his hard length, rocking his hips into my hand.

"Fuck, Brianna." His voice is rough as gravel.

His free hand slides around and squeezes my ass, and he pulls me away from the door toward his bed.

He sits on the edge of the mattress and pulls me into him, my legs straddling his body. He leans in, kissing the space between the lace edge of my bra and the rounded top of my breast, each kiss more urgent and desperate, his tongue tracing to the next spot. He nips at my skin as his left hand moves to cradle my breast and he bites harder.

I gasp at the sharp pain, his nose tracing over the spot as his mouth moves to the fabric over my perked nipple.

"Sit," he commands as he pulls at my hips. I sit on his bent legs, my knees digging into the edge of the bed. He reaches for my bra, unsnapping the hooks with ease and tossing it across the room. "Damn," he says, admiring my perky breasts, standing at attention just for him.

I feel myself dissolving under his intense stare. His hand traces light circles on my breast as he hovers his mouth over mine, the anticipation of his kiss maddening. My fingers trail down his chest to the bottom of his shirt and I pull up. His torso is tan and sharp, every line of him carved for battle, built by the Navy. A smile stretches across my face.

Kevin smirks. "You like what you see?"

I trace the pads of my fingers back down his chest, savoring every moment before I meet his gaze.

"*Mmm hmm.*" I instinctively lick my bottom lip.

"Stand," he demands, and gives my ass a playful smack.

"Yes, Sir," I respond, twitching a smile as I rise and take a step back.

He tilts his head, eyes narrowed.

"Fuck, you're going to be the death of me."

He prowls forward, power caged beneath the surface like a predator savoring the heartbeat before he seizes my mouth again, his grip fisted in my hair.

Lost in intensity, I barely notice his hands clamp around my hips, yanking me off the floor and tossing me onto the bed, the frame protesting beneath my weight. My hair fans out around me, arms stretched above the crown of my head.

A groan escapes him as he takes in every piece of me.

"I love the look of you . . . naked on my bed." A sly grin tugs at his lips. "Move up," he demands as he climbs on top of me, his arousal grazing my leg as his mouth dives between my breasts. He moves side to side, giving each one their own attention. Through the intoxicating sensations and the breathless pants, I can no longer think straight.

He sits up, kneeling beside me, undoing the button on my shorts.

"These need to come off now," he orders, and in one tug, they're also across the room. He grins, looking at the apex of my body, covered by a pink lace thong. His breath becomes ragged as his fingers hook the strings near my hips, gently pulling down. "These are too pretty to rip," is all he says as he slides them slowly down my body.

I'm lost in him, in this moment . . . and I have no words. The last time I felt anything like this, it barely touched me. This . . . it wraps around me, pulling me under, leaving me breathless. I want to reply, to tease, to say anything, but I'm undone, adrift in something entirely new.

He leans over me, his mouth inches from mine, scanning my face like he's looking for answers to an unknown question.

His fingers slide down my stomach, and the closer his hand gets to my hips, the further my mouth opens, sucking in air. His touch is electric. He captures my mouth as his hand cups the apex of my thighs, and I moan at the pressure of his grip.

He slips in one finger and my back arches in response. Then two, and the knot of pleasure builds.

"Kevin . . . " is all that comes out as my body squirms, and I react to each thrust. His bicep flexes with each movement and I'm about to combust. It's all happening so fast. All I can do is whimper against the back of my hand, as he pumps his fingers in and out of me. A sexy smile grows on his face and then he curls his fingers against my inner walls and I gasp.

He has no idea how long it's been for me.

"Oh, shit." I gasp, as my pleasure looks for its escape. I want to hold it in, to feel the buildup a bit longer, but my body refuses. The energy inside me surges, a torrent that threatens to burst into flames. My breathing becomes quicker and my muscles clench as my orgasm washes over me. I cry out in a pleasure I haven't met before, every nerve ending singing his praise.

Wasting no time, his lips are on mine once more, his one hand bracing against the bed, the other trailing up my thigh to my breast. My nipples are tight and sensitive as they brush against his chest.

"I will burst apart if you're not inside me in the next two seconds," I say, panting.

"We can't have that, can we?" he says as he reaches for the side table drawer, pulling out a condom.

He slowly drags the latex down his shaft like the calm before the storm. In seconds, the swollen head of his arousal is pressed against my bundle of nerves and I am consumed, drowning in the sensation.

"It's been more than two seconds," he says, teasing me. He can sense it—every shuddered inhale, the hunger etched across my face—how desperate I am for him.

"Please," I beg him as he dances around my entrance.

"Keep begging like that and I won't hold back."

He pushes in with one long roll of his hips, consuming every inch of me. There's nothing cautious about how he thrusts into me. He's taking what is his. And the power he unleashes is the hottest thing I've ever witnessed. He's so fucking deep that I feel him everywhere. I brace one hand against the headboard to keep us from sliding up any more.

He slams into me over and over and I surrender, helpless and alive. I stare up at the ribbing of muscle all around me as waves of heat roll through me with each thrust.

"God, you feel good," he says, pounding himself into me.

"Harder," I call out, my voice breathless. It's been so long, but I want to be broken by him. A tidal wave of sensation rolls over as he penetrates me with great force. Fire floods my veins, and my eyes roll to the back of my head, focusing on the sounds our bodies make together.

Kevin pierces his arm underneath my back and pulls my torso up until I'm kneeling over his hips.

"Ride me," he orders, palming my ass. He pulls me up, then drops me onto him, and I land with a gasp. Each motion sends stars spinning across my vision, and I can't catch my breath. I'm drowning in this sensation.

I can tell the storm is about to break inside him. His breathing comes in ragged gasps, matching his rhythm. His neck muscles tighten, his breath spilling like heat into the air. He buries himself to the hilt inside me one last time, his eyes rolling back in pure pleasure, lips parting with shallow, urgent exhales. The growl that escapes him is the sexiest sound I've ever heard.

His abdominal muscles contract and he quivers before sinking against me.

"Fuck, that was incredible," he says as he buries his face in my neck.

He lowers me onto the bed and we lie together, tangled and catching our breath. Pure bliss.

A smile forms on my face as I replay the last few moments.

"You're smiling," he says.

"You're supposed to have your eyes closed like me."

I open one eye to look at him, only to close it again.

He chuckles at my silliness.

"I can't help but admire the beautiful woman lying in my bed right now."

My body still tingles everywhere he touched me, and I peek at him once more. His hand wanders around my waist before pulling me onto my side and closer to him. Smiling, he reaches for my butt and gives it a smack.

God, I completely forgot it could feel like this. Forgot how everything inside me could ignite like Fourth of July fireworks.

The walls I've built so carefully over the years, the ones that kept me safe and lonely, feel like they've crumbled in the span of an evening. Why did I resist this for so long? Why did I convince myself I didn't need anyone, didn't want to feel this vulnerable, this alive? I want to freeze this moment, bottle this feeling so it never slips away. I don't know how to go back to pretending I don't need this.

Chapter 12

Hawaii

My eyes blink open, adjusting to the morning light. The room is quiet and warm, sunlight spilling across the sheets. Outside the window, palm trees sway lazily against a cloudless sky.

For a moment, I just lie there, letting the stillness wrap around me. Then I reach behind me, fingers searching for the heat of another body.

Nothing.

The space is empty and cold.

Disappointment creeps in before I can stop it. I haven't woken up next to someone in a long time. I didn't realize how badly I wanted to.

But this is *his* house. He can't leave me. Can he? Where do you go on Sunday mornings? For all I know, he's sitting in a pew somewhere, praying for forgiveness for what he did to me last night. I hate that I don't know him well enough to guess.

Sitting upright, I push the covers back like I might find him hidden underneath. The floor is a scattered mess of clothes. I grab mine, dressing in silence. Each movement feels louder than it should, as though I'm disturbing a moment that never fully belonged to me.

I tiptoe down the hallway, though I'm not sure why. It's not like he forgot I am here, but something about waking up in a man's house—one I met two days ago—makes me instinctively quieter.

The kitchen is empty, but the smell of coffee drifts in the air, rich and grounding. I peek around the corner into the living room.

There he is.

He sits in a wide, modern gray chair with sharp lines and silver legs—clean, intentional, just like him. One leg crossed over the other, a black coffee mug resting in his hand, a book open in his lap. I didn't think it was possible to fall harder, but here we are.

He looks completely relaxed, like this morning is just another Sunday. Like I didn't break apart in his bed eight hours ago.

I step into the room and he looks up from the page.

"Good morning," he says, his eyes meeting mine.

"Good morning."

I hover on the far side of the living room, fingers fidgeting. Do I sit on his lap? Kiss him good morning? Pretend last night never happened? Walk straight out the door?

"Can I get you some coffee?" he asks, breaking the silence.

Relief floods through me. "Yes, please. Thanks."

I force a smile, taking a deep breath to settle the flutter in my chest.

The plush carpet cushions my steps as I move closer to his chair, curiosity pulling me toward the book in his hands.

He sets the book beside his coffee mug and stands, squeezing my shoulder—a small touch, familiar but careful—before heading to the kitchen.

Great. He regrets sleeping with me. I was as bad in bed as I feared, and he's being polite, offering coffee like some consolation prize. I don't even want the damn coffee anymore. All I want is to run out of this house, run far enough that he can't find me. Run until I forget this morning ever happened.

"Lucas has been blowing up my phone all night," Kevin says, pouring coffee into a mug.

I blink, my eyes wide. Lucas was the furthest from my mind last night.

"I totally forgot to text him."

"He's fine," Kevin says. "I told him what happened to your car and we came back here to swap it out."

He reaches into the fridge. "Milk?"

"No, thanks." I shake my head, grateful he filled Lucas in.

He pads back from the kitchen barefoot, and something about the domestic sight of him carrying coffee makes my pulse quicken. The mug appears in front of me, and when his thumb grazes my knuckles as I take it, something warm spreads through my chest. I follow him back to the living room, claiming the chair next to his. Shit. I think I really like this guy.

This feels so awkward though. I hate mornings after—the stilted politeness, the careful distance, the way passion from the night before feels like something that happened to someone else entirely.

But what I hate most is the creeping doubt that's already settling in my chest. Was I just convenient? An opportunity for him to get laid while showing the tourist a good time? The questions feel ugly even as they form, but I can't shake them.

I replay last night in my mind—the way he touched me, looked at me, commanded me. It felt real. It felt like more than just scratching an itch. But sitting here watching him move around like nothing earth-shattering happened, I second guess everything.

That unwelcome thought twists deeper because this wasn't some random hookup for me. It's been so long since I've been with anyone, so long since I've wanted to be with anyone. Last night felt monumental, like emerging from emotional hibernation into the warmth of real life.

And maybe that's the problem. Maybe what felt like a revelation to me was just another Saturday night for him.

I shift awkwardly as Kevin swipes through his phone, his attention elsewhere.

I need to know what comes next. Every question I want to ask feels like a landmine waiting to explode.

If I ask what he's doing today, will he think I'm clingy? Or that I want to spend every moment with him until I leave? The truth is, I don't even know what I want. I wasn't expecting this.

"So, what are your plans today?" I blurt out.

I take a hasty gulp of coffee, the steam stinging my eyes.

"I told Dom I'd go fill bottles at the dive shop later," he says, voice casual. "There's a beginner dive I might help on too, if they need extra hands. You never know how a newbie will react underwater."

He lifts his mug to his lips, and for a second, I wish I were that coffee cup—close, warm, and important.

"Oh, that's nice of you. Those new divers would be lucky to have you as one of their guides."

I instantly regret how formal I sound. Like I'm complimenting a coworker, not the guy who just made me forget what planet I was on.

Kevin sets his mug on the side table.

"I was wondering," he says, glancing at me.

I lift my mug to my lips for another sip.

"Would you like to go to dinner tonight?"

My coffee goes down the wrong pipe. I sputter, hand flying

to my mouth as I choke on the inhale. Kevin's expression shifts to concern, ready to spring into action.

I wave him off with one hand while coughing into the other, eyes watering . . . again.

"It's just breathing, Brianna," he teases, the corner of his mouth lifting.

I toss my hands up, wheezing. "Then why is it so hard?"

We both laugh, even as I keep coughing, my face probably the same shade as a fire truck.

But beneath the embarrassment, I realize his question is still hanging there. He asked me to dinner. Which means I'm not just a quick lay, and he wants to see me again. Maybe this isn't as hard or as complicated as I thought. He wouldn't ask me out again if he wasn't interested in something . . . with me.

"So?" He tips back the last of his coffee.

"I'd love to," I say, swallowing down the last of my cough.

"Great. Want to meet me back here around five thirty?"

"Sounds good," I reply, doing my best to mask the Cheshire cat grin threatening to take over my entire face.

I sit in my new rental car outside Kevin's house, rushing through my usual rental car routine, hoping to get out of here before he heads off to the dive shop.

I adjust the side mirrors, then shove my hand between the seat and door to find the seat's adjustment lever. I push forward—too far. I push back—too far. Forward again. Perfect.

My phone buzzes in my front pocket.

> Mr. GQ Griffin: Hey Beautiful. I'm back in NY and was thinking about our first date. I hope you're enjoying Hawaii. I'm really looking forward to date #2 in San Antonio. I haven't been there in a few years.

I let out a grumble, rolling my eyes at Griffin and his grand romantic gesture of flying to Texas for a date. I still haven't decided if it's flattering or stalkerish, but that's a problem for later. I toss the phone in my purse, shift into drive, and hit the gas harder than usual.

My phone rings again from somewhere deep in my handbag, and I fumble blindly while steering, fingers catching on lip gloss and a granola bar wrapper before finally finding it.

Lucas. Of course. I swipe to answer just before it goes to voicemail.

"Hey, you little hussy, you," he says without a trace of shame.

"Shut up," I say, trying not to laugh. "My rental car was vandalized and my laptop was stolen." I toss it out like a headline, hoping he grabs the bait. Anything to steer him away from the real story.

His tone shifts, softer now, and I exhale with relief. Let's see how long I can keep him off the topic of Kevin.

"I'm sorry that happened, B. That sucks. Unfortunately, it happens all the time here." Not exactly comforting, but sincere. "Kev said it was your work laptop though? So you don't have any personal data on it?"

"I don't."

Lucas hesitates. "Did you tell your boss yet?"

"No," I admit. "I'm heading to that coffee shop you took me to last year to make some calls."

I fumble with my phone charger at the red light.

"So. Last night, huh?" Lucas's voice oozes mischief. I can practically hear the grin spreading across his face.

I roll my eyes. *Here we go.*

"Oh, my God, Lucas. I am *not* talking to you about this."

"What? We're all adults here," he says, all mock innocence. "And I think it's great. I support it. Encourage it. You should do it again . . . and again . . . . And—"

His voice gets more breathless with each word, like he's narrating a late-night Cinemax scene.

"Lucas!" I bark, yanking the wheel as I turn left.

"I'm done, I'm done," he says, barely holding it together.

I exhale as I turn into the shopping plaza.

" . . . and *again* . . . And *again! Oh, Kevin!*" he screams into the phone.

I snatch my phone from the cup holder and press the red button. "That's enough of *that*."

In all honesty, I still need to process everything that happened last night. It's a lot. Especially for someone like me, someone who's spent the last few years pretending desire is optional.

It's too much right now to have Lucas busting my chops.

Ding.

I glance down at my phone resting on my lap.

> Lucas: and again!!!!

A laugh escapes me before I can stop it.

God, I love that kid. Even though he's not really a kid anymore—just five years younger than me. We grew up in the same town, went to the same elementary school, shared the same circle of friends. He used to complain that teachers would say, "Lucas, I expect you to be as well-behaved as your cousin, Brianna."

He wasn't. Ever.

I toss my phone into my purse, still smiling. Leave it to him to make everything feel a little less overwhelming—even when he's being an absolute menace.

Time to focus. I have some tough phone calls to make.

Later, I can freak out about dinner.

I unzip my suitcase and riffle through my clothes, searching for something that says *dinner with an ex-Navy guy who's way smarter and hotter than I'm ready for, and possibly way out of my league.*

Nothing feels quite right. I press my palm to my forehead with a long, slow sigh. Sweat beads at my hairline. I'm from Dallas; I know humidity. But today, even the air feels overwhelming.

I didn't panic this much when I went out with Rental Car Guy or Mr. GQ, did I? Is this what it feels like to embrace something I wrote off a while ago? The thought twists my stomach in a mix of nerves and something more terrifying—hope. Hope that maybe this guy could be different. That maybe *I* could be different.

"B!" Lucas calls from the kitchen.

I push the door open to find him popping the cap off a beer by the fridge.

"What's the update on the work laptop?" he asks, holding up the bottle and mouthing, *Want one?*

I nod, walking a few steps to the kitchen counter.

"My boss is ordering me a new one. Said my team was due

for an upgrade next quarter anyway, so . . . silver lining, I guess."

Lucas slides a cold beer across the counter.

"Oh, good. Damn."

I take a sip, the cold fizz slicing through the heat that clings to my skin.

Lucas leans on the counter, head tilted downward, but his eyes flick up with mischief.

"I hear you have plans tonight."

The way he says it makes my stomach flip.

"Yes. I do. And I have nothing to wear."

Lucas raises an eyebrow. "He's a Navy guy."

"Exactly. Which is why I want to look nice." My face crumbles into an exaggerated pout.

"Fair." He takes a sip, eyeing me over it. "Where's he taking you?"

"I don't know. I'm meeting him at his place at five-thirty."

Lucas smirks.

"So, I shouldn't expect you home tonight, then?" He waggles his eyebrows, and I roll my eyes so hard I might sprain them.

I scoff and wave him off. "Don't be gross."

But his comment sticks, replaying in my head as I take another sip. I hope I don't come back here tonight.

For Kevin, this could be casual—just dinner with the girl he hooked up with last night. A fun time. No pressure. But for me? Everything feels charged with possibility. The possibility of the one thing I've been too scared to let myself want. Like a door I thought was locked has swung open and now I stand at the threshold, heart hammering as I decide whether to step through.

"Well, make sure you take my spare key. I work early on Monday mornings."

I grin.

Chapter 13

Hawaii

I pull into Kevin's driveway at five-thirty. Excitement and nerves tangle in my chest.

Kevin holds the front door open as I walk up the path. His gray collared shirt and dark denim should be ordinary, but on him they look anything but.

"Hey," he says, smiling as the wind catches my yellow sundress. He leans in to kiss my cheek as I reach the front door. Goose bumps rise on my arms. He steps aside, letting me through the door.

"You ready to eat?" He reaches for his keys on the kitchen island and I smile, remembering last night—me leaning against that same island for our first kiss. That first kiss changed everything for me.

"I am." I smooth down the sides of my dress in an attempt to calm my nerves, and follow him into the garage.

"The passenger side is unlocked," he says, pointing toward the car as he gets in the driver's side. The interior is spotless—black leather that smells faintly of cleaner and that new car scent, though I can tell it's not a current model.

"You look beautiful," he says, pulling out of the garage.

"Thank you," I respond, warmth spreading through my chest.

"How'd everything go with the laptop?"

"Good, actually." I shift in my seat. "My boss said our team was scheduled for an upgrade anyway, so I'll just get mine early."

He nods. "I'm glad it worked out."

My phone dings. I fish it out of my purse.

> Mr. GQ Griffin: What is my princess up to?
> Are you catching any sunsets?

I grip my phone tighter before shoving it back into my purse.

"So," I say, turning my attention back to him, "How was this morning? Did you end up helping with the beginner dive?"

"I did," he responds, eyes on the road. "Got paired up with a nineteen-year-old kid named Cody. He was solid—handled the basics, didn't panic. His sister, though"—he lets out a breath, the corner of his mouth twitching—"She couldn't sink. Kept floating to the top, had to climb back in the boat twice to add weight. We finally get her down, and two minutes later she's signaling she can't breathe."

My eyes widen. "Was something wrong with her gear?"

"No. Cody checked everything—bottles, pack, lines. All fine. She just panicked. Said she *felt* like she couldn't breathe, so I took her up while Cody stayed with the rest of the group."

He says it so calmly, like none of it rattles him. There's something about his competence, the way he takes charge in dangerous situations, that makes heat pool in my stomach.

"She okay, though?" I ask.

"Yeah, just nerves. Happens all the time. New divers think they're ready until the water closes over their heads."

He runs his hand through his hair, messing it perfectly. I focus on his hand, remembering how those same fingers felt last night against my skin.

"That's got to be hard. Not knowing how someone's going to react until they're already under."

Kevin shrugs, a small smile on his lips.

"You learn to read the signs. You can't control everything, but you can be ready for the moment things go sideways." He taps the steering wheel lightly. "It also helps if you're comfortable with mouth breathing. For some reason, new divers try to breathe only from their nose and it feels restricting in most masks."

I raise an eyebrow. "Oh? I think I'd be fine mouth breathing."

He smirks. "Yeah, I figured that out last night." He laughs, unbothered, clearly enjoying himself.

"Wait—was I *snoring*?" *Please don't say yes. Please say you're kidding.*

"Just a little," he says, his voice warm with amusement. One corner of his mouth quirks up, and I catch a glimpse of that devastating smile. "It was cute."

I groan, slumping back against the seat and pressing my hand to my forehead.

"Great. I probably drooled too."

He doesn't answer, but I see him bite his lower lip to keep from laughing, confirming every fear I have.

As we pull into the restaurant parking lot, he finally speaks —just one little phrase, under his breath.

"Worth it."

The restaurant rises two stories, its glass walls folded back like an accordion, erasing the boundary between inside and out.

The parking lot, however, is a different story. Dirt and

uneven gravel make my wedges wobble with every step, and I have to slow down to avoid twisting an ankle.

Kevin walks ahead, completely unfazed, moving across the rough ground as competently as he walks through sand.

Inside, we're led to a small table tucked into the front corner. It's private enough to escape the bar chatter, but close enough to the open windows that I can see the ocean across the street.

The light outside is shifting, casting everything in golden-pink tones that make Kevin's skin look even more tanned.

The server drops off our water and introduces herself. I order a local IPA, and Kevin nods to me before ordering the same.

As she walks away, I lean in. "So . . . last night you said you've owned your house for five years, but how long have you been in Hawaii?"

"Seven years," he says, folding his hands loosely on the table. His forearms rest against the wood, and I find myself staring at the way his muscles shift under his skin. "Once I got out of the Navy, I knew I wanted to stay near the water. I ended up at the NSA."

My eyebrows shoot up. "The NSA? Like, National Security Agency?"

He shrugs.

I nod, wide-eyed. "That's impressive."

"It's really not," he says, but the way his mouth lifts tells me he doesn't mind the compliment.

"You have to have, like, top-tier security clearance to get a job there," I say. "That's not nothing."

Kevin smiles again, his eyes steady on mine.

"Again, not that impressive. Honestly? My job is boring. Explaining it would put you to sleep."

I lean forward, resting my chin on my hand. "Try me."

He studies me for a second, something amused in his gaze.

"You really want to hear about data models and signal patterns?"

"Maybe," I tease. "Depends on how good you are at telling stories."

And he is. Kevin transforms intelligence analysis into compelling storytelling—explaining how he dives through oceans of data searching for anomalies that could signal threats. What could be boring technical work becomes fascinating detective stories, and I find myself completely absorbed in his world of digital patterns and hidden connections.

Beer, dinner orders, and another thirty minutes of the kind of conversation that makes me realize how long it's been since I genuinely enjoyed someone's company.

Our food shows up almost as an afterthought. The scent of grilled fish and citrus hits me first, while Kevin's prime rib looks like it was carved off the cow five minutes ago.

"Wow," I murmur, adjusting my napkin over my lap. "I didn't realize how hungry I am."

"You picked a good one." He nods toward my ono. "That's the best thing on the menu."

"I usually do," I say with a soft grin, cutting into the macadamia-crusted fillet.

He doesn't take the bait, just smirks as he lifts his beer and studies me before taking a sip. My stomach does that somersault thing it only started doing again in the last forty-eight hours.

We eat in comfortable silence, the low crash of waves and distant conversation filling the space between us.

"As I was saying earlier," Kevin says, picking up our earlier conversation, "There's a popular wreck site about ten minutes off the coast of Waikiki. We charter out to it from the marina."

I pause mid-bite, fork suspended. "You just dive into a sunken ship?"

He shrugs, that easy, confident gesture I'm starting to recognize.

"It's calculated. The Sea Tiger wreck sits about a hundred feet down, so we monitor our air and take decompression stops on the way up. Remember what I told you about narcosis?"

"This sounds terrifying." My eyes must be saucer-wide. "And you're talking about it like ordering coffee."

"Because it's routine if you know what you're doing," he says, settling back in his chair.

I laugh, the sound escaping before I can stop it.

"Can you actually go inside the wreck?"

"Multiple entry points. It's mostly stable, but the real risk is getting your lines caught. That's why having a dive buddy matters. You look out for each other."

He delivers this with complete matter-of-factness. No smugness, no bravado. Like being the kind of person who swims inside sunken metal coffins is just another Monday.

"People enjoy this?" I laugh at the absurdity. "I mean, it sounds amazing, but also like you need a PhD in not dying."

He smiles. "Takes some training. But it's peaceful once you're down there."

He leans forward, forearms settling on the table. "I'll take you." His eyebrows lift in challenge.

I burst out laughing. "Absolutely not."

He sits back and reaches for his beer. My traitorous eyes follow the movement of his lips against the rim.

"You don't trust me?" His voice carries that light curiosity, like the answer doesn't matter but he's filing it away.

"Oh, I trust *you*," I say. "After everything I've heard this weekend, I trust you with my life." I pause, pressing my hand to my chest. "I just don't trust *myself*."

His smile deepens. His chest seems to expand, and he settles back in his chair, satisfaction radiating from him like heat.

Our food disappears between stories and laughter until the server eventually appears with the check. Kevin reaches for it before I can even think to offer, and after settling the bill, we step into the parking lot where the restaurant noise fades behind us. The sun has melted into the horizon, painting the sky in watercolor streaks of blues and purples.

"Thank you for dinner," I say as we walk toward his BMW.

"Of course."

The drive to Kevin's hums with tension. The good kind.

Kevin glances over, a smirk pulling at his mouth. "So, have I convinced you to start diving yet? We could get you fifty feet down before you leave."

I scoff. "I'm happy existing above the water's surface. But I might look into taking a course back home so I won't be a complete air-wolf my first time."

He chuckles. "You don't need a course. You've got me and Lucas."

His hand finds my thigh. Not a pat—a claim. Heat burns through the fabric of my dress.

Please don't move your hand. Please.

He doesn't. His fingers trace slow lines against the light cotton, like he knows the effect he's having.

Electricity zings through my nerves. I want to keep breathing like a normal person, but it's impossible when every brush of his fingers feels like a request.

Is this his official invitation? Yes, I accept. I'll attend your bedroom. Yes, I'll be naked. And yes, I can guarantee mouth breathing when we fall asleep later.

His fingers move higher. My dress has ridden up enough that he's touching bare skin halfway up my thigh. My breath catches, but I stay perfectly still. I don't want to do anything that might make him stop.

When he pulls into the garage and cuts the engine, his hand slips away from my leg, leaving behind an unexpected chill.

I open the car door and glance toward the right side of the garage—then freeze.

Hanging from a tall metal rack in the shadows is something vaguely humanoid. My pulse spikes. For a split second, I'm staring at a figure cloaked in black, lurking in the corner.

Then I exhale hard.

"Oh, my God. That's your scuba gear?" I slump back in my seat, hand pressed to my chest like I've survived a ghost encounter.

Kevin chuckles. "Yeah. That's what I wore for the dive this morning. It has to dry or it gets moldy and rank."

I squint through the low lighting and take in the full-body wetsuit hanging from a tall aluminum stand, clips securing the arms and legs. There's a hood draped over the shoulder like a shroud, booties dangling beneath like lifeless feet. Totally normal... now.

"That thing is nightmare fuel."

Kevin shuts his car door and pauses, following my gaze to the wetsuit. "What, the dive gear?"

"It looks like a body hanging there. Very serial-killer chic."

He looks at it, then back at me with a slight smile. "Never thought about it that way."

"Well, I'll never unsee it now."

He laughs under his breath as he strides into the house, his keys landing on the kitchen island with a sharp clink.

"You want something to drink?"

I follow him, stopping a few feet away. "No, I'm good."

He turns from the island, his expression changing in real

time. The playful smirk fades into something more serious, more focused. On me. My pulse picks up as he takes a step forward, then another, slow and purposeful. Each footstep seems to steal more oxygen from the room. The dim light catches the edge of his jaw, the slope of his shoulders, the shadows in his eyes.

He doesn't say a word.

He lifts his hand to brush a loose strand of hair from my face. His fingers graze my cheek, then trail down my neck. My breath stutters.

"You want dessert?" he asks, his voice low, eyebrow lifting.

I nod. Barely.

Chapter 14

Hawaii

His lips curve into that half-smile that's been undoing me since the minute I met him.

"Good," he murmurs, and then kisses me without hesitation.

His mouth is warm, hungry. His hands find my waist, pulling me closer, and I let him. Let myself sink into it. Into him.

The press of his body, the scratch of his stubble against my cheek, the familiar heat winding through my veins—it all hits at once.

I gasp as his mouth leaves mine to trail down my throat, and my hands grip his shoulders, anchoring myself as the rest of me starts to float.

The room disappears. It's just the two of us again.

And I don't want it to stop.

Energy zip-lines through my veins. I'm so happy to be doing this again.

He kisses me again, deeper this time, his hands traveling—fingers sliding over the curve of my hips, the dip of my lower back. One hand finds the back of my thigh, and with a slight tug, I get the message. I jump, wrapping my legs around his waist, and he carries me without missing a beat.

God, he's stronger than he looks. For someone so lean, he lifts me like I weigh nothing. At thirty-five, I'm not exactly light, but he doesn't even strain.

His mouth stays locked on mine, warm and insistent, even as he navigates the hallway.

By the time we reach the bedroom, I'm breathless. Dizzy. Like I've had three more glasses of wine without drinking a drop.

Kevin lowers me onto the bed, his body covering mine in a slow press of heat and weight. His mouth moves along my collarbone, my shoulder, my chest—his focus shifting into something primal. He knows exactly what he wants. And right now, it's me.

I let him take the lead. Let myself fall into the pleasure of being wanted. Touched. Taken.

His hands are confident, his rhythm controlled, and the sounds he pulls from my mouth are so unfamiliar I barely recognize them as mine. I arch into him, chasing every sensation. I'm not thinking. I'm not overanalyzing. I'm not wondering what happens after.

I'm just here.

My hands clutch at his back, my legs tangle with his, my breath comes fast. He's everywhere, and it's everything—raw and consuming, electric and loud.

And for the first time in a long, long time, I feel beautiful.

Not because he says it—he doesn't. But because of the way his hands move, the way he groans when I respond, the way his body tells me what words don't.

Kevin knows exactly what he's doing.

And I'm drunk on the way it feels to be wanted this much—

even if I'm not sure what any of it will mean when the sun comes up.

His hands find the hem of my dress, fingers skimming the fabric. "Is this okay?" he asks, his voice low.

I nod, unable to find words. He lifts the dress slowly, his knuckles brushing against my skin as the fabric slides upward. I raise my arms, letting him pull it over my head. Cool air hits my skin, but his gaze is warm as it travels over me.

"Beautiful," he murmurs, and heat rises in my cheeks.

My hands move to his shirt, fingers fumbling slightly with nervous energy. I push the shirt from his shoulders, revealing the lean muscle I glimpsed last night.

His chest is marked with a few small scars that I didn't notice before. I trace one with my fingertip, and he inhales sharply.

"Your turn," he says softly, reaching for the clasp of my bra.

The last barriers between us fall away, and for a moment we just look at each other. The vulnerability should terrify me, but instead I feel powerful under his appreciative gaze.

He pulls me closer, skin against skin, and the sensation makes us both shiver.

Time dissolves. There's nothing but us and heat and the way he whispers my name against my throat like a prayer. His mouth finds the sensitive spot just below my ear, and I gasp, my fingers digging into his shoulders.

"You're so responsive," he murmurs, his voice rough with desire. His hands map every curve, every hollow, like he's memorizing me. When his fingers find the sensitive peak of my breast, I arch beneath him, a sound escaping my lips that I didn't know I could make.

"God, Brianna." His breathing is uneven, his control starting to fray. "I want to taste every inch of you."

He moves lower, his mouth trailing fire down my body.

When he reaches the apex of my thighs, I tense with anticipation. It's been so long—too long—since anyone has touched me like this. His tongue finds that bundle of nerves and I cry out, my back bowing off the bed.

"That's it," he breathes against me. "Let go."

I'm already spiraling, lost in sensations I forgot existed. His fingers join his mouth, and the dual pressure sends me spinning higher. Every nerve ending is alive, electric, screaming for release.

"Kevin, I—" I can't finish the sentence. Can't think past the building pressure.

"Come for me," he says, and the command in his voice, combined with the precise pressure of his tongue, shatters me completely.

My orgasm crashes over me in waves, starting at my core and radiating outward until I'm shaking, gasping his name. He doesn't stop, drawing out every tremor until I'm boneless beneath him.

When I finally come back to myself, he's kissing his way back up my body, his throbbing arousal hard and ready against my thigh. I reach for him, wrapping my fingers around his length, and he groans low in his throat.

"Your turn," I whisper, but he catches my wrist.

"Not yet," he says, positioning himself between my legs. "I want to feel you around me when you come again."

He reaches across the bed, grabbing a square packet from the night stand. He rips the foil with his teeth and guides the latex down to the hilt. He hovers on top of me, his one arm holding his body weight while his other positions his cock between my thighs. He enters me slowly, letting me adjust to the fullness, and I moan at the sensation of being completely filled.

"Fuck, you feel incredible," he breathes, his forehead pressed to mine. "So tight. So perfect."

He starts to move, setting a rhythm that has me clinging to him, my nails leaving marks on his back. Every thrust hits that spot inside me that makes stars explode behind my eyelids.

"Harder," I gasp, surprising myself, again, with my boldness. "Please."

He complies, his movements becoming more urgent, more desperate. The slap of skin against skin fills the room, mixed with our ragged breathing and the soft moans I can't contain.

I feel myself building again, impossibly fast. "Kevin, I'm close—"

"Come with me," he commands, his hand finding that sensitive bundle of nerves again. The added stimulation is my undoing. I shatter around him, my body clenching, and he follows with a harsh groan.

We collapse together, breathing hard, sweat cooling on our skin. His arm stays draped across my waist, fingers tracing lazy patterns on my hip. I turn my head to study his profile—the way his dark lashes cast shadows on his cheeks.

"That was . . ." I start, then trail off, not sure how to finish.

"Yeah," he murmurs, pressing a kiss to my shoulder. "It was."

I want to ask what happens now. Want to know if this changes anything between us. But the words stick in my throat, and instead I let myself sink into the warmth of his body, the steady rhythm of his breathing.

Tomorrow can wait. Right now, I'm exactly where I want to be.

My lips are swollen, my skin hums with the lingering touch of his hands, and for now, I let myself feel good. Wanted. Reconnected to something I thought I buried.

He gives a soft, satisfied grunt and settles deeper into the mattress.

I stare at the ceiling, a lazy smile tugging at my mouth. I should probably go to the bathroom. Or find my underwear. But I don't move. I don't want to break the moment. Not yet. Because when I do, it might start to mean something else. Something more complicated.

And right now, I just want to stay here. Floating in the warmth of being touched. Being seen. Even if I'm not sure how long it'll last.

Chapter 15

Hawaii

A sudden thud rustles me out of my sleep. I reach my arm around to where Kevin should be but it's empty. A disappointing groan rumbles in the back of my throat as I reach for my phone on the side table. Six thirty-five in the morning.

I check my messages.

> Sara: Please tell me you were in Scuba Steve's bed last night.

An airy laugh escapes me as I remember Sara's obsession with Adam Sandler.

> Me: I can neither confirm nor deny the presence of Scuba Steve in this bed.

> Sara: OMG YES! Details. NOW.

> Me: It's 6:35 AM Sara.

> Sara: And? I've been up for hours with the baby. SPILL.

I pull the pillow to my face, biting down on a smile that won't quit. The room looks different in the morning light. Less mysterious, more real.

Sitting up in Kevin's bed, I pull the sheet around me, suddenly self-conscious even though I'm alone. More diving gear hangs neatly in the corner, and the house is completely silent.

The thud must have been him leaving for work.

I inhale the faint scent of him still clinging to the pillow before finally pushing the covers aside.

I stretch, limbs loose and sore in places I forgot could feel sore, and pad into the bathroom.

My dress from last night slides on easily and I head down the hall, a bit more relaxed than yesterday morning. The smell of coffee lingers in the air but the coffee pot is rinsed and drying upside down in the sink.

Ding!

"This phone, I swear to G—" I stop mid-curse as I swipe to read the message.

The part of me that woke up smiling wilts a little.

> Marina Man Preston: Good Afternoon Brianna. I hope you're enjoying your trip. If you haven't already, I recommend getting a towering burger from Seven Bros. It's delicious! I am looking forward to meeting up when you get back. -Preston.

I place the phone on the island and curiously open the fridge. Eggs, oat milk, hot sauce, two perfect rows of energy drinks, and a container of leftover poke.

Of course he eats clean.

The fridge door shuts with a soft thud. I twist my hair into a messy knot and press my palms against the cool granite countertop.

Ugh. I don't even know what to do with this Kevin thing.

He seems interested. I think. He invited me to dinner. He slept with me—twice. His hand was on my thigh, scratching soft circles like it was second nature. But then he left this morning like it was any other Monday. I mean, it *is* Monday... but still.

It's not just the palm trees and golden hour lighting that are making my heart swoon.

It's Kevin.

It's the way he talks about diving with quiet certainty, like the ocean is just another room he's learned to navigate. It's his Navy stories, his quick wit, the way he can command a room with ease and still smile like a kid. It's the house that looks like it belongs on HGTV—clean lines, perfectly hung photos, the wine fridge. It's the career I barely understand but find wildly impressive, and the fact he teaches beginners to dive like it's his mission in life.

Before leaving, I memorize it all—how the light slants through his windows, how everything smells like salt and coffee and him. Who knows if I'll be back here. But something in my gut says this isn't the end of our story.

I close the front door behind me and step into the humid morning, a smile tugging at the corner of my mouth.

My phone starts ringing as I double-check the lock. It's Sara. I look at the time—six-fifty-five a.m.

"Hey," I say, walking down the driveway to my rental parked on the street.

"Did you sleep with *Scuba Steve?*"

My grin could be cast on a Colgate commercial.

I fill the day with everything to avoid thinking about Kevin. Packing becomes an excuse to reorganize my suitcase three times. The beach provides the perfect distraction when I discover sea turtles nestled into the sand. I take about fifty photos of them. Shopping for souvenirs kills another couple of hours, and I devour an acai bowl.

Somewhere between the sandy beaches and the smell of salt water in my hair, it hits me—Kevin woke something in me. Desire. Lust. Hunger.

For years, I've been flatlining emotionally. Functioning, performing, checking boxes. But I wasn't really *living*. I shut down any part of me that dared to hope for love again. I told myself I didn't need it. That I was better off focusing on work, on routine, on being "fine."

But then Kevin comes along, out of nowhere, like a match striking dry wood. It's not just the sex, though that's been a nice reintroduction to my own body. It's the way he makes me laugh, the way he looks at me. The way he talks about diving with the same intensity most people save for love.

He reminds me I'm still a woman who wants things. Who feels things. Who's allowed to want and feel and *burn a little*.

Before Kevin, I was living in grayscale. Now I see in color again.

Lucas texts around lunch time, saying they are all meeting up after work for drinks. After touring the macadamia nut farm, I head inland to meet them.

The concrete floors of the restaurant make sense when I see

the open sides of the building. No windows, few walls, and pillars holding up the roof while trade winds sweep through.

I spot the crew at a picnic table near the front of the restaurant. Kevin's sitting across from Lucas, deep in conversation with Hag and August. Demi's laughing at something on his phone.

"Aye! Brianna! Over here!" Lucas shouts, waving his beer in the air like a man signaling a rescue plane. The floor muffles the sound of my flip-flops as I head to the picnic table they're sitting at.

"Yo, Lucas, I don't need a shower, man," Hag says, ducking and swatting at the beer hovering over his head.

Demi points up to the pint glass. "I thought you *liked* golden showers, Hag."

Kevin, mid-sip, chokes on his drink. August reaches over and smacks his back a few times.

"Guys," Lucas groans, gesturing to me. "We have a lady in our presence. Let's not be total assholes."

Kevin turns. His eyes find mine and hold for a long moment before his mouth curves into a subtle smile. It's not huge. It's not loud. But it's for me.

"There she is," Kevin says, sliding down the bench to make room.

I squeeze in next to him, our thighs brushing under the table. The contact sends a spark up my leg, tightening something deep in my stomach. I want to lean into him. I want him to lean into me. I want something from him, and *that's* the part that makes me nervous.

As if he can sense it, Kevin wraps his arm around my waist and gives me a soft squeeze.

"Yes, please excuse these assholes, Brianna. They were raised by wolves," Demi says, wagging a finger around the table.

"Yeah, but you're the royal asshole," Hag fires back, swinging his legs out from under the bench.

"Where's my crown, bitch?" Demi grins, making a circle on top of his head.

"Up your ass. Go fishing," Hag calls over his shoulder as he heads for the bar.

"Beer, B?" Lucas asks, holding up a pitcher of what looks like light beer, judging by the color.

"I'll grab an IPA. Thanks, though," I say, scooting out from the picnic table. Kevin's hand grazes my ass as I stand, casual but deliberate, sending a buzz down my spine that follows me all the way to the bar.

I step up next to Hag, who's already ordered.

"Anything else?" the bartender asks Hag.

"Yeah, whatever she's having," Hag jerks a thumb in my direction.

"IPA, preferably non-hazy," I add, stepping up next to Hag.

"I got you." The bartender grabs a pint glass, gives it a quick spin in his palm, and scans the tap handles before reaching for the far-right lever.

"I thought they all were hazy," Hag turns toward me, confusion on his face.

"No. West Coast IPAs aren't. They have less of that orange juice taste. I like the hoppy kick."

"I drink Coors." Hag shrugs and hands the bartender his credit card.

I sit down close to Kevin, hoping he wraps his arm around my waist again. He doesn't.

I try to catch up on the banter. Something about August being naked in a field, and I just don't know if I want to hear the ending. Kevin must have picked up on my lack of interest, because he leans over and gently bumps my shoulder with his.

"Day good?" he asks, pouring beer into his half-full glass.

"Yeah, it was. I spent the morning packing, and then at the beach."

"That's right, you leave tomorrow."

His tone is casual, like he forgot. But I've mentioned it more than once this weekend. He should know.

"Yep. Back to Texas tomorrow morning. I'm going to miss it here."

You. I'm going to miss you.

"We're gonna miss you," he says, rubbing my knee under the table.

It is hard to find a private moment to talk to him about what happens after tomorrow. What *we* are. What this *is*.

We'll be separated by two time zones. I calculate the difference in my head—Oahu to Dallas. When Kevin's getting off work, I'll be getting ready for bed. Not ideal, but not impossible.

"Earth to Brianna!" Lucas waves his hand in front of my face, pulling me back to the present.

I blink, startled, lifting my gaze from where it had been fixed on the table.

He grins. "Do you need another beer?"

I glance down at my empty glass. One more beer would buy me more time with Kevin. But if I stay, I'll miss the sunset. And a part of me hopes Kevin might follow if I go.

"No, I'm going to get going. I want to catch a sunset one more time."

Lucas nods, finishing the last of his beer in one long gulp.

"All right, cool. I'll see you later tonight, then?" he asks, pouring himself another beer.

"Absolutely," I say, sliding out one leg at a time from the picnic table.

One of them catches, and before I can stop myself, I stumble right into Kevin's lap. His arms open instinctively, catching me as though it's the most natural thing in the world.

"Have a seat, Brianna. Please, stay a while," he says in a dry tone, his chest vibrating with laughter beneath me.

Ugh. I hate picnic tables.

"Sorry, Kev. I just find your lap cushier than the wooden bench." I wrap my arm around his neck in a quick half-hug.

"Wait a little longer and you'll definitely feel some *wood*, Brianna," August yells from the end of the table.

Lucas lifts a single eyebrow and shakes his head as Demi, Hag, and August burst into synchronized laughter.

I roll my eyes, but I'm smiling.

"Come on, I'll walk you out." Kevin gives my butt two quick pats and knocks back the rest of his beer.

August reaches for my hand and kisses it. "My lady."

Kevin shoots him a look. "Don't be weird, August."

As we make our way toward the back exit, I feel the same dread I did on Saturday after the beach barbeque. My time with him is ending and I don't want it to. I mentally rehearse what I'll say once we're out of earshot.

"I'm glad you came out today," Kevin says, walking close beside me.

His tall, solid frame casts a shadow across the hood of my rental car, shielding me from the early evening sun. Even in the fading light, I can see the definition in his forearms, the way his T-shirt pulls slightly across his chest.

I stop at the driver's side door and turn to him.

"Me, too. I'm glad I got to see you." I offer a smile—soft, a little dreamy. Maybe too dreamy.

A breeze kicks up and I catch a whiff of his scent—salt air and sun-warmed skin, something distinctly *him*. It wraps around me, pulling me back into memories from last night—his arms braced on either side of my head, muscles taut. His breath against my neck. The way his voice dropped to that low rumble when he said my name. My pulse flutters at the memory.

"Hey . . . " Kevin shifts his weight, swaying from foot to foot. "I really had a good time with you this weekend."

"Me, too," I say, adjusting the strap of my purse on my shoulder. "Thanks . . . for everything. The car, dinner, letting me crash at your place . . . "

I take a breath. *This is it.* I lift my eyes to his and start, "So, do you wa—"

"Let me know when you're back in town again," he cuts in. "I'd love to meet up."

My purse strap falls off my shoulder into the crook of my elbow. Heat flashes across my cheeks.

"Wait, what?" My chin juts forward like I didn't hear him right. No way that just happened. That sounds like a truncated goodbye. My pulse quickens, and something cold settles in my stomach.

"When you come back to Oahu, let me know."

"I don't have a return date. I don't know when I'm coming back."

I let the annoyance occupy my expression, sharp and immediate. What. The. Hell. Did I misread everything this whole weekend? My jaw clenches as I process his dismissive tone.

"Okay. Whenever you're back, hit me up." He leans in and kisses my cheek. My cheek. Just like that, I'm shoved straight into the friend zone.

The casual peck feels like a slap. My hands ball into fists at my sides.

"Whoa. Hold on a minute."

I stand there, staring at his perfectly sculpted jawline and American flag hat, gathering my thoughts. Anger bubbles up from somewhere deep, but I force it down. I can't sound like a pining, whiny girl begging for his love. Though that's exactly how I feel.

Let's be clear. I'm not *opposed* to begging.

"This whole weekend—you, me—I enjoyed our time together. Enough that I'm curious if there's something here. Something worth exploring." I gesture between his chest and mine, my voice strained with the effort to stay calm.

His face tightens like he's tasted something sour. In that moment, I know he has no intention of exploring anything further.

His rejection hits like ice water, and my composure begins to crack.

I *consider* begging.

"I'm sorry. I thought we both knew we were keeping it casual. I enjoyed my time with you, too, but—"

"That's just it," I interrupt, my voice firm and rising slightly. "For both people to be on the same page, it has to actually be discussed."

He doesn't say a word. My cracked composure breaks like a dam—all the frustration and humiliation I've been holding back flooding out in a surge I can't control.

"So, I'm the dumb one for not realizing this was just casual for you?" I jab a finger hard into my chest. "I'm the idiot who didn't know I was just entertainment. Great. Good. Got it."

I fling my arms up and let them fall heavily against my thighs, the slap echoing in the space between us.

"No, that's not what I'm saying." He sighs, pulling the bill of his hat up to rub his temple. "I'm sorry. You're not dumb. I just thought you'd want to keep things casual."

"This wasn't casual for me, Kevin. What if I want to see if something real is here?" I swing open the car door and throw my purse onto the passenger seat.

"I'm sorry, Brianna. I can't do long distance. It's not something I'm willing to entertain."

Entertain?

"But you sure as hell had no problem entertaining yourself with me *in your bed*." The words come out like venom and I realize I'm making myself look like a fool in front of him.

God, Brianna, stop.

The more I yell about the last forty-eight hours, the more desperate and pathetic I sound. I need to get out of here before I embarrass myself further. I shake my head in frustration, and climb into the front seat, slamming the door behind me.

Kevin says nothing. He doesn't chase after me or call my name. Just silence as I pull away.

His complete lack of response feels like another slap. My vision blurs, not from tears, but from pure, unadulterated rage. How could I have been so dumb? So hopeful? *So dumb.*

I wanted more. But that was me, lost in a fantasy spun by sunsets, palm trees, and salt air.

Here I am again. Feeling used. Feeling tossed aside. Feeling like a placeholder, a nice weekend distraction, but never the real thing.

I'm not just losing Kevin tonight. I'm losing the piece of myself I thought had healed.

Chapter 16

Dallas

I collapse onto my bed, too tired to do anything but appreciate being back in my own space. It's just a bedroom, but it's mine, and it welcomes me back like an old friend. I'd be lying if I said I was over the Kevin situation. It's hard to let go of the fantasy. For a moment, a romantic life in Hawaii with a chiseled scuba diver seemed within arm's reach. It was enough to risk everything I've tried to keep safe.

Am I so out of the dating loop that I don't even know the rules anymore? Was I stupid to think Kevin and I could have a happy ending?

"Scuba Steve is an asshole, B. Those military guys are all the same. They're used to women throwing themselves at them. Women are a dime a dozen." Sara's voice echoes from my phone, muffled under the pile of clothes on my bed.

I ignore her words as I debate bringing a larger suitcase for my San Antonio trip. I'll be at The Elysian Hotel for five days, and I'm not someone who packs light. What if I don't feel like wearing a skirt? What if it's raining? What if it's unseasonably cold that day? I like to be prepared for anything.

"My great uncle told me that when he arrived in Europe on his ship, there was a phone number for locals to call to basically adopt an American serviceman. But half the calls were from girls looking for a good time," Sara says.

I hold my white blouse with black polka dots in front of me. "Is it too early to wear white?"

"What? Oh, my God. Stop changing the subject."

I drop my arms and look at my phone, nearly buried under potential outfits.

"Your uncle is sixty-seven. I'm not sure what relevance that has to today. I don't even think they do that anymore."

"My point is, there's a long history of servicemen getting any girl they want just because they wear a uniform."

I don't doubt Sara is right. I remember Lucas talking about all the girls who threw themselves at him whenever he's in uniform.

"I guess I thought Kevin was mature enough to understand the value of a real woman. Someone who sees beyond the uniform."

"Oh, my little grasshopper. You have so much to learn. You have definitely lost your dating smarts."

I fall backward onto my bed, my arms draped above my head, cradled by thirty pounds of fabric that used to hang in my closet. I stare up at the fan blades spinning above me. Am I that naive? Has dating changed so much in the last several years that I don't even know the rules?

"So, is it too early?" I ask, in an attempt to avoid feelings.

"Too early for what?"

"To wear white. I want to wear my white blouse this week."

Sara knows when it's time to move the conversation along. But she never forgets. She holds on to it, the lesson she thinks I need to learn, and brings it up later.

Static comes through my speaker, Sara's exhale of defeat.

"If it's over seventy degrees and the sun is shining, you can wear white."

"Okay," I say, focusing on one fan blade as it spins around and around.

"How long are you in San Antonio?"

I sit up, bracing myself on my elbows.

"Well, Chris nailed the sale, as usual, so he and I will be there for the full week."

"I mean, is there anything Chris can't sell?"

"Newspaper ads."

"Newspaper ads? He sold newspaper ads?"

I stand and walk back over to my closet.

"Yep. His first job out of college. He said he was terrible."

"Interesting. I thought I knew everything there is to know about this Chris character. Finally, something he's not good at."

I chuckle as I continue to sift through my closet for something that speaks to me. My favorite is a black A-line dress. Simple. Understated but powerful. Unfortunately, I was mistaken for a hotel employee during my first stay at The Elysian.

"It's okay. He's totally going to be jealous of my new laptop. It's at least four generations newer than his, and half the weight."

"Good. He can't have the upper hand in everything."

There's silence as I contemplate the blouses on my bed. Then Sara clears her throat.

"What about Mr. GQ and Marina Man? You still going to explore those opportunities?"

I know she's tiptoeing around this topic. I also know she's not going to let me off the hook with this dating challenge.

A few days ago? I couldn't wait to go sailing with Preston. Now? I want to swear off all men. And Mr. GQ? His love-bombing texts suffocate me. I still haven't responded to his last message.

What if I'm building up another fantasy? I let my guard down with Kevin and look what happened. Before Hawaii, I was excited about going out again with Marina Man. Now, I just feel exhausted.

But Kevin ignited something inside me that had been dormant. I liked that feeling of possibility, connection, infatuation. I want that again. I just don't know if it's worth risking getting hurt.

"I don't know," I answer after a long pause.

"I'm proud of you for getting this far. And I really hope you continue. I mean, you get to go *sailing*. Aunt Elise would be so proud."

"All right, let me focus on packing so I can get some sleep. I'll keep you posted on my dating status."

"Please do. You are four dates down, eight to go! Remember, they have to be single and interested, and they have to pay for it to count. If he mentions his ex more than twice, it doesn't count. That's therapy, not a date. And if you spend the whole time talking about work, it's a business meeting, not a date."

I roll my eyes. "Got it. Bye."

I'm in a stand-off with my closet. I keep staring, hoping new outfits will magically appear. They don't.

My eyes drift to the bottom of my closet, where the cardboard box sits pushed against the back corner. The familiar weight settles in my stomach. I try to ignore it, but it calls to me like a siren song.

I should grab any dress and leave. Shut the door like I have dozens of times before and ignore it. Instead, I find myself kneeling on the carpet, my knees pressing into the rough fibers.

The box feels lighter than it should when I pull it toward me. Lighter than the weight it carries in my chest. My hands tremble as they hover over the sealed edges, and the faint scent of fabric softener from the clothes above mixes with dust and something else. Something that makes my throat close.

My finger finds the spot along the sealed edge where I always touch it. The cardboard is soft there, worn thin from handling.

This is what happens when I let my guard down. When I believe in possibilities and happy endings. When I think I deserve something beautiful.

Heat builds behind my eyes. I blink hard, willing it away, but my vision blurs anyway. One tear escapes, hot against my cheek. Then another.

No. Not today. My level of disappointment is already at an all-time high. I can't handle any more.

My tears break free, hot and relentless, and I collapse forward, pressing my forehead against the box, surrendering to the breakdown. The cardboard feels shockingly cool against my fevered skin as my shoulders convulse with sobs I can't swallow back.

All the pain I've been pushing down since coming home from Hawaii, since everything, comes flooding back. It crashes over me in waves, stealing my breath. I can't think. I can only hold this box and remember what it feels like when dreams crumble in your hands.

The weight of loss crushes me—not just the loss of Kevin or what we could have been, but something bigger. Something that carved out a hollow place inside me that nothing seems to fill.

My arms wrap around the box, holding it like it might disappear. Like everything else has disappeared. The tears continue to fall, and I'm mourning something I can't even name, something that lives in the space between what was and what could have been.

I think about futures that dissolve before they can take root. About dreams that die before they can breathe. About the way hope feels like betrayal when it blooms in your chest, bright and dangerous, only to wither away.

This is why I'm terrified of letting anyone close. Because losing what you never really had still breaks you in ways that never fully heal. And no one understands.

Downtown San Antonio sprawls beneath us through the windows of the twelfth-floor conference room. The view draws my attention away from the empty chairs. Chris hunches over his laptop at the far end of the table. Our client, Mercury, is running late, again, but the extra time gives me more time to prepare.

From my bag, I pull out my new laptop and boot it up. My pen clicks against the table as the screen loads. *Click. Click. Click.* The rhythm soothes me.

Chris glances up at me, then at my pen, then back at me. I stop.

He raises his eyes over his archaic laptop toward mine. A few seconds pass before his nose wrinkles.

"Is that the shit we're getting next quarter?"

I lift my laptop in one hand, twirling it around to show him the keyboard and log in screen.

"You mean this lightweight, slim, fastest processor of your life, next-gen laptop that I'm holding in one hand?" I graze my fingers along the edge like it's a masterpiece.

Chris laughs as Mercury's director of technology opens the door to the conference room.

"Sorry we're late. A few fires to put out," Gus says as he flops into the chair closest to the door, oblivious to my Vanna White moment. "Michele is right behind me."

I nod, remembering Michele from the finalist meeting—the project manager who asked more technical questions than Gus.

"How was your weekend, Gus?" I attempt small talk.

"It was fine." He reaches for his phone and starts swiping.

Chris raises his eyebrows at me before looking back to his screen.

My leg bounces, heel tapping against the floor. I reach for the HDMI cable coiled in the center of the table and plug it into my laptop. The screen flickers to life on the wall-mounted TV.

"Sorry I'm late, everyone. I hope you're all doing well." Michele bursts into the room holding a few blue folders, a notebook, and her laptop. Her blonde bob swings as she sits next to Gus.

"Not to worry. Gus has been great company."

Chris gives me a wink.

She looks at Gus, whose eyes remain glued to his cell phone, oblivious that we're talking about him.

"All right, let's dive in." She opens her laptop, fingers flying across the keys. "We're thrilled about partnering with VerityLens. What's our first move?"

Chris leans forward, hands clasped. "Today we'll map out the implementation plan, discuss roles and responsibilities, and lock in your Go Live date. Brianna will be your guide through everything."

I flip to the project timeline on my laptop and glance up to the TV.

"What we're looking at is a phased rollout. We'll integrate VerityLens with your existing systems. Then we'll train your team on the new analytics dashboard before we flip the switch company-wide."

Michele nods, taking notes.

"And timeline-wise?"

"About four weeks, depending on how quickly your IT team can provide system access," Chris says. "Brianna's worked with companies your size before. She knows exactly what potential roadblocks to watch for. She'll be partnering closely with your Marketing and IT teams to ensure a smooth integration."

Chris nods, my cue to take it from here.

"Exactly, I'll be partnering with you and your PR team to connect your business's social media platforms so we can pull sentiment from Mercury's Facebook, X, and other accounts. I'll also need a list of news outlets, trade magazines, and high-traffic bloggers where your company, your competitors, and your product show up most."

Gus chimes in with, "We show up everywhere."

"Okay, what would be the top three news outlets?" I say.

Gus barely glances up from his phone.

"All of them."

I look to Chris to jump in.

"Gus." Chris's jaw tightens. "We can't sweep every news outlet that exists for keywords, hashtags, and mentions of your company. It'd be too much data and completely useless to you."

Gus drops his phone with a clatter.

"*WSJ, Times, Tech Today,* and *San Antonio Express.*"

I look at Chris, my pulse jumping as panic floods my system. He gives me a confused look and continues.

"Great. *Wall Street Journal, The Times, Tech Today,* and *San Antonio Express.* Those will be the *four* news outlets we focus on for the first quarter. We'll need specific hashtags, keywords, and competitor names for the sweep. Brianna can partner with your marketing team to help with that."

Why do I have to be the bearer of bad news?

"To clarify, we don't have a license for *The Wall Street Journal*." Heat creeps up my neck as all eyes land on me. "We do have access to FactVera, which holds tens of thousands of articles from various news sources, including *some Wall Street Journal* content. We just can't guarantee complete coverage."

Michele looks at Gus, her face unreadable.

Chris leans back in his seat, cool as a cucumber even though the confusion is guaranteed his mistake. Sales guys. They promise the world and then leave it up to the rest of us to clean up their overpromising. Michele tucks her blonde bob behind her ears.

"Well, that clarification would have been appreciated before we signed the contract." Her voice is steady, but there's an edge to it.

"Wait, what?" Gus has officially joined the meeting. "We specifically requested *WSJ* coverage. That was a major selling point."

My chest tightens. This is exactly what I was afraid of.

"We have an indirect line to *The Wall Street Journal* through FactVera. But FactVera chooses articles for their database based on relevancy and trends." I try to make it sound like a selling point. Gus abandons his phone.

"You say database. So, whatever you get from FactVera isn't breaking news? What's the point? If I can walk down the street and grab *The Wall Street Journal* quicker than your software can pull from a database, what are we paying you for?"

I ignore Gus's question and search through the shared drive to find the presentation that shows which news outlets we access directly and which are delayed through databases.

Chris adjusts in his seat. *Finally.* He's uncomfortable.

"Gus, our agreement with FactVera gives us breaking news within thirty minutes. But you're forgetting about *The Times, San Antonio Express, Technology Today*, and dozens more news outlets that are live feeds. When news breaks with the keywords you choose, our software flags and pulls it immediately, alerting you."

I switch the presentation to a slide addressing Gus's concerns, hoping we can move on before this meeting gets completely derailed.

"As you can see on the screen, seventy-eight percent of our data is breaking news, meaning our software searches these twenty-nine media outlets every second, looking for your hashtags, mentions, and keywords."

"All right, we need to focus on those," Michele says, brushing her bangs off her face.

An hour later, we've covered everything on our agenda. Gus seems satisfied with the data breakdown, and Michele has her action items. As they file out of the conference room, Chris puffs his cheeks and blows out a breath.

I turn to him with a hard stare, anger flashing in my eyes.

"Chris, this is not the first time you've oversold *Wall Street Journal*. Conversations like today? They don't have to happen."

He packs up his laptop, unbothered by my annoyance.

"Every company wants *Wall Street*. I don't understand why we don't have that subscription. I'm losing sales because some guy in an office decided it's too expensive." He stands, shoving the chair in. "What's expensive is me losing sales because of it."

A sharp zip cuts through the air as I close my laptop bag, the sound louder and more rushed than usual.

Chapter 17

San Antonio

Our flights landed around the same time this morning, so we're sharing a rental car even though we stay at different hotels. We pull up in front of my hotel, The Elysian. The tension from earlier has melted away, replaced by our usual rhythm. Chris gets out to help me with my suitcase.

"You brought the big one this week, huh?"

I ignore his observation. I wasn't in the right mindset to select outfits last night, so everything that was on my bed ended up in my suitcase.

"Thank you," I say as he pulls my suitcase onto the sidewalk.

"Pick you up tomorrow?" he asks, rounding the back of the car.

"Sounds good." I smile and turn, dragging my suitcase up the sidewalk toward the hotel entrance.

Between the meeting and Hawaii memories, my head's a mess. I'm ready to escape to my hotel room.

With each step closer to the door, I feel my shoulders relax. The boutique hotel's entrance offers refuge after a long day. I'm focused on those beautiful bronze door handles when my heel wedges deep in a crack between the sidewalk slabs.

I take another step, and a sharp *snap* echoes under me.

My broken heel remains trapped in the crack as my foot slips forward, throwing me completely off balance. I stumble, arms flying out like a deranged conductor, but my momentum carries me down. The suitcase tips with me, its weight nudging me from the back enough to send me sprawling to my knees in what I can only imagine looks like I'm bowing to the hotel gods.

Why does this always happen to me?

The hotel door swings open with a soft *whoosh*, and chatter from the lobby spills out onto the city street.

"Miss Whitmore, are you okay?" A pair of brown loafers appears in view.

I look up to find an extended hand, soft yet strong. It pulls me upward as my quads struggle to push me the rest of the way. I really need to start working out.

An arm wraps around my waist, supporting me to a full stand.

I brush my wavy strands from my face and smile as I lock eyes with Javier, his eyes wide with concern.

"Are you okay?" He leans in, searching my face.

Glancing behind me, I spot my thin black heel protruding from the sidewalk.

"My shoe."

"Yeah, you killed it." He laughs, his hand grazing my back. "Let's get you inside."

He grabs my luggage and offers his arm. I hobble toward the hotel door, completely off-kilter with one three-inch heel and one bare foot.

"I'm so embarrassed," I say as Javier opens the door for me.

I realize I've been entertaining several guests in the lobby with my blunder. Two women in business suits offer sympathetic smiles, while two kids giggle at my expense.

"Angelina! Dominic! Manners!" Javier calls to the children who circle the large floral arrangement in the center of the lobby. "Come sit down over here." He gestures me toward the seating area to the left of the entrance.

Each step toward the chair is a lopsided limp, three inches of heel on one side throwing off my entire gait. My left foot arches high like a Barbie doll's, except I'm nowhere near as graceful.

I collapse into the chair, elegance abandoned, with my legs stretched out and my arms falling limp in my lap. The custom scent of white tea and verbena is the only comfort at this moment.

Javier sits on the coffee table across from me. There's a gentle contrast in him—the tailored lines and sophistication of his suit against the soft concern in his eyes as he leans forward.

He examines me from bottom to top, his gaze lingering on my scraped knees and my palms where they throb in my lap.

As if it couldn't get worse, I see the general manager, Diane, approaching like a storm cloud. She stops about three feet away, hands planted on her hips, and fixes me with a withering glare that could freeze hell over.

"What happened here?" She waves her hand in my direction, her tone dripping with irritation.

I don't want to look at her. It's bad enough that all the guests in the lobby witnessed my tumble. But now Diane has even more ammunition to use against me, for whatever campaign fuels her apparent dislike of me.

"Miss Whitmore took a stumble on the sidewalk." Javier holds up my black heelless shoe as evidence.

"Well, it's a talent to trip on a flat surface. You should be more careful next time." Her words slice through the air with precision.

Why does this woman hate me? I don't get it. I've tried to be nice to her, respectful, given her the benefit of the doubt, but there's no breaking through the ice wall that surrounds her.

And the sidewalk isn't even that flat. Clearly.

My chin lifts to respond to her when I feel a gentle grasp on my left hand. Javier turns my wrist over, and I look down at the abrasion and flakes of skin peeling up from my palm. My thumb got the worst of it—a small flap of skin stained crimson.

"Diane, would you grab our first aid kit? It's in the printer room." Javier's fingers graze my palm, avoiding the tender spots.

Diane stalks off toward the printer room, muttering something under her breath.

"I'm fine, Javier. Really. My pride is the most bruised." I give him a half smile, and he lets go of my hand.

"You have nothing to be embarrassed about. I'm just glad you're okay." His face is drawn tight.

Sara always teases me that I'm accident-prone, and I'm starting to believe there's some truth behind it.

"Other than your scrapes, do you have any pain or discomfort?"

He looks over to the kids standing by the flower arrangement, gawking at me.

"Angelina. Take Dominic upstairs and get changed for the pool."

As the kids scatter from the lobby, Diane returns, her face like stone.

"Here's the first aid kit." I wince as she shoves the red plastic box so close to my face I wonder if she's trying to add another injury.

Javier opens it, sifting through the band-aids.

Diane shifts on one hip. "I'm sure Miss Whitmore can bandage her own wounds."

Javier ignores her as he peels apart the paper wrapper.

"Javier." I glance up at Diane's disapproving stare before looking back at his hands. "I can handle a band-aid."

"Oh, sorry." He pushes the half-opened bandage toward me. "I do this for Angelina and Dominic all the time." He clasps his hands in his lap.

"Are they your kids?"

"Sometimes they feel like it." He laughs, leaning back on the coffee table. "My sister's kids. But sometimes I forget they're not mine. I love them like they are."

A slow smile blooms on my face. "How lucky are they?"

"I'm the lucky one." A nervous laugh slips out before he can stop it. "As cheesy as that sounds."

"That's not cheesy at all." I place the fabric band-aid across my thumb, smoothing out both sides with my finger.

His smile turns sheepish, and he tugs on the cuff of his sleeve, fumbling with his watch.

"My sister travels a lot for work so when she's away, the kids stay with me. I take them to school, make sure they get their homework done, and that Angelina gets to piano lessons."

"Wow, that's a lot of responsibility for an uncle! How do you juggle it all?"

Javier seems to work around the clock. I've encountered him at breakfast, after client meetings, even during my late-night wine sessions at the bar.

"The hotel is their second home, too." He smiles. "They have their own room where they can hang out, watch TV, do homework, that kind of stuff. Angelina loves the pool. And they've grown accustomed to ordering room service." He rolls his eyes, shaking his head.

"And the owner doesn't mind them spending so much time here?"

He shakes his head. "He's okay with it. Besides, there's no way I'd be able to do both if they weren't allowed to be here. Those kids are my world. I think even when I have my own kids, Angelina and Dominic will still be my favorites."

I nod at what he says, but it's distant, delayed.

"I should let you get settled in. Please do not wobble through the lobby on one heel." He eyes my right foot, smirking.

"I can't walk around barefoot," I say, offended.

"You are family here. You can walk around however you want." He stands, smoothing out his suit jacket. "I mean it, Brianna."

That was kind of him to say, but The Elysian has a reputation to uphold as a sophisticated boutique hotel, which means no size nine footprints across the tile of the lobby.

Javier grabs my broken shoe, lying dead on the coffee table, and reaches out an open palm for the one I'm still wearing.

"I'll take care of these."

I peel off the second heel with a long sigh, then hand it to him. I pad over to the check-in desk, looking behind for sweaty footprints.

Grace smiles behind the desk. "Welcome back, Miss Whitmore."

I'm grateful she doesn't mention my stumble, although I'm sure she saw it all.

"Thanks." I position my suitcase to block my bare feet from other guests.

"If you want, I can have pastries delivered for you?"

Of course, Grace noticed the absence of my pink box and latte which accompany me every time I check in. And who wouldn't want to shove conchas in their mouth after that embarrassing escapade.

"No, thanks. Actually, I need to buy a new pair of black heels. Any ideas where?"

Even though I packed half my closet, I only brought flip flops, sneakers, and a pair of blue flats with sequins.

"I can have someone draw up a list of nearby shops and have it sent to your room." She slides my key cards across the counter and winks. "1010, as usual."

I can't wait to get into my room.

Dropping my cell phone and key cards in their usual place, I walk over to the window to get a bird's-eye view of the pastry shop line across the street. Only a couple stands outside the front door of La Panadería, which means the line is still about 15 people deep inside. I glance over at the time—three o'clock. They'll be closing in a couple of hours.

The sound of quacking ducks comes from my cell phone, a ringtone that never fails to amuse me. If he knew, he'd kill me and demand I change it. I grab the remote and turn on the local news before seeing what his highness needs.

> Chris: Hey. Where are we at on the Delefont visuals?

Shit.

Chapter 18

San Antonio

I started the presentation for the Delefont bid but after they rescheduled our meeting, it sat on the shared drive and I forgot about it.

> Me: Nearly done. Just putting final touches and I'll send it over.

> Chris: What about the data for Chremsoft?

"Shit!" I reach for my laptop bag.

Chremsoft wants more hand holding than usual now that their CEO was caught making out with sales reps at an offsite team building event, and I was supposed to reach out to their PR team.

> Me: Still waiting for their PR team to schedule a meeting. Will follow up.

> Chris: Are you logging on soon?

> Me: So you can cast your demands from multiple communication channels? Yes. Ordering room service. Should be logged in shortly.

> Chris: Hurry up

> Me: I will now take an additional 5 minutes.

My relationship with Chris makes me laugh. We're impossibly close, yet somehow not at all. There's this connection between us that I can't articulate, where we just get each other in a way that translates to perfect work chemistry. We're both sassy as hell, trading barbs like it's our second language. No other sales executive would get away with what Chris does, and I'd never dream of mouthing off to anyone else the way I do with him. Calling out another exec about *The Wall Street Journal* like I did today? Never would happen.

I crank the AC down to sweatshirt weather and open my laptop. The bed beckons, but I force myself toward the desk instead.

My fingers tap at the keys, taking my sweet time. I swivel my chair to the right, admiring the sun reflecting off the building across the street.

Ding!

I sigh, dragging my gaze from the window and swiveling back around. It's a shame my phone didn't get destroyed when I tripped downstairs.

> Mr. GQ Griffin: Good Evening my beautiful flower. I was hoping I could see you soon.

My face scrunches reading the first line. Beautiful flower? Are you kidding me? There's a disconnect between his written and verbal communication. He speaks normal in person. But these texts? They give me secondhand embarrassment. They can't actually work on women.

How do I blow this guy off?

> Me: So sorry, Griffin. It's been hectic since I got home from vacation. I'm only here in San Antonio for the next 3 days. Sorry about that!

I flip through the room service menu to decide on dinner. *Ding!*

> Mr. GQ Griffin: I'll see you tomorrow after work then. How about a late picnic at Mission Concepcion after you get out of work? I'll swing by your hotel around 4:30pm?

The pleather folder holding the room service menu makes a *thud* as it hits the desk.

What the fuck?

I stare at my phone, waiting for the bottleneck of thoughts to settle so I can focus.

> Me: I don't want you to make a last minute trip just for me. I'm sure the flights are expensive from NYC. We'll find another time soon!

Doubtful.

> Mr. GQ Griffin: Actually, I'm going to be there anyway. I have some business meetings lined up. There's a small twenty-bed hotel interested in selling and I found a historical society that has Talavera tile for sale. It'd look great in Vivante's hotel entry.

If he's coming here on business, then it's not like he's flying across the country last minute just for me. He's an entrepreneur; of course he wants authentic materials for his hotel. It makes sense.

San Antonio's architecture tells the story of Spanish colonization dating back to the 1700s, with that influence woven through every corner of the city. This place is a gold mine for someone looking for real history and character. I've always wanted to visit the missions around San Antonio—soak in the history myself—but never have the time.

I huff out an exhaustive breath and make the decision before I overthink it any further.

> Me: That sounds great. I've love to go on a picnic.

Only time will tell if this is a bad decision. At least I'll finally get to see one of the many historic missions in the area.

Okay, moving on. I need to focus on completing the work Chris is waiting for. He never needs to follow up with me on work tasks. Being on Chris's bad side? Hard pass. He made another employee cry because she didn't respond to a client email within forty-eight hours. He is cutthroat when it comes to anything impacting his sales.

I slip my reading glasses on and dig into the shared drive where the client data and presentation decks are stored.

I spot my phone light up from the corner of my eye.

"Who the hell is calling me now?" I say to no one.

Sara.

"Hey, boo!" she says after I answer. She's in a cheerful mood. "I won Coffeegate."

"I'm sorry, what? Coffeegate?"

"Yes! Didn't I tell you? Evan and I have been at a standoff on coffee pots for the last three weeks."

I swivel in the office chair, annoyed by the distraction but curious about Coffeegate.

"You know the one-cup coffee pot we have? I keep getting coffee grounds in my coffee and then the coffee gets weaker and weaker. I have to press and hold the top for it to come out properly."

She pauses, and I know she's waiting for me to jump on the Coffeegate train, telling her how ridiculous and unfair this is.

I comply. "That's ridiculous. Does he expect you to press the top for the full three minutes it takes to brew a cup when you're barely awake?"

Satisfied with my reaction, she continues.

"I know, right? So I was, like, eff this. I ordered the newest model and it arrived three weeks ago." She pauses again before shouting into the phone, "He won't use it. He continues to use the broken one and has been drinking weak-ass coffee with a crunch for weeks."

Maybe everything about being single isn't bad—like having a functioning coffee pot all to myself.

"Why is he being so stubborn?" I ask, feeding into Sara's rage.

"I'll tell you why. It's be—" Her words abruptly cease and I push the phone closer to my ear, waiting. "Hold on. Baby's crying. Probably drank some of Evan's weak-ass coffee." She chuckles as her voice fades.

I swivel back and forth in my chair for several moments, my patience dwindling as I stare at my laptop and wait for her to return. When she does, she jumps right back into the conversation like she never left.

"Ever since my in-laws arrived, this kid cries day and night. All the time, B. And as his mother, I shouldn't say he's annoying, but it's annoying. And my in-laws are too, hovering like vultures. Telling me how to hold my child, bathe my child, soothe my child. Making me feel like I'm an unfit mother."

I want to tell her how lucky she is. Crying means life, it

means presence, it means everything some people would give anything for. Instead, I say, "You're a great mom, Sara. Don't let them make you doubt that."

"Thank you. I am, right? So, I need a boy update. I'm keeping score and date count."

"Griffin—I mean, *Mr. GQ*—is picking me up tomorrow for a picnic at one of the missions."

"When the hell did that happen?" she says, sounding shocked.

"Um . . . twenty minutes ago. Apparently, he has investment opportunities here, so he planned the trip anyway. I don't know. For a normal guy, this would feel weird. But this guy is far from normal. He owns three hotels and likes to pick out expensive tile."

"B. Don't write him off just yet. The guy can afford to fly across the country. Enjoy it. Remember. Explore. Have fun. Dating someone who is the opposite of you has its perks."

I try not to internalize her response, and continue. "Marina Man and I are talking every few days and planning to meet up when I'm in Irvine in a few weeks."

"Is he taking you sailing? That is so romantic."

"Let's just focus on exploring and having fun. No romance." I toss up my invisible walls again.

"Got it."

My stomach growls and I look at the clock. It's starting to irritate me how Sara seems to get entertainment value out of this whole dating challenge. She sits back like she's watching her favorite reality show, offering commentary and rules, completely oblivious to the emotional toll and time this requires.

"This dating challenge is a lot. My phone goes off all hours of the day. I've had to schedule time on my calendar just to reply to text messages. Dating is like a part-time job and my work is slipping, which never happens. Chris had to remind me he was waiting for visuals for two of our clients."

"Chris needs to learn that you aren't at his beck and call. He's smart enough to figure out how to get what he needs. You need to do some change management on his ass. You might have been available twenty-four-seven before, but not anymore."

The reality is, Chris is used to the level of service I provide as the implementation manager, and I have high expectations of myself, too. I won't let my personal life bleed into my work or damage my professional relationships.

"Any new dating app prospects?" Sara asks, and I hear the tub start running.

"I haven't opened the app since Mr. GQ. I have no time to date. Who am I kidding?"

"I can be your virtual assistant. Give me some spreadsheets to play with. I can stick Grady with my in-laws and hide in my office. Brianna Whitmore's personal assistant." She groans. "God that sounds wonderful. Who would've thought I'd miss spreadsheets, deadlines, and endless meetings?"

I need to wrap this up—I actually do have deadlines.

"Question for you. Even though I'm going out with Mr. GQ again tomorrow, does that still count toward my twelve dates?"

"Sure, that can count. Any date where the guy asks you out to dinner and pays. Or you ask him. And he's single. It counts."

"Okay. Hey, I'm going to go. I have to work on these presentations for Chris."

"Okay. Tomorrow is date number five out of twelve! You are on your way, sister. Keep it up!" She pauses. "And I'm serious about the personal assistant thing. Let me know!"

Chapter 19

San Antonio

I tap my room key against the black lock pad adjacent to the hotel's gym door. I'm still mortified by how much I had to lean on Javier to stand after yesterday's sidewalk disaster.

The hotel's custom scent is overpowered by the smell of rubber and sweat the moment I push the door open. I reach for a rolled white towel nestled in a wicker basket. A thin, older gentleman jogs on the treadmill closest to the door, his tiny shorts leaving little to the imagination. A blond guy who looks about my age pumps his arms back and forth on the elliptical machine at the far end. Why people choose to work out before the sun rises is beyond me. I feel groggy, cranky, and in desperate need of caffeine.

The elliptical is usually my go-to machine when I work out, which isn't often, but I don't want to be right next to that guy. I step onto the open treadmill, one machine away from blondie and one machine away from Mr. Tiny Shorts.

Blondie's stare is palpable as I figure out how to turn on the machine. I slap the start button and the belt lurches to life beneath my feet. I jab the speed button until it settles into a pace I can handle this early in the morning.

I resist looking, though I feel his eyes on me.

In a normal gym, people ignore you. At least, that's what I've heard. I don't go often enough to test this theory. Sara tried to get me to join her a couple years before the baby came, but I declined. I never know what time I'm going to get out of work. If Chris calls, I must answer. And he usually does.

"Good morning!" he says, a Colgate smile that is too blinding this early in the morning. His long, shapeless arms extend from his sleeves as he pushes those arm things forward and back.

I force a smile, his light blue eyes locked on me. "Morning."

"I love a woman who takes her health seriously." He nods my way, brushing the sweat from his forehead.

If only he knew how many chocolate conchas I can pack away.

"Yeah. Success is mental and physical." My tone is dry, but all he hears are the words, and his face shows it. I know this type. I've worked with several of them in the past.

"A girl after my own heart. I'm Trent." He might think he looks sexy, but he looks like one of those smiling ladies on the NordicTrack commercials from the eighties.

"Brianna."

"Pleasure to meet you, Brianna." His gaze holds. I look back to my treadmill, hoping this conversation will end.

"I don't want to interrupt your workout."

Then please don't.

"But I hope we can continue our conversation later, if you're interested."

I'm not.

Normally, I'd shut him down, but I have a goal of twelve

dates. I could easily knock another one out with this jokester and never have to hear from him again.

"I'd love to." My smile strains.

"I'm pretty busy, but I can squeeze you in Thursday between four and five. Are you still here? We can meet across the street at La Panadería?"

He comes to a stop before stepping off the elliptical, and wipes his face with a towel.

"How kind of you to work me into your schedule." I drape my towel over the timer, regretting saying yes.

"Something tells me it'll be worth it."

Through the gym mirrors, he steals a glance down my body when he thinks I'm not paying attention. "Great. I'll meet you over there at four, Trent."

He winks at me, tosses his towel over his shoulder, and struts out.

Gross.

After thirty minutes on the treadmill, I stroll down the hall to the lobby, the smell of fresh-baked croissants and hot coffee lifting my mood. The area is empty except for a few business professionals grabbing a quick bite before their workday starts.

Javier sits at his desk, his attention focused on the computer screen. A pressed blue suit jacket drapes over the back of his chair.

"Brianna, good morning." He leans back in his chair, taking a sip of coffee. His salmon-colored silk tie is a nice pop of color against his dark gray dress shirt. "I have my team working on your . . . shoe situation. Don't you worry about a thing."

My head drops, remembering my public tumble from yesterday. Thank goodness my face is already flushed from the gym. It's embarrassing that he has to assign a team of people for this.

"Thank you, Javier. I appreciate it. Just let me know what

stores are in the area and I'll do a quick shopping trip later tonight." I don't have time for shopping. My date with Mr. GQ at Mission Concepción is this afternoon. I'll be cutting it close, but my blue flats will only work with today's outfit. "You're here early," I add, distracted for a moment by fresh croissants being dropped off on the breakfast bar. I don't expect the concierge to be at his desk at six in the morning.

"I like to get a jump start on email before it gets busy." He stands, leaning against the desk, his arms crossed. "How about you? Is your work week going well?"

Javier's back in full professional mode this morning, a sharp contrast to the gentle man who carefully peeled the paper off my band-aid yesterday.

"It is. We just landed a new client." The scent of his cologne—something fresh and aquatic—makes me forget my train of thought for a second.

"Congratulations, that's wonderful." Javier has kind eyes that feel almost too perceptive. "Was that your colleague who dropped you off yesterday?"

"Yes, that's Chris, our sales executive. We're sharing a car this week."

"Now that you've landed the sale, does that mean we will see less of you?"

"On the contrary, you'll see more of me for the next few weeks."

A smile grows across Javier's face but quickly disappears.

"It will be our pleasure to have you."

Ding! I glance at my phone.

> Griffin: I can't wait to see you this afternoon. I'll meet you in your hotel lobby at 4:30pm.

"Please, don't let me distract you." Javier drops his arms to his sides, pushing off the desk.

"Thanks, Javier. I'll see you later."

The workday flies by. Chris and I spend four hours with Mercury's project team—two employees from their PR team, Michele, and Gus. They catered lunch, which feels like a small luxury. Chris rarely participates in meetings after contract signing, but I suspect he feels guilty about the *WSJ* issue. He remains quiet as we dive into the nitty-gritty of systems, territory where his expertise doesn't help much.

With our laptop bags strung over our shoulders, we leave the Mercury team and head toward the elevator and back to our hotels. A bounce in my step returns as we approach the elevator bays.

"Ready?" Chris asks as his finger hovers over the digital display.

"Do it." I hold my breath, staring at the display. I choose my elevator, but say nothing.

He presses the button, then turns to me with that mischievous grin, counting down on his fingers.

"Four!" I shout.

"Two," he says.

We both lean in, tension crackling between us as we wait for the display to tell us which elevator to go to.

A large number one pops up on the display. We both lose.

I trudge toward the elevator, bummed I guessed incorrectly. Chris has already moved on, his attention buried in his phone. I pull out mine and follow suit.

> Sara: Good luck tonight on your date!

> Me: This dating life is destroying my work schedule. I'm so far behind, I'll be up all night catching up.

> Sara: Let me help! Evan and his parents can watch Grady. Send me some stuff to work on! Dooo it.

I smile despite my stress.

> Me: You're funny.

Back at The Elysian, I pull open the door, wrestling with my laptop bag and purse as they tangle around my shoulder. Grace is checking in guests at the front desk with Tobias, who usually works the front desk at night. She catches my eye and waves me over.

"No pastries?" she asks, her elbows resting on the counter.

"Sadly, no, but I'll grab some tomorrow."

"Good. I wanted to ask how you're feeling after your spill yesterday."

I want to hide my face. These people need to forget about yesterday's disaster.

"I'm recovering, thank you. Speaking of which, did you get a list of nearby stores? I need to buy another pair of shoes to get me through the week."

"It's all taken care of. You'll find it in your room."

"Thank you. You're the best."

Before I have a chance to turn away, Tobias leans conspiratorially close to Grace.

"Looks like someone is requesting another round." His eyes widen as he pulls me into his gossip circle with Grace.

The three of us turn toward the bar, where Javier leans against the polished mahogany surface. He's deep in conversation with a blonde, her gorgeous waves cascading over her shoulders as her contagious laugh fills the space between them.

"Tobias! We do not gossip in front of guests." Grace elbows his waist.

"Brianna is family. Besides, she's here enough. I'm sure she's seen the fortune hunters prowling around Javier."

"Fortune hunters?" I ask.

He nods, his eyebrows climbing toward his hairline.

"Mr. Forever-a-Bachelor attracts them like gnats on a dewy face. I just hope he gets tested regularly." He purses his lips and shoots a pointed look toward Javier.

My stomach twists.

"Tobias! We do not disrespect other employees of the hotel." Grace's voice carries a sharp edge.

He throws his hands up in exasperation and stalks away from the desk.

I can't say I've noticed women hovering around Javier, but I don't make a point of watching him—like I'm doing right now. She's touched his forearm three times since I've begun staring. He leans into her touch, a smile playing at the corners of his mouth. Who wouldn't be drawn to him? His dark hair sweeps in a pompadour-ish wave, and that fitted dress shirt beneath his suit vest shows off his broad shoulders.

I force myself to look straight ahead as I walk past the bar toward the elevator. His dating life is none of my business. At least he's open to it. Good for him. But his cologne reaches me as I pass by him, cutting through the hotel's scent. It's no wonder Blondie can't resist him.

My phone buzzes in my purse. I fish it out and use it to hit the elevator button before reading the message. Mr. GQ's text fills the screen.

> Mr. GQ Griffin: I can't wait to see that beautiful face of yours. I have a wonderful afternoon planned for us. See you soon, mi amore.

I'd really like to slap the woman who previously encouraged this weird way of talking to women. His words feel manufactured, like he's reading from a script entitled *How to Woo Women 101*.

I wish he'd drop the act. Underneath the designer clothes and private jet lifestyle, I think he's a genuine guy. But he buries that authenticity under layers of forced ick.

> Me: Can't wait 😵

Chapter 20

San Antonio

I tap my keycard against the door lock to Room 1010 and push it open, stepping into the familiar comfort of my space. Afternoon light filters through the gauze curtains, casting soft shadows against the walls. Everything looks exactly as I left it this morning—except for a shoebox sitting in the center of my bed.

"Whoa." The word escapes before I can stop it.

My laptop bag slides off my shoulder, hitting the floor with a soft *thud*. My purse follows, landing beside it. I move toward the bed as if drawn by invisible strings, my eyes fixed on the ivory box with its gold-foiled emblem—a stagecoach pulled by two rearing horses.

"Why is there a Coach shoebox on my bed?" I murmur to the empty room.

I pivot left, then right, my hair whipping across my face as I scan the room for anything else out of place.

There's no way they bought me shoes. No one does that. How would they even know my size? My style? I circle the bed, studying the box from different angles like it might suddenly explain itself.

I resist opening it because I know I'll fall in love with whatever's inside. And I can't accept designer shoes, not from anyone, especially not from strangers at a hotel.

But it would be rude not to look at them, right? Maybe I should try them on so I can explain specific reasons why I can't accept them. They pinch, the back rubs against my heel, they're too wide, they're too narrow.

I approach the box like I'm approaching a sleeping dragon, my fingers tracing the edges of the pristine packaging. Even the container feels expensive under my touch.

Fear and excitement twist together in my chest as I lift the lid.

I pull apart the tissue paper and my breath stills. Nestled inside lies a beautiful pair of black leather pumps with three-inch heels that gleam like polished obsidian.

These are stunning.

I sink into the office chair and kick off my blue flats. The leather feels like silk beneath my fingertips as I lift one pump from its nest of tissue. It slides onto my foot as if custom-made, the supple material conforming to every curve.

They fit. Why do they have to fit?

The insole cradles my foot, and the toe box gives me room to breathe.

A small cry escapes me as I realize how much I love them. I stand and test them out, strutting back and forth across my room like I'm on a runway. My mind races through calculations. How much could they cost? Two hundred? Three? I've never owned designer shoes like this before.

It's not that I can't afford them. I budget carefully, and luxury shoes fall into my 'unnecessary splurge' category. Except wearing them transforms me into someone who belongs in boardrooms and fancy restaurants. Maybe my categories need updating.

Still, I can't accept these.

I glance up at the clock and panic. Griffin is going to be here soon. I slip off the heels with reluctance and change into something more suitable for a picnic—a soft pink button-down with cap sleeves, jean capris, and my trusty white sneakers. The transformation from elegant to casual feels jarring after those beautiful shoes.

I grab my purse and head downstairs, hoping to catch Javier before I leave.

His desk is empty. I crane my neck toward the breakfast area, scanning for any sign of him, then pivot toward the check-in desk where I find him holding a portfolio, talking to another man in a business suit.

Clarification: Javier is talking to the business suit guy, but staring at me.

His grin is contagious, and mine follows before I can stop it.

I lean against the bar, waiting as they finish what appears to be a formal conversation.

The weight of two additional stares presses against the side of my head. Tobias and Grace stand at check-in grinning ear to ear.

Of course they know about the shoes.

Javier walks toward me after saying goodbye to the businessman, his hands clasped in front of him.

"So?" he asks, eyebrows raised.

"Oh, my gosh, Javier. They're beautiful! And completely unexpected. I mean, I can't—"

"Good. They're yours. A gift from The Elysian."

My chest warms from his generosity. "You have to let me pay you for them."

"Nonsense. It's already taken care of." He brushes the palms of his hands against each other.

"I can't accept a pair of Coach pumps that I didn't pay for. Please, who can I pay?"

"You are family, Brianna. This is what we do for family."

"How did you even know my shoe size?"

Javier's gaze drops to the marble floor. "I may have gotten it yesterday when I was holding your broken shoe." His eyes peek up, gauging my response.

"Sneaky, sneaky, sneaky." I smile.

Tobias and Grace look like they're watching their favorite TV show when I glance over at them.

Javier's touch is warm on my arm. "Please, it's a gift from us to you." The sincerity in his voice is overwhelming.

Out of the corner of my eye I see Tobias cup his hands around his mouth like an amplifier.

"If you don't accept the shoes I'll take it as a personal insult, Brianna! I chose them!"

Laughter washes over all of us and I decide to give up the fight, for now.

The sound dies abruptly from the check-in desk. I turn to see what caught their attention, and there's Mr. GQ framed in the hotel's entrance. Sunlight streams behind him, casting his silhouette before he steps inside. Even from across the lobby, he draws every eye. There's something almost theatrical about the way he moves.

"Brianna, you look beautiful."

His voice carries across the marble as he approaches with long, measured strides. He's holding a tote bag that I assume contains our picnic, though it looks flat.

"Griffin, hi. . . This is Javier, concierge here at The Elysian. Javier, Griffin."

Javier extends his hand to shake Griffin's.

"Griffin owns and operates hotels in Europe," I add.

That perks Javier's interest. "Oh, really. Which hotels?"

"Eh, you probably wouldn't know them."

"Try me. The Elysian has connections throughout the globe." His voice is steady, almost amused.

Griffin shifts closer to me. "Vivante and Amore Albergo are just outside of Rome, and Gold Crest is in Spain."

Javier's eyebrows lift with interest. "Are you sole owner, or are you part of a corporation?"

"They're my hotels," Griffin says with a hint of arrogance.

"Interesting. I feel like I've heard of Amore Albergo. Was that once owned by the Bianchi Group?"

I watch Javier with new appreciation. I expect him to know other hotels in San Antonio, but not across the globe.

"No, you must be mistaken. It must be another hotel you're thinking of." Griffin turns to me. "Are you ready to go?"

"Yes," I say, before turning back to Javier. "Thank you so much for going above and beyond. I really appreciate it."

"You are most welcome." He nods toward me, then turns to Griffin. "Great to meet you, Griffin." Then he turns to walk away.

I follow Griffin outside. We stand in silence for a few seconds. Was that tension back there? Javier was nothing but professional, but Griffin's arrogance was noticeable.

He glances up from his phone. "Ride share should be here in three minutes."

I search his face for something unsaid and find nothing, just smooth planes, careful neutrality, and those artfully messy curls framing the top of his head. Before my thoughts can spiral, his arm settles around my shoulders and he presses a kiss to my temple.

"Are you close with that concierge?" The question comes out sharper than casual curiosity.

"I wouldn't say close. I see him coming and going."

I catch the slight easing in his posture.

"As long as he's not making a move on my girl." He kisses my temple again.

I laugh for two reasons—the idea of Javier being attracted to me, and the possessive way Griffin just claimed me.

"I couldn't wait to see you," he says, a soft, genuine smile returning.

"I'm excited for our date. I've been dying to go to the missions, but I never get a chance."

His face lights up. *Excited for our date* carries only half the truth. I'm excited to explore the mission, not necessarily to be on a date. But I'm going to make these dates work for me, even if all I can think about is the work waiting for me.

"I can't believe you flew out here to take me on a picnic date," I say as the ride share pulls up.

"Of course I would. You've been on my mind since New York. Nothing would stop me from seeing you again." He throws his palms out in a gesture of transparency. "If I'm being honest, I wanted to scout out some hotels while I'm here. But I couldn't wait to see you."

My shoulders relax. This is the normal Griffin—the one who doesn't send cringy texts.

"Any hotels in particular?"

He glances back, opening the passenger door for me. "Nothing I can disclose yet. Most hotels don't like to announce they're trying to sell."

We fall into normal conversation during the car ride. Griffin tells me about his recent travels while I share work stories. I can't tell if he's interested in my work. His eyes have that polite-but-distant look people get when they're waiting for their turn to talk. I get it, though. Most people would rather discuss anything besides work. But he does find every excuse to touch my knee—when I say something funny, when he laughs at his own jokes, when we hit a bump in the road.

The car slows as we approach the historic mission, gravel crunching under its tires, the old stone walls rising ahead of us. The ride share drops us off in front of the Mission Concepción sign, and Griffin immediately tells me to pose in front of it.

I feel like a tourist cliché as I stand here, my arms dangling at my sides while he takes what feels like twenty photos of me.

"You're beautiful," he says, and heat creeps up my neck.

We walk the grounds, the thick grass cushioning each step like a green carpet. Puffy clouds drift across the sky like cotton balls, casting shifting shadows as we approach the mission's weathered stone facade.

The mission rises before us like something from a dream, its honey-colored limestone walls glowing warm against the Texas sky. Twin bell towers frame the entrance, their surfaces weathered smooth by centuries of wind and rain.

Ancient oak trees stretch their gnarled branches over the courtyard, their roots probably older than the mission itself. The whole place hums with quiet history, making Griffin's chatter about hotel acquisitions sound small and temporary by comparison.

I feel Griffin's eyes on me. "You look happy."

"Of course. The mission is stunning."

"Not nearly as stunning as you."

And there it is.

My smile fades and I focus on random patches of dry grass crunching beneath my sneakers.

"Let's go over here," Griffin says, nodding toward a shaded area.

His hand grazes my back as he guides us toward the side of the mission. The church stretches before us, its walkway punctuated by three arched openings that frame the courtyard like windows into the past.

Reaching into his tote, he pulls out a large white bedsheet. With a flick of his wrists, he catches the wind to help it unfurl before it settles on the ground.

"Take a seat," he says.

My focus shifts between the breathtaking view of the historic structure and the items Griffin pulls from his bag. Unless it works like a magic hat, I'm not sure where the food is hiding. I try not to stare as he produces two plastic cups wrapped in cellophane, a bottle of red wine, a variety pack of sliced cheeses, and a small box of crackers.

Wine on an empty stomach is never a good idea, especially when I haven't eaten in hours.

After the sharp crack of a screw top, Griffin holds out a bottle of red wine, his hand covering the label.

"May I?"

"Yes, please." I tear the plastic from my cup.

Cheddar slice in hand, I snag one of the crackers that tumbled onto the sheet.

"Are you a big wine drinker?" he asks, taking a sip.

"No. I mean, I drink wine, but it's not serious." A memory surfaces, and I laugh. "After college, my best friend and I decided we were going to become wine drinkers. We visited wineries and pretended we were sommeliers until we were crying with laughter. Sara once said the wine danced on her tongue like a tipsy gnome doing a jig."

My laugh fades. It was the same weekend she found out her mom had cancer, and we both needed the escape.

"That's adorable. I always wonder if the sommeliers are just making it up. I've been to tons of wineries and I never taste what they describe," Griffin says.

Then, in mocking gestures, he lifts his cup of wine to his

nose, sniffing so hard it must hurt. He moves the cup in small circles, swirling the red liquid, his face pursed in concentration. He drags the cup to his mouth, pinky out, and takes the tiniest sip before making that satisfied quench-your-thirst sound.

"This is medium-bodied with a brilliant hue." He looks at me, his face barely holding back a smile. "I taste overripe cherries, a hint of rose petal, and subtle undertones of shoe leather and aftershave."

I burst out laughing, steadying my cup to keep it from spilling onto the sheet. He leans back on one arm, pleased with my reaction. Those dark curls catch the breeze, aviators glinting atop his head in the afternoon light, and for a second, he transforms from the polished GQ guy on the dating app into someone I might actually want to know.

"That's a disconnect I feel with my guests. I'm not into caviar, expensive bottles of wine, imported duck eggs." He smirks. "I had to order imported duck eggs because a guest was offended by the ducks in Spain."

I burst out laughing at the audacity.

"I mean, don't get me wrong. I like the finer things in life, but there's a line for me. For my guests, no ceiling exists."

Griffin is an enigma—a puzzle I can't seem to solve. His thoughts, his feelings, his motivations, even his true nature feels unclear and contradictory.

"How's all your remodeling and upgrades going?" I ask, grabbing another slice of cheddar.

"Great! We just installed a beautiful sculpture of Aphrodite at the entrance of Gold Crest. It's breathtaking." His hand kneads the grass through the sheet. "They say Aphrodite represents beauty and self-love. I think self-love is so important, especially today when people are so willing to break you down with just a few words, you know?"

He plucks a few blades of grass at the edge of the sheet.

I chew my cheese, watching him roll the green slivers between his fingers. He shifts his body, crossing his legs.

"Enough about me. I want to talk about you. Your job sounds incredible. Do you get to keep all those travel points and miles? I bet you have platinum status everywhere."

I laugh, thinking of how I prioritize pastries over points.

"I do. The air miles are nice. I used them to visit a college friend in February."

"Nice. I assume you don't own a home since you travel so much?"

The assumption irritates me. "Actually, I have a condo in Dallas. It's perfect for me right now."

"Smart investment." He draws his sunglasses down from his head. "You can't go wrong investing in land and buildings. I watched my parents make smart decisions on their properties."

"That's really nice that they were great role models."

"Well, it doesn't come without family turmoil. When there's so much money on the line, it can strain relationships. I don't speak to my mother anymore because of it. She . . . " Griffin glances up at the mission, hesitating. "She said some nasty things to me that a mother should never say to a son. I had to separate myself from her, to protect myself." He glances at the mutilated blades of grass in his hand. "Are you close with your family?"

My smile tightens. "Pretty close, yeah."

He leans forward, his sunglasses slipping down his nose. "Have you mentioned me yet?"

The grin that spreads across his face makes my stomach tighten, though I'm not sure whether it's good or bad.

I let out a nervous laugh. "I haven't mentioned that I'm dating. I usually don't until it gets serious." I turn the interview back on him. "What about you? How long have you been active on the dating app?"

"Not long. You were the first person I saw after signing up." His voice drops. "Exactly what I've been looking for."

"Lucky me," I say, tipping the cup back, taking a bigger sip than I intend.

He watches me swallow before continuing. "Can I ask you something?" He pauses, studying my face. "Have you ever had your heart broken? Like, really broken?"

My cup rests on my lip as his question floods my brain with answers.

Yes. I have. And it was debilitating.

"A few times," I say.

"Really? Tell me about them." Griffin leans in, like a kid during story time.

"I'd rather not cover that on date two." This question feels too personal, too early.

His body tenses. "Sorry, I was curious. We don't have much time together, and I want to know everything I can about you."

I smile, but it feels painted on.

Where are the *How do you take your coffee* questions? *What's your favorite movie? Do you like to hike?* The easy ones that don't require excavating old wounds.

"Can you pour me some more wine?" I ask, holding out my cup.

"Of course," he says, filling it with a heavy hand.

The rest of our time passes in a blur of interrogation disguised as getting-to-know-you questions while I drink more wine than I should on an empty stomach. By the time we pack up, the sun is setting and I'm half drunk.

Chapter 21

San Antonio

The ride share pulls up to The Elysian, and I need real food stat. This guy knows how to leave a girl wanting more. Too bad it's just more calories.

Griffin hops out to open my passenger door.

"Can I see you again tomorrow?" His hazel eyes are full of hope.

A third date? More interview questions?

"Oh, I don't know. I have a lot of work—"

"Come to the movies with me." He reaches for my hand. "The new rom-com with Maya Sterling and Jake Westbrook is out. It's getting rave reviews on Rotten Tomatoes."

Damn it. I want to see that movie. I met Maya Sterling at a hotel I was staying at when they were filming. We talked for thirty minutes at the bar before her director called her back to the shoot.

"Please? I'm a guy. I can't go see that movie by myself." His puppy dog eyes seem honest and real.

Against my better judgment, I say yes. He kisses my cheek, his lips soft against my skin.

I'm never going to get my work done. But also, the faster I get to twelve dates, the faster I can put this whole fiasco behind me. Movies also mean less talking and no interrogation.

Sara offered to help with my workload, I might as well see if she meant it.

> Me: Hey- Are you still willing to pass Grady off to the in-laws and help me wrangle some data?

Sara might be my Hail Mary this week.

I arrive at the movie theater just before six p.m. A man in brown slacks and a crisp white shirt is taking photos of the building while families scurry through the front doors. I head toward the entrance. The humidity is out of control today and I'll be happy to wait for him in the AC.

"Hey, Brianna!" The man in brown slacks calls over to me.

"Oh, Griffin. I didn't recognize you."

"You look beautiful as always," he adds, grabbing my hand and kissing it.

My smile feels fake.

He guides us to the ticket booth and I wait off to the side, sweat beading on my nose. Who uses the ticket booth these days?

Once he has our tickets, we head inside and the blast of air conditioning hits me like a wave of relief. I walk up to the ticket taker, not realizing Griffin stopped several feet behind me, tapping something into his phone with intense concentration.

The ticket taker, a woman in her fifties with graying hair,

leans forward from her stool. She extends her hand with practiced efficiency, waiting for Griffin to hand over our tickets. There's a brief pause—just long enough to feel awkward—before he finally passes them to her.

"Thank you," I say, offering her a smile.

"Yes, Thank you, Priscilla," Griffin adds.

Griffin takes the tickets back from her and we walk into the lobby where the theater's back wall is one long concession wonderland with popcorn poppers, candy dispensers, and drink machines creating an almost overwhelming display of movie snacks.

"There's nothing better than movie popcorn, right?" Griffin says, his hand finding the small of my back as he guides us forward. The scent of butter and salt make my mouth water.

I glance around the busy lobby as we wait on line, observing families juggling drinks and candy, teenagers clustered around the arcade games, employees in red polo shirts restocking the nacho station.

Griffin's eyes move systematically across the lobby—customer service desk, cleaning crew, finally settling on the popcorn scattered around our feet. I track his gaze, wondering what he's looking for.

"Griffin?"

"*Mmm?*" His face transforms from straight concentration to a bright smile.

"How was your day?"

"Oh! It was good. Met with the hotel owner. They're not willing to budge on the price and it needs a lot of work, so I won't be putting in an offer."

"That's disappointing. How about the tile you were looking at?"

"I'll get my eyes on the tile tomorrow before my flight. I'm—"

The teenager at the register waves to get our attention. "What can I get for you?"

Griffin steps forward. "Two medium popcorns and two medium sodas. Coke and . . . " He points my way.

"Root beer, please."

The teen nods. "Sure. Anything else?"

Griffin looks at the employee for a long moment, as if he needs to reboot his internal system.

"Griffin?" I swat his arm.

"Oh, sorry. No, that's it for now."

The girl leaves to grab our popcorn and drinks and I glare at the side of Griffin's head.

He turns and whispers in my ear. "She didn't ask us if we wanted to add candy."

"Do you want candy?" My voice is low and my tone flat.

"Oh no, no. I'm okay for now."

He must notice my *what-the-hell* expression because he shifts on his feet before adding, "Being in the business of customer service, it's so important that your employees are upselling and educating customers on these things."

Boarding school clearly skipped the social skills curriculum for this guy.

We find our seats as the previews begin, and Griffin's commentary during the coming attractions turns into an impromptu list of movies he wants us to see together, his enthusiasm growing with each trailer. But his attention wanders during the actual film. He sneaks out during a pivotal moment and comes back armed with Mike and Ikes and Whoppers. He offers me some, but I shake my head. By the time the credits roll, both boxes are empty.

As we exit the movie, I drop our empty containers in the garbage can outside the theatre door. Griffin taps away on his phone, nearly walking into it.

Really? He can't put his phone down for two seconds?

Griffin glances up from his phone, catches my expression, and his face drops a fraction.

"I'm sorry, Brianna. I know I was distracted tonight. The truth is, my CFO texted and told me a guest is filing a lawsuit against me because she slipped and fell by the pool." Something flickers across his face—a mix of fear and sadness that makes me pause.

"That's terrible! I'm so sorry to hear that."

Guilt creeps in about my irritation with his phone obsession. A lawsuit would send me into complete hermit mode, but Griffin still came out tonight. I have to respect that, even if his mind is clearly elsewhere.

He insists on waiting with me for the ride share even though I say I'll be fine.

"The last two days have been great for me, Brianna. I really enjoy spending time with you."

"It's been fun. I appreciate you coming out this way, even with business."

"Can I fly you to New York next weekend?" Hope flickers across his face. "I don't know if I can go longer without seeing you."

Do I hear him right?

"Oh, wow. Griffin, that's . . . " *So crazy.* "So generous of you." I hesitate. Is this normal dating behavior now? I mean, I haven't been out of the dating scene that long, but this guy is insane if he thinks I'll say yes to flying me to New York after three dates. "I need to think about it, look at my work schedule. Can I get back to you?"

His face falls. "Of course. But I'll warn you, I don't like to take no for an answer." He winks, kissing my temple.

I sit in the ride share, uncertainty washing over me. The date was kind of weird. But Griffin is kind of weird. I've never met someone who went to boarding school, and there's definitely some social cue training that wasn't covered during his education. Still, his boyish mannerisms seem genuine, even if extremely awkward. What I am certain of is that I will not be flying to New York anytime soon.

Walking into The Elysian brings me comfort. The staff, the service, the ambiance—everything feels like an embrace. The custom scent of white tea and verbena drifts through the air, and I breathe in a healthy dose.

The front desk sits empty, and the lobby stretches quiet around me as I pause to admire the new bouquet displayed in the center of the space. Yellow flowers dominate this arrangement, brighter and more cheerful than yesterday's.

That's when I spot Javier behind the concierge desk, and something about his expression makes my stomach turn. The scraping of his chair against the marble floor echoes through the lobby as he stands.

"Are you okay? Are you safe?" he asks as he strides closer to me, his hand reaching for my shoulder, his eyes darting over my face as if he's searching for something.

"Yes, why?" My pulse quickens at his intensity.

"Where's that guy you were with yesterday?"

Javier's eyes dart to the entrance, his body coiled tight.

"Griffin? Probably at his hotel, I guess?" My heart is hammering against my ribs. Javier is in full panic mode, nothing like his usual calm demeanor. "Javier?"

"Brianna, I'm so sorry. Yesterday, when he said he owned those hotels in Europe, something felt off. I recognized one of those hotels and knew the Bianchi Group owned it. I met one of the Bianchi brothers at a conference a few years back." He pauses. "He lied to you."

His words land like stones, but I can't process them. "Wait, what? No, that's . . ." I shake my head as if that'll make sense of what he's saying. "Maybe you misheard? Or maybe he works *with* the Bianchi Group?"

Even as I say it, doubt creeps in. Griffin was so specific about those properties, so proud when he talked about them. Javier's jaw tightens.

"He doesn't own those hotels. He doesn't even work there."

"But he . . ." I trail off, my mind racing back through our conversations. All those details about renovations, guest complaints, the duck eggs. How could someone fake all of that? "Are you sure? Maybe there's some explanation."

But even as I scramble for reasons, pieces click into place, things that didn't quite add up, moments when his stories felt rehearsed.

What. The. Fuck.

Griffin lied to me? My stomach churns. What else was fabricated? The art knowledge—was that fake too? All those hotel stories—just research? The romantic flight to New York— Christ, how starved for attention was I that I fell for this? I'm smarter than this. I used to be smarter than this.

The picnic date floods back, and my stomach twists. The cheap wine, the precut cheese and cardboard crackers. Those weird, probing questions. I'm such an idiot.

The lobby spins around me. Griffin's lies, his fake charm, the whole elaborate performance—all crash down at once. I want to crawl under a rock. Hide from my own stupidity. But as I stand here drowning in embarrassment, another thought surfaces.

"Wait." I look up at Javier. "You did research on my date?"

His head drops with a forced exhale, and for a moment he looks almost embarrassed.

"I'm so sorry, Brianna. My intent wasn't to research your date." He meets my eyes, and I catch something unguarded in his expression. "It struck me as odd that he owned these hotels when I knew the Bianchi Group owned one of them."

He fidgets with his tie, already pulled loose from its perfect knot.

"I used my Elysian contacts to fact check." His voice drops. "They got back to me a couple of hours ago. I wasn't sure where you were, but I couldn't leave until I knew you were safe." He pauses, searching my face.

I scan the hotel lobby as if the marble columns might hold answers to the questions flooding my mind. That bastard lied to me the whole time. Who knows if anything he said was true.

"Yes, I'm safe." I press my palm against my forehead.

"We can increase security. If you have a photo of him, I can print copies for our staff. If he tries to enter the hotel, he'll be escorted out immediately." Javier watches my face carefully. "I assume you don't want to see him again?"

"No. I'm done with that lunatic." My head drops into my hands. "I'm so stupid. How could I let this happen?"

I turn and start walking, as if the distance alone could carry me out of this moment.

He follows, his hand grazing my arm. "You're not stupid. He convinced me."

"No, he didn't. You sent your emails!" I snap.

"Brianna. Stop." He catches my arm gently as I try to keep walking. "Your hands are trembling." He runs his other hand through his hair. "Look, I know this is a lot to process. I don't want you going up to your room upset like this. Can we just . . . sit for a minute? Can I get you a drink?"

I'm not even present as he steers me into the bar. My mind is racing through every text and conversation I had with Griffin over the last few weeks.

"What can I get you, boss?" The bartender nods toward Javier while emptying a box of limes into a large glass jar.

"I'll take my usual, and whatever Brianna would like."

I look at Javier, then the bartender, not even sure I want to be here.

"Red wine is fine."

I can sense Javier's gaze but I'm too deep in my thoughts to acknowledge him. Griffin doesn't own hotels. He acted so strangely tonight at the theater. But he flew here to see me. You can't do that if you're broke, right?

"Brianna." Javier pulls me out of my spiral. I focus on the soft creases at the corners of his eyes. "I didn't mean to intrude, but I was really worried you were going to be put in an unsafe position." He pulls out the bar stool. "Please, sit for a moment."

I struggle with the bar stool—still too tall for me—before I respond. "Thank you, truly. I appreciate you looking out for me. I'm embarrassed that you had to. That I couldn't see it myself."

"You have nothing to be embarrassed about. He was convincing, and you wanted to trust him. That's not a flaw; that's being a good human. I only caught it because of a lucky coincidence."

I don't mention that I was with Griffin tonight too. It will just make me look like a complete idiot. How did I not see this coming? And to think I was justifying his weird, clingy texts. They were red flags from the beginning.

Javier nods to the bartender as he slides my wine and an old fashioned across the bar.

As if things couldn't get worse, the general manager appears next to the bartender.

"Why are you still here? You have important things to do tomorrow." Diane doesn't even glance at me as she addresses Javier.

I take a large gulp of wine.

"Everything is ready to go. No need to worry." Javier gives her a smile and turns back to me.

Her presence and judgment are more than I can handle right now. I need to get away from her, from everyone, and process what happened.

"I should let you go, Javier. Thank you so much for your concern and investigative skills. I really appreciate it."

"Let me know what else I can do for you. I mean it." He gives my arm a quick squeeze.

I smile and nod, taking my wine with me as I head upstairs.

Chapter 22

San Antonio

I didn't sleep much last night. I spent hours rehashing my dates with Griffin, analyzing everything he shared with me, looking for missed red flags. The way he talked about his hotels with such specific detail—the thread count of the sheets, the tile for the pool. How could someone fabricate that so convincingly? The truth is, I didn't see any warning signs—well, other than his love-bombing texts. What does that say about me? Why do I minimize the warning signs, twisting obvious signals into quirks?

Maybe it's because I wanted to remember what it felt like to be chosen. Maybe I'm so desperate to prove Sara wrong that I ignored my instincts.

The betrayal carves into me, but what stings even more is the realization that I fell for exactly what I thought I was too smart to fall for.

I texted Sara everything first thing this morning. It was her challenge that put me in this situation anyway. Her reply was in all caps, something about him being a serial killer. Very helpful.

This is the last thing I need before my date with Trent tonight. I'm already not looking forward to going out with the gym guy. I only said yes because I need twelve dates for this stupid challenge. But now, after discovering Griffin lied about everything? I have zero emotional bandwidth left for pretending to be interested in someone I'm not even attracted to.

At least I get to see Beck later. She's in town for a basketball tournament for the high school girls' team she coaches, and even though she's not exactly the shoulder-to-cry-on type, I'm looking forward to the distraction. Beck has this way of keeping things light, which is exactly what I need right now—or it might be the opposite. I can't tell anymore.

I'm sitting in one of the wingback chairs in the breakfast area, picking apart my croissant. The buttery layers crumble between my fingers as I take a bite.

Javier's face appears around the wing of my chair. I gasp, and the flaky pastry catches in my throat. His charcoal gray three-piece suit looks crisp this morning, the vest accentuating the muscle of his chest.

"How are we doing this morning?" He sits in the chair next to me, his elbows on his knees, leaning in.

"Other than complete embarrassment and being mortified that half the hotel knows I have poor judgment when it comes to dating?" I fall back into the cocoon of the winged chair, taking another bite of my croissant.

"We talked about this. Master manipulators can deceive the most intelligent of people." He pauses. "And only I know all the details. Dustin, our bartender, might know a little based on our conversation, but he also knows that he does not repeat any conversations that I'm a part of."

"What about Miss Mean Face?" I ask, curling my fingers around the warm coffee mug.

Javier's face twists before breaking into a laugh. "Miss Mean Face? Who is that?"

"The general manager, Diane."

Come on, he has to notice how she treats me.

He leans back into the chair, still laughing, the blue wings swallowing him, too. I don't think it's that funny.

"That woman does not like me and I don't know why."

I take a sip of my coffee and brush away two drips that fall to my black pants. I lift the white porcelain mug above my head to check for leaks.

"Everything okay over there?" He nods toward my mug.

I inspect the mug once more and place it on a napkin.

"It's fine." I redirect my attention back to him.

"About Diane, or Miss Mean Face," he says, "I can have a conversation with her."

"No!" I thrust my hands toward him. The last thing I need is for her to have more fuel. "It's not your problem. You're not her boss. Please don't say anything, Javier. It'll only make it worse."

"Okay, I won't. Promise." His attention shifts to above my chair, and his expression changes to something more professional. "Good morning," he says.

Chris appears out of nowhere.

"Good Morning, Javier. Morning, Brianna."

These chairs will be the death of me, if this dating challenge doesn't kill me first.

"I'll let you two talk shop. Brianna, let me know if you need anything, okay?" Javier's focus turns serious.

Chris looks at Javier, then me, then back at Javier. The silence stretches.

"I will, thank you," I say, forcing a smile.

Chris sits in Javier's chair and grabs the croissant from my plate. "What was that all about?"

"Hey!" I frown as I mourn the pilfered buttery goodness.

Chris inhales the croissant in two quick bites. I turn to see if there's any more on the breakfast bar. He follows my gaze and stands.

"Get me one too," I call out as he heads to the food.

He comes back holding two croissants wrapped in a napkin. "Let's go. The first time I met with this client, I was ten minutes late because there's no parking."

He grabs my laptop bag as I stand, and before he can say anything, I snatch a croissant out of his hand and turn on my heel before he can grab it back. I grin, hearing him mutter something under his breath as I walk ahead.

The lobby buzzes with movement, more than usual. Businessmen and women in expensive suits cluster in small groups, chatting or checking their phones. There's a low hum of conversation and the clacking of dress shoes across the tile.

The sound of my name cuts through the chatter. I pivot to find Javier among a cluster of well-dressed men, blending in seamlessly while still managing to catch my eye.

"Those are lovely shoes," he says, glancing down at my new black pumps. The rest of his group look down at my heels.

"Thank you, they're Coach," I say, lifting my foot slightly to show them off.

Javier nods and returns to the circle of suits.

I push open the heavy exterior door and step outside.

Our meeting with the potential new client, Northpoint Publicity, a public relations firm for mid-level celebrities, goes well. They sought us out when one of their clients was arrested and charged with a DUI. They're eager to sign a contract to track whether public opinion is positive or negative now that their famous performer has been in jail. Chris let me tag along even though they're still in the early negotiation phase. I love seeing him in full-pitch mode.

After the meeting, we set up shop at a local cafe for lunch and to strategize our next steps for Northpoint. This is our first PR firm client, so we're brainstorming which celebrity magazines, entertainment blogs, and social media platforms we need to monitor. Since our AI tracks mentions and keywords across the Internet, we have to anticipate which outlets are covering the DUI story, how fans are reacting to the arrest, and whether it's gaining traction or dying down.

I would be happy to continue brainstorming, but my date with Trent is coming up. On a positive note, I get to sink my teeth into a chocolate concha, and I get to see Beck later. I'm excited to hear how her basketball team is doing since they made it to playoffs.

The sweet smell of pastries and espresso fills my senses as I step inside La Panadería. The restaurant is packed, as always, but I snag the only open table near the window. I settle into a deep green cushioned chair and pull out my phone.

I missed a call from Sara during my brainstorming session, and I have a text from her waiting for me.

> Sara: Data has been wrangled. I emailed you the final presentation deck. That was SO MUCH FUN! Send me more work! Love, your personal assistant.

It's the least she can do, putting me through this nonsense.

I scan the restaurant, my gaze settling on a mother cradling her little boy. He looks like Grady. Time seems to slow as I stare, my eyes growing distant, breath catching in shorter intervals. The mother notices me watching and offers a gentle smile that I return before tearing my attention away to a group of college students and their scattered textbooks.

And then I see him. Trent. He stands at the door, scanning the room like a lost tourist, with several tote bags and a laptop bag hanging from both shoulders. The bags dwarf his frame.

Maybe he won't recognize me and leave.

Please let him leave.

The odds are not in my favor. He spots me and makes his way over, the tote bags bouncing with each step like eager puppies. Whatever energy this date requires, I don't have it. I glance down at the bags as he reaches our table.

"You always come with this much baggage?" The words slip out before I can stop them.

"My clients come with me everywhere." His chest puffs like a peacock showing off its feathers.

"Is that so?"

I'm going to need something stronger than coffee to survive this.

He drops his bags with a heavy *thud* that makes nearby diners look over. I lean forward in my seat to see what's so important that he needs to haul it around like a traveling salesman. Blue folders and white binders poke out of the bags.

I look up at him. "Want to grab something?"

He turns, hands placed firmly on his tiny hips in a power stance that would be impressive if he wasn't five-foot-six, staring at the menu board for what feels like forever. I've seen people choose mortgages faster.

I study the back of his head and the blond locks that are one bad haircut away from full mullet status.

"No, I think I'm good," he says as he turns and sits down.

Are you *kidding* me? This is supposed to be a date. He invited *me*. That entire menu meditation was for nothing?

"Well, I'm going to grab something."

I stand, my chair scraping against the floor, and head to the end of the line. Each step feels like I'm walking deeper into dating hell.

This is ridiculous. I'm standing in line *alone* while my *date* guards his precious file folders like they contain state secrets. This is what I get for following through on commitments. Next time, I'm staying in my hotel with room service and Netflix.

I snag the last chocolate concha in the case along with a decaf coffee and walk back to our table. Trent is hunched over his phone, fingers flying across the screen, oblivious to my return. I could probably set the table on fire and he wouldn't notice.

"So, busy day?" I say, using both hands to lift my oversized bistro mug.

He says nothing for a few moments, just keeps tapping away on his cell phone like I'm invisible furniture.

Finally, he acknowledges me. "I don't know how this company would run without me."

"Really." My voice comes out flat as I take another sip of my coffee, buying myself time to formulate a response that won't get me kicked out of this place.

The rest of the date becomes the Trent Show. He talks about how wonderful he is, how his clients adore him, and how everyone else in his industry is a complete buffoon. The next twenty minutes shifts to his nonprofit work and how someone has to help "these people."

Lucky for humanity, he's willing to sacrifice himself for the cause.

I place a bet to see how long it takes him to ask me a single question about myself. Current count: forty-three minutes.

After complaining about how often he gets friend-zoned, he finally asks what I do for work. Fifty minutes about his greatness, and I get a measly ten-minute consolation prize. But not even that—after five minutes, he interrupts me.

Of course he does.

"I've actually got a Zoom call in five minutes, so I'll need to wrap this up."

I stare at him, dumbfounded. A Zoom call. He's ending our date for a Zoom call. After fifty minutes of the Trent Show, he's dismissing me like I'm a staff meeting that ran over.

"No problem." I gather my things and stand, my movements sharp and deliberate.

"I'll send you a friend request on Facebook, but I have to unfriend someone because I'm at the max friends count."

"Please don't." My words come out flat and final.

And I walk out of my pastry paradise, leaving Trent and his ego to their very important Zoom call.

As I stand on the street corner waiting for the walk signal, I pull out my phone and Google *What is the maximum number of Facebook friends?*

Five thousand.

Chapter 23

San Antonio

I can't get to the Riverwalk to meet up with Beck fast enough. The fifteen-minute walk from the coffee shop feels like an escape route from my own personal hell. Each block takes me further from Trent and his precious file folders, his nonprofit savior complex, and his Facebook friend crisis.

Three blocks later, my shoulders finally start to unwind, loosening the tension that's been coiled tight around my ears.

The city streets give way to stone staircases as I approach the river, and the tightness in my chest melts away.

The Riverwalk stretches out before me like a different world—cypress trees draped in Spanish moss create a canopy over the water, their branches swaying in the breeze. I take my first full breath in over an hour.

Tour boats float past, their guides pointing out landmarks to clusters of travelers who seem to be enjoying each other's company. *What a concept.* I watch an older couple lean into each other, laughing at something on their phone. My smile grows before I realize it.

The walkway curves along the San Antonio River, and my

pace slows. I'm not racing away from something anymore; I'm walking toward something good.

Thank God for real friends.

The red umbrellas of Bella Vista come into view, and I feel almost human again. When I arrive, the hostess points me toward the patio, and I see Beck's familiar silhouette at a riverside table—and she has two glasses of red wine waiting for us.

"So . . . how did your date go?" she asks as I approach the table.

She has no idea what a loaded question that is.

"Well, I learned the Facebook friend limit is five thousand." I reach for my wine glass like it's a lifeline. "So there's that."

Her eyebrows shoot up. "Huh?"

I spend the next ten minutes recounting the last hour with Trent—the power stance, the file folders, the fifty-minute monologue about his greatness, and the grand finale: being dismissed for a Zoom call.

Beck leans back in her chair with her arms crossed as her expression cycles through an entire spectrum of emotions—confusion when I mention the bags, disbelief during the nonprofit savior story, and pure horror when I get to the Facebook friend limit excuse.

"Wait, wait, wait." She holds up her hand. "He actually said he had to *unfriend* someone to add you?"

"Word for word."

She stares at me for a moment, then throws her head back and laughs.

"Oh, my God. What a douchebag."

"Oh, it gets better."

Then I update her on Griffin and the picnic date, and how weird he was acting at the movie theater—asking if I caught employee names, if I saw managers, what the concession stand employee should have been doing. I'm about ready to drop the bomb about what Javier uncovered when she interrupts me.

"Shit, B. He was doing a secret shopper event."

"A what?" I set down my wine glass and lean forward.

"Secret shopping. Companies hire people to go to their locations and evaluate the service, cleanliness, employee behavior, all that stuff. I did it during my first few years of teaching. They pretend to be regular customers but they're actually taking notes on everything." She shakes her head. "His questions about employee names, managers, what people should be doing—that's classic secret shopper behavior."

Her words hang in the air between us—"secret shopper event"—and suddenly everything clicks into place with sickening clarity. The way he insisted on this specific theater. How he kept checking his phone and jotting down notes. That weird moment with the concession worker.

Of course. I sit back in my chair, the truth snapping into focus. Waves of embarrassment mixed with anger pump through my veins.

"So, he wasn't on a date with me. He was working."

"Sounds like it. Did he take photos while you were there?"

I play back the date in my head. He was texting on his phone but . . . *the front of the movie theatre.*

"He was taking photos of the theater when I arrived. I didn't even recognize him at first."

"You were basically a prop in his work assignment. He gets paid for doing it, and reimbursed any money he spends on tickets and food."

A prop. I was a freaking prop in his professional con job. While I was trying to figure him out, he was evaluating bathroom cleanliness and employee uniforms.

"I can't believe this." I bang my hand on the table. Beck steadies my wine glass.

I should have known. Everything about him was off from the start. Normal conversation one minute, then those intense, over-the-top texts that made my skin crawl. I kept trying to figure him out, like he was some puzzle I needed to solve, when I should have trusted my gut that something was wrong. His whole life is apparently built on deception, and I was too naive, too trusting, to see it. The weight of the humiliation presses me deeper into the chair.

No wonder I couldn't connect with him. No wonder every conversation felt like I was talking to a different person. I was talking to whatever version of himself he thought worked best in that moment.

We finally get around to ordering appetizers, and I fill her in what Javier discovered.

"Well, I'm glad he didn't kidnap you."

Comforting, Beck.

I hunch over my wine, staring at my hands. "Okay, I'm really done talking about my shit dating life. Please tell me about the basketball tournament. How's it going?"

"It's been good. We won our first game yesterday, and the girls are playing smart. Tomorrow we face a stronger team, but I think we're prepared for it." She checks her watch. "I need to be back at the hotel by eight for our team meeting."

"How's your star player doing this year? Still causing trouble?"

Beck raises an eyebrow. "You mean the locker room incident?"

I nod, remembering something about her getting caught in the boys locker room.

"She's team captain now. Turns out she just needed to focus."

"See? Some people can turn their disasters around. I'm just collecting them." I gesture with my wine glass. "Seven dates, all a waste of time. Wait—actually six. Today's date doesn't count because I had to pay for my own damn coffee. Damn it!"

"So, quit." She bites into the mozzarella sticks the server delivered a few moments ago. "Sara's not the one going on these dates."

"Right? What's with the married woman forcing the single one to date?" I wag my mozzarella stick at Beck.

"Look, I know Sara's heart is in the right place, but dating today is different than when we were in college. This shit isn't easy." Beck lifts her glass. "Do I think you're in a slump? Yeah. You basically shut down after that asshole. Do I think you need to go out with anyone who has a dick? No." She takes a drink. "I think you need to be open to opportunities, which you haven't been, but I don't think you should be forced into this rapid-fire dating challenge."

I stop chewing, the warm cheese suddenly feeling like glue in my mouth as her words settle over me. Everyone sees it. I thought I've kept my walls invisible, seamless. But everyone sees the cracks—Beck, Sara, even Lucas. I'm not as good at hiding it as I imagined.

Our conversation transitions to something lighter after our dinner arrives. Beck doesn't like to stay in the emotional zone for long, where Sara and I thrive in it.

After dinner, we walk in opposite directions to our respective hotels. I step into the stream of tourists wandering the Riverwalk. A father ushers his twin toddlers off the tour boat as the mother carries two small backpacks, a plastic dinosaur and a small blanket. She looks exhausted, but she plasters on a smile when one of the twins asks her to carry him. A mariachi band plays near one of the stone bridges, their music mixing with laughter from the boat tours drifting past.

I climb the stone steps to the first bridge, my heels clicking against the worn surface. Below, the water catches the string lights from the restaurants, fracturing them into a thousand tiny pieces. *Like me*, I think. I'm tired of being broken.

A couple passes me, the woman laughing at something her date whispers in her ear. They look so easy together, so natural. When did dating become this impossible? When did I become this person who pays for her own food and gets lied to about imaginary hotels?

I continue up the incline toward street level, leaving the river behind. My calves burn slightly in my new heels, but the physical discomfort feels better than the emotional weight I'm carrying.

Maybe Beck's right. Maybe I don't need to force myself through more dates with random strangers.

But what if one of them isn't terrible? What if date eight or nine is worth it? If I stop, if I give up dating again—*he* wins.

Something fierce rises in my chest. Dirtbag has stolen enough of my confidence, enough of my hope. I won't hand him my future too.

I emerge onto the city street, the noise of the Riverwalk replaced by cars and the hum of air conditioning units. The sidewalk stretches empty before me, and for the first time all evening, I'm truly alone with my thoughts.

They can't all be assholes, right?

Tobias and Grace are huddled over the computer as I enter the lobby and pass the check-in desk. My heels clack against the marble floor, and Tobias looks up.

"Lookin' good in those pumps, girl," Tobias says as I walk by.

"My friends have impeccable taste," I call back, titling my head and winking at him.

"*Mmm hmm*, damn right they do." He laughs before turning back to the computer.

My phone buzzes in my purse as I press the elevator button.

> Marina Man Preston: Hey Brianna, I plan to take the boat out again soon. I'd love for you to join me. We can dust off those sailing lessons from college. Let me know if you're interested.

Here's what normal looks like. Preston's living his life, not obsessing over mine. No ten texts per day, no love bombing, no desperate need for my attention. Just a simple invitation to go sailing when I'm ready. If I received this text twenty four hours ago, I'd be elated. But after the horrible date with Trent, and finding out about Griffin, this text falls flat for me.

I feel myself shutting down. My walls going back up. I crave the comfort of protection, from everything and everyone who could hurt me.

The doors open to the tenth floor and I step out, fumbling in my purse for my key card.

"Miss Whitmore, good evening." Javier strolls toward me.

"Please, call me Brianna." I insist and he raises his palms apologetically. "Why are you here so late?"

Javier settles against the wall with one shoulder, hands disappearing into his pant pockets, his charcoal suit perfectly tailored, even in this casual pose. What is it about his matching vest that frames his body like a five-star meal?

"We had an event tonight at our rooftop bar. The elevator was packed with guests, so I got off here. Then I heard a grinding noise in the ice machine room and figured I should check it out." His gaze flickers down to my shoes, then back up to my face.

"Everything okay with the ice machine?" If that ice machine goes down, I'll be pissed. It's part of my nightly ritual.

"Oh, yeah. It probably needs a new filter. I'll let maintenance know in the morning." He nods to my feet. "The shoes working out okay?"

"They're wonderful. I can't believe you did that." I gesture to my feet. "Most hotels would've just shrugged and said 'sorry about your luck.'"

Javier quirks a brow. "We are *not* most hotels, Miss Whitmore."

"Brianna."

"Sorry, I'm still peeling off my professional mask from the day." He smirks and then shrugs. "It's a shame you're not staying the weekend. San Antonio goes wild on St. Patrick's Day. They dye the river green, bands play on the Riverwalk, green beer . . . It's a good time."

"That does sound fun, but I fly home tomorrow night."

"A shame." His stare lingers, a hint of a smile tugging at his lips. "Well, I'll let you settle in. Have a good night."

I press my key against the door of 1010, watching him walk to the elevator. As he steps inside, he looks back at me, smiling.

I flip off my Coach heels, each one performing aerial acrobatics before landing softly near the bed. I place my phone on the nightstand, Preston's text staring at me. He seems legit. Nothing like Trent or Griffin. I already met him once, and I did some snooping with the project team at my company that he consulted with from years ago. They all had good things to say about him.

I flop back onto the bed with a heavy exhale. Is this challenge worth it, though? I'm swamped with work. So swamped that Sara finished my presentation for tomorrow, just like she did in college. The last twenty-four hours have been such a buzzkill. At least Griffin stopped texting. Maybe he realized how weird he was acting, or maybe he's just moved on. Either way, his exit is a relief. I let out a long sigh.

If I quit, *he* wins. If I quit, then I continue to believe my value is based on chemistry. That I'm only worth what I can give someone else. If I quit, I continue to believe I'm easily tossed aside. Disposable. If I quit, my body remains not good enough. It will always be defective.

The phone is blurry through my tears, but I type anyway.

> Me: Hi Preston, I'd love to go sailing. I won't be in Irvine for another 2 weeks. I can drive down after my Friday meeting and join you on Saturday if that works?

I take a deep breath and send the text, the sting behind my eyes subsiding. I wait for the familiar dread to settle into my chest, but it doesn't come. Maybe I made the right decision. We'll see.

> Preston: I can make that work. I'll send you the address closer to the date. I look forward to being your sailing coach '-)

Chapter 24

San Antonio

We arrive at the Mercury building just before nine on a breezy San Antonio morning. After our usual elevator bay bet—I win, guessing bay two—we make our way to the conference room.

Now we sit in our normal spots. Chris takes the head of the table, and I settle beside him. We open our laptops. His eyes linger on mine.

"Did they say when the rest of us are getting new laptops?"

I know it kills him that I have a new laptop before he does. Chris is great, but he's not without his ego and faults. He's used to having the best of the best as the sales executive.

"Everyone but you gets one next month." I smile.

He squints at me and starts to say something when we see movement at the doorway.

"Good morning," Michele says as she drops into the chair nearest the door.

"Good morning, Michele. How are you?" I ask as I reach for the cable to connect to the TV monitor.

She rambles about traffic, but I tune her out as I open Sara's email with today's presentation. I double-click the file and share my screen.

"I'm looking forward to our first round of results. Some of our leadership team thinks we wasted money on your technology, especially since we learned we won't have full access to *The Wall Street Journal*."

Michele flips open her notebook. Chris responds first.

"We're very pleased with what we found. As Brianna shared in a prior meeting, we're focusing on your top news outlets for the first sweep, and what your competitors are doing." He leans back in his chair, shoulders relaxed, signaling he's done talking.

"Our slide shows favorable res—"

The words stick in my throat.

Something's wrong. The numbers on screen don't match what I remember when I started pulling them. These look like data from another client—RexMar Group. Did I send Sara the wrong data? My heart hammers against my ribs, a drum I can't control, and my stomach twists into knots.

I blink. The data doesn't change. Sentiment numbers that should read positive are showing unfavorable. These aren't even the keywords and hashtags we used.

This is not the right presentation.

The silence stretches. Michele's pen hovers above her notebook. Her eyes dart between the screen and my face, confusion creeping across her features.

Chris's glare sears into the side of my head.

Heat crawls up my neck.

"I'm so sorry, Michele, there must have been a mix-up in the slides." The words tumble out too fast. Embarrassment burns down my face like acid.

My fingers hover over the keyboard. Every second that passes feels like an eternity. Michele watches me, her pen still suspended in the air. Chris shifts in his chair and the metal creaks.

I click through menus, buying time. My brain scrambles for solutions. Close the presentation? Pretend the laptop froze? Tell them I need to step out for a call?

The cursor blinks, mocking at me.

"Technical difficulties happen," Michele says, but her voice has lost its earlier warmth. She's trying to be gracious, but I can hear the doubt creeping in. The same doubt her leadership team already has about wasting money on our technology.

"While Brianna gets the correct slide, I'll share what we found. The keywords resulted in some interesting hits from your competitors. A company based out of Atlanta is getting some heat online because their object detection model alerted the security guards of an active shooter. It was the corporate photographer carrying a tripod to a photoshoot. Apparently the photographer used the tripod to point to something, and the system flagged it as a shooter. The news article focused on the unreliability of AI technology and the risks of such mistakes."

Michele shakes her head. "Of course it's confused—that company cut every corner possible. They probably used blurry photos from the seventies and called it a 'data set.'"

I'm still opening random documents, so Chris continues.

"We also found a generalized article around facial recognition and human rights. But it had less than a thousand views. We'll monitor it and see if it gains traction."

Chris has stalled as much as he can, and I can't find the data to save my life.

"I'm really sorry, Michele. There was a mix-up with the slides, and I'll need more time before I can send them over to you. I will say that your social media sentiment is positive, with the exception of traffic cameras. There are several complaints about inaccuracy. Residents are posting photos to show they were cited in error for running a red light."

Michele lets out a rough sigh, and I slump into my chair.

"Okay. I'll have my team look into the traffic camera issues, but it'd be nice to have the actual data in front of me." She brushes her bangs off her forehead.

"I will have the correct data for you later today," I assure her.

Michele leans forward, her hands clasped in front of her on the table.

"We have another issue that I need your help with. Our director of technology, Gus, is on extended leave. I have no one to lead the systems team and finish the onboarding of your program and assist with training, not that we have any data that shows this will even be worth it."

Chris jumps in. "Michele, you will be happy with the data once we're able to properly share it. How can we help?"

I sink deeper into my chair. I cannot believe this happened. This was so irresponsible of me. I risked the reputation of our company, Chris, and myself.

"I need someone to lead the transition in Gus's absence."

"Fine. Brianna can handle it." Chris's glare pierces my temple. My brows drop as I recognize the classic *this-is-your-retribution* look. "Right, Brianna?"

"R-right. Absolutely." I scramble for words and next steps. "I'll need to understand your infrastructure, the team, and where Gus left off. But I'm happy to step in and facilitate a smooth transition."

I exhale loudly, and it's not discreet.

"I was hoping you'd say that. I've already initiated system access for you, mirroring the access that Gus had for the legacy system. You'll have admin privileges, and I'll email you the names of the team who've been working on this. I expect you'll get in contact with them and foster the partnership we all need to make this successful."

She leans forward, her chest resting on the table.

"I don't think I need to remind you that all of our asses are on the line. You don't have buy-in from my leadership team, and they'll cut this project at the first sign of failure."

Chris's glare scorches the side of my face.

Michele continues. "Brianna, you are now a part of Mercury. Welcome. Please, for all of us, don't screw this up."

Shit.

Chris says nothing as we leave the conference room. He walks beside me in silence down the hall toward the elevators, staring straight ahead. He doesn't even guess an elevator bay.

I have to guess alone. I pick five, but it's bay three.

I wish I had my own rental car. Am I going to have to ride in silence back to the hotel too? I can't be that lucky. As soon as we're out of earshot of any Mercury employee, he's going to let me have it. And I deserve it. This presentation was my responsibility. I was accountable for getting it done. I passed it off to Sara, and it bit me in the ass. I have to own it and accept it.

I just don't know how I'm going to explain to Chris how I botched these numbers. Of everyone, I know the data best. I don't want to lie to him, but if he finds out I passed it off to Sara, I'll be in trouble with more than just Chris. Sharing internal data with Sara broke several protocols.

Chris pushes open the exit door of the high-rise with such force, I'm afraid the glass will shatter as it knocks against the building. The hot sun beats down as we walk toward the parking garage, and it doesn't help my already flushed face. The silence kills me, but I know better than to say a word. My feet hurt as I hurry to keep up with his pace. He doesn't even take out his phone, his normal post-meeting behavior. He's too busy loading verbal ammunition.

I slide into the passenger seat of our rental vehicle and pull the door shut with deliberate care. Even the sound of it closing too hard might set him off.

The car feels smaller than usual. Suffocating. I can feel him watching me. Waiting. The weight of his stare presses against the side of my face. My hands find my lap, fingers twisting together.

I have to look at him eventually. He isn't going to drive until I do. The seconds stretch out, each one heavier than the last. Finally, I turn my head. Slowly.

His jaw is locked tight. His knuckles are white where they grip the steering wheel. His eyes burn with the kind of controlled fury that's somehow worse than screaming.

"What the fuck was that?"

When we arrive at my hotel, I can't get out of Chris's car fast enough. I'm pretty sure he feels the same way. There are two versions of Chris—the one who thinks I'm brilliant, and the one who can destroy my career with a phone call. I've seen both over the years, which is why I'm always careful to stay in his good graces.

I pull open the door to The Elysian, the smell of white tea and verbena hitting me in the face. The scent has become a comfort. The lobby is pretty dead for a Friday afternoon. Those traveling for business are halfway home by now, and tourists have checked in and are either at the Mission or the Riverwalk.

Chris ordered me to stay the weekend and get up to speed on Mercury's system. It's punishment for the botched data, and as the sales executive, he can do it.

As if I need to be reprimanded even more, Miss Mean Face is at the check-in desk. Great.

I approach her with caution. I don't need more hate today. Chris delivered enough for the whole city.

"Miss Whitmore," is all she says, her eyes glued to the computer as she types away on her keyboard.

"Hi, Diane."

"Uh-uh-uh," she waves her finger at me. "Ms. Barthow."

Are you kidding me? Her name tag says Diane, and after all this time, she's insisting I address her more formally?

"Ms. Barthow, I need to extend my stay through Sunday."

She looks up with an evil smile. "I'm so sorry, my dear. We're all booked."

Chapter 25

San Antonio

I stand in disbelief. Random thoughts charge through my brain all at once, and my mind is about to explode from the bottleneck of thoughts pushing through.

The familiar scent of cool water cuts through the white tea and verbena, and I know Javier's here before I even turn around.

"Diane, Brianna, my two favorite people. Happy Friday."

Relief settles over me as I turn. Javier strolls up to us wearing his tailored vest, sleeves rolled up.

Diane lifts her pointed chin to interject, but I beat her to it.

"I need to stay the weekend, but Dia—" I stop to correct myself. "Ms. Barthow says you're all booked this weekend."

Javier looks at Diane with a quizzical expression.

"*Ms. Barthow* must be mistaken. We always have room for our VIP guests." His chin drops as he looks down the length of his nose at her.

I lean back, witnessing what feels like a stare down between the concierge and general manager. It's the best thing I've seen all day.

Diane huffs as she looks at her screen and taps on the keyboard for a few seconds.

"You are in luck." She lifts her head, forcing a smile. She's not looking at me; she's staring at Javier the entire time. "We just had a cancellation."

I look at Javier, who continues to glare at Diane as she types randomly on the keyboard.

She drags her eyes from her computer screen to me.

"We are happy to have you this weekend, Miss Whitmore." No smile. Forced pleasantry.

"Excellent. Thank you, Diane." Javier's voice sounds genuine.

Diane gives a strained smile and walks away toward the bar area.

I tilt my head toward Javier. "I'd be hotel-less if you didn't step in. Thank you."

"My pleasure." His face brightens with hope. "So, did I convince you to stay and enjoy St. Patrick's Day?"

"Not quite. I need to work this weekend and be close to our client."

Javier's eyes widen. "You can't work all weekend." His hand grabs my shoulder. "Let me be your tour guide tonight. Nobody works past five on Friday anyway."

It's so tempting. I'm exhausted from everything this week, and something inside me aches to let loose, to step outside this cage I've built. Javier is the concierge, and this is what he does for a living. The worst has already happened, so it can only get better.

But will it be weird going out with him? It's not a date though, this is his job, taking care of guests. He probably feels bad that Diane wasn't going to let me stay here this weekend.

I hesitate, and he sees it. He knows part of my hellish week, so he must understand why I'm holding back.

"I guarantee you a fun, light, and enjoyable night," he says. His hand drops from my shoulder to my wrist, giving it a gentle squeeze before letting go. It's as if he understands the importance of specifying *fun* and *light*.

I might regret this. I will probably regret this.

"Okay," I say.

Javier disappears to change clothes, then meets me in the lobby twenty minutes later. He's traded his formal work attire for dark jeans and an olive green polo that makes him look less like the professional concierge and more like an average guy. The Riverwalk is only a few blocks away, but our walk stretches longer than expected as Javier points out historical details about every landmark we pass.

"Watch your step, the stone can be slippery," Javier says, staying close behind me.

I turn back to him as I take my first step. "Please turn off Mr. Concierge and activate regular Javier. Or I'm going to throw myself into the river."

His smile turns sheepish. "Well, the river is only three feet deep, so..."

I laugh despite myself. "So, I'd just be standing there, soaked and embarrassed?"

"And wouldn't that be a sight to see," he teases.

Stepping onto the Riverwalk is like stepping into another world. The city above is cold, gray, and full of cement, but down here, everything pulses with life.

The San Antonio River flows emerald green—dyed for the holiday weekend. Irish flags flutter from every restaurant balcony, mixing shamrocks with fiesta banners. It's a riot of green, orange, and white. People stroll past clutching clear plastic cups filled with green beer, their laughter mixing with fiddle music spilling from open doorways.

The air smells like river water, fried food, and something floral—maybe the jasmine climbing the old stone walls.

"Would you mind if I made a recommendation for dinner?" Javier says as we navigate the crowds.

"You? Make a recommendation?" I press my fingertips to my chest in mock shock.

He winks. "Oh, that's right. I'm not the concierge tonight."

"Like you can even turn it off," I tease, but my smile softens. "I'd love your recommendation."

"I was going to give it to you anyway because you're right. I can't turn it off."

We laugh and I appreciate that he's following through on his guarantee—a fun, light night.

"There's a restaurant attached to the Riverview Hotel. They have incredible food, and if we time it right, we can hear the local band echoing around the river bend."

"Sounds great," I say, making an effort to avoid staring at how nicely the shirt fits across his shoulders.

A restaurant's patio opens up before us, tables scattered under cheerful striped umbrellas that flutter in the evening breeze. The air carries the mingled scents of grilled steak, garlic, and something faintly sweet, like roasted peppers. Candles flicker on the tables, while the murmur of voices and the clink of glasses blend into the rhythm of water lapping against the stone banks.

"Do you want to take a look at the menu first?" he asks, as if second-guessing his tour guide skills.

"You haven't steered me wrong so far." My eyes nearly close as I grin, and I catch him watching my expression.

A young lady appears from the restaurant's interior, smoothing her apron as she approaches the hostess podium.

"Party of two, please," Javier says. "Is Stefan here tonight?"

She straightens her stance.

"He is, sir. Should I let him know you're here?"

"Please. Tell him Javier is hungry." Javier's smile is pure charm, and I snort before I can stop myself. How does someone manage to be funny and professional at the same time?

When Javier catches my reaction, his grin widens.

The hostess clamps her lips shut to stifle a laugh. "Yes, sir. Follow me."

We follow the woman into the outdoor patio area, gated off by low black iron fencing. She gestures to a corner table with an unobstructed view of the river.

"Thank you," Javier says, pulling out my chair for me. The gesture feels old-fashioned, sweet.

I sit, trying to look graceful. As Javier pushes my chair forward, I instinctively pull it in at the same time. The table lurches forward, and glasses wobble dangerously while utensils rattle against plates. The salt shaker topples over, rolling across the surface as white crystals scatter everywhere—mostly on his side of the table.

"Oh, geez." Heat floods my cheeks. "I'm so sorry. I just—" I grab my napkin, reaching across to brush salt off his side of the table, sending it cascading onto his chair.

Javier's laugh is warm, not mocking, as he comes around to help. He grabs the salt shaker, standing it upright.

With an easy smile, he settles back into his chair, completely unfazed. "Don't worry about it," he says, reaching for his menu as though I didn't just assault the table setting.

I'm still brushing invisible salt off my hands when he looks up from his menu, that same patient smile that got me through the hotel disaster this afternoon.

"So, do you know the restaurant manager?" I ask, thinking of his question to the hostess.

"Oh, Stefan? Stefan and I go way back. He was a mentor

when I started in hospitality. I usually send guests here, so he'll be surprised to see us."

I raise an eyebrow. "Surprised to see you as a customer instead of working?"

"I don't always work, Brianna." He gives me a teasing look.

"That's a lie. You live at that hotel." Javier shifts in his seat, and I backtrack. I can't judge him for the same thing I do.

"So, what's good here?" I ask, lowering part of the menu.

"I'll tell you what's good." A strong, raspy voice cuts through the air behind me. Javier's face lights up as he stands and extends his hand to the hefty guy approaching our table.

"Stefan, always a pleasure," Javier says, shaking the man's hand.

"About time you made your way over here. Took a beautiful woman to drag you out, I see." I crane my neck past the man's considerable belly to meet his flushed, cheerful face.

"This is Brianna. Brianna, this is my dear friend and mentor, Stefan."

I lean back to take in the large, happy man towering above me.

"Well, you are one lucky lady. I've never seen Javier with a date," the jolly man says. Heat floods my cheeks.

I glance at Javier, who is smiling. I study his features, waiting for embarrassment to creep across his face. It never comes.

"How's business, Stefan?"

"Great, thanks to your referrals."

"Don't make a liar out of me." Javier grins and sits down.

"Did you see what they're building at the edge of town?" Stefan lowers his voice so the other tables can't eavesdrop. "Some say it'll put us old-timers out of business."

My eyebrows furrow.

"Yeah, I saw that. They're dumping a boatload of money

into that project." Javier fidgets with the fork and knife on his side of the table.

"Yep. Hundreds of guest rooms, a water park, several restaurants, and an amphitheater where concerts can viewed from the hotel room balconies. So, if you wanted to see Dierks Bentley, you could book a front-facing room and watch the concert from your balcony," Stefan explains.

That sounds like so much fun.

"Wow, that sounds excessive," is what comes out of my mouth.

Even though Sara and I would have a blast listening to Dierks Bentley from our own hotel room balcony with our own cheap wine, I understand why it threatens traditional hotels and other conventional music venues.

"Well, my darling, excessive is the selling point for travelers these days. It's like Kellerman's Mountain House from *Dirty Dancing*, but for the next generation. All-inclusive with top dollar experiences and Instagrammable backdrops. We can't compete."

"There has to be room for both experiences. Not everyone wants an Instagrammable vacation," I say, coming to his defense.

Javier studies me with quiet appreciation.

Javier and Stefan talk business for a few minutes longer as I sip my wine, pretending to study the menu while zeroing in on their conversation about commerce, community, and San Antonio's future.

After Stefan says his goodbyes, curiosity about him lingers.

"Does Stefan own the restaurant?" I ask, running my thumb and forefinger up and down my stemmed glass.

"Stefan owns the hotel." Javier smiles and returns to his menu like he knows he just dropped a bomb on me.

I lean forward, speaking low, and letting my curved menu carry my voice across the table.

"Excuse me? He owns the *entire hotel?*" I crane my neck back, counting the floors as they stack fifteen stories high, making me feel small at the base.

Javier's smile turns into a smirk, as if he knows he's being coy, before he returns to his menu.

"I thought hotel owners were like fictional characters that don't exist."

I return to my menu, but feel his stare.

"Hotel owners are fictional characters?" He laughs as he leans back in his chair, crossing his right leg over his left knee, considering. "You might be right, actually." He laughs.

"I've never met a hotel owner, and I travel for work."

"Well, maybe they're hiding in plain sight and you don't even realize it." Javier smiles as he flips through the menu. "I don't know why I bother looking. I always get the same thing," he says, letting the menu fall to the table.

I look up at him, and a smile spreads across my face. Not just any smile—the kind that comes when I glimpse someone's genuine nature. In this moment, he's adorable. The way he dropped his menu, so casual and unguarded. I like this version of him.

"What do you usually get?"

"It's delicious," he says, throwing his head back as his arms gesture upward. Then he leans in closer, elbows on the table. "It's shredded carne asada over a whole cactus pad, with rice, beans, cheese, and a roasted jalapeño. Incredible." His palm smacks against his chest.

"Yeah, I don't know if you sold me on that dish," I say, a wry smile tugging at the corner of my mouth. "All that body language—the head tosses, the hand over your heart. I mean, who in their right mind eats a cactus?"

He laughs and I join him, but there's something behind my laughter. An added feeling I can't quite identify. It's probably that I've had terrible dates lately, and Javier is reminding me that there are still good, fun guys out there.

"How about this. I'll share some of mine with you and show you just how good my recommendations really are." He winks at me. Leaning back, my smile reaches my eyes.

The server approaches to take our order. I debate ordering something completely different—maybe fish tacos or enchiladas—just to see if Javier will actually follow through on his promise to share. It seems so intimate. Sara and I swap bites constantly, but Chris and I have never shared so much as a French fry.

I end up ordering the same carne asada cactus dish.

Another glass of wine later, our sizzling skillets arrive. Steam carries the smoky scent of barbecue and charred jalapeños toward my face. Shredded beef mingles with melted cheese, bell peppers, and onions, while the nopal cactus pad presses against the skillet's edges.

Javier's smug smile widens as he takes another sip of wine, brows raised in anticipation. "I'll wait." He gestures toward my plate.

I lift the fork to my mouth. His unwavering stare makes me pause, and the weight of his expectation hangs between us. I take the bite.

The flavors explode across my tongue: smoky, savory, with the perfect kick of jalapeño heat. The cactus has a texture I wasn't expecting, almost like a tender green bean but with more substance. Melted cheese binds everything together to perfection.

"It's okay..." I scrunch my nose and shrug.

Javier's hands fly to his head in mock horror.

I can't hold back my grin, and his face shifts from despair to recognition. He knows I'm messing with him.

"I almost stood up and left," he says, pointing behind him.

He picks up his fork, shaking his head, and we dive into our meals.

After dinner, we stroll along the river toward the outdoor theater. Javier mentioned that local bands perform on a small stone stage built into the water's edge—a perfect half-moon carved into the other side of the riverbank.

The terraced stone steps bend with the curve of the river, each row carved into the hillside like ancient stadium seating.

Across the river, musicians tune their instruments and adjust microphones.

"If we sit four rows up, we'll have a clear view of the stage."

"You think of everything." I follow him as he climbs the stone steps.

We step past a family of four seated in one of the rows. The little boy squirms away from his mom as she wipes ice cream off his cheeks.

My body tenses as I sit, suddenly aware that I'm out on a Friday night with the hotel's concierge. We just shared dinner and wine, and now our knees are touching as we wait for a band to start. This should feel weird, shouldn't it? I should feel awkward about being here with someone I barely know, a hotel worker.

"That little boy reminds me of Dominic. He would fight everything. He'd walk around with spaghetti sauce all over his face because I wasn't allowed to wipe it off." He shakes his head. "I sent him to bed one night, dried sauce all over his face, and he didn't care. I thought my sister was going to kill me."

My eyes stay fixed on the little boy as he squirms away from his mother's napkin. "You're really lucky that you have that connection to your niece and nephew."

"I know. I treasure it." His gaze shifts from the family to me. "Do you want kids?"

I smile, smoothing my pink tank top down my stomach. "Since I was a little girl."

I meet his gaze and we search for the untold stories behind our eyes. Something shifts in his expression, but then the band starts their sound check. I glance across the river, the lead singer adjusting his mic. Javier was right. With all the people walking along the river in front of us, I can see the stage perfectly from here.

We settle into our seats as the Celtic band warms up. A gentle breeze rustles the leaves overhead.

"What's it like being a concierge? I'm sure you have some stories." I turn toward him, tucking one leg beneath me on the stone seat.

He leans back, resting his elbows on the stone behind us, and rolls his eyes with a grin. "Let's see, there was the time I had to find three hundred white roses before a guest's girlfriend arrived."

"Three hundred?" My eyebrows shoot up.

"Yeah, I searched all of San Antonio." He shakes his head, chuckling at the memory. "Technically, they only got two hundred and seventy three, but she said yes, so I guess that's all that matters." He shrugs.

"That's so sweet."

Around us, other couples and families find their seats on the stone steps, and the Celtic band's warm-up music grows more melodic.

"Then there was this woman who requested dinner in our private dining area with seven successful and single men of our choosing. They all had to be under thirty five." He shoots me a sideways look, his mouth quirking up at the corner. "She was in her sixties."

"Damn, cougar." I laugh, and the sound escapes louder than I intended.

"Yeah, at the time, I was thirty seven." He leans forward, resting his forearms on his knees. "She tried to get me to do it." The fiddle music swells behind his words.

"Did you?" I'm more invested in this answer than I expect.

"No."

"What else?" I scoot closer, my eyes lighting up.

"Ah, let's see. . ." He tilts his head back, thinking, then snaps his fingers. "There was a YouTuber who asked us to hire people to follow him around so he looked popular. And then there was the woman who said if I got her tickets to an exclusive gala, she'd give me a Rolex and, I quote, 'a memorable evening.'"

"Ew! Gross!" I scrunch up my face. We dissolve into laughter.

"The scary part was she was serious, and came back from the gala looking for me to keep up her end of the bargain." He shudders dramatically, and across the river, the band launches into their first song. The lively Celtic melody mixes with our laughter.

"To be clear, I was at Angelina's piano recital that night. Thankfully, the woman checked out the next day." He grins, and his dimple appears in his left cheek.

I lean against the stone step behind me, still smiling. "Smart man. Family first." I find myself staring at him, the way his dark brown hair sweeps high off his forehead in a dramatic wave, not a strand out of place. "These requests are outlandish, though. I can't believe people ask for those sorts of things."

Javier nods. "Yeah, the expectations of a boutique hotel are different from hotels like Stefan's. In a boutique hotel, the concierge is your personal curator, creating rare moments and exclusive touches that transform an ordinary stay into something extraordinary. And making the impossible feel effortless."

We ease into our seats as the band plays, content to sit quietly and let the music fill the space between us for the next half hour. Javier drums his fingers on his knees and I notice the way his long fingers move, precise but relaxed, like he was born with rhythm in his veins.

The lead singer's voice carries across the water as he adjusts his microphone. "This is our final song of the night. Thank you everyone for joining us. We are Clan of the Craic!"

The crowd around us erupts in applause, and I clap along, glancing at Javier as he whistles through his fingers. The air cools as the evening deepens, and a shiver runs up my arms. Above us, the first stars peek through the darkening sky.

We wait for the crowd to filter back onto the Riverwalk before leaving our seats. Javier looks at me, smiling.

"Dessert?"

Chapter 26

San Antonio

We walk along the river as Javier points out historic buildings. His animated storytelling makes me watch his hands as much as listen to his words.

"The ice cream shop is on the other side, so we'll take that bridge over." He gestures toward the stone arch ahead.

At the top of the bridge, I pause, watching the pink tour boat drift toward us in the distance. The stone railing is cool beneath my elbows as my fingers explore the grooves between each block. Javier stands beside me, his hand close to mine.

He turns to look at me. "I'm curious, Brianna. What drives you?"

I turn my head, his face only inches from mine. "What drives me?" It feels like a question Griffin would ask, but somehow, it lands differently with Javier.

"Yeah, I'm curious." His face reflects pure curiosity, no agenda.

I look down the river, focusing on the pink riverboat full of happy tourists. "Happiness. Success. Helping others."

He smiles, a soft chuckle escaping. "That's the easy answer."

My eyebrows furrow. Easy answer? I shift against the stone, my fingers tightening against the ledge. That actually took some thought.

I lean back, extending my arms, fingertips gliding lightly over the stone as I think harder. My answer won't be graded, but I still want to give the best response, something impressive. I've already failed.

"I want to live life financially stable. I want to make an impact."

He nods slowly, processing. *Still not deep enough.*

"What drives you, Javier?"

He throws his head back and laughs, then looks at me with that dimpled grin.

"Touché." He turns to face the water, mirroring my position against the stone. "Growing up, my uncles told me we have to work twice as hard just to get by." He looks across the river. I follow his gaze toward the now-empty stage off in the distance. "I started to believe it. My grandfather said to me once, 'Javier, people like us don't go places like that. Just find something that pays the bills so you can provide for your family.'"

He lets out a sigh, looking down at his clasped hands.

"The scary thing is, I believed that. People like me need to work twice as hard to just get by."

I hang on every word as his fingers fidget against each other.

"Because of their guidance, I half-assed it through school—B's and C's while working the front desk at a hotel. One day, this man walked in wearing an expensive suit with an entourage behind him. I stood there like an idiot, just staring. He looked like my uncle. He looked like me. And he was wearing a suit that probably cost two weeks of my pay." He pauses, seemingly caught in the memory. "He walked up to me and we started chatting. Asked me what I was studying, what I liked about working at the hotel, stuff like that."

Javier pauses, taking a deep breath and slowly turning toward me.

"He then asked me the most ridiculous question I'd ever heard in my life. He said, *Do you want to run a hotel one day, Javier?* I looked at him like he was crazy. He became my first of many mentors and . . . " He straightens, a small smile breaking through. "Well, the rest is history."

This is why Javier feels different. He knows what it's like to fight for something, to prove people wrong.

He angles his neck toward me, his face serious.

"So, you asked what drives me. It's that I've fought internal battles, limiting beliefs, and a generational curse to be where I am today. I had to deprogram what the men in my family—the men I idolized—ingrained in me as a child." He takes a long breath. "What drives me is never limiting myself the way my family has."

I'm completely awestruck. He just shared something so real, so raw, and I gave him some surface-level bullshit about happiness and success. I wanted to impress him and chose three meaningless words. He didn't try to impress me at all. Instead, he ripped open his soul and shared something vulnerable, something I wasn't willing or aware enough to do.

"Thank you for sharing that," is all I can say.

His eyes find mine, his smile genuine and warm. We hold each other's gaze and something passes between us—an understanding that he trusted me with something important. The moment stretches, intimate and fragile.

The spell shatters as someone shouts, "Got it! I got it! That was perfect!"

I tear my gaze away and follow the sound to a man with a

digital camera jogging up the bridge toward us. Javier steps out beside me.

"Look at this shot. You two are perfect!" the man says, shoving the back of his camera at us. "The lighting, you two leaning over the bridge, the tour boat halfway under, that long stare. This shot is perfection!"

I didn't think our stare was that long.

Javier hands the camera back to the photographer. "This is a great shot. Can we get a copy?"

The photographer nods, pulling out a business card. "Sure. Reach out to me here." He hands over his card. "This photo is going to win the Local Love contest. I know it!" He taps the side of his camera excitedly.

Local Love? We're not . . . This isn't . . . We barely know each other.

The Elysian hotel stretches skyward, warm lights accenting the stone exterior. Golden light spills from the restaurant windows where a few guests linger over late dinners.

Javier stops and turns to me, leaning against the exterior wall. "I had a great time tonight."

"Javier, tonight was perfect. Thank you for being so generous and welcoming. You really went above and be—"

"Oh, I wasn't working tonight." He reaches for the ornate gold door handle. "Have a great weekend, Brianna. Don't work too hard." He holds the door open for me, but doesn't follow me inside.

As I walk through the lobby, his words echo in my mind. *I wasn't working tonight.* I pause near the elevators, frowning.

That doesn't make sense. He showed me his usual guest recommendations, shared the Riverwalk's history, pointed out the oldest buildings downtown. How was that not work?

Whatever it was, I needed it.

I press the button for the elevator, enjoying the peace and quiet of the lobby. I wish every date I went on was as easy as tonight. It would make this stupid challenge so much easier.

I wonder if tonight can count as part of the challenge. It's too late to text Sara. Since her mom's been sick, she keeps her phone ringer on loud in case her dad needs to reach her.

I open my laptop and start an email instead.

My Dearest Sara-
We need to discuss the fine print of my dating challenge. The concierge at the hotel I'm staying at took me down to the Riverwalk tonight. He paid for dinner—well, technically, I think we ate for free because he knew the owner of the hotel. Side note, do you know any hotel owners? Like, not general managers, but owners? Just curious. Anyway, we had dinner, listened to a live band, and he bought us ice cream. I'm pretty sure he's single?
Therefore, I'm submitting this request to be reviewed and approved for Date #7. Thank you for your consideration.
Love your face.
B-

I change into my llama pajamas and settle into bed. Grabbing the TV remote, I flip to the local news, letting the familiar drone of weather reports wash over me.

My phone buzzes once. Then again. Then it's going off

non-stop, vibrating on the nightstand. I glance at the clock. Ten-thirty. Who the hell is texting me at this hour?

> Mr. GQ Griffin: Brianna. I need your help.

> Mr. GQ Griffin: I was robbed at gunpoint. He stole my laptop and wallet. I need money to get back to New York. Can you please help me? I'm desperate. Look what he did to me.

Attached is a photo of Griffin, his face a mess of angry red cuts and purple bruises that make him barely recognizable.

What the fuck?

I bolt upright in bed, my right hand gripping the phone, my left clutching the bed sheet. I scan the room wildly, as if the walls might offer some answer or solution. Panic claws at my chest.

Is he okay?

Did he call the cops?

Why is he texting me?

Should I call the cops?

I can't think straight. My thoughts crash into each other, creating a traffic jam in my brain. I'm completely short-circuiting.

I look at the clock again; I can't wake Sara. She barely gets enough sleep as it is. Beck might be awake?

"Hey, chica," Beck answers.

I explain the texts I got from Griffin. Panic courses through my body as I feel the pressure to act.

"Hold on a sec, Bri. Is this the Secret Shopper dude?"

"Yes."

I don't have a second to hold on. Neither does Griffin.

"Send me the photo he sent you."

It's annoying how casual Beck is about this while I'm a tornado inside.

Just as I send the photo to Beck, another message comes through from Griffin.

> Mr. GQ Griffin: Brianna? Please help me! I need you. 💜

I'm scared for him. I'm scared for me. I'm angry that he's made this my problem.

"He's scamming you," Beck says, her voice certain.

"What? How do you know?"

"Look at the photo again. It's AI generated. The bruises are flat against his curved nose. And he said this just happened? Bruises don't turn that dark purple until day three or four."

My brain seizes as I process her explanation. His texts, the photo, all his lies.

"This is fake?" I ask, still not convinced.

"Yeah, Bri. He's scamming you. Haven't you seen that documentary, *The Tinder Swindler?* Some guy used the Tinder app to con women out of money to support his lavish lifestyle." She pauses. "But you're a smart woman. You know this."

"Clearly I'm not that smart because I called you like a damsel in distress. You're the smart one. What the hell, Beck. This guy thought I'm such an idiot that I'd give him money?"

"Guaranteed, he knows you're not an idiot. He knows you have a heart, and he's playing full out on your caring, empathetic nature." She pauses. "I wouldn't even respond. Block his number and get rid of him for good."

How dare he try to take advantage of me. How dare he target me for his schemes.

"I'm done with dating forever." I collapse back into the pillows.

"Now, now, Bri. That's a little drastic. Everyone needs the

D. Well, except me of course, for obvious reasons." She coughs. "But you know what I mean."

"I don't need the D either. I ordered the dildo you recommended."

She chuckles. "Nice. It won't disappoint."

My phone dings again.

> Mr. GQ Griffin: Please Brianna, I don't have much time. I need you.

"Did you get the waterproof one? Julie and I use it in the hot tub. It's ah-mazing."

I admire Beck's ability to move on from the chaos. When I need a comforting hug, she's usually not who I call. But I go to her when I need honesty. She's loyal and brutally direct. I appreciate that about her.

"Delete that bastard and move on. They're not all swindlers, Bri. Shake it off, sister."

"I feel like one of your basketball players right now."

"Good. Now, get your ass back in the game and get me a damn win!"

We laugh and say our goodbyes.

I climb out of bed and pace my room. How dare he think he can use me for money. How dare he waste my time, and for what? It was all a ploy. Love bomb me, throw around a little cash, then cash in.

Asshole.

I'm furious with myself. How could I not realize he was a manipulative asshole? How did I miss something so obvious?

Chapter 27

San Antonio

I find an empty row near my gate in the San Antonio airport, claiming a chair near USB ports. My laptop is settled on my knees and I fire it up to sift through work emails. Michele replied early this morning, acknowledging the corrected information I'd provided on Saturday.

Since taking over Mercury's project team, my inbox overflows with requests for direction. Direction I'm still figuring out myself.

A flashing icon commands my attention at the bottom of my screen.

> Chris: Hey- What progress did you make this weekend?

"Hello to you, too," I mutter while rolling my eyes.

> Me: Pulled the org chart, added team emails to contacts, introduced myself to all points of contact, and researched their system integration options. About to give the team direction before my flight leaves in 20.

The typing bubble starts and stops. Starts and stops.

I don't have time for this.

I minimize the chat and draft an email to the Mercury team as their interim manager. Anything for a sale, right? Chris left me no choice, exploiting my guilt from the data snafu. That's what makes him successful—his ruthlessness keeps him on top.

My phone rings with Sara's face lighting up the home screen, and I shove in my earbuds.

"Hi," she says, as if gauging my mood.

"Hey," I say, pounding the keys on my laptop before Chris sends a firing squad. "How's it going?"

"Peachy. Grady exploded his diaper, Evan pretended not to notice so I had to deal with it. I'm not frustrated with Grady, but Evan's being lazy, enjoying his crunchless coffee while I handled the poopy diaper. How are *you*?"

I exhale, hands going limp on the keyboard as I stare out the airport windows.

"I'm fine."

"B, I'm a girl. I know when a female says *I'm fine,* she's anything but."

"I'm annoyed. Frustrated. Angry. Disappointed."

"Go on."

"Everything is shit. Chris is riding my ass. I have to manage the client's project team because the guy in charge is on an extended leave. Chris overpromised and undersold, so they're extra cranky. I'm still processing the swindler thing, and mad at myself for not seeing it sooner."

I never told Sara her data was wrong and that's why I'm in hot water with Chris. She'd feel terrible, and ultimately, it's my fault. I'm accountable for what we communicate to clients.

"B, I'm sorry about Mr. GQ. He's a shyster, but you didn't fall for it. You sensed something was wrong and called Beck.

These guys are master manipulators. They target emotion, not intelligence."

"Does everyone know about master manipulators except me? Both Javier and Beck said the same thing." My jaw clenches.

"Well, yeah, haven't you seen the documentary?"

How has everyone seen it except me?

"I think I need a break from dating."

"That is the last thing you need. Another excuse to write off men because some assholes sneaked their way in."

"Stop." The word comes out sharper than I intend. "Just stop. I'm tired of being the project everyone wants to fix. Maybe I write off men because they keep giving me reasons to."

"Maybe you're digging for reasons like you're combing the carpet for a lost earring." Sara huffs into the phone.

"I didn't have to dig far with Griffin."

"Look, I don't want you giving up when there *are* nice guys out there. Chris is nice, that concierge guy is nice, Marina Man seems nice, too. We stalked his LinkedIn and you got intel from coworkers who remembered him from his consulting days. He might be the nice guy you need."

I grind my teeth, jaw protesting. This is a game for her, entertainment while she complains about her life, her husband, and her baby. I'm not a puppet she can control to escape her domestic drudgery.

"I gotta go, my flight's boarding." I hit send on my email to Mercury and close my laptop, shoving it into my bag.

"Okay, but you're not off the hook with the dating challenge, Brianna. You only have four more. And Marina Man seems nice. You want to go sailing, right?"

I side-eye no one in particular.

"I'll think about it." I zip my bag and stand. "Also, I have a package coming to your house in a couple of days."

"I still have your Amazon order from two weeks ago."

"I know. Thanks for letting me ship packages to your house."

"Not a problem. It's my sneaky way of ensuring more visits from you. You're barely home these days."

She's right. I volunteer for every out-of-town assignment I can get, helping the sales executives in the eastern, central, or pacific northwest regions. Anything to avoid my condo. It's easier to stay in hotels than face my own four walls and everything they remind me of.

"Thanks. Talk to you soon." I shove my phone in my purse and head toward my gate.

Portland, Maine is a breath of fresh air, literally and figuratively. I love the ocean, cool breeze, and fresh lobster.

Working with our eastern region sales executives is refreshing too. I spent today with Marsha, helping with her finalist meeting. It's always stressful, the final meeting before the customer decides. The stakes are always high. But she did great and the potential client seemed pleased.

After checking into my hotel, I walk a block to my favorite bar, Four Dollar Freddie's. As I pull open the door of the historic downtown building, the smell of popcorn hits me in the face. The self-serve machine stands proudly in the dining area, surrounded by towers of red baskets.

I turn right toward the L-shaped bar. Sara once asked me to describe this place since I come here every time I'm in Portland. I said, "Wood everywhere." It's a vibe and I love it. Cozy and true to its early 1900s roots.

Scanning the bar, only two seats are unoccupied. One near the kitchen entrance on the far left, and one straight ahead between two guys in flannel.

I squeeze between the flannel shirts, thankful the stool isn't as cumbersome as The Elysian's.

"What can I get ya?" The bartender places a white napkin in front of me.

"Coal Porter, please."

He nods and vanishes behind the beer taps crowding the bar.

I hop off my bar stool and beeline to the popcorn machine. Popcorn tumbles to the floor as I shovel it into the red plastic basket.

Clutching my popcorn prize, I head back to my stool. There's my beer, looking like dark coffee with a tan, foamy head. This is the only dark beer I drink because it's fabulous.

"Good choice," the guy to my left says as I take my first swig, quickly wiping the foam from my upper lip.

Forest green flannel catches my eye first—sleeves rolled to his elbows, revealing freckled forearms. His faded ball cap sits low, casting shadows across his eyes.

"Thanks." I glance at his beer. "What are you drinking?"

His weathered hand cradles the glass. "Irish Red." He stares ahead as he takes a sip. I sneak a look at the lobster tattoo covering the inside of his forearm.

Well, he's a local.

He doesn't say anything else so I dig into my popcorn, waiting for the bartender to return.

"The menus are there," Mr. Flannel says, pointing to the condiment corral.

"Thanks, I don't need it. I always get the same thing." He

glances at me, taking in my white blouse with thin black stripes and black slacks.

Over the next twenty minutes, I order my buffalo chicken wrap with fries, and respond to work emails and questions from the Mercury team. Sara replied to Friday's email—dinner with Javier counts as date seven.

Why I agreed to this challenge is beyond me. I thought meeting new people would be easy, a piece of cake. Instead, I want to swear off men forever. Marina Man seems normal—professional, driven, successful, has a sailboat in San Diego. Well, I think he has a sailboat. That could be a lie, too.

The fries have gone cold by the time I sense Mr. Flannel's stare. I turn my head, peering into the shadow beneath the brim of his hat.

"They're no good after twenty minutes," he says, looking at my plate.

My smile lifts. "That's exactly what I say. Once they start to cool, it's all downhill from there."

Nothing bonds strangers like French fry standards, even to rugged Mainers, apparently.

"Where you from, city girl?" he asks, raising his empty glass to the bartender. His question sounds lazy, like he's killing time more than anything.

"Dallas. I'm here for work."

"What do you do?"

"I work for a software company." I've learned to keep it short—if they want more, I'll elaborate.

He nods, his mouth tight.

The bartender places another beer in front of him. He's got that mysterious loner thing down, whether he means to or not.

"You haven't asked what I do for a living." He gives me a sideways look.

Is this guy toying with me? He barely looks at me, his

communication skills are terrible, yet he's insulted I didn't ask about his job?

"I already know."

The brim of his hat lifts with his eyebrows. He turns his body, his right arm resting on the back of the chair.

"What do I do, then?"

I lean toward him, eyes narrowed. "You're a crustacean wrangler."

Dead silence. He stares, face unreadable. Then, like a dam breaking, he starts laughing—deep, surprised laughter.

He *is* capable of emotion.

"That's some funny shit," he says, tipping his glass toward me before taking a sip.

I file that laugh away as a win. Now to see if I can make it happen twice.

"Yeah, you spend your days battling armored crusaders at sea."

He tips his head back with laughter, and I finally see the weathered lines around his eyes. I try for three times.

"You deal with clawed chaos."

Like the dork I am, I lift my hands and do my best lobster claw impression.

The bartender lets out a low chuckle while drying a pint glass.

Mr. Flannel's face turns soft. His smile fades but his eyes stay warm.

"What's your name?"

"Brianna. What's yours?"

"Caleb." He lifts his cap, runs his hand through thick brown hair that curls slightly at the tips, then pulls the cap back down. "Nice to meet you, Brianna."

Caleb and I talk for a while. He tells me how he got into lobster trapping, how it's been in his family for four generations. He shares how warming oceans affect their business, forcing longer days as they travel farther.

Our conversation breaks when an older guy approaches Caleb.

"Hey, buddy, thanks again for helping Jimmy last week. His wife was going to peel him like a shrimp if he didn't get that boat running." He glances at me, nods, then returns to Caleb.

"No big deal. I said I'd stop over tomorrow and check the rest of the motor so Sheila can rest easy."

"Good man, Caleb. I'll see ya out there."

With a final squeeze to Caleb's shoulder, he's gone.

Caleb takes another sip of his beer.

"What's the issue with Jimmy's boat?" I ask, like I'm a local who'll make sure Sheila rests easy.

"Jimmy's a great fisherman. But boat mechanic?" He shakes his head. "He ignores everything until it becomes a big problem. His engine wouldn't turn over and he had a full day of trap hauling planned, so I helped him out."

"Did you get it started?" I lean my elbow on the bar, chin resting in my hand.

"After a few trips to the store and half the day."

"What about your boat?"

"We had a rookie crewing with us, so they went out and I stayed to help Jimmy."

The rough lobsterman has a caring heart. Go figure.

"So it worked out for everybody."

He gives me a side eye. "Not quite. The rookie is . . . a lot. My boss told me the kid is never allowed onboard without me again."

The bartender motions to us for refills. We both refuse.

"The kid has heart, but the water will humble the best of us. First week he was with me, he grabs a lobster from the trap but doesn't band the claws quick enough. The lobster fights back, grabbing the tip of his glove. Kid freaks—thrashing around the deck like a landed fish, hollering the whole time. The lobster goes airborne, with the glove, and sails back into the sea. That's the last time I lent the kid my gloves."

The visual of the lobster sailing through the air with a glove in its grip is hilarious. Lobster vengeance, if you will.

"I can't imagine that life, but I have so much respect for it."

I let admiration for Caleb and his crew settle on my face as I picture myself on a fishing boat miles off the coast, green from seasickness.

He chuckles. "Well, I can't imagine your life either. My buddy got me this pet cam for my black lab, Archie. It's cool—I can watch him on the app anytime I want to." He pauses, pushing his beer glass forward. "Speaking of, I should probably get home and feed him. He gets cranky when he doesn't eat on time."

I shift back into my seat as Caleb motions to the bartender, slapping a few bills on the bar before standing.

"It's been fun chatting with you, Caleb. Good luck with Jimmy's boat and the rookie. But it sounds like they're in good hands."

"Thanks. Appreciate it."

He pushes the bar stool in and nods before leaving.

I flip through my email one last time before flagging down the bartender for my bill.

"Caleb got it," he says.

Confusion must have been written all over my face because the bartender lets out a laugh as he pulls on the tap in front of him.

Caleb bought my dinner? But . . . why? He left. I'll never see him again. How is it that a stranger bought me dinner when I couldn't get Gym guy to buy me a damn coffee?

For a moment, I consider counting this as a date. I can't,

though. He didn't ask me out—we just happened to sit next to each other. There was no romantic interest, no intention of seeing each other again. It wouldn't be fair to call this a date just because he was kind.

Caleb's act of kindness sticks with me as I walk the Old Port's uneven cobblestones, the breeze mixing salt with hints of seafood. Caleb was nothing like I expected. The way he stayed behind to help Jimmy fix his boat, his patience with the rookie, even buying my dinner without making it a big deal, not needing the acknowledgement. Selfless, generous, *and* kind?

Maybe good guys do exist.

Chapter 28

San Diego

I fly to Irvine a few days later, a renewed excitement to see Preston after leaving Portland.

Chris flies out last minute to oversee my meeting with the client because God forbid someone drop the ball on his clients. I nail the data, though Chris will credit our pre-meeting review for that success. Now, I can focus on tomorrow's early morning sail with Preston.

I sit at the hotel bar in San Diego, fifteen minutes from Preston's marina, responding to emails from the Mercury team. They're easy to work with and patient with my questions. With Gus out on leave, they're having to cover additional projects, so our system implementation is taking longer.

I trace the stem of my wine glass with my thumb and forefinger, the movement calming me. I keep thinking about Caleb—not in a romantic way, but as proof. Proof that there are still good men in the world. Men who show up for people, who care without expecting anything in return. If there's a Caleb out there living his best ocean life, maybe there's someone like that for me too. Someone real. Someone worth all these terrible dates.

I set down my wine glass and reach for my phone as a group text flashes on the screen.

> Evan: Miss Brianna. Your dildo, the Maniac Rabbit 7000, has arrived and is eagerly awaiting pickup. Please get it the fuck out of my house. I can't compete with this thing.

"Oh, shit!" I gasp as heat floods my cheeks. I glance around the bar, paranoid that somehow everyone can see my phone's screen.

> Sara: Don't let him dildo-shame you. He opened the box before checking who it was for. He brought this on himself.

I press my fingers to my forehead, mortified. Of all the packages, it had to be *that* one.

> Me: WHY DID YOU OPEN MY BOX, EVAN?!

Evan left the chat

> Sara: He was waiting for lawn mower parts. Sorry B.

> Sara: That thing is impressive though! 😳 It makes me see Beck in a whole new light. Haha.

I sink in my seat, wishing the floor would open and swallow me whole. Evan knows plenty about my dating disasters, but some things should stay private. Knowing him, I'll never live this down. At least I won't leave this challenge empty-handed. Just dateless.

I review Preston's text from earlier with all the details—where to park, what to bring, how to find him at the gate.

Six a.m. comes quick. I keep it simple for a day on the water—crisp white V-neck, navy shorts, and flip flops. I stuff my tote with sunscreen, sunglasses, the long-sleeve from Hawaii, and my Texas Rangers hat before leaving my hotel room.

> Marina Man Preston: Looking forward to seeing you! Txt me if you run into any trouble.

Nerves buzz through my body. There's been such buildup to this date—finding his ID, our Dallas encounter where I launched through the front door, and now, sailing.

I'm not entirely sure whether this is a romantic gesture or his way of saying thanks for returning his ID. He seemed interested at lunch, but his texts remain professional. This might just be a sailing lesson. Still, if he feeds me, it counts as a date—which means only four more left.

I snag the last parking spot at the marina. My rental car looks cheap compared to the luxury cars filling the lot. I slide sideways past an Alfa Romeo, careful not to brush my tote against it.

Preston steps out of a sailboat two docks down as I approach the marina gate. His reddish-brown hair catches the morning light, his light blue button-down and dark shorts looking effortlessly nautical.

"You made it," he says, opening the gate and leaning in for a hug. The mixture of sunscreen and salt air wraps around me. My hands wrap around his back, his linen shirt doing little to mask the muscle underneath.

He leads me down the second dock, a narrow wooden walkway flanked by sailboats. Masts tower above us like a forest of poles, creaking as the boats sway side to side.

"Here she is," Preston says, stopping beside a pristine white Catalina. The name *Second Wind* curves across the bow in gray vinyl.

I bite back a smile. "*Second Wind?*"

"Fresh start after a rough patch." He shrugs. "Plus she handles beautifully in light wind."

Preston boards the boat, turning to extend his hand.

"Step on the side rail first," he says.

I grip his hand and time my step with the boat's sway, but my flip-flop snags on the rail. If I fall in front of him again, I'm throwing myself overboard.

Preston's other hand steadies my waist. "I've got you."

The boat shifts beneath my feet as I step in.

"Want the tour before we head out?" His excitement reminds me of a toddler wanting to show off his toy collection.

"Lead the way, Captain."

Preston opens the hatch and gestures below. "Watch your head."

I duck into the cabin, where everything is compact but intentional—a small galley with a two-burner stove, a navigation station with nautical charts rolled in cubbies, cushioned seating that probably converts to a bed.

"This is cozy," I say, running my fingers along the wood trim.

I follow him out and watch as he conducts his pre-sail routine. His movements are confident and methodical. And . . . it's hot.

"Can I help?" I ask, feeling useless.

"Just sit back and enjoy. Next time, I'll put you to work."

Next time. The casual confidence in those words sends a small thrill through me.

The engine purrs to life, and within a few minutes, Preston guides us away from the dock. The marina falls away behind us.

"Want to help raise the mainsail?"

My nerves jump. "Sure, just tell me what to do."

"Pull this line. Don't worry about technique. Just pull."

The big white sail climbs the pole in stuttering jerks as I pull, Preston calling out encouragement. When it reaches the top, he secures the rope and moves to the smaller triangular sail at the front.

He cuts the engine and the sails drink in the coastal breath. *Second Wind* tilts slightly, cutting through the water with a gentle hiss.

I breathe in the salt air, gripping the rail as Preston grins, in his element.

The boat glides forward powered by nothing but wind, and I understand why people become obsessed with sailing.

"Sit next to me and take the wheel."

I slide across the bench until our thighs touch, and grab the wheel in front of us. His chest brushes my shoulder as he reaches around me to point at the smaller sail at the front.

"See how the jib is flapping? Turn just a touch to port—left."

I adjust the wheel, hyperaware of his hands settling over mine, guiding. The sail fills properly, and *Second Wind* picks up speed.

"Nice job," he murmurs, but doesn't move away.

The compliment sends heat through me that has nothing to do with the morning sun. For a moment, we stay like this—his hands near mine on the wheel, his chest warm against my shoulder. Then the wind shifts, and Preston straightens, alert.

"Feel that?" His lips are nearly brushing my cheek as he speaks. "We need to trim the jib."

The romantic moment crashes into sailing jargon, and I can't help but giggle. Preston moves around the boat, adjusting a few things before turning back to me.

"Your turn to take the reins," he says, patting the winch handle. "Don't worry, you won't break her."

My nerves spike. This boat probably cost a fortune, and I'm supposed to operate machinery I don't understand? But Preston's confidence is infectious, and I want to impress him.

"Wrap the rope around three times, then turn clockwise. Put your back into it."

I grip the handle and crank it in circles, each rotation pulling the rope attached to the sail, hyperaware that Preston's eyes drop to where my shirt rides up from my shorts. The attention sends a flutter through my stomach, but the sail barely budges.

"Here." Preston steps behind me, his hands covering mine. Every nerve ending fires where his skin touches mine.

"Feel the rhythm of the boat," he murmurs against my ear. "Pull when she dips into the trough"—he hesitates, then rephrases—"Pull when she tilts toward you."

The quick correction makes me smile. He's self-aware enough to catch his own jargon, patient enough to adjust for me. It does something to me.

We crank together, his chest solid against my back, our bodies moving as one with the boat's rhythm. I can feel the power in his arms as we work the crank, the way his whole frame envelops me like a protective shell. The sail tightens with a satisfying snap, but I'm more focused on the hard curve of his biceps against my shoulders.

"Perfect," he says, but doesn't step away. His breath warms the sensitive spot behind my ear, and I have to resist the urge to lean back further into him.

We sail like this for another thirty minutes, Preston constantly in motion—adjusting this line, tweaking that sail, reading the wind like a language I don't speak. Every time I start to ask a question, he's up and moving to adjust something.

"See that gray ship on the horizon?" He points northwest while adjusting the big sail. "Navy destroyer heading back to base."

I squint against the glare off the water, spotting the gray silhouette he's pointing at.

"There's a shipwreck about two miles that way," he says, nodding southeast. "Scuba divers love it; sits in perfect diving depth."

The mention of Navy and scuba divers sours my mood. I try to change the subject, but it's like having a conversation with someone conducting an orchestra—his focus constantly divided between me and his boat.

Gradually, the wind begins to die. His constant adjustments slow, then stop altogether.

"Looks like we're losing our breeze," Preston says, scanning the water. "Perfect excuse to duck into a cove for breakfast." He guides the boat in, where the water turns from deep blue to turquoise. Cliffs rise around us as we motor in.

Preston cuts the engine and moves to drop the anchor. A few other boats bob quietly in the distance. The anchor chain rattles as it plunges into the water.

"Stay put," Preston says, disappearing below deck.

I hear him moving around the galley, and when he emerges, he's carrying a wicker basket and a bottle of wine.

"You came prepared," I say, impressed despite myself.

"I always get hungry on the water." He sets the basket

between us and pulls out fruit, cheese, crackers, and chocolate. This is what a picnic should be. Not the half-assed nonsense Mr. GQ threw together. My mouth waters at the sight of cheese and grapes threaded along wooden skewers. The strawberries are freshly cut, like he cut them himself, and the crackers glisten with buttery goodness.

He pours wine into stemless plastic wine glasses—not wrapped in cellophane—practical for onboard a boat.

He raises his cup, his eyes locked on mine.

"To returning marina IDs," he says.

I laugh. "To marina IDs." I clink my glass against his.

The wine softens everything—his laugh, the way his eyes linger when I talk. And the heat building between us? That's not from the sun.

"You look good on this boat . . . with me." His confident stare makes me hyper-aware of every flaw, every reason I might not deserve someone like him.

Panic flutters in my chest. I reach for humor like a life raft. "Good thing, since we're kind of stuck out here together."

He laughs and sets the picnic basket on the floor. Then he takes my wine glass from my hand, leaning past me to set it in the cup holder. His body cages me for a moment, linen shirt soft against my bare arms, carrying that mix of sunscreen and salt air.

As he pulls back, everything goes quiet except for my heartbeat. His nose skims slowly along my cheek, the touch feather-light, until our foreheads rest together. He says nothing, but I can feel his breath against my lips.

My heart hammers against my ribs. This can't be real—me on a sailboat with this gorgeous executive who looks like he wants to devour me.

He plants one hand on the rail beside me, the other cupping my face, and kisses me. Deep. Urgent. Everything. He commands the kiss with controlled intensity, his lips firm and insistent.

I brace myself against the seat, caught between wanting to pull him closer and needing to steady myself. Then a swell rocks the boat unexpectedly, the momentum pulling us apart. Disappointment is instant and sharp. I want that kiss to continue, to see where it would lead. But with other boats dotting the cove, the last thing I need is to become someone's entertainment through a pair of binoculars.

The rest of the morning passes in easy conversation, my body finding a comfortable rhythm with the boat's gentle rocking. Preston's whole face transforms when he talks about the boat—how he refinished the wood decking himself, upgraded the electronics, spent weekends sanding and varnishing until his hands were raw. There's a boyish pride in his voice as he points out each improvement, and I find myself charmed more by his enthusiasm than the actual renovations.

But underneath my enjoyment, there's an ache building. I'm dreading our goodbye.

The sail back to the dock happens in comfortable near-silence, the kind where words aren't necessary. Preston handles the boat with the same easy confidence, and I find myself watching him more than the coastline slipping past.

When we reach the marina, he ties off the boat with efficient movements while I gather my stuff. The magic of being out on the water fades into the reality of timelines and flight schedules.

"I've got to head straight to the airport," I say, hating how final it sounds.

He straightens, closing the distance between us on the dock. "I know."

There's a moment when we just look at each other. Then his hand slides to the back of my neck, pulling me in for one more kiss. This one's different, slower, as though he's memorizing it. When we break apart, I'm breathless.

"Safe flight," he says, voice low.

I nod, not trusting myself to say anything that won't sound desperate or presumptuous. Instead, I squeeze his hand once and head toward the parking lot, forcing myself not to look back.

Chapter 29

San Antonio

I spent a few days at my condo in Dallas after getting back to Texas—long enough to remember why some days I love the familiarity of my own space, and other days I can't stand it. Every corner holds a memory of what used to be here. What I lost.

On the bright side, I grabbed my packages from Sara's in Dallas. Evan promises he'll never let me live it down, and I had to swear not to discuss my dildo's performance with Sara.

But that's behind me. Now, I'm in San Antonio with Chris for work.

Preston's been texting every couple of days. He's in San Antonio touring office spaces since his company's looking to expand outside California, and he's taking me to dinner tomorrow.

Sara keeps hinting that I would've missed out on a good guy if I quit the challenge. I'll never tell her she's right. Four dates remain. I'm hopeful Preston fills all of them.

Chris and I spend the morning with Chremsoft. The media is having a field day reporting on their CEO, who was caught making out with several reps at a sales conference. Our team is already working on their crisis communication, anticipating the contract will be signed this week. We spend the rest of the afternoon in our separate hotel rooms, emailing back and forth about our strategy until I can't stare at my laptop any longer. A glass of red blend is calling my name.

The closer the elevator gets to the first floor of The Elysian, the stronger the white tea and verbena scent becomes. I breathe it in, happy to be in my home away from home.

I round the bar and spot Javier in a blue three-piece suit, hands gripping his hips so hard his knuckles are white against his thick black belt. He listens to an older couple, jaw ticking, shoulders rigid, posture radiating tension. The guests lean close, keeping their voices low.

I steer to the right when Javier calls my name. Concern flickers in his eyes before he forces a smile. He motions me over. The couple's attention snaps to me, and my steps slow as I feel their glare.

Whatever's happening has wiped Javier's trademark smile clean off his face.

"Is everything okay?" I ask.

A shadow crosses his features. He leans in, worry carved across his brow. I move to his side—us against the older couple in the middle of the hotel lobby. I offer a cautious smile to the woman, but her stoic expression matches her companion's.

Javier gestures to the couple. "This is Marianne and Richard Walker. Griffin's parents."

The world narrows. Background noise disappears, leaving only the frantic thud of my heartbeat. My eyes drift back to Javier, needing somewhere safe to land.

"Mr. and Mrs. Walker would like to speak with you about Griffin. You can absolutely say no. You are under no obligation to speak with them."

"We can't find him. We're worried," Marianne says, sounding like a concerned mother—nothing like the woman Griffin described on our second date.

"We need to find him," is all Richard says.

"Please . . . Brianna," Marianne says, smoothing the sides of her shirt.

Javier can see my hesitation. I want to tell them what a complete asshole their son is. I want to tell them they're shitty parents for raising him to believe he can use and manipulate women. I want them to know the pain and anxiety their son has caused me. But I also want to forget he exists. Forget the betrayal, the con artist.

"If you choose to speak with them, I would like to be present for the conversation." Javier turns toward me, more serious than I've ever seen him.

Even through my fear of this conversation and my anger at their son, I catch a glimpse of Javier's kindness—his quiet protection wrapping around me. That small reassurance is enough.

"You have five minutes," I say to the couple before looking at Javier, drawing strength from his presence.

"Let's give ourselves a little more privacy. This way." Javier leads us past the breakfast area and fitness center, down a long hallway to a plain door marked "Mr. De La Vera." He opens it and guides us into his office, motioning for the Walkers to sit in chairs facing his large wooden desk. Richard practically falls into his seat while Marianne sinks slowly into hers, clutching her purse in her lap.

Javier grabs a conference room chair and positions it behind the desk, gesturing me to sit.

As the neutral party, he begins. "I understand your concerns about Griffin, but I don't know how Brianna can help.

She was a victim of your son's manipulative tactics. You should feel lucky she's willing to give you any time."

He leans forward, hands clasped on the desk.

"We know. And we are. We're very sorry, Brianna, for any trouble Griffin caused you. He's . . . unwell," Marianne says, pressing her delicate fingers through her hair.

My jaw tightens. *Unwell*. Like he has a cold.

"I ask again, why is that Brianna's problem?" Javier pushes as Richard shifts in his seat.

"Look, we're sorry for any trouble our boy has caused . . . " Richard looks to Marianne, and back to me. "Do you know where he is? Do you have a contact number for him? That's all we need and we'll be on our way."

Look. That single word—so casual, so dismissive—shatters whatever control I've been clinging to since I found out who they are. When I finally speak, every word burns on the way out.

"Do I know where your son is?" I look Richard straight in the eye. "I don't give a shit where your son is. I've been trying to forget he exists. He's your son. You should know where he is."

Silence fills the room and I'm aware of how sharp I sound, like an overly-dramatic teenager.

"He keeps changing his phone number every time we contact him," Marianne says, her tone defeated.

Javier leans back in his chair, his expression stoic.

"Have you involved the authorities? Put out a missing person's report?" he asks, looking at Marianne.

"No. We don't want to involve the authorities," Richard jumps in.

"Oh, that's rich. You must be as shady as your son."

I immediately snap my mouth shut, shocked the words escaped. Stupid, heartbroken teenager. Javier looks at me with understanding, then back to Richard. His hand rests on my knee for a moment, the touch gentle and protective, before he returns it to the desk.

"We understand Griffin hurt you. We're very sorry," Marianne says, her face long.

"Hurt?" I let out a bitter laugh. "How dare you. This isn't a simple heartbreak. Your son is a predator. He manipulates women, lies, and then tries to take their money." Marianne's face winces as if she were physically slapped. "Your son is a con artist who ruins lives for sport. Excuse me if your concerns and worry die at my feet."

Adrenaline floods my system, hands betraying my fury with their tremor.

Javier leans forward, probably afraid of what else might come out of my mouth.

"I understand your position, Mr. and Mrs. Walker. I just don't know how Brianna can be any help. He lied to her about everything. She can't trust any detail he gave her. And given what he has put her through, I don't see it necessary to drag this conversation out any longer." He stands.

Marianne and Richard both stand, appearing reluctant to leave. I stay seated, afraid my legs will give out.

"Can you email or call if you think of anything that will be useful for us to find our son?" Richard places his business card on top of the desk.

"We'll be in touch if anything comes up," Javier says.

As Marianne and Richard walk toward the door, Javier gently touches my arm.

"Stay here. I'll be right back." He gives me a soft smile before slipping out and closing the door.

I sink into my chair and bury my face in my hands. How did I end up here? Thank God Javier stayed. While I fell apart, he held everything together.

I reach for Richard's business card:

Richard Walker
Walker Construction & Remodel
Norfolk, Virginia

I turn the business card over and see, *Family owned and operated since 1990.*

Griffin lied about everything. His parents aren't venture capitalists. They own a construction company... in Virginia.

Javier opens the door and steps inside, concern etched across his face.

"Are you okay?" He settles into the leather high-back chair beside me.

I shake my head and stare at the ceiling, searching for the answer. I swivel my chair until our knees touch.

"I'm furious. I'm spitting fire." I pause. "But also... seeing the worry on his mother's face made me feel sad and helpless."

Javier leans back, letting the rich leather cradle his shoulders.

"Because you're an incredibly intelligent, caring woman. And you're fair, even when you don't have to be."

I roll my eyes. "Look where that got me."

"You have to stop beating yourself up." Javier's voice turns firm. "He's a master manipulator. I guarantee he's fooled smart, caring women before you."

I don't want to hear that. It's bad enough I got duped, but knowing this bastard is destroying other women's lives turns my stomach.

"He lied about everything." I pick up the business card and stare at it. "His parents are in construction." A bitter laugh escapes me. "I'm such a fool."

Javier leans forward until his knees press into mine, placing both hands over mine.

"You are no fool." His voice drops. "And believe me, I've met several." He pauses, waiting for my eyes to meet his. "If one of those other women came to you for help, would you call her a fool?"

I have to think about it. Silence stretches between us before I finally answer.

"No. I wouldn't." My voice softens. "They were tricked."

"Exactly. And so were you. Don't let—"

A sharp knock interrupts him.

"Come in," Javier calls toward the door, swiveling away from me.

The door opens slowly, and Diane's face appears in the gap.

"Your meeting is starting. They're wondering where you are." Her gaze shifts between us, expression unreadable.

"Thank you, Diane. Please tell them I'm on my way."

Javier waits until the door clicks shut, then turns back to me. Our knees don't touch this time.

"Do you need anything?"

His attention makes me squirm. I want to erase this whole experience from my mind and pretend it never happened. Pretend Javier didn't have to get involved in my dating disasters twice now.

"I'll be fine." I force a smile. "Just a bruised ego." I stand and smooth my skirt, avoiding his gaze. "You're late for your meeting."

He moves toward the door, but stops with his hand on the handle. He turns back to me, studying my face.

"Join me for a drink later, up on the rooftop. My favorite bartender is working tonight."

I should say no. The last thing I want is to burden him further with my mess.

But something in his voice stops me from declining. Maybe it's the way he's looking at me—not with pity, but with genuine concern. Or maybe it's because he's the only person who knows the whole ugly truth and isn't making me feel like an idiot for it.

"Okay," I hear myself say. "What time?"

"Seven."

"I'll be there." I pause as he opens the door. "And Javier?"

He turns back, and his eyes—steady, searching—find mine.

"Thank you. For everything."

"No need to thank me, Brianna."

He flashes me a quick smile before stepping into the hallway. I follow him out, pulling the office door closed behind me.

Chapter 30

San Antonio

Right at seven, I push open the glass door leading out to the rooftop. Wind scatters dried leaves around my feet. Teardrop lights drape overhead, casting warm light across empty lounge chairs and high-top tables.

I expect it to be bustling with guests, but no one is here.

"Shit!" someone shouts.

Scratch that—someone *is* here.

Javier pops up from behind the bar, wiping his hands on his slacks.

"Brianna! Sorry, I thought I was alone." His familiar smile returns as he leans on the black bar top.

"It's nice to hear you curse once in a while." I wink and slide onto the barstool. "Where's your favorite bartender?"

I glance around the empty space as an employee tapes a white sign to the rooftop entrance and disappears.

Javier spreads his arms wide. "You're looking at him. What can I get you?"

"Should I test your bartending skills, or play it safe with wine?"

"I like a good challenge." His voice is low as he grabs a glass tumbler. "Stand by and watch the magic." He wiggles his fingers and grabs a bottle. Rum, I think.

Javier works behind the bar with serious bartender flair. He grabs four different bottles, pouring from each into the shaker, along with what looks like red fruit puree. The shaker bounces between his strong hands with surprising force as he shakes it beside his ear, grinning at me.

"You're loving this, aren't you?" I say, feigning boredom.

"Oh, I am." He pops the top off the shaker and strains the mixture into the tumbler. A large strawberry goes on the rim, followed by a tiny yellow umbrella. He slides the glass toward me and stands there grinning, waiting, just like he did at dinner when I tried the cactus dish.

I can't help but smile as I reach for the glass. Something sweet and innocent in his expression makes my chest warm.

I take a sip and my taste buds explode with flavor. Coconut, strawberry, and the perfect tang of alcohol. Incredible.

"It's okay." I scrunch my nose as I set the glass down, fighting to keep a straight face.

"Are you kidding?" He reaches for the glass. "Hold on." He dips a lowball straw into my drink and traps the liquid inside by covering the opening with his fingertip. Then he tilts his head back, and removes his finger from the straw, the liquid trickling onto his tongue. He pauses, savoring it before looking at me. I can't hide my grin.

"Oh, you got me. I thought my skills were slipping."

"Is there anything you're not good at?" I steal my glass back.

"Plenty." He laughs as he rounds the bar. "Come sit with me. Best view in the house."

He guides me past the bar to a small table—the only one set with a cloth cover, wine glasses, and silverware. He pulls out my chair.

"I gambled that you probably skipped dinner."

"You would be correct."

"I took the liberty of ordering dinner. You need something substantial in your stomach besides alcohol." He pushes in my chair as I sit. There's no salt shaker for me to knock over this time.

He settles across from me. His crisp gray shirt sleeves are rolled up, fabric pulling slightly around his biceps as he leans forward.

"Thank you for this, Javier. For everything."

He waves dismissively as he opens his beer—a local IPA. "It's nothing. I'm happy to do it."

"It's not nothing. It's everything." I pause, meeting his eyes. "You've been the calm in my Griffin storm. I would have completely unraveled today without you." My voice softens. "I can't tell you how much I appreciate you just . . . being you."

His smile fades into his beer as he takes a sip. "I'm happy to do it."

An easy silence settles between us. I lean back in my chair and take in our surroundings for the first time. The city spreads out around us, twinkling lights scattered like diamonds across the dark landscape.

"How was your meeting?" I ask, guilt creeping in about making him late.

"Fine. Half the time I don't know why they include me. It's good to be aware, but I'd rather be helping guests."

"You really love your job. I see it. You radiate joy all over that lobby."

He laughs softly. "I don't know about radiating joy. Like any job, there are pros and cons." He leans forward. "Most of the time it feels like I'm being pulled in every direction. Which is why Diane is a stickler about my schedule. But I love helping guests build memories, finding restaurants for business travelers hosting important dinners, connecting them with local businesses. This hotel is more than just rooms and beds to me. I'd like to think we make an impact on the people who stay here and on the local community."

"I admire that you don't only think about your job duties as a concierge. You think more broadly. I hope your boss appreciates that."

He stares at the top of his beer can as if pondering what I said. He lets out a laugh before saying, "He probably thinks I'm crazy." He smiles, lifting the can to his lips.

"You are far from crazy." Ice clinks as I drain my cocktail. "Is Diane your boss?"

His brows lift, as though he's surprised. "Um . . . no. I like to think we're peers."

I'm about to ask more when an older employee appears, cutting off the conversation.

"Mr. De La Vera, dinner's almost ready. May I refresh your drinks?"

"Thank you, Frederick. I'll take another beer. Brianna?"

"Same." I point to Javier's empty can.

"Brianna drinks IPAs? I keep learning new things about you," Javier says.

I explain how Chris gave me grief about drinking light beer and created a "ramp-up plan" to train my palate for IPAs.

Javier rests his head against his hand, listening. At first I think he's mocking me, but then he responds, "I love that you challenge yourself and try new things. It's an admirable trait—one I had to learn."

"Well, it's worked out pretty well for you."

"Let's just say some lessons come with a price."

He glances toward the bar as two employees approach with a room service cart.

"I hope you like Chicken Francese?" he asks, grabbing his beer from Frederick.

The aroma rises up—buttery, citrusy, with a hint of garlic—and my stomach answers before I can.

"This is one of my favorite dishes." I look up at him. His pleased expression does something to me.

Javier and I fall into easy conversation during dinner. He shares funny stories from his childhood while I tell him about the ridiculous scenarios Sara and I got into during college. After my second beer, the words almost spill out about Evan opening my dildo package. I catch myself and take another sip instead.

"You travel a lot," he observes. "I know it's hard on my sister when she has to leave Angelina and Dominic. Does it ever get old? Living out of a suitcase?"

Neither of us wants to hear the real answer, so he gets my fabricated response. The one I've perfected over years.

"I love to travel. I love the opportunity to explore places I'd never see if I only worked out of Dallas."

I pause, the way I always do before delivering my scripted finale. But something shifts inside me. He's been nothing but honest with me tonight. I let out a breath.

"Yeah, it does get old. The travel wears me down. Airports blur together, and scheduling doctor appointments around flights becomes this constant juggling act. And I miss grocery shopping." I pause, realizing how strange that sounds.

I gave him more than I give others—these surface complaints I can share safely. But the real reason sits heavy in my stomach, making me queasy.

We talk through dinner—work, travel, random observations that make each other laugh. It's easy, natural, the kind of conversation that doesn't require effort. The server returns to clear our dinner plates, replacing them with small dessert plates. I welcome the distraction.

"I have a special dessert tonight." Javier stands and heads behind the bar. "It's a delicacy from its country of origin—thoughtfully made and sculpted. Close your eyes. I want it to be a surprise."

I close my eyes reluctantly. The darkness strips away my defenses, leaving me vulnerable as his footsteps approach.

I hear a clunk as another plate hits the table.

"Open."

I open my eyes and stare at the center of our table. Then I laugh. The sound bursts out of me. Javier stands there grinning, pleased with himself.

How did he know?

I reach for the delicacy, a soft, pillowy, sugary goodness shaped like a seashell.

"I always see you with a box from across the street," he says, sitting across from me.

I tell him about my concha obsession, and why I always request Room 1010. Normally I'd feel embarrassed sharing this, but Javier has seen me at my worst and hasn't judged me.

After we devour our pastries, we settle back into our chairs. The sky has gone dark, and the evening feels complete.

"I should let you get settled in for the night." Javier gathers the plates, his movements slower than necessary. "I have an early morning myself."

He places the plates on the bar, then pauses and turns to me.

"Want to go on our own little adventure first?"

I can't resist that smile. "What kind of adventure?"

He leads me to an unmarked door at the end of the hallway on the twelfth floor, then unlocks it and steps inside. I trail after him and walk straight into his back.

"Close the door," he says, turning to face me. He pulls a light chain, barely illuminating the cramped closet.

"Did you just bring me into a broom closet?" My nose is inches from his. Energy hums through my body. He laughs and points left.

A narrow wooden door stands there, curved at the top.

"Are there hobbits behind this door?" I ask, only half-joking.

He laughs, flicks on a light switch, and opens the door. I peer into a tight, dusty hallway. The paint looks like it was yellow a lifetime ago. Now it's faded to a dusty, tired brown.

If it were anyone else, I'd sprint from this serial killer setup so fast . . .

Javier leads us into the narrow, hidden hallway. My sleeves brush against the walls as I take a few steps inside.

"What is this?" I ask.

"It's an old servants' passage. Back then, staff needed to move around without guests seeing them. They used these routes for room service, housekeeping duties."

I follow his silhouette down the hall, fascinated by the history of it.

"We use it today for maintenance—electricians, plumbers—so guests aren't disturbed." He slows as we approach a narrow metal staircase.

"Watch your step." He descends backwards, facing me, his warm grip steadying me as I follow him down. "Did we just go down to the next floor?" I ask as we start down another narrow, dimly lit hall.

"Yep. This is the eleventh floor."

I read the age-stained signs hanging on the wall: "Staff must remain unseen after 7 p.m."; "Quiet Zone—Suite Overhead"; "Bellboys Must Shine Shoes Before 7 a.m."

Javier doesn't expect me to stop at a sign mentioning dumbwaiters. His chest bumps into my right shoulder, and instinctively one hand braces my lower back, the other my stomach. For a moment, we freeze.

"You might want to warn a guy first," he says. As his hands drift away from my body, my stomach tightens.

"This sign had more words." I turn toward him, my pulse quickening more than it should, here in the servants wing with the concierge.

"It's cool, right?" he asks, searching my face for reassurance. "I walk through these passages when I need to connect with the heart of the hotel."

I realize this means more to him than showing off hidden spaces. These corridors represent everything he believes about hospitality—rooted in tradition, built on invisible service.

"Shall we?" He motions toward another door, and I'm curious what's behind door number three. I pull the door handle. Nothing. I try again—still nothing.

"Here, let me try." He moves to slide past me in the cramped space. We turn to face each other, our bodies brushing as we attempt this awkward dance, slowly sidestepping to our left in perfect unison.

He stops.

His breath is warm against my cheek, soft and unsteady. His chest rises and falls, pressing against mine with each breath. When he looks at me—really looks at me—it's as though he sees straight through every carefully constructed wall I've built to keep men at arm's length. The vulnerability should terrify me. It should send me running back down that narrow corridor. But I don't want to look away.

He leans in closer, and my heart hammers against my ribs. Our breathing synchronizes, chests rising and falling together as if we're sharing the same air. His lips hover mere inches from mine, close enough that I feel the warmth radiating between us.

He's waiting, letting me decide whether to close the distance or pull away.

The spell breaks with the groan of door hinges. Light floods the narrow space, forcing our guilty bodies apart. A tall figure stands silhouetted in the doorway, hands on hips like a disapproving parent.

"You left the twelfth floor door open," Diane says.

Of all people, at this exact moment.

"Thank you, Diane." Javier steps around her as she continues glaring at me. "Come on, Brianna. I'll walk you to your room."

As I squeeze past her, she leans forward, glaring the entire time. What is this woman's problem? I escape and hurry to catch up with Javier.

We say nothing as we wait at the elevator, but grin as we exchange "we've been caught" looks.

We step in, giggling like children. He tilts his head back, eyes crinkling at the corners. That rare, unguarded laughter spills from him, and I just stand there, stunned by how handsome he is. Like someone took a charm and carved it into a man.

We exit the elevator one floor down. He stays close as we walk to Room 1010, our shoulders nearly touching.

"Thank you for a lovely evening, and thank you for joining me on my adventure."

I laugh at him for a few reasons, but mostly because he's just adorable.

"Are we going to be in trouble?" I ask, thinking of Diane's death stare. This woman already wants me out of this hotel, and I'll feel bad if Javier gets in trouble or written up because of our little hobbit hopping.

"Nah." He waves it off. "I'll smooth things over with Diane. It'll be fine."

"Diane is going to make my upcoming stays hell ... because of our adventure," I airquote "our adventure."

"She won't. I'll make sure of it."

I give him this skeptical look. "You're untouchable here, aren't you?"

He laughs, shoving his hands in his pant pockets.

"No, definitely not. Diane has high expectations of everyone, including me. She knows what it takes to run a hotel and she's ... unwavering in making sure the hotel runs smoothly. Sometimes a little too much. But I'd be lost without her." He shifts his stance a few times. "Key?" He reaches out for my room card and I hand it over.

The familiar beep sounds and Javier pushes my door open.

I get the general manager has high expectations about the hotel. But it doesn't explain why she's so mean to me.

"Thank you for your company tonight. I hope it helped put your mind at ease," Javier says, holding the door open to my room.

"It was exactly what I needed. Thank you."

"I'll see you tomorrow, then?"

I smile and nod, suddenly self-conscious. We've gone from concierge and customer to friends, and now ... *what?* Is he interested? Am I reading this wrong?

The door shuts behind me. I lean against it, catching my breath. What was that energy in the storage room? Why does my body react like *that* every time he gets close?

Chapter 31

San Antonio

I didn't see Javier in the lobby this morning before I left for work. That's probably a good thing since the more I think about our almost kiss, the more I get uncomfortable about it. I mean, in the moment, I wanted it more than I wanted air.

But now, in the cold light of day, I can see how messy it would've been. We work together, sort of. I'm a guest; he's the concierge. And I genuinely like having him as a friend. One kiss could ruin all of that and make the rest of my stay here unbearably awkward.

It also would complicate things with Preston. He's in town scoping out corporate spaces for his company's expansion and taking me out tonight. I've never been the type who dips my toes in several waters at once. Not that Preston and I are exclusive, but for the first time in a long time, I'm hopeful about what this could become.

I open the door to my room, and sitting on my bed is another box. This one I'm very familiar with. It's pink, the same pink box I get from La Panadería. I rush over and flip open the tiny note card,

Brianna,
Thank you for the adventure!
-J

I read the note twice, a warmth spreading through my chest that I don't want to name. Then reality kicks in. This is a problem. He's leaving me gifts, almost kissed me, and I'm *happy* about it. But I can't afford to be happy about it. My life is already a disaster of avoidance and half-truths. Adding Javier to that mix? Recipe for more heartbreak.

My cell phone dings from my purse.

> Marina Man Preston: I'm 5 minutes out. I'll meet you in the lobby.

Shoot! I only have time to change my shoes. I hop across the floor, taking off my heels and exchanging them for my tan flats. I grab my purse and phone before swinging open the door. I come to an abrupt stop so I don't plow into the body that stands on the other side of the door.

Diane.

"Miss Whitmore. I don't know if you understand the level of sophistication and professionalism expected at this hotel. Our guests hold themselves in high regard, and I expect the same from you."

I don't have time for this shit.

"Yup. Got it." I squeeze past her and head toward the stairs. I am *not* going to wait for the elevator while she's still on this floor.

I walk through the lobby just as Preston is walking through the front door.

"Hey," I say embracing the sailing captain in a hug. His arms feel strong, like armor wrapped around me. "You look like you've been touring corporate spaces," I add, taking in his tan suit jacket and olive green tie. Unlike Javier, he doesn't have a matching vest.

"Ugh, it's so boring touring empty office buildings. But I think we might have found one." He glances around the lobby. "So, this is the hotel you're always staying at."

Grace and Tobias are snickering to each other at the front desk.

"You ready to go?" Preston asks.

As I'm about to say yes, I hear the voice I haven't heard all day. I glance behind me as Javier chats with the bartender. Our eyes lock and the secrets overwhelm me. The secret that we almost kissed, the secret that my body feels things around him even now.

My face betrays me as a smile spreads wide across my face.

"Brianna," he says, and holds his hand out to Preston. "I'm Javier, the concierge."

Preston shakes his hand, "Preston. Nice to meet you, Javier."

I awkwardly stare at the guy I almost kissed and the guy I definitely kissed.

Say something, Brianna.

"We are about to head to the Maison du Soleil, the restaurant you recommended I take clients to."

"Oh, great!" Javier's demeanor shifts, all polished concierge now. "Perfect choice. The chef spent twenty years training between France and Italy. You're in for an amazing meal. Enjoy."

Preston turns toward the exit but I pause, my gaze lingering on Javier.

"Hey"—I lower my voice—"Thanks for dessert." I grin.

"Enjoy." He tilts his head down, lifting his eyebrows.

I catch up with Preston, who's oblivious to my few extra moments with Javier.

I step into Preston's rental, a dark blue Audi SUV that makes me a little jealous. It suits him—sleek and efficient. He's animated during the drive, updating me on today's real estate tours, weighing airport convenience against parking access.

At Maison du Soleil, we're seated right away. Wine arrives, we toast, and slip easily back into work talk.

"How's everything going with Mercury?" he asks.

"It's good. I demonstrated the dashboard today. The project manager still struggles with the term *snapshot*. She wants all the data at her fingertips."

Preston laughs. "She doesn't know what she wants, then. They're the worst clients because they end up drowning in data, and then the company does too."

"I know, but I'm getting her to see that less is more."

"What did they think of the competitor comparison chart?" he asks, leaning back in his chair. "That was added based on my input." He waggles his eyebrows.

I smirk. He's the expert consultant on these products, and it's clear he knows them inside and out.

"They loved it, of course," I say with some dramatics. "What they didn't love was your recommendation to ax *Wall Street Journal*. It nearly killed our sale before it even started."

Preston purses his lips, shaking his head.

"They don't need *Wall Street Journal*. They have FactView. If I remember correctly, FactView pulls something like eighty percent of *Wall Street's* articles."

"My sales executive nearly flipped a chair a few years back after he found out we didn't subscribe to *Wall Street Journal*. He claims he lost money because of it."

Preston shakes his head. "Then, he's a shitty salesman."

I raise my eyebrows. I don't appreciate him talking that way about Chris. But the certainty in his voice is the sexiest thing in this restaurant right now.

"He is, and I'll tell you why." Preston puts his wine glass down. "I recall something like twenty plus media points to choose from. Are you telling me of all those subscriptions, he couldn't figure out how to keep that sale?"

Something protective flares in me. Chris closes deals other reps can't touch. But Preston's confidence—sharp, unapologetic, earned—sparks a need low in my belly.

I open my mouth to defend Chris, but Preston's already moving on, his intensity softening as he signals the waiter. The moment passes, but that heat lingers between us.

As our entrees arrive, the conversation shifts naturally. Preston shares his career plan, which includes getting out of the start-up space and into more established corporations, and taking longer sailing excursions.

He asks me the same question Javier did, about my travel schedule. With Preston, I give the highlight reel. He travels as much as I do, and the way he leans in, like he'd finally found someone who understands, makes me bury the exhaustion I shared with Javier.

As he drives me back to the hotel, his hand rests on my thigh and the city lights blur past in a wash of gold.

"I'm sorry we didn't have time for dessert. I was hoping my flight home got delayed so we could spend more time together. The crème brûlée looked delicious. It's one of my favorites," he says as he pulls into the curbside bus stop next to La Panadería.

"Actually, I'd love to take you to my favorite restaurant in San Diego. Their crème brûlée is exquisite."

"That sounds great. I'll be in Irvine next week, if that works?"

I unclick my seat belt, wishing we had more time.

"I'll make it work."

I lean across the center console. "Thank you for dinner, especially before your flight back home."

"For you? Of course." He cups my face, thumb brushing my cheek as he leans in. The first touch of his lips is soft. When I lean closer, his other hand slides to the back of my neck, and our kiss deepens. The noise of the city streets fades to a dull hum, and all I can focus on is the warmth of his mouth, the press of his fingers in my hair.

"Looking forward to next week when you're in San Diego."

I look back at him before closing the door. "Me too."

The short walk to the front of the hotel passes in a blur, my face aching from smiling. Thank God I didn't abandon the dating challenge.

The Elysian's door won't open. Shit. My watch says 10:07—seven minutes past lockdown.

My hand's still digging through my purse for my room key when a voice crackles through the small speaker beside the door.

"If you got a goodnight kiss, we'll let you in. If you didn't, you better go find that boy and get it."

Tobias. Through the window, I see him grinning at the check-in desk. Grace's hand comes down on his shoulder before she leans over to buzz me in.

"I am so sorry, Miss Whitmore, Tobias is out of his mind tonight. He didn't mean to be so rude. Right, Tobias?"

He scrunches his face at her and says, "Oh, no. I meant

every word." He turns to me. "So, did you get a smoochy smooch?"

I shift on my feet. "Sorry to disappoint you, but the highlight of today will be crawling in bed and stuffing my face with—"

Tobias raises his hand to his cheek. "Oh, we're going there." He waves his hand as if ready to hear more.

"Pastries. From next door," I say, smiling.

He leans in and whispers, "Is that the code word?"

Grace smacks Tobias again in the arm.

"*Ouch*. What? Brianna is a beautiful woman. I'm sure she meets a buffet of men when she travels. Or women. Whatever you're into."

I smile at his boldness. If Diane heard this, she'd give him an earful about maintaining the hotel's standard of professionalism.

"It's fine. It's funny. I hate to disappoint you, Tobias, but I'm quite boring."

"*Mmm hmm*. And I'm a virgin who only drinks tap water." That earns another slap from Grace and a chuckle from me. "Good night, Miss Whitmore," Tobias says, grinning ear to ear. "Enjoy your pastries."

Chapter 32

San Antonio

The next morning, I stuff a croissant into my mouth from the wingback chair I hate. Chris and I need to prep before meeting our potential client, Delefont. I'm brushing pastry flakes off my blazer when a wave of dark brown hair suddenly appears around the wingback.

"Oh, my gosh, Javier." I smack my chest, grinding any remaining crumbs into my clothing. "I need to find a different chair."

"Sorry," he says, unbuttoning his suit jacket before he sits. The rich brown vest underneath hugs his torso like a second skin, and I forget about croissant crumbs entirely.

"How did dinner go last night? Did Preston like the restaurant?"

My stomach churns.

"He did. Thanks again for the recommendation."

"My pleasure. It's a great place to schmooze clients." He nods toward the breakfast bar. "I'm glad the croissants are such a hit."

I twist in my seat and lean over the armrest, practically

folding myself in half to peer around the chair's wing where Chris is grabbing two.

"I think we found the source of those extra ten pounds, Chris," I say to him.

He pretends to throw one at me, and I duck behind the chair's wing.

"I'll let you two get to it." Javier stands, amused. "See you later?"

"For sure."

He fastens each button slowly, his hands drawing my eyes down the length of his torso.

Chris sits, a half-eaten croissant in hand. "All right, let's talk Delefont."

Chris drops me off at the hotel around three-thirty after a successful day of meetings, and I drop my stuff in my room before heading to La Panadería. I still have pastries in my room thanks to Javier, but I need coffee to get through the rest of the day.

I stand in line, responding to Preston's earlier texts. He's confirming our plans to meet in San Diego next week, and I can't help but smile.

I'm still looking at his text when I catch the scent of cool water.

"Why am I *not* shocked to see you here? Did you already eat the conchas?"

Heat flashes over my skin at the sound of his voice.

"You can never get enough pastries, Javier. Never."

"Clearly." He crosses his arms, biceps crowding against his brown vest, smirking, and damn him for looking that good.

"I'm loving the conchas, thank you for those. Just hunting for caffeine now." I look at him more closely. "Wait, you left the hotel?"

Javier laughs, embarrassment pulling his gaze down to his feet.

"Yes, to meet with a potential partner for the hotel, but he canceled last minute. I've been enjoying the time away, honestly. How did your meeting with the client go?"

"It went well. Chris usually doesn't pull me in until the finalist presentation, but these guys are a technology company so he wanted me in the earlier conversations."

I step up and order my latte, Javier waiting patiently behind me.

"Join me. Tell me about your day before we have to go back," Javier says as I turn with my latte in hand, pushing the cardboard sleeve up the cup.

"I'd love to," I say, following him to a table near the back, and continue to update him on the Delefont meeting. He seems interested, which I appreciate.

"We could've used your company months ago when they broke ground on that Instagrammable hotel-concert-resort place. It took the hotel community by surprise. I think they intended it that way."

"They were trying to hide it?"

"We think so. They negotiated a massive multi-year tax break with the city. They knew we'd throw a fit."

"I would think their target market isn't the same as The Elysian's, am I wrong? Your guests don't seem like the Instagram type."

I peel at a corner of my coffee sleeve.

"You're right. Our guests are looking for a much more elevated experience, so I don't think it'll impact us as much. But I worry about the hotels downtown. I worry about Stefan and his hotel."

I sit quietly, absorbing his words. The way he worries about Stefan, about other hotels—it's not just business strategy. He genuinely cares about people's livelihoods, their dreams. This is what makes him extraordinary, and it terrifies me how much I'm drawn to it. To him.

"What do you do for fun, Javier?" I realize I know a lot about the concierge, but little about the guy outside of those three piece suits.

"Fun? What's that?" He laughs. "Honestly, the hotel takes up a majority of my time. If I'm not working, I'm at an event representing the hotel, city meetings, chamber meetings . . ." He lofts his hands in the air. "If it wasn't for Angelina and Dominic, I probably wouldn't see family."

He laughs, shaking his head. "Wow, I just realized how boring I am."

"You're far from boring. And I get it. My work is a big piece of my life."

He leans forward, his arms resting on the table.

"I do enjoy soccer. I played when I was a kid, and there are a few bars nearby that follow some UK teams. They'll open the bar at seven a.m. and serve beer and breakfast sandwiches while the game plays on every TV."

"That sounds like a good time." I mirror his stance, my elbows stretching across the table.

Two employees holding brooms and a mop enter the dining room. I glance at my watch—four-forty-five.

"Is it that time?" Javier asks.

"I think so."

Reluctance tugs at me. The hotel is always chaotic—guests,

demands, Diane's watchful eye. But out here? It's just us. No performance, no professionalism.

We clean our table together, and I walk to the trash can with my hand full of napkins and empty cups. We head toward the door that leads to the side street between The Elysian and La Panadería—the side of The Elysian where my room is—when an employee calls out behind me, "Bye, Brianna!"

Javier turns. "Of course they know you here."

I slip through the door he holds open for me, smiling at the gesture. The expression falls as I imagine Diane at the front desk, ready to glare at us walking in together. I don't know what I did to earn her hostility.

As if reading my thoughts, Javier says, "Why don't we use the back door to avoid any. . ." His voice trails off.

"Any Dianes?" I insert, and Javier laughs. "You're scared of her, aren't you?" I tease.

We wait until a delivery truck passes, then hustle across the street.

"I'm not scared of her. It's just that Diane knows everything I have on my plate. She doesn't like me distracted from my work. She's not a bad person, just a little intense sometimes."

Am I a distraction?

Javier guides me around the back of the hotel, pulling keys from his pocket as he stops at a metal door that blends into the stone building.

The sharp smell of cleaner hits me as soon as we're inside. Employee-only territory—bare hallways and the distant hum of industrial washers.

"This way." He guides me down a long hall. Voices drift from somewhere ahead as we weave between tall racks of white linens. The hum of washing machines grows louder with each step.

Javier gasps and stops abruptly. I look up, but it's too late—I collide with his back, my nose pressed between his shoulder blades. The scent of cool water mixed with cleaning chemicals surrounds me, and my pulse stutters. He reaches back, his hands finding my hips, fingers spread wide to steady me. The gentle pressure pulls me closer, and heat blooms everywhere our bodies meet.

I hold my breath, straining to hear over the washing machines. Muffled voices come through but I can't tell if one is Diane's.

"Oh, shit," he hisses, turning to grab my arms, pushing me between two linen carts. We press our backs against the wall.

Javier's body convulses in laughter. Thank God for the laundry room noise. I can't help laughing—at him, at us. We're grown adults hiding in linens. He points down the hallway, mouthing, "She's right there!" His eyes bulge. When he starts laughing again, something flutters in my chest.

The voices fade. Javier leans forward, checking the hallway. Without looking at me, he grabs my hand and pulls me from between the carts. It feels natural, until awareness hits. I'm holding hands with Javier.

Javier holds my hand until we reach the elevator at the end of the hallway. When he lets go to press the button, the disappointment catches me off guard. I stare at him as if he could explain this feeling.

The utility elevator doors creak open, protesting every inch. Inside, thick padding covers each wall. Javier hits the tenth floor button and leans back, his head dropping against the wall.

"Oh, my God, that was hilarious. We almost got caught by Diane." He's breathless between laughs. His eyes follow mine as I lean my shoulder against the wall, facing him.

"I feel like a teenager hiding from the principal," I say, watching Javier laugh.

He looks like temptation wrapped in expensive fabric, and

here we are playing hide-and-seek. He shifts to face me, bringing us only inches apart.

"You're fun," he says, his playful smile fading into something more serious.

"You're fun, too. You and your adventures." I playfully roll my eyes.

"I want to finish something that I started on our last adventure," he says.

For a moment, we just stare at each other, the air thick with something unspoken. Then he makes his move.

The kiss happens in the space between floors, suspended between moments. His lips are warm, insistent. Shock dissolves and I return his kiss, pressing into him. He pins me against the wall of the elevator, his body against mine as his tongue slips through. A whimper escapes from low in my belly, surprising me. Javier's hands move from my arms to my waist, tracing up my sides as his kisses a trail down my jaw to my neck. The scent of cool water fills my senses.

The sensation overwhelms me. My breath turns ragged as he kisses my collarbone, his hands tracing just under my bra line of my blouse. Alarm bells clash with desire, my body at war with itself.

The door creaks open, but we don't stop. Javier works his way back up my jaw, crushing my lips once more. His hands leave my torso, brushing my chest as he cups my face. My attention splits between the bliss of this unexpected kiss and wondering whether we're heading back down to the bottom floor.

He presses three gentle kisses to my lips before pulling back just enough that our foreheads touch. We stand there, breathing hard, his hands cradling my face. The silence stretches between us, not awkward, just full.

"I've been wanting to do that for quite some time," he says, a boyish smile spreading across his face.

Javier's never been on my radar like this. He's the friendly concierge, the guy who makes my mornings better. I don't know what to say. *Thanks? Can't say the same, but it was enjoyable?*

So I kiss him again.

Two days later, I'm back in Dallas, sitting across from Beck and Sara at our usual corner table at Magnolia Press. I've barely finished telling her about last week in San Antonio when—

"You made out with the concierge in a utility elevator?" Beck shouts.

"*Shh!*" My hand shoots out, covering her mouth. The barista glances up, his mustache curving with his smile.

"Eww!" I jerk my hand back, wiping it on Beck's shirt.

"Did you just lick her?" Sara laughs.

"Gross, Beck. I need sanitizer." I grab my purse.

"So, what happened after the elevator kiss?" Beck breaks off a piece of her coffee cake, crumbs scattering.

"Nothing. I flew home."

"You haven't heard from him?" Sara asks, sitting down with her gigantic iced green tea.

"No. Why would I?"

I look at Sara, who looks at Beck, who looks at me. Great. We've formed a triangle of judgment.

Sara leans onto the table. "Oh, I don't know, B. Because he's been your knight in shining armor for weeks? Because he closed the rooftop bar for a private dinner? Because he left you pastries and a cute note? And let's not forget the Coach shoes." She ticks off each point on her fingers.

"He bought you designer shoes?" Beck's voice pitches high.

"He's the concierge. It's his job to be nice." I shrug.

They stare at me. I shrug again, wondering why they're making this such a big deal.

"It was a mistake. I'm sure it won't happen again. We were just in the moment."

I trace the rim of my mug.

"Sounds like you've had several moments," Beck says. "So, what's wrong with him?"

"Nothing's wrong with him."

"Then, what's *right* about him?" Beck crosses her leg, perched for my response.

I think for a moment, taking a gulp of coffee under the pressure.

"He's safe, reliable, familiar."

"That's how my grandpa would describe his 1970s station wagon," Beck says dryly.

"He's hot," Sara butts in, lifting her iced tea. "And he wears waistcoats for fun."

"The dude wears three-piece suits?" Beck asks. "Also, don't call them waistcoats, Sara. You also sound like my grandpa."

Sara frowns.

"Yes, and they're tailored. No adjustable strap in the back," I add.

"So, what's the problem?" Beck presses.

"I'm focused on Preston."

Beck looks at Sara. "Is she hearing me? What's the problem with Javier?"

"He's the concierge at the hotel I stay at for work."

Sara goes still, her expression shifting.

"Hold on. Is the problem that he's a concierge?"

"Wait, you're discounting him because of his job title?" Beck asks.

Prickling tension creeps across my shoulders, every muscle on edge. It's not his job title—it's his schedule, his responsibility for Angelina and Dominic, the way I picture myself with someone else entirely. Someone like Preston.

Sara sets her tea down with deliberate care.

"Do you judge my husband because he drives a garbage truck?"

Her voice is quiet, controlled—which is somehow worse than yelling. The tilt of her head tells me everything I need to know. I can't escape this conversation unscathed.

"No, that's not what I'm saying. I just want someone who understands my world."

Sara sits back, crossing her arms and legs, every line of her body sharpened with fury.

Great.

"I get that," Beck affirms, popping a piece of coffee cake in her mouth.

Sara's mouth twists, one eyebrow arched, like she's loading the perfect comeback. I brace for impact.

"You should stop judging people by their occupation, and judge them by their character instead. Maybe then you'll actually find someone."

My head snaps back from the blow. I don't know what set her off today or why I'm the unlucky target.

"Shots fired, Sara. Damn." Beck leans back, rubbing her forehead. "Let's get back on track. I get what Bri's saying. Remember when I dated that software consultant? She didn't know anything about basketball and I didn't understand her drama with some database called Oracle."

Beck's gaze darts between us. Sara crosses her arms, jaw set. I hold her stare, refusing to back down first.

"Let's table the concierge. Who's the next victim—I mean *date?*" Beck's elbows hit the table, breaking our stare. I shake off the tension.

"I have a date with Preston in San Diego next Friday."

"The marina guy?"

I nod.

"How many more after that?"

"One."

"Awesome! You're almost done."

"Yeah—and she's learned nothing from it," Sara bites out.

"Oh, I've learned something. I've learned not to take stupid challenges from my best friend because I may end up murdered by the Tinder Swindler."

Sara straightens in her chair, voice tight. "That wasn't my fault."

"This whole dating challenge was your idea. Here's what I've also learned—my married best friend thinks she knows better than I do about something she's never experienced."

Beck huffs. "You two make me wonder why I date women."

Sara's face goes slack, recognition washing over her features.

"Oh, I see. We're not even talking about dating anymore."

Wait, what? My mind scrambles to catch up, replaying what I said. And then it clicks.

How did this conversation take such a hard turn? Ten minutes ago, we were laughing about Beck's coffee cake addiction, and now I'm sitting here having thrown my deepest wounds at Sara like grenades. I hate fighting with her. Sara's been my anchor through everything—the losses, the endless work trips, the nights when I couldn't stop crying. And here I am, acting like she's the enemy because she has what I've always wanted.

Maybe I am judging everyone. It's easier to reject them

first, safer to find reasons why they won't work than to watch them leave when they find out what I can't give them.

The dating challenge was supposed to help me find my light again, but all it's done is prove that Sara doesn't understand what it's like to be me. I let that anger sit for a moment, righteous and sharp. But that's not fair either, is it? She's helping the only way she knows how, and I just punished her for it.

My phone quacks and Beck stares at my purse. Impeccable timing.

"Sorry, it's Chris from work. He leaves Wednesday for vacation and won't stop bugging me with his to-do list."

"Chris is actually taking a vacation?" Sara says, emerging from her angry shell.

"Alaska. He's going on some fishing trip with his college buddies. He'll be gone for a week and he's freaking out. I've gotten seven texts today, and I guarantee I have double that in my inbox."

Chris has been prepping me for this Alaska trip for months, planning meetings around it since January. He's technically only gone five business days, but he acts like he's taking a month off.

"Is Chris hot?" Beck interjects.

"Chris is the kind of specimen that should be studied by science. Ridiculously attractive. And we get along well. But he's not for me." I drain the remainder of my coffee.

"So, Preston next Friday," Beck says, breaking the quiet. "Date eleven."

I nod, but for the first time since this whole challenge started, I'm not sure what I'm hoping for.

Chapter 33

San Antonio

Pulling open The Elysian's heavy door feels different today. Chris is on the east coast with another client, and I haven't seen Javier since our elevator kiss four days ago. What if he regrets it? The last thing I need is to feel awkward here.

"Welcome back, Miss Whitmore," Grace says at check-in. "I see we didn't make it to La Panadería in time."

"No, so you know where I'll be tomorrow morning."

Grace laughs as Tobias joins her behind the desk.

"That man must get around," Tobias announces, fishing for someone to take the bait.

I bite. "Who?"

"Javier. Women flock to him like he's giving away free cocktails. He just walked another one back to his office." He shakes his head. "I bet Dotty needs industrial-strength disinfectant for that desk."

My stomach tightens. Why should I care if Javier entertains women? We kissed . . . once. It means nothing. I'm focused on building something with Preston.

"Tobias Brown! Stop making assumptions about Mr. De La Vera. Most are salespeople trying to sell him something."

Tobias grins at his private joke.

"Oh, they're selling something." He winks at me.

"Don't ruin an employee's reputation because you're jealous, Tobias." Grace's tone could cut glass.

"I'm one hundred percent jealous," Tobias says with a dramatic sigh. "But come on, that man will never settle. He treats relationships like seasonal allergies—tolerable in small doses. Probably breaks out in hives if a woman asks what he's doing next weekend."

Grace hands me my keycard to Room 1010, and I can't help but ask, "Why do you think that?" My thumb traces the keycard's edge while I wait for his answer.

Tobias leans on the counter, arms folded, all casual menace.

"He's never seen with the same woman twice. He takes them out—wine, dinner, laughter—and then? Gone."

Grace rolls her eyes. "Maybe he's just private."

Tobias lifts a brow. "Oh, please. He's committed to one thing and one thing only." He nods toward the lobby. "This hotel. Anyone else? Always second fiddle. He doesn't play duets."

Grace looks at him like he's live-streaming government secrets to a TikTok audience, eyes wide and afraid of the aftermath.

His words sink in, but so do the memories—the late nights he waited for me, the easy conversations, the unexpected closeness, the kiss in the elevator.

"Maybe he's really good at hiding it," I say, now fidgeting with my keycard.

"I see everything." Tobias purses his lips and nods before pushing off the counter to assist a guest.

I sit in my room thinking about what Tobias said. Is Javier

really a player? Does he reject commitment? Although I don't like to feel like I'm *one of many*, it might also work out well for our current situation. If he's not seen with women more than once, then maybe that kiss was just a one-time thing and we'll go back to normal.

My phone dings.

> Marina Guy: Hey Brianna- hope you had a safe flight into San An. Looking forward to our dinner on Friday. Bring a light jacket - we'll be sitting outside and it gets breezy by the water. I hope you have a good work week, talk to you soon.

> Me: Hey Preston, trip was uneventful, thanks for asking! Can't wait for our dinner on Friday 😊

A knock at the door interrupts my thoughts. If this is Diane ready to scold me for gossiping with Tobias, I'll lose it.

I swing the door open, bracing to confront her lanky frame in a black dress and Mary Janes. Instead it's sleek loafers, gray trousers with a matching vest, and a white shirt so crisp it could crack. The look whispers confidence wrapped in classic lines.

"Welcome back. How was your trip in?"

Javier's stare lasers right through me, as usual. He leans against the doorframe, arms crossed over his chest.

"Good. Chris is back east, so I'm holding down the fort. How did you know I was here? Tobias tell you?"

"No, I checked the system. Once the front desk checks someone in, it updates the room status. Since you always stay in 1010, I knew it was you."

He was looking to see when I checked in?

I rock back on my heel. "Do you want to come in?"

I step aside, back pressed against the door, hoping he doesn't think I'm propositioning him.

"Actually, I was hoping you'd come to dinner... with me."

His boyish grin melts my insides. Eyebrows raised slightly, as if afraid of my answer. Is he worried about the same things? About me regretting the elevator kiss? *Do I regret it?*

"I'd love to but I have some work I need to do for a client."

Lies.

"We won't go far. There's an Italian place across the street. Quick and easy." I study his face, cataloging every detail. A freckle above his left eyebrow, another beside his nose, one at his jawline.

"Come on, it'll be light and fun."

He's hacked right through my defenses with those two words, found the exact algorithm to make me say yes. And it's a guy who's paying for dinner, a qualification that counts as date number eleven. One to go and I'm done with this nonsense.

My traitorous smile gives me away before I can stop it. "Okay."

Tobias isn't in the lobby when we walk out. I wonder what he'd think—would he feel bad about his warning or judge me for becoming one of those women? Am I one of those women?

I'm anxious about this dinner. What if Javier gives me the "it's not you, it's me" speech because he regrets the elevator kiss? I've spent years building walls against rejection, only to walk straight into it with a hotel concierge during what was never even a real date.

Dinner is easier than I expected. Javier asks about my projects, and I tell him about the upcoming finalist meeting for Chremsoft. He seems to know a lot about them, and offers helpful intel about their community initiatives that I can share with Chris.

He spends most of the meal talking about his niece and nephew, Angelina and Dominic, who'll be visiting the hotel later this week. The way his face lights up when he mentions them makes my chest tighten—not in a bad way, exactly. It's sweet watching him get so animated, describing Dominic's obsession with the elevator buttons and Angelina's elaborate tea parties in the lobby. I could listen to him all night.

But there's something else there too. A hollow ache that settles somewhere behind my ribs. He says he wants kids someday, and I have to look down at my pasta, twirling my fork just to have something to focus on.

Maybe he just likes the *idea* of them—weekends with Angelina and Dominic where they entertain themselves around the hotel then go home isn't exactly real parenting. That's what I tell myself anyway.

Not once does he mention the elevator scene, or establish his bachelor lifestyle or lack of commitment.

"Let me ask you something," he says as we step in the front door of the hotel lobby.

Oh, no. Here it comes. Why couldn't he have done this at the restaurant, away from everyone we know?

"What do you think of our hotel scent?"

"Hotel scent?"

"Yeah, we chose this custom scent four years ago, but I'm wondering if it's outdated."

I bite the inside of my cheek to stop the giggle threatening to escape—he's serious about this.

"Outdated?"

But then again, I consider cucumber melon and sun-ripened raspberry and it all makes sense.

Javier looks toward the breakfast area as a man with an expensive suit and confident stride approaches.

"Javi, Jack is waiting on your approvals. It needs to be in tonight." The man doesn't even look my way.

"Oh, shoot." Javier presses his hand to his forehead. "Brianna, I'm sorry—I need to handle this."

"Of course. Have a good night, Javier." I turn toward the elevator, straining to hear their conversation, but catch nothing.

I decide not to overthink the Javier situation. He didn't mention our elevator shenanigans, as if they never happened. Tonight felt more like friends—maybe that's my answer. Things are back to normal.

My phone quacks as I enter my room. I was hoping to hear from Sara. Our communication has been sparse since that coffee date with Beck.

> Chris: Where you at? I've sent you several IM's. You logging on tonight? Otherwise I'll just text everything here.

> Me: I was having wild, passionate sex but I'll stop and log in to work.

> Chris: No you aren't.

I'm insulted by how easily he calls my bluff.

My phone rings.

"Is it too far-fetched that I could be having sex?" I bark into the phone, pulling my laptop from its bag.

"Yes. Do you have the Chremsoft data ready?"

"Of course. It's in the slide deck on the shared drive. Did you even look?"

"No. And you're set with Mercury? Their IT guy returns from his extended leave next week."

"Yes, we're good. Don't worry, Chris. I've got everything covered. You're only gone a week."

"I know, but Mercury isn't fully onboard, and Chremsoft could be my biggest sale in two years. Plus, my partnership with them might lead to the Texas hospital system."

"I'll take care of your babies while you're gone, Chris. Focus on your trip. Did you pack yet?"

"No."

"Well, why don't you grab your little suitcase and pack some undies and warm socks, and your hair gel."

Chris scoffs. "Whatever. Text me with any questions or concerns. Anything. You hear me, Brianna?"

"Yes, sir. Now stop bothering me—my male companion will be here soon for wild, passionate romp in the sheets."

"Gross. Okay, have a good week. I'll be in touch."

"We can guarantee that."

I hang up the phone, annoyed. I really don't need my hand held through any of this. One slip-up and I'm treated like an intern. Chris acts like he's the only one capable of closing deals, like I haven't been managing implementations for three years. He's supposed to be on vacation, but knowing him, he'll find ways to helicopter parent from three time zones away.

I have one more week managing the Mercury team before Gus returns. I'll be happy to hand that role back—the team's great and easy to work with, but managing them and the integration adds hours to my day. I'd spent several hours working from a coffee shop a few minutes from the hotel, and now it's nearly 5:30 p.m.

Chris is on a plane to Alaska, probably half-drunk by now. No laptop doesn't mean no contact—he has his tablet, same access to everything.

As I open the door to my room, I spot a small cream-colored note propped on my bed, embossed with the Elysian logo. I can't get across the room fast enough.

> Brianna-
> Please come to my office when you get in. I have a question for you.
> J-

Curiosity propels me to Javier's office, wondering what this question is and why it required a note on my bed. I knock on Javier's office door and hear a faint, "Come in."

I peek inside.

"Brianna." Excitement in his voice puts me at ease.

I never really looked around his office before. The last time, I was too distracted by Griffin's parents. It's all rich chocolate browns and buttery leather, like stepping into an expensive whiskey bar. Soft lighting makes everything feel intimate and expensive.

"How was your day?" He stands from his high-backed leather chair and walks to the front of his desk.

"Good. Gus returns next week, so I can hand the reins back to him. We're nearly done with the software integration—should be running in two weeks."

"Gus is the IT guy?"

I nod, impressed he remembers.

"And Chremsoft? I hope I gave you good intel on them.

They're hosting a charity event next month for the children's hospital."

Javier leans back against his desk, arms and legs crossed in that effortless way that makes his button-down stretch in all the right places—commanding and completely unfair.

"Great intel. I shared it with Chris and he's really excited about Chremsoft's potential. It would be a monumental sale for him. We both appreciate you."

Silence fills the space between us as we stare at each other, smiling. Everything feels different with Javier now. The professional lines we maintained for months blurred the moment he kissed me in that elevator. Now I don't know which version of myself to be. Professional Brianna who talks about project timelines? Or the one who let him pin me against the wall?

I shift my weight from foot to foot, suddenly hyperaware of where my hands are.

"So . . . I got your note. You had a question for me?"

"Oh, yes. I'm checking out a new installation called Luminary Dreams at the museum—illusions with lights, mirrors, and angles. They're hoping we'll feature it in our guest recommendations."

He pauses, his confident posture faltering slightly. "I wanted to know if you'd like to go with me. Tonight."

My brain stutters. Wait, is he asking me out again? He probably just wants a guest's perspective on it, right? He's the concierge. This is research. But illusions and glass *do* sound cool. It's practically educational.

"I'd love to go." I lean against the doorframe. "So what's the story with this exhibit?"

Javier's eyes light up. "The art museum's been struggling with attendance the past couple of years. They brought in an installation artist who works with glass and mirrors to create these optical illusions. It should be fun."

"Great! What time should I be ready?"

"Six-thirty should give us plenty of time."

"Perfect. I'll go change."

I rush to my room to change. Since we're going to the museum at night, I pick the dress I brought for Friday's date with Preston—sapphire blue, with a surplice neckline and a dark blue satin ribbon at the waist.

Twenty minutes later, I return downstairs and knock on Javier's office door.

"You look stunning," Javier says, closing his office door. He studies me for a long moment, his professional composure slipping as his gaze follows the lines of the dress before he catches himself.

"And you look handsome as always." The words escape before I can stop them.

"As always, huh?" He steps toward me.

Why did I say that?

"You're all right," I correct, scrunching my face. Javier laughs, his stride confident and easy as we leave his office and I follow him down the hall.

"We're taking the hotel car, if that's okay?" He motions toward the hall with the elevators. "I just need to grab the keys from the printer room."

I didn't even know this room existed, just past the elevators on the right. I peek in, leaning against the doorframe. Large floor printer, L-shaped counter lined with packing supplies, three suitcases stacked in the corner.

"We can use this side door." He pockets the keys and heads toward the hallway's end.

We exit to a small parking lot behind the hotel, where the hidden door to the laundry room is. Heat pools low in my belly, remembering our hide-and-seek session between the linen carts last week.

Javier opens the passenger door of a black Cadillac SUV, and waits for me to step in before gently closing my door.

"I haven't seen Angelina or Dominic recently. Does that mean your sister gets to be home for a while?" I ask as we merge onto the highway.

He shakes his head. "They'll be here tomorrow." He's quiet for a moment, eyes on the road. "My sister's hell-bent on proving we're not where we came from. Like, if she makes enough money, works hard enough, no one will remember we grew up eating rice and beans for every meal because that's all we could afford." His jaw tightens. "I get it. I do. But Angelina asked me last month if her mom was ever coming to her piano recital. She's seven. She shouldn't have to ask that."

My hands clench in my lap. Some people don't realize how lucky they are. Sara complains about being home with Grady all day—the mess, the noise, never getting a moment to herself. I pretend I understand.

"That's hard," I finally say. "For all of you."

He's quiet for a beat. "She doesn't see it that way. To her, I'm the one wasting my life."

"What do you mean?"

"She called today. Asked when I'm going to stop playing house at the hotel and actually settle down." He laughs, but there's an edge to it. "Apparently, Angelina told her I'd make a good dad."

I glance at him. "I agree with Angelina." My voice softens. "You would."

"I don't know. Maybe?" He drums his fingers on the steering wheel. "My family is very traditional. Get a reliable job, then marriage, then kids. Like, everyone's life is supposed to follow the same script."

Something tightens in my chest. "Not everyone's does."

"No." He glances at me. "Is this how you envisioned your life when you were younger?"

The city buildings blur past the window. "I thought. . ." I inhale a sharp breath. "I thought it'd be different."

Dirtbag's face flashes through my mind. All those conversations about *our future*, about what we'd build together. I blink it away.

"Career-wise, I'm exactly where I want to be. But everything else?" I shrug, keeping my voice light. "I guess I thought there'd be more."

"Like what?"

His question catches me off guard. I can't tell him the truth, that I thought my Saturdays would be spent on soccer field sidelines, that I'd be the team mom with snack schedules and carpool spreadsheets.

"I don't know. Just . . . more." I turn it back on him before he can press further. "Do you want kids?"

He's quiet long enough that I think he won't answer. Then, "I want them. I think." He glances at me. "My sister says I use the hotel as an excuse. That I hide behind work so I don't have to commit to anything real."

"Is she right?"

"No? Maybe?" He chuckles as we pull into the museum parking lot. "I love what I do. But people see the hotel, the connections, the life . . . and they make assumptions about who I am." His jaw tightens. "Turns out I'm better at reading hotel guests than I am at reading relationships."

I study Javier's profile as he stares out the window, his fingers twisting together in his lap.

I unbuckle my seat belt and reach for the door handle. "Come on," I say, forcing brightness into my voice. "Let's go see some illusions."

Chapter 34

San Antonio

The museum building—all historical architecture meets contemporary glass and steel—looks like a modern-day castle. Inside, Javier talks to the desk clerk while I wander toward a sculpture that catches my eye.

My stomach drops. Its sharp angles and polished metal remind me of the pieces at Bryant Park. The ones Griffin stood beside, spinning lies about his art knowledge on our first date.

I turn away before the memory can settle.

"Ready?" Javier's voice pulls me back to the present. I follow him down a bright hallway where ceiling lights bounce off white walls. Signs for the Luminary Dreams exhibit loom ahead.

"Do you like art?" Javier asks as he opens the exhibit door.

I stare at him. Harmless question for most people. For me, it's loaded.

"Sure," I say, forcing a smile.

The moment we step through the door, darkness swallows us whole. My hand shoots out instinctively and finds Javier's arm. He covers my hand with his and guides me forward through the black, toward a faint purple glow ahead.

An employee gestures toward a dark hallway. "Please enter through the tunnel of lights. Hang on to the railing if you get dizzy."

We follow the corridor, and with each step, color bleeds into the darkness—vibrant pinks, electric blues, deep purples. Then we step through, and the world explodes into light. The tunnel stretches before us, ribs of neon arching overhead in waves. The lights pulse and shift, creating the illusion of movement—like we're being pulled forward through a liquid vortex.

I step forward and stumble, bumping into Javier's back.

"Sorry. I'm off balance," I say as he grabs my arm to steady me.

"I got you," he says. I grip the railing and hurry across the walkway, my stomach churning.

The next room blazes with light—a kaleidoscope of endless corridors. Walls, ceilings, and floors covered in squares of white, yellow, and green. Two hallways stretch ahead—one real, one illusion.

"Exploration of perception and reality," he says. "The spatial illusion challenges your sense of space, depth, and orientation. It invites you to question: What do we trust—what we see versus what we know?"

Based on the last several weeks, I'm going to fail this test.

I take a breath, trusting what I know, and walk forward.

Javier turns when he hears my head hit the wall.

And once again, I fall for the wrong one.

"Are you okay?" He turns me around and examines my face. My dumb ass face.

"I'm not great with spatial illusions." I rub my forehead.

I let him lead us through the real hallway this time. We move along the walls, searching for the hidden exit among the dark squares. My hand disappears into empty space on the third try.

"I found it!" Relief bubbles in my voice.

Javier follows as I step through the opening and into the next room, which is made entirely of mirrors. Panels of glass in varying sizes and angles line the walls and ceiling, casting back a thousand versions of me and Javier as we step into the center.

Javier drifts off to explore, leaving me alone with a thousand versions of myself.

Does my ass really look like that? I twist at my waist to get a better look.

"Brianna, this way!" Javier calls.

I turn toward his voice, but the mirrors throw it everywhere —bouncing it back from every direction. Arms outstretched like a zombie, I inch forward, wary of slamming face-first into my own reflection. Again.

I don't know how, but I've entered a different part of the mirrored room. Now it's just him. No trace of me, no corners, no exit signs. Only Javier, multiplied and inescapable. As if the room can read my mind.

He waves, and dozens of mirror clones wave back.

"Where are you?" I squint to make sense of the endless reflections.

"Over here," Javier's voice calls out, calm and steady.

I reach out, fingers brushing empty space. "Javier, where the hell are you?"

"Over here," he says again. Then he turns around, and all I can see are the broad, strong lines of his back reflected a dozen times over in the mirrors. There's something magnetic about the way his shoulders stretch beneath that dress shirt, a quiet promise of strength. My pulse quickens as I imagine what it would be like to reach out, to touch. But the maze of reflections keeps him just out of reach, teasing me.

I shuffle over to another area and swat at air. "You're enjoying this, aren't you?"

"Maybe," he responds, turning to face the mirrors again.

I decide to walk to the right. Javier spins in place, disorienting me as I step forward.

Confident, I take one last step and smack into something solid.

Strong arms wrap around my waist, steadying me. I rub my forehead, aware of every place our bodies touch.

Javier chuckles, lips brushing my ear. "Smooth move."

My breath catches as his hands glide across the dress fabric. I can barely find my voice. "I'm so sorry."

Javier lets out a soft laugh, his nose close to mine. "You okay?" His arms stay locked at my sides. The closeness feels both familiar and unsettling.

"You'll need to provide some heavy disclaimers if you're going to recommend this to guests." My voice comes out breathier than intended.

He releases me and I step back—not because I want to, but because I think I should.

"Only a couple more rooms," he says.

I sigh. "I might not make it out alive."

"I've got you." He grabs my hand, pulling me forward.

We enter the next room—more mirrors, but now with glowing purple columns creating maze-like walkways. Another sigh escapes me.

"Stay close." He squeezes my hand.

He moves to the right, pulling me with him down a narrow walkway. The room pulses with neon light—purple columns rising like pillars in an electric cathedral, the floor crisscrossed with teal and violet lines.

Every step feels suspended, like we've slipped into another reality where it's just him and me, multiplied infinitely.

He turns to me, and I catch his reflection first—just a flicker in the mirrors ahead. Then another. And another. All of them moving in sync, like a slow, glowing dance.

The air shifts between us. In every reflection, I see the same thing—the way he's looking at me, like I'm something precious he's afraid to break.

"Brianna." My name sounds different in his voice, rougher.

I can't look away from his eyes. The purple light catches the gold flecks I never noticed before.

He takes a half-step closer. The space between us shrinks to nothing but electricity and anticipation.

Javier leans in, his intent mirrored and magnified.

The scent of cool water clings to the space between us, clean and crisp, pulling me closer. He hovers, giving me the chance to step away.

I don't. Maybe I should, but I don't want to.

Then his lips meet mine.

Even though I saw it coming—from five different reflections of him—I still lose my breath.

The kiss is soft, certain, a little greedy. As though he's been waiting for the perfect moment. My lips remember, moving instinctively, answering with hunger. His arms snake up my sides, around my back, pulling me closer. My body melts into his—willing, wanting.

My eyes flutter open, catching reflections in the surrounding mirrors. In one, his hand slides to my shoulder blades. In another, his other hand settles at the small of my back. Heat flashes through me as his fingers trail down my body. Then he gently pushes me backward.

My spine meets cool glass and I let out a soft gasp, his mouth still on mine, our kiss deepening as he presses into me—every point of contact sparking, igniting. My hands explore his shoulders, fingertips tracing solid muscle beneath his shirt.

Voices echo in the distance—laughter, footsteps. Javier breaks our kiss, but doesn't move. His forehead rests against mine, our breaths mingling, hearts racing.

He pulls back slowly, eyes locked on mine, seeing straight through me, like he knows exactly what this means. Around us, the evidence lingers, reflected from every angle. Our closeness. Our kiss. The way I didn't hesitate. The way I wanted it.

He takes my hand again, warm and sure, and I follow without a word as we step out of the mirrored room—changed.

The drive back to The Elysian is quiet, but not uncomfortable. Javier's hand rests on the console between us, close enough that our fingers brush at stoplights. We don't mention what happened in the mirror room, but it lingers in the air between us.

He parks, and we walk around the side of the hotel. Across the street, I peek into La Panadería's kitchen, where the bakers are prepping their stations for overnight baking.

"I need to drop off the keys," he says, and I follow him into the printer room.

He hangs the keys on their hook, then turns to face me.

"Thank you for tonight," I say, softly.

He steps closer, the small space between us shrinking. "Thank you for coming with me."

His hand lifts to my face, thumb brushing my cheek. Then he kisses me, slow and deliberate, as if we have all the time in the world. My back presses against the wall as his other hand slides to my waist. Heat spreads through my chest, catching me off guard. I'm not supposed to feel like this—not with him. Still, my fingers curl into his collar anyway, and I hate that I don't actually hate it.

When he pulls away, I'm left with the faintest brush of his lips on mine.

"Goodnight, Brianna," he whispers.

"Goodnight," I reply.

I slip out and make my way to the elevator, my steps wobbly, warmth pooling through me. By the tenth floor, I feel weightless, as if gravity forgot I exist.

I close the door to Room 1010 and lean against it, heart still racing. He kissed me like I was something worth holding on to.

I sink into the desk chair, slipping off my shoes. His kiss lingers on my lips, and I can still feel the memory of his touch across my skin.

What am I doing? Preston's taking me to dinner on Friday. I should be thinking about him, not replaying the way Javier's hands felt on my waist.

But I can't stop thinking about it. About him. About the way he looked at me in those mirrors, like I was the only real thing in a room full of illusions.

A knock rattles my door.

Chapter 35

San Antonio

Fear drips through me. If Diane is on the other side of this door, ready to scold me for distracting Javier, I will lose it.

I tiptoe to the door like it might bite and press my eye to the peephole. Brown eyes. Dark waves of hair.

"Fancy seeing you here," I say as I open the door, immediately regretting saying something so stupid.

"Can I come in?" Javier's eyes are hopeful.

I open the door wider and he steps inside.

"Thanks again for such a fun night," I say. He takes in the room before his gaze returns to me.

"I had fun, too. So much that I want to see you one more time." He smiles, glancing down before meeting my eyes again.

"Oh?" I ask, feigning shock. He steps toward me, tunnels a hand through my hair, and cradles the back of my head. His gaze drops to my mouth. Anticipation floods my veins. I know we won't stop at a kiss this time.

His lips find mine and steal my breath. His hand finds my waist and trails up my side, leaving fire in its wake. I circle his neck with my arms, fingers threading through his perfectly cut hair. My lips part and he slips his tongue inside, his hand gripping at my dress just beneath my bra.

He pulls me closer, and every inch of space disappears between us. Heat builds low in my stomach, spreading outward as his lips find my jawline. Each kiss is gentle, caring.

His breath warms my skin as he moves lower, finding the sensitive spot just below my ear. When he lingers there, my knees nearly buckle. A soft sound escapes me.

"Brianna," he whispers against my neck, and my name has never sounded so sweet. I tilt my head back, his mouth becoming more insistent as his hand slides down the back of my dress, palming the curve of my ass.

The warmth of his breath travels down my neckline. He pauses, looking up at me with those dark eyes, seeking permission. I lean in and his mouth plunges along the fabric's edge, silk parting to reveal skin along the V-neck's tempting path. My hands slide up his shoulders, feeling the muscle beneath my fingers.

I take a breath and guide him backward. One step. Then another. Until the back of his legs hit the bed.

"Brianna," he says, hovering over my lips. The air between us crackles with anticipation.

I can see the want in his eyes, but also something else: patience. Like he'll wait if I need him to. The moment stretches between us, heavy with possibility. Once we cross this line, there's no going back to whatever we were before. I think about all the reasons I should stop this. Then I think about all the reasons I don't want to.

I crush my mouth against his, my hands working quickly to unbuckle his belt before reaching for the zipper. The sound of metal separating as I pull makes my toes curl.

He kisses me so deeply I disappear into him, into this fire between us.

He spins us around, his thumb pressing into my hip bone. Heat shoots up my spine. His other hand drags my dress sleeve down my shoulder, his mouth following with hungry kisses.

"Tell me to stop," he begs before his teeth graze my earlobe. I shake my head and yank at his shirt, desperate to feel his skin.

His hand drags up my spine, gripping my hair and drawing my head back in a way that makes me feel claimed. His teeth rake down my neck and I let out a soft moan.

"This dress needs to go," he says as he lifts the fabric's edge along my neckline, his knuckles grazing my skin, sending chills up my spine. He pushes the fabric down my other shoulder. I feel air rush against my legs as my dress pools at my feet.

His eyes drink me in. "You are stunning." His voice drops low. "I want to know every inch of you."

He traces my lips with his before covering them completely. His breathing changes and he kisses me harder, claiming every part of my mouth. Desire floods through me and I feel how hard he is.

"I love this black lace bra"—he kisses my collarbone—"But it's in my way."

Within seconds, it joins my dress on the floor.

Javier places his hands on the center of my chest and pushes gently. I fall back onto the bed with a soft bounce, breathless with laughter as he stares down at me.

"Incredible," he whispers, shaking his head.

He prowls on top of me, muscles shifting under his skin, and my breath catches.

His tongue traces a path up my stomach. His gaze lifts to mine as his mouth closes over the peak of my breast. My body reacts on its own, arching into his touch. The caress of his mouth and the strokes of his tongue steal every logical thought.

Sliding his hand between our bodies, fingertips trail up the inside of my thigh. Those fingers move between my legs, delicately dancing over the thin material of my panties.

"Geezus . . . " I gasp, his light touch tormenting.

The sides of his lips curve up.

I rock my hips against his hand for more.

Javier takes my mouth again, desperate and consuming, his tongue sliding against mine as his fingers stroke me through the fabric.

Then he's sliding off the edge of the bed, his hands gripping my panties, pulling them off.

A smile grows on his face as he wraps his arms around each ankle, pulling my body across the soft duvet to the edge of the bed. Dropping to his knees, he moves my legs over his shoulders.

Before I can get a word in, his mouth is between my thighs. I pull in a sharp breath, bracing myself on my elbows, watching in pure amazement. He kisses my inner thigh before bringing the flat of his tongue up firmly between my folds.

"Holy shit, Javier." I gasp as sensations flood through me, too many to process.

His smile presses into my skin.

He presses the V of his fingers over my center and I throw my head back at the sheer pleasure of his tongue, licking and swirling around my core. He flicks his tongue over that sensitive bud, and I moan.

Pleasure, hot and insistent, spirals from my stomach and I'm lost in the sensation, my hips rising and falling as I chase the sensation with every stab of his tongue.

"Oh, fuck." I throw my head back at the pleasure.

"I love hearing you curse. Especially when it's because of me." He grins and slides his middle finger deep as he settles back between my thighs like he has nowhere else to be.

My mouth falls open in a silent moan. Long gone is the professional concierge, and I couldn't be happier.

Every touch of his mouth ignites my skin like flame to kindling. My thighs tremble as he takes up a rhythm against my clit and drives two fingers inside me. I'm nothing but ragged breaths and raw hunger as he lingers on my sensitive spot, taking his time.

I breathe his name as the pleasure builds.

Javier works his fingers in and out, his tongue flicking its way up to my swollen bud before pausing. I wait. I wait for what I need to send me over the edge.

"Please, Javier . . . " My voice cracking with need. A low growl vibrates on my skin just before he wiggles his tongue roughly. It's my undoing. I cry out as the coil of tension releases with each wave of my orgasm.

Javier finds my mouth with his own, winding our tongues together while I feverishly unbutton his dress shirt.

"You are so beautiful, Brianna." He tugs his shirt sleeve over his watch.

"I finally get a look at what lies beneath those vests of yours," I say, taking in his body on top of me. I pictured lean lines and defined abs, but reality is better. His body has substance—broad shoulders, a strong chest, the kind of frame that looks like it belongs to him rather than something built from vanity.

"And how long have you been wondering what's under my vest?" he asks playfully.

The truth is, I'm not sure.

"I'm not telling." I trace the lines of his back, feeling the dip between his shoulder blades. I glance down at his pants. "Those need to come off . . . now."

He laughs as I shove his pants and boxer briefs past his

hips, freeing his thick shaft. It's hot and hard in my hand, and his quiet groan makes me feel powerful.

Javier's caught off-guard when I roll us over. Rising to my knees, I crawl on top of him, straddling his lap. He reaches behind me, his hands gliding down my back and cupping my ass. I lift forward, the head of his shaft rubbing against my entrance. His eyes flare, and then he kisses me like I'm the air he's been missing.

I feel him reach across the bed for something—his wallet from his pants. He pulls out a condom and rips the foil. The hunger I see in every line of his face is unmistakable.

He guides me down onto him, his eyes rolling back, jaw falling open in a moan.

"Fuck, Brianna."

The pressure, the stretch, the fit of him is beyond words. I roll my hips, pressing my hands to his chest and finding my rhythm. My head tilts back, the friction pushing me to the edge of mindless bliss. His knuckles find the juncture of my thighs, brushing against my bundle of nerves on each descent, and I know I won't last much longer.

"You had to put your knuckles there." I breathe through the words.

"Oh, just wait." Without elaborating, his thumb presses tight against my clit finding a rhythm that pushes me to the limit of pleasure—and then tips me into a freefall. Pleasure takes me in waves, rolling through me again and again, clenching around his cock.

"Oh, shit, Bri."

Javier clutches the nape of my neck and kisses me long and hard, stealing every breath, every thought.

His hands glide down my backside, yanking me up and back. And then we tumble sideways until he's on top of me.

Javier's gaze captures mine as he hovers above me, bracing his weight.

"Nice move," I say and our mouths collide in a ravenous kiss.

"I'm just getting warmed up." Javier reaches between us, rubbing his cock up and down my entrance. It's too much and not nearly enough.

I let out a small, torturous cry and he grins, knowing he has me right where he wants me.

He pushes inside that first inch of me, and I gasp. Hard, deep, and slow, he sets a rhythm that has me arching for every thrust.

Our mouths collide once more, the kiss hot and hard and completely out of control.

Pleasure pulses through my body like rocket fuel, and I groan against his mouth. A cue, permission to go harder, faster, and he does, pressing our moaning mouths together.

He pushes my knee up toward my chest, taking me even deeper. I rock my hips to meet his, sweat beading on our skin. He adjusts the angle so he hits my clit with every thrust, and I surrender completely, melting into him.

"Holy shit," I say as sensation floods through me like a dam ready to break.

He drives toward his own release, groaning into the side of my neck as his core contracts.

For a moment, neither of us moves. His breath is hot against my throat, my fingers still clutching his back. My heart pounds so hard I'm sure he can feel it.

He lifts his head, eyes finding mine. There's something vulnerable in his expression as if he's seeing me for the first time, or maybe letting me see him. He brushes a strand of hair from my face, his touch gentle despite everything that just happened.

"You okay?" His voice is soft, almost hesitant.

I nod against his skin. More than okay. Which is terrifying in its own way.

He presses a soft kiss to my forehead, then rolls to the side, pulling me with him, his fingers tracing lazy patterns along my shoulder blade. Our breathing has finally evened out, but neither of us moves.

I tilt my head to look at him. His eyes are already on me, dark and unguarded in the dim light filtering in through the curtains. There's something in his expression I can't quite name. Something heavy that doesn't match the softness of his touch.

He brushes a strand of hair from my face, his thumb lingering against my cheek.

"Brianna..."

But he doesn't finish. Maybe he doesn't need to. Maybe I already know what he's not saying because I feel it too—this shift between us, this realization that we've crossed into territory neither of us planned for.

I press a kiss to his chest, just over his heart. "Get some sleep."

He pulls me closer, and I let myself sink into the warmth of him. His breathing gradually slows, deepens. Mine follows.

For once, I don't overthink. I just let myself be here, in this moment, wrapped in something that feels dangerously close to right.

Later, the click of the door wakes me. Javier slips out as I lift my head to check the clock. Four a.m.

Chapter 36

San Antonio

My phone buzzes against the nightstand, pulling me from sleep. Not only is my prescription ready at CVS, but there's a barrage of texts, voice memos, and emails from Chris—all sent late last night. Right now, he's the least of my worries.

Did I really sleep with the concierge last night? It must have been a dream, because it was the best sex I've had in years, way better than Scuba Steve from Hawaii. He worshipped every part of me. Multiple times. Like I was something sacred he's been searching for.

But he didn't stay the night. I guess the concierge can't be seen leaving a guest room with disheveled hair and yesterday's clothes.

Now I'm wondering if he regrets it. Maybe I do, too. I'm supposed to be focused on Preston, the challenge, my job. Javier was never part of the plan.

Last night, I knew crossing that line would change everything between us. But my hormones staged a coup, and logic didn't stand a chance. I don't have any meetings until this afternoon, so I let myself linger in bed longer than I should, scrolling mindlessly through my phone.

Eventually, I force myself up for a shower, letting the hot water wash away the confusion—or at least trying to. I sit by the window with coffee from the in-room maker, watching the city move below. Anything to delay the inevitable.

But I can't hide in this room forever. By the time I'm dressed and heading downstairs, I've almost convinced myself I can act normal around him.

Javier's laugh fills the lobby as I exit the elevator, and my heart drops. He's talking to a couple of guests as I cross the lobby. The first thing I notice is his fresh three-piece suit—off-white dress shirt, dark brown tie, light brown slacks, vest, and jacket. I can't help but remember those shoulders hovering over my naked body last night, and heat shoots through my core. He nods at the couple and they head toward breakfast, papers in hand.

As if he can sense me, he turns, his eyes finding mine with the weight of our shared secrets.

"Hi," he says as I approach, his smirk taking on a whole new meaning for me.

"Hi," I reply, my smile so wide it probably takes up my entire face.

"So, how was your night?" His cheeky grin makes me shake my head as he lifts his eyebrows in anticipation.

"Nothing noteworthy." I fight to keep a straight face.

"Really? Nothing earth-shattering? Mind-blowing?"

I pause, pretending to consider this seriously. "Nope. Pretty forgettable, actually."

"Forgettable?" He steps closer, lowering his voice. "I must be losing my touch."

"Your touch was . . ." I let the words hang there, biting my lip.

His laugh is low and dangerous. "Careful, or I might have to refresh your memory."

"In the middle of the lobby?" I raise an eyebrow, matching his energy.

"I'm very thorough in my customer service."

"Oh, you're thorough, all right." I give him a wink. The playful moment hangs between us, but I can't let my worry go. I lean in, lowering my voice. "I didn't hear you leave."

Lie.

"I left around four," he says, his voice softer. "I had to prepare for a meeting this morning."

My eyes widen. "You didn't go home?"

"No." Javier waves to the couple he helped as they walk past.

"You just have spare outfits lying around?" The words come out sharper than I mean them to.

"As a matter of fact, I have my dry cleaning delivered here since they're usually closed by the time I leave work." His hand moves to his hip, but there's amusement in his eyes as he explains away my accusation.

"Oh, well, that makes sense," I say, though I'm not sure I trust my own judgment anymore.

"I was hoping I'd get to see you before you left town. I wanted to—"

"Mr. De La Vera." My body stiffens. I don't need to turn around to recognize that dreaded voice.

"Steve is requesting some information from this morning's meeting. He says it's urgent," Diane says as she glances my way.

Of course, I'm the distraction again.

You keep spoon-feeding her more ammo to hate you, Brianna.

"Thanks, Diane. He has what he needs." Javier nods in assurance, and her mouth purses.

She stands there as if contemplating something else.

I glance at her witchy profile. She looks at me, eyes narrowed, mouth twisting down. Then she leaves.

"She hates me," I mutter.

"Follow me." He nods toward the elevators.

I trail him down the hall, studying his back as if I can see through his clothes—those muscles, the scar under his right shoulder blade that I traced with my finger, the way he whispered my name. My face flushes remembering how he made me gasp.

I follow him into the printer room. He presses the door closed behind me, and before I can turn around, his hands cup my face. His lips crash into mine with desperate hunger. The scent of cool water floods my senses as my fingers dig into his back, pulling him closer. I arch into him, already craving more.

He turns me around and pushes me against the commercial printer. I hear several beeps and a buzzing sound. He pulls me away from the printer and guides me back toward the counter. His hands reach below the curve of my ass and lifts me onto the counter. My legs spread as he steps forward, his hands rubbing up and down my thighs. I regret not wearing a skirt today. I run my fingers through the back of his hair, careful not to mess his perfect wave. He drags his lips down my neck, knowing it destroys me.

I'm swept away by his touch when the door handle jiggles. I lean back, his lips leaving my neck. The spell breaks.

"I locked it," he breathes out, already reclaiming the territory his lips had mapped.

The handle rattles again, but Javier acts as though nothing else exists but us.

I hear two soft voices on the other side of the door.

"Uncle Javier? Let us in!"

His smile grows against my neck, and his head falls to my shoulder.

"They're off from school today. They won't leave until I open that door," he murmurs, his hands trailing down my thighs.

I tilt my head back, giggling. Javier closes his eyes and grimaces, clearly torn between duty and desire. The pounding on the door intensifies.

"Let us in!" a young girl's voice calls.

Javier helps me off the counter, his touch gentle as I straighten my clothes. He reaches for the door while I walk over to the printer, pretending to push the buttons.

"Why was the door locked?" Dominic asks as they tumble in.

"It must have locked by accident," Javier says, his voice instantly warm and patient.

"We're going swimming!" Angelina announces, bouncing on her toes.

"Do you have your towels?"

His tone is so caring, so paternal. I can't help but turn around to witness it.

"Yes!" Dominic responds proudly.

"Angelina, do you need help with your swimmies?"

Javier kneels to her level, checking the inflatable bands on her arms.

"No, they're fine."

"Dominic, do you have your ear plugs?"

The way he remembers every detail about keeping them safe makes my throat tighten. Dominic goes quiet for a moment, his face falling.

"I forgot them in the room. I won't go under the water."

Javier stands, hands on his hips, but his voice stays gentle.

"Dominic, you know the rules. Ear plugs or no swimming."

Watching him with these kids—the way he knows exactly what they need, how naturally he slips into parent mode—makes something beautiful and painful bloom in my chest. He'll make an incredible father someday. The thought hits me like a physical blow, and my eyes burn. I turn back to the printer, blinking hard as I dab at the corners of my eyes.

I pretend to examine the printer settings while straining to hear their conversation, torn between wanting to witness this tender moment and wanting to run before I get too attached to the fantasy.

"I'll be in the pool room in ten minutes, and Dominic, if you don't have your ear plugs in, there's no movies tonight." Angelina giggles. "Same for you, Angelina. I bought you backup swimmies, so you have two pairs here. You better be wearing them."

I turn around to see Angelina beaming at her uncle. The love they have for him warms my heart. It's adorable watching him try to be the authority figure—judging by Angelina's expression, she thinks so, too.

"Bring it in," Javier says, arms wide open. They both jump into his embrace before bolting out the door as he shouts after them, "No running in my hotel!"

"They're so lucky to have you," I say as he turns to me.

"I'm lucky to have *them*. They're such good kids, most of the time."

He laughs, and I can't help but wonder who Javier really is. Is he the forever bachelor that Tobias says he is, married to the hotel? Or is he the man who was made to be a father?

My face falls as realization settles in. Whichever Javier exists, I can't have either. I can't have the forever bachelor, and I can't have the future father.

Whatever I've been feeling is fleeting. I was stupid to fall into his arms repeatedly. I got caught up in the moment.

Maybe I needed the tryst with Javier to open me up—emotionally and, well, physically—to love again. He was the safe adventure.

I have my date with Preston to focus on, and it's unfair to straddle lines with someone I can't be serious about.

Chapter 37

San Diego

Chris's texts have slowed now that he's immersed in his Alaskan vacation, but there's not much more we can do until closer to the date. The presentation is finished, we have our data, and I've researched the philanthropy efforts Javier mentioned. I captured talking points and emailed them to Chris for his Tuesday flight home. We'll prep all day Wednesday for Thursday's finalist meeting with Chremsoft.

> Marina Man Preston: Here's the restaurant address. I made a reservation for 6pm. Let me know if you have trouble finding it. Don't forget a light jacket- it gets breezy by the water. See you soon!

I'm excited for this date with Preston. But I'd be lying if I said I wasn't thinking about Javier and last night. It wasn't just good sex—it was sensual, as though he was honoring my body instead of taking it. The energy was different.

I step out of the ride share into the warm San Diego

evening, smoothing my dress as the low sun paints the sky golden. A playful breeze catches the fabric and lifts it.

"Careful there," I hear from behind me.

A handsome man approaches in white pants, sneakers, and a flowy, light tan linen shirt with the cuffs folded up. My heart jumps as he gets closer.

"Well, hello there," I respond, accepting his hug and soft kiss on my forehead.

"How was traffic?" he asks as we walk toward the restaurant.

"As expected." I look up at him and smile. *This* feels right.

I glance around the restaurant as he checks in with the hostess. My gaze skims past the oval bar, through floor-to-ceiling windows, to the deck overlooking the Pacific Ocean.

"Right this way." The hostess zigzags through the tables toward the outdoor deck.

Preston gestures for me to go ahead, and I follow the hostess to a table for two overlooking the water. He pulls out my chair before settling into his own.

"This is beautiful." The ocean stretches endlessly before me.

"This is one of my favorite restaurants. Great food, perfect location." He points behind me. "My sailboat is just down there."

The server pauses at our table. Preston orders a bottle of Cabernet Sauvignon. "And we'll start with the calamari," he adds.

He slides on his black-framed glasses. The effect is immediate—suddenly he's Clark Kent meets beach god. Our eyes meet over his menu.

"See something you like?" His smile is pure trouble.

My cheeks burn, but I hold his gaze. Screw embarrassment. I like him, and clearly the feeling's mutual. Why hide it?

"I'm enjoying the view," I say.

He glances behind him at the elderly couple at the next table. "I didn't know you liked them older. I could dye my hair gray if that's what you're into." He quirks his eyebrow before returning to his menu.

We make quick work of the calamari and half a bottle of wine over the next twenty minutes. Preston shares updates on opening a new office in San Antonio while I fill him in on the Mercury client and the looming Chremsoft presentation. Chris's constant texts from Alaska earn an eye roll from Preston.

"That sounds like an important account for him." Preston takes a sip of wine. "I used to be like that—needed control over everything. Every decision had to go through me. But I learned that burns out relationships and teams."

I nod, absorbing his words.

"He'll learn." Preston leans back as the server places his steak and shrimp beside vibrant green beans.

"Want some?" he asks, chasing a shrimp around with his fork.

"Shrimp, please." I cut into my salmon. "Want some?"

"I'm salmon-ed out. Used to order it every time I came here." He drops a plump shrimp on my plate. "But yours looks perfect."

The food is too good to rush. We eat in easy silence for a few minutes, occasionally pointing out bites the other should try. Preston's right about the salmon—it's perfectly cooked, flaking apart under my fork.

"So, you're a regular here." Envy edges my voice.

"Yes and no. They don't know my name yet." He chuckles softly. "I found this place the day I signed my marina lease. One of those life moments, you know? I've dreamed of having a wet slip here since I was young. They handed me my marina

ID—the one you returned—and I needed to celebrate somewhere special."

I catch myself wanting to read meaning into him bringing me here—to his sentimental place. Old Brianna would have spun this into something bigger. The Brianna who accepted Griffin's second date would have. This version of me? It's a good restaurant with a sweet story.

"I love that. So, now that you've achieved your childhood dream—"

"In a wet slip—that's key. My parents dry-docked their boat when I was growing up. Every time we wanted to go out, the marina had to put it in the water. Better than nothing, but the wet slip means I just turn on the motor and go."

"Do your parents still have it?" I chase a garlic potato around my plate.

"Nah, Dad sold it after their divorce."

"I'm sorry. That had to be hard."

"He was an asshole; my mom deserved better." His jaw tightens. "It all worked out."

I file that away for later—or never.

We finish our meals in companionable quiet, the topic clearly closed. Preston pushes his empty plate aside and catches the server's eye.

"Want some dessert?" he asks me. "My favorites are the crème brûlée or tiramisu. I love cheesecake, but theirs is too dense." He shakes his head in disapproval. "Want to order both and share?"

A few minutes later, the server places our desserts between us. The tiramisu sits tall on its white plate, each layer precisely defined. The crème brûlée hides in a shallow ramekin, caramelized sugar concealing the rich custard beneath.

Preston's face lights up as he reaches for the crème brûlée, then pauses.

"Actually, you may have the honors of cracking the top."

A smile spreads across my face as I lean forward. "I didn't even know that was a thing."

"My sister used to make a wish before breaking it." He slides the ramekin closer, his fingers brushing mine as he adjusts the spoon's position. "Go ahead, make a wish first."

I hover the spoon over the golden layer. So many things I could wish for, but one keeps pushing to the front of my mind. I glance up at Preston's encouraging smile and bring the spoon down. It strikes the sugar with a sharp *crack*.

"Perfect." His smile reaches his eyes as caramelized shards glisten on my spoon's edge. "What did you wish for?" His voice is softer now.

"If I tell you, it won't come true."

Smirking, Preston takes his spoon and dives confidently into the tiramisu.

"Now that you've achieved your childhood dream of a sailboat"—I lean forward and point at him for emphasis—"in a wet slip, what's the next goal?"

Preston sits back, his chair creaking softly. He holds his spoon near his mouth, the metal tapping a gentle rhythm against his bottom lip as he considers. His eyes drift toward the water beyond my shoulder.

"I've been debating buying a vacation home. Mountains, maybe, or somewhere with seasons." He gestures toward the endless blue. "But for only a few weeks a year? Renting might make more sense." He cuts into the tiramisu, then lifts his gaze to mine. "Would you come with me?" The question hangs between us like the salt air.

It catches me off guard. A vacation together? We've had two dates. But something in his expression makes my heart skip.

"Come with you on vacation?"

"Yeah, in the future." He attacks his tiramisu again, nervous energy making his spoon move quickly.

"I'd love to." I'm not sure if it's shock or sugar making me dizzy.

"Good, I enjoy spending time with you. It seems like we're on the same page about a lot of things. Big goals, Career driven." He picks up another heaping scoop of crème brûlée. "Hopefully, we can achieve some of them together."

He turns the spoon in his mouth and pulls it out, bottom side up. I never thought eating dessert could be sexy, but here we are.

A genuine smile transforms his face, creating those attractive crinkles around his eyes. I'm completely gone. Maybe Sara's challenge isn't so crazy after all.

"When can I see you again?" he asks, abandoning his dessert entirely.

"You're seeing me tomorrow for my sailing lesson." I sip my wine and grimace—wine and tiramisu, terrible combination.

"After that." His voice drops to that register that makes my stomach flip.

"I'm all over—San Antonio, Seattle, back to San Antonio, then Dallas."

"Seattle sounds fun. I can take you to my favorite restaurant there, out on Bainbridge."

"I won't say no to that." Excitement ripples through me thinking of the future . . . with Preston. This feels right. This is what I've wanted.

"The last bite is yours." Preston scoops up the final piece of tiramisu, reaching across the table with a gentle smile.

I lean forward instinctively, lips parting, caught up in the intimacy of the gesture. This feels like something couples do—something real and tender and—

His hand jerks suddenly to the left, the spoon smearing custard across my cheek instead of finding my mouth.

"Tiramisu. My favorite." The voice behind me is ice-cold, dripping with venom. My blood freezes.

Preston's face drains of color. His eyes squeeze shut as his free hand moves to his jaw, rubbing it as if easing a sudden, sharp pain. The spoon clatters to the table.

I turn slowly, tiramisu still sticky on my cheek, to see a woman about my age standing behind my chair. Her hand rests on her hip, her entire body radiating fury. But it's her eyes that make my stomach drop—they're not looking at me.

They're looking at Preston like she knows exactly who he is.

"New flavor of the week?" She tilts her head toward me with mock sweetness, her smile razor-sharp.

Wait. What?

Her words hit me like ice water, but I don't fully understand. Flavor of the week. Why would she—

"Desiree, don't cause a scene." Preston's voice is strained, desperate.

Chapter 38

San Diego

"Cause a scene? Me?" The woman Preston called Desiree presses her manicured fingers to her chest in exaggerated shock. "I'm not the one having dessert with random women while my wife sits at home."

Wife.

The word slams into me with brutal clarity.

I am such a fucking fool. Again.

"How long have you two been dating?" she asks, her voice dripping false curiosity as I wipe the smeared tiramisu from my face, unable to look up.

Silence stretches between us. I can't form words. Can't even breathe properly.

"Does she talk? Oh, you found a mute one this time. How refreshing—bet that makes things easier for you, doesn't it, Preston?"

"Desiree, go home." His voice is barely above a whisper, defeated.

"Why would I do that? I got the confirmation email for this romantic little dinner"—she gestures around the restaurant with theatrical flair—"So I figured I'd drop by and meet whoever you're parading around town this week."

She leans down close to my ear, her voice dropping to a venomous whisper that only I can hear. "You should get tested, sweetheart. You're definitely not his first side piece."

The words hit like a physical blow.

Around us, other diners are starting to notice. Their stares burn into my back.

Preston's and the woman's voices fade to white noise as they bicker over my head. I can see their mouths moving, see Preston's desperate gestures and Desiree's animated fury, but I can't process the words anymore.

My thoughts crash over me in brutal waves. *I'm so stupid. I fell for this shit again. Made a fool of myself again. Picked the wrong one again.*

Sara was wrong. They're all dirtbags. Every single one of them. This whole challenge, this idea that I could find someone decent—it's hopeless. I'm hopeless.

My chair scrapes against the floor as I stand slowly, my legs unsteady. I fumble for my purse with numb fingers, avoiding eye contact with anyone. The other diners pretend not to stare, but I feel their pity burning into my skin.

I push past his wife. His *wife*.

"Brianna, wait—" Preston's voice cuts through my fog, desperate and pleading.

I don't stop. I can't stop. I push through the restaurant's front door and into the night air, my chest tight and burning.

My hands won't stop shaking. I fumble for my phone, nearly dropping it twice before I get the ride share app open.

I tap to request a ride, but it asks for a destination.

Where am I going?

I stare at the empty field, my mind completely blank. The hotel. What's it called?

Nothing. There's *nothing* in my head.

Breathe. Just breathe.

I close my eyes and force air into my lungs. The hotel name lurks somewhere in my mind—I just have to find it.

The wind picks up, and the cool night air hits my flushed skin, offering momentary relief from the heat of humiliation burning through me.

The Roosevelt. My fingers fly across the screen, typing before I lose it again. I hit "Find Driver" and clutch the phone like a lifeline.

Five minutes away.

Five fucking minutes feels like a lifetime when you're falling apart on a public sidewalk.

Behind me, the valet is talking to someone. Please, God, don't let it be Preston. Or his wife. She didn't even seem shocked by finding him with another woman. Like she expected it. Like he's done this before.

Flavor of the week.

The words echo in my head, each repetition twisting the knife deeper. I'm one of many. Just another stupid woman who fell for his act.

Fuck me. I give up.

I glance back at the valet stand. Desiree. She's staring at me with pure hatred.

Perfect. I escaped their table fight only to end up in an awkward sidewalk standoff.

I stare at my phone, pretending to be absorbed in the app, but her scrutiny burns into my skull. She steps closer, deliberately moving into my line of sight.

She wants a confrontation. And I'm trapped here for four more minutes.

I didn't ask for this. I didn't know. *He* pursued *me*—

The wait time updates. Six minutes now. How the hell did it go from five to six?

"I don't blame you. Not really." Her voice cuts through the night air. I keep staring at my phone, unable to look up. I can't engage with this woman. What am I supposed to say?

Sorry your husband is a cheating piece of shit? Thanks for the STD warning? Hope you find someone better?

"I know you didn't know about me. Most of them don't." She's staring straight ahead, talking to the wind more than to me.

Despite myself, I glance over. She's not the furious woman from the restaurant anymore. She's hollow. Beautiful but empty—blonde waves cascading over her shoulders, expensive blouse fluttering in the breeze. But her eyes hold nothing.

I know that look. I've worn that look.

Oh, God. The recognition hits me like a physical blow. She looks exactly how I felt when I found Dirtbag with that woman in our bed. The same emptiness. The same devastation of someone whose entire world just crumbled.

How many times has she stood outside restaurants like this? How many nights has she wondered what she did wrong, why she wasn't enough?

This is what I looked like. Broken. Discarded. Pushed to the side. Fighting for scraps of a man who never deserved me in the first place.

And here I am, several years later, falling into the exact same trap. Being the other woman this time instead of the one betrayed, but ending up in the same goddamn place—standing on a sidewalk, shattered and humiliated.

We're both collateral damage, from the same selfish bastard.

"I didn't know." My words come out barely above a whisper.

She turns, her eyes scanning me from head to toe with cold assessment. She lets out a long, weary sigh, as though she's done this dance too many times to count.

A white Lexus sedan pulls to the curb. The valet holds open her door. She slides in and drives away, and just like that, I'm alone. Standing on a sidewalk with my shame, and a ride share that still hasn't arrived.

The San Antonio heat hits me the moment I step out of the ride share. The Elysian rises before me, but I can barely appreciate it. The Chremsoft presentation looms over me, and Chris will be back from Alaska tomorrow, which means I need to be at the top of my game.

I'm far from it.

After updating Sara and Beck about the disaster, Sara officially released me from the dating challenge. But dinner with Preston was date number twelve.

The challenge didn't just fail—it crashed and burned. Spectacularly. Multiple times. Like a dumpster fire that keeps reigniting.

Maybe Sara's challenge was doomed from the start. How can I trust myself to pick the right person when I've proven, over and over, that I can't?

I thought I had it all figured out with Dirtbag—the perfect life, the man I wanted, the family we planned together. Everything I'd dreamed of since I was little, all mapped out and ready to unfold. Then he discarded me like a broken appliance he couldn't be bothered to fix.

And here I am, several years later, managing to put myself

right back in the exact same hell. Different city, different cheater, same stupid me.

I drag my suitcase through the lobby, past potted palms and hand-painted tiles, and do my best to shake off the lingering humiliation. The Chremsoft presentation is what matters now. Not Preston.

Work. I can do work. Work makes sense.

I am relieved not to see Javier in the lobby. According to Tobias, he's "entertaining someone" in his office, though he doesn't specify whether it's business or pleasure.

Not that it matters anymore. I'm done, with all of it. The games, the hope, the disappointment. It's not worth it. Not the emotional whiplash, not the distraction from work, not the energy I could be spending on people who actually deserve it.

I lay on the bed flipping mindlessly through TV channels. Normally, I'd be glued to the local news, but nothing stays on screen long enough for me to process what it is before I'm clicking away.

I glance toward my window. The late afternoon sun reflects off the downtown buildings, casting warm shadows across my wall. I love this time of day, the way the light turns everything golden and soft.

Knock knock knock.

My gaze stays fixed on the window. Sherbet orange and pink hues dance across the glass and concrete nearby.

Knock knock knock.

I know exactly who it is. And I don't want to see him.

But my legs betray me, moving without permission as they carry me across the room. Before my brain can catch up and stop this terrible decision, my hand is already turning the handle.

"Welcome back." Javier's face lights up with genuine excitement.

He must catch my dead-eyed stare, because his smile falters the moment we make eye contact.

"Are you okay? What's wrong?" His concern appears genuine, which somehow makes it worse.

Should I tell him?

Oh, hey, funny story. My best friend convinced me to do a dating challenge, and I've been seeing other guys this whole time. You know one of them. But wait, there's more! I also went on a date with another man you met, assuming he was just a client. Plot twist: he turned out to be a lying, cheating piece of shit. So now I'm licking my wounds and planning to avoid anyone with male anatomy for the foreseeable future.

Yeah, that conversation would go well.

"I don't feel well." It's all I can manage, and hope that's enough to make him leave.

"Aw, Bri, I'm so sorry. Germs are everywhere in airports lately."

Did he just give me a nickname? It's more serious than I thought.

"I was going to ask if you wanted to grab dinner, but I totally understand if you're under the weather."

"Yeah, don't want to get you sick," I lie.

Hey, all the men do it. Why shouldn't I?

"Can I get you anything? We need you better for the finalist meeting Thursday."

"I'll be fine. Thank you. I just need to sleep." Actually true for once. I spent the entire weekend in bed in Dallas and plan to continue that trend here.

"Of course. Totally understand. Wait." He fishes out a pen from his shirt pocket and a receipt paper from his perfectly pressed trousers. "Here's my direct line downstairs, and my cell."

He scribbles numbers on the back of the receipt and hands

it to me. I smile, already knowing this paper will hit the trash the second I close the door.

"Thanks, Javier. I appreciate it. I'll be okay. I'll talk to you soon."

I don't want to seem like I'm rushing him out, but I am.

I close the door, crumple the receipt in one fist, and toss it into the wastebasket by the desk before falling back onto the bed. Remote in hand, I resume my mindless channel surfing.

I settle on some TV show about surviving life in Alaska. Not that I need a reminder of Chris and the finalist presentation in three days, but the show features isolated people who are cold, hungry, and miserable.

I can relate.

The next episode is starting when I'm interrupted again.

Knock knock knock.

Javier needs to take a damn hint. He doesn't get exclusive access just because we've had sex.

My legs carry me to the door and I peek through the peephole. Not Javier.

"I didn't order takeout," I say as I open the door.

"Brianna Whitmore?"

"Yes."

"This is for you. I was told I am not allowed to go back down to the lobby holding this bag. So, uh, I need you to take it or I won't get my tip."

I sigh, grab the bag, and close the door. I already know who it's from. His kindness makes me want to throw up.

I press my finger on the receipt stapled to the side of the bag.

Brianna Whitmore
Elysian Hotel
Room 1010

Notes: Tip will be provided after food is delivered. See Javier in lobby.

I rip apart the bag and pull out a cup of what smells like chicken noodle soup, a roll, and a clear container with two pieces of baklava.

"Weird combo, but whatever," I say as I leave it all on the desk and crawl back into bed.

Not ten minutes later, the aroma of the soup reaches me in bed, and it smells incredible. All I've eaten today is a banana at the airport and a stupid salad at lunch.

I crawl across the bed like I'm slogging through the final mud pit obstacle of a Spartan race. I haven't done one, but I cheered on Beck when she did. I grab the soup, spoon, and container of baklava, and crawl back into bed.

I eat without tasting—soup first, then one piece of baklava before I give up and set the rest aside.

My phone sits powered off in my bag. I couldn't stand the groveling texts from the cheating asshole, so I turned it off.

I settle into bed, my neck angled uncomfortably by the six pillows behind me. I'm ready for sleep to take me away from this nightmare.

Ring ring ring.

"Fucking hell. Just let me die, people."

I reach over to the nightstand and pick up the hotel phone.

"Hello." The annoyance in my voice is palpable.

"Well, hello to you, too," Sara says on the other end.

A long sigh escapes me as I fall back into my six pillows.

"So, it's going well, then?" she says.

"If by well, you mean that I hate the world, I hate men, and I hate emotions? Then yes. It's fantastic, actually."

"Wow, B."

"How did you get the number to my room?"

"Um . . . I called the hotel and said please connect me to Brianna Whitmore's room?"

"*Mmm*," is all I reply. I lie there, my eyes closed, phone receiver lying close enough to my ear that I can still hear her.

"Did you eat?"

"Javier sent me soup."

"Are you sick?"

"No, I just told him I am."

"Awe, that was sweet of him."

"Don't."

"Sorry. What a fucking asshole for caring about your well-being. How dare he."

"I know, right?"

I get she's being sarcastic. But I'm not.

Sara sighs into the phone and I wait because I have nothing to say.

"I'm so sorry, Brianna. This dating challenge has been an epic failure. I had good intentions, but rather than helping you find love, I feel like I've caused more heartache, and the immediate need for therapy. Can you forgive me?"

Her words are sincere. I have been avoiding dating, and I know exactly why. I just didn't realize everyone else knew, too.

"Your heart was in the right place," I say after a few moments pass.

"I promise it was. I just hate to see you so closed off. After Dirtbag, it was like you turned into a different person. I mean, you were still you, but some part of you died with that relationship."

My anger spikes.

"It wasn't just me who died," I snap back.

"I know, B, and I'm sorry. I'm so, so sorry. Losing . . ." She worries I can't hear it spoken out loud.

"Say it."

She sighs, most likely debating whether to continue or not. The bandage is off already, so go ahead and shove the knife through.

"Losing a baby is unfathomable. Losing a relationship and a baby at the same time is heart wrenching. You have every right to feel every damn emotion that you feel. And you have every right to feel it as long as you want to."

She pauses, but all I heard is, *losing a baby*.

Sara doesn't know what it's like to lose a baby. She doesn't even know I lost two babies. She has a beautiful, healthy boy that she gets to complain about daily. She doesn't know what it's like to have a life planned out and then have it ripped from your clenching fists. Evan never left her.

Dirtbag left me. He left me because I wouldn't be able to carry a baby to full term, to carry on his bloodline like it's the fucking medieval times. And therefore, I was no longer a part of his long-term plan. And because he's a coward, he stepped outside our relationship so I'd break it off with him. Because how would it look if he broke up with me after I lost our babies? Fucking asshole.

"But Brianna . . . " I roll my eyes even though they're closed. "You can't give up on life, or on *you* because there are assholes out there. They're not all dirtbags. Most of them. But not all of them."

I let out a quiet laugh.

"Lucas said I'm waiting until I hit menopause to start dating."

"That's a bold statement coming from a twenty-somethin' year old."

"He's not wrong. I didn't realize it until he said it. But maybe that's what I was doing, subconsciously. No one will expect me to have kids, and I won't disappoint anyone."

"You are not a disappointment."

"Tell that to Dirtbag. I was so easily tossed aside."

"You can't control what your body can or cannot do on the inside, Brianna."

There's my name.

"Well, *Sara*, producing a child is the expectation of every fucking woman on this planet, and I can't do it. So, how do you think I feel when I have to tell every guy I date that I'm defective? That I'm incapable of protecting the life inside me? And then watch their interest in me die, right there. Fuck everything else—my personality, my character, my success. Fuck all of that if I can't shoot out a kid from my vagina. If you can't have a kid, you're worthless."

"You are not worthless. I'm so sorry. I don't think I realized . . . " Her voice fades out.

Of course she doesn't realize. She had a happy and healthy pregnancy, and I'm happy for her. I mean that. I wouldn't want her to go through what I did. Grady is a blessing, and her uncomplicated pregnancy was a blessing. The fact she gets to complain about him on a regular basis is a blessing. It's hard to hear, if I'm honest. She complains about something I'd give fucking anything to have.

I'd give anything to not have to tell guys I date, "Sorry, can't have kids," so I can get ghosted and blocked within the hour.

"I'm defective," I whisper. Tears stream down my face, grazing my ears before absorbing into the pillows.

"Oh, B. You are not defective. Please don't believe that. I wish we would've talked more about this. I just knew how much it hurt, and I was afraid to breach the topic."

I appreciate that she cares. But talking to her about it feels impossible when she's living the life I can't have. There's a part of her, no matter how hard she tries, that just won't get it. And there's a part of me, no matter how hard I try, that will always resent her.

Chapter 39

San Antonio

I can finally say I'm getting sick of The Elysian breakfast buffet. Even the croissants. I've changed my seating and opted for one of the tables on the perimeter with normal chairs. This way, no one can sneak up on me. The downside is, I'm more distracted by the commotion and noise from the lobby. Also, these large potted plants that separate the breakfast area from the rest of the lobby need to be trimmed. I just pulled a green frond out of my coffee cup.

The breakfast hour is blissfully silent. No messages, no calls. I turned my phone back on when I woke up, and other than a thoughtful text from Sara, nothing. Nothing from Chris, Preston, or anyone else who might want to stick a pin in my balloon today.

I should find Javier at some point and thank him for the food last night. It's the right thing to do.

My phone rings the moment I lift the last piece of croissant to my lips.

"Fucking hell. I almost made it through breakfast," I mutter as I lift the phone to my ear.

"Where are you?" Chris asks before I even say hello, a bit demanding this early.

"I'm where I always am at seven-thirty in the morning. Shoving a croissant in my face."

"My flight home was canceled. There's a snowstorm coming in, and air traffic has been grounded. I'm trying to find a way out, but I haven't had luck yet."

"Come again?" I lean forward in my chair, uncrossing my legs. "You aren't coming home today?"

"I'm working on it. I'll find a way. I'm waiting for my boss to call me back to discuss a backup plan. Maybe we can get Marsha from the northeast region to fly in and cover for me. I've already texted her."

No. Not now. I earned my right to be miserable today. I have plans to be pathetic. This disaster requires competence I can't muster right now.

"My God, Chris. The finalist presentation is in forty-eight hours!" I say a little too loudly. Several guests walking through the lobby look my way. I duck behind the oversized plant.

"No shit, Brianna. I'm working on it. I'll call you when I have an update. But I need you to prepare all the documents in case Marsha has to do it."

Shit. Shit. Shit.

I hang up with Chris, still promising he'll hire a private charter to get home the moment the snow stops.

I'm not entirely sure why, but as I exit the breakfast area I turn left past Javier's empty desk and then take another left toward his office. I don't know if he'll be there. I don't know if he'll be alone. I don't know why I'm walking to his office.

Knock knock knock.

I hear a faint, "Come in," so I open the door.

To say that my body is put at ease when I see Javier at his

desk, alone, is an understatement. There's something about him that still feels . . . safe.

He scribbles something in a ledger, his hair perfectly combed in a wave.

He glances up and smiles before closing the ledger and stepping around to the front of his desk.

"How are you feeling?" He continues to close the gap between us, and I stop, not wanting him to.

"Better, thank you. And thank you for the soup and baklava. You didn't have to."

The smell of cool water immerses my senses, and I push away the flashbacks of our night together.

"It was no problem at all. I know you have a big week. Do you need me to pick you up anything? Cold medicine? Cough drops? Vaporizer?"

"Vaporizer?"

"Yeah, Dominic can't live without one when he's sick. It's like his security blanket. It's loud and leaves water stains on the furniture, but he says it makes him feel better, so. . ."

He's such a great uncle.

"No, I'm good. I'm feeling better. Thank you, though." The tone of my voice contradicts what I say, and Javier knows it.

He hesitates, shifting his weight to his left foot. "Are you okay? Is anything else going on?"

Isn't that a loaded question? Part of me is on a warpath to ruin every interpersonal relationship around me.

"Chris's flight was canceled. All flights out of Alaska are grounded due to weather."

"Oh, shit." He rubs his palm up his forehead. I love when he curses. It reminds me that he's a normal person outside of his formal job.

"Yeah, so now we're all in panic mode to see who can fly in to lead the meeting."

"Why can't you do it?" he asks, so matter-of-factly.

I laugh at the audacity of the question.

"Because I'm not a sales executive?" The answer seems obvious to me.

"So? You know the client and the material as well as Chris does, probably better. There's no reason why you couldn't do it."

I appreciate Javier's belief in me and my skillset, but he's wrong. I can't do Chris's job. I'm an implementation manager. Anyway, I barely have enough energy to sustain this conversation; there's no way I can transform into a sales executive in forty-eight hours.

There's no way I could land this client. It'd be an epic failure, just like my dating life, and Chris would have me fired because I cost him the biggest client and bonus in two years.

"Thanks, Javier. They're probably going to fly in the other sales executive for this."

"Okay. Well, let me help. Let me write up additional insights into Chremsoft's executive leadership so the other sales executive, *or you*, can land that deal for Chris. I don't know them personally, but the company has been rooted in this city for over fifty years."

I don't know why he's so insistent on helping me, but I'll take anything I can get.

"That would be great, thank you." A weak smile tugs up my cheeks.

"I . . ." Javier shifts back on his right foot. "I've missed you. I know you have an important meeting this week, and even more so now that Chris is delayed. I won't bug you for dinner, though I want to"—he rolls his head back and forth—"but I wanted you to know I missed you. I'd love to celebrate with you after the finalist meeting on Thursday, before you fly home."

He doesn't understand that I can't handle any of this right

now. What I really want to say is, *Please don't miss me. Please don't want to celebrate with me. Please don't think about me. Please don't want to help me. Just forget about me. Forget I exist.*

"That sounds great."

It *doesn't* sound great. I don't want to be near him. I don't want to be near anyone right now. I just need to survive the next two days.

He leans forward, placing a soft kiss on my forehead. My eyes close for a long moment, and I fight back tears that threaten to spill.

Oh, God, get me out of this office.

"I'm here if you need me," he affirms as his hands slide down my arms to my hands, his touch stinging me like bees.

Relief settles over me as I walk to the elevators, leaving the Mercury team behind for the last time. I've grown fond of their technology team, grateful for what we built together. But now that we've integrated the systems, my job is done. We pass responsibilities to our client care team, who maintains the relationship until the contract is up for renewal.

The project team hosted a party for Gus's return and brought me a box of conchas—apparently my reputation as a sugar fiend precedes me. Small gestures like this remind me that not everything has to carry hidden meaning. And closing the book on Mercury feels good. No more references to that *Wall Street Journal* article that plagued our integration meetings.

Large caramel latte in hand, I walk back to the hotel with renewed energy. The Mercury team energized me today.

Michele and Gus gave me what I needed—kind words reminding me I matter.

In a job where I'm constantly moving between cities and clients, they've become my anchor. Learning to trust them during this partnership felt risky at first, but they never let me down. When everyone else feels temporary, they feel solid.

Now, I need to put my personal stuff aside and focus on this finalist presentation. Time to be for Chris what the Mercury team was for me—dependable, trustworthy, and skilled. Well, Chris will have to settle for reasonably skilled.

I pull open my favorite door, admiring the gold half-moon handles, and breathe in the familiar scent of white tea and verbena.

At the front desk, Grace types behind an enormous vase of roses while Tobias works beside her. He spots me, smacks Grace's arm, and points. Grace's head pops up, eyes wide.

I approach the desk, confusion mixing with curiosity.

"Brianna. I'm sorry. I didn't know. I would've kept my mouth shut." Tobias's face twists with pain.

What is he talking about?

Grace shoots him a sharp look. "You should always keep your mouth shut."

"You guys, what's going on?" They both look guilty as hell, and I have no idea why.

Grace taps the vase with her fingers. "These are for you."

"Oh. Thank you." I scan the obnoxious display of red roses, looking for a card.

"I'm sorry, Brianna. I read the card out loud, and Javier overheard." Tobias winces. "The look on his face . . . and then he just left. A minute later, I heard crashing coming from the printer room." He glances at Grace. "I had no idea you two were . . ."

His voice trails off.

I pull the card from the bouquet and read it.

> Brianna—
> Please forgive me.
> I don't want us to end.
> Preston.

"Fuuuuck." I stare at the card, piecing it all together.

Javier knows about Preston. He told me he missed me this morning, kissed my forehead, and now he knows about the roses. I turn and scan the lobby, searching for him. My heart hammers against my ribs, anxiety coursing through me like ice water.

"He hasn't been at the desk all day," Grace says.

I turn back to her. "I need you to get rid of these flowers. Donate them, throw them in the trash, but please get them out of here."

Grace nods, and I turn away from the front desk, my legs unsteady. The lobby stretches out before me—polished marble floors, clusters of leather chairs, guests chatting over coffee like nothing has changed. But everything has changed. I cross the lobby toward the hallway that leads to Javier's office. The bar area buzzes with early evening energy. Glasses clink, conversations blend into white noise. I'm nearly past the bar, almost to the hallway, when movement catches my eye. Javier steps into view, adjusting his tie, completely absorbed in whatever's on his phone. He hasn't seen me yet.

"Javier," I say, my voice trembling.

His head snaps toward me mid-stride and his expression crumbles into pain, then hardens into anger. He holds a finger up at me.

"Don't." He keeps walking, past the elevators.

My feet move before my brain catches up.

"Javier—"

He stops, spinning on his heel to face me.

"Brianna. I cannot talk to you right now." His hand forms a fist against his mouth.

"Just give me five minutes to explain," I plead, aware that every word bounces off the marble floors.

He laughs, but it's hollow. "No. No explanations are necessary." He turns away. "I need to go."

I don't listen. I follow him into the printer room before he can shut the door.

He stands in the middle of the room, shoulders dropped, staring at the floor. His back expands as he takes a slow breath.

"Jav—"

He turns around, palm out. "I don't care what your explanation is. That's what I meant to say. I don't care about your explanation." His voice cracks. "I don't care what happened."

He glances over at the counter where only a few days ago, he'd been kissing me. His face breaks like shattered glass. "You played me."

"No. Javi—"

"You're all the same. All of you." He shakes his head. "I thought you were different. I thought . . ."

Tears burn behind my eyes. "It's not what you think."

His jaw works silently before he speaks.

"Was I just a fun distraction for you? Entertainment? Another one to add to your collection?" His harsh laugh cuts through me. "I'm so stupid. I actually thought you cared about *me*." He presses his hand to his chest. "And not what I could give you."

What he could give me?

Tears stream down my cheeks. "Those flowers mean nothing. *Nothing*. If you would just—" Pain shoots through my chest.

"Nothing? A three-hundred-dollar vase of *red* roses means nothing to you? Now I kind of feel bad for the guy. I guess I'm not the only one you're playing."

"Javier, please. He was a consultant for my company years ago. I found his ID in my rental car. I returned it and—"

"And he sent you *three* dozen roses for returning his ID?" His gaze turns glacial. "I'm so stupid. I broke every one of my rules for you. I let my guard down . . . for you. I convinced myself that you were worth the risk, that you saw me for me. That you liked me for me. Not as a hotel—" he pauses, swallowing. "Not as a man who lives a glamorous life, who gets invited to fancy events, exclusive restaurants. Who has access to influential people."

I stare at him, struggling to understand everything behind his words, what he's not saying.

"But I do like you for you," I say, still trying to grasp everything he's not saying.

He shakes his head, annoyance cast from his features.

"No, I'm not a "one of many" type of guy. I'm the one and only, and you . . . you seem to have many."

My words scrape out as a whisper. "It wasn't real . . . with Preston." I reach out for him, desperate. "It's not what it seems. With you it's . . . it's real."

Javier's shoulders tense and he takes a step back. "This . . . isn't real."

He pushes past me and out the door. I inhale the scent of cool water one last time.

"Shit," I whisper, wiping tears from my cheeks.

The flowers weren't supposed to happen. *This* wasn't supposed to happen.

I keep my head down the whole way to my room, hiding my tear-filled eyes. Only when I reach my door do I realize I left my coffee downstairs.

The door shuts behind me and I don't move.

I thought we were just . . . casual? Something fun? But the way he looked at me—it was like I'd ripped out his soul.

The flowers were from a cheating asshole, but Javier doesn't know that. He can't, because telling him about my dating challenge would mean risking the warmth in his eyes, the careful way he touches me, the attention that makes me feel like I matter.

When did this become real for him?

I said it was real for me. Did I mean it?

I search the room for answers. Answers I wonder if I'm hiding from myself.

The bathroom mirror reflects my puffy eyes and streaked makeup—evidence of how quickly everything unraveled. I move to the window, pressing my forehead against the cool glass, watching people hustle across the city streets below like nothing has changed.

But everything has changed.

I turn back to the room, feeling restless and trapped. That's when I notice it—a navy blue folder on the bed that wasn't there when I left this morning. There are several printed sheets inside, and what looks like a handwritten note.

Brianna—

I hope this additional info is enough for you to land the sale.

You've got this! Looking forward to celebrating with you Thursday night.

—J

My tears begin to fall again. I crawl into the bed and just cry. Ugly cry. Every emotion that I've been shoving deep down comes up and I cry it all out. I cry until I can't cry anymore, and then I pass out.

Chapter 40

San Antonio

Javier is nowhere to be found. I've been camped in the breakfast area for three hours, hoping he'll show up. Four croissants later, I'm studying his Chremsoft notes and reviewing the presentation deck. I grab another coffee before our conference call with Chris and our bosses to discuss the backup plan and Chris's return to Texas.

I log in to the video conference early and dig through my purse for headphones. A loud "Hey" makes me spring up, looking around for Javier.

"Whitmore. Down here."

I look at my laptop screen to see Chris waving.

I exhale and plug in my headphones. "Hey, Chris. How's it going?"

"It's going. How are you? You look rough."

"So generous with your compliments." I roll my eyes and force a smile.

"I'm the one stuck in Alaska. I should be the cranky one."

He's right. I can't let my personal life interfere with business. How many times do I have to remind myself of that? If

Chris realizes what a wreck I am, he'll banish me from the finalist meeting.

"You're right, I'm sorry."

"You miss me, don't you, Whitmore."

I scrunch my nose. "I miss you like I miss a migraine."

I smile into the camera as Chris throws his head back laughing. His face shrinks as another box pops up.

"What are we laughing about?" Jerry, Chris's boss, asks as his camera turns on.

"Brianna says she misses me like a migraine."

"Ah, that's funny," Jerry replies flatly before jumping into updates. "So. Marsha can't get there in time for tomorrow's meeting. Everyone else is booked. Unless you can ask Santa for overnight delivery, we may have to reschedule."

Chris's brow furrows. "I've been working on this account for months. We can't reschedule. We could lose them."

"Why can't Brianna do it?" My boss, Loraine, jumps in as her camera turns on. "Sorry I'm late."

Chris and Jerry both laugh once. I press my lips together.

"Why can't she? She's partnered with Chris for years, pulls all the data, creates the presentations. She's well positioned, and our best chance at landing this account without Chris."

Of course they're laughing. Chris believes in me right up until his commission check is threatened. All those late nights I spent making sure he had everything he needed, and this is how conditional our friendship really is. At least my boss sees what I'm actually worth.

I watch Chris and Jerry's faces for any reaction. Their silence is maddening. If Chris doesn't trust me to lead tomorrow's meeting, it says everything about our so-called partnership. I've been wrong about every other man who's waltzed into my life, why would Chris be different?

I keep waiting for Chris to speak up, to say he believes in me. That he's confident I can pull it off. That he trusts me.

"I'll defer to Chris on this," Jerry says, tossing his hands up and leaning back.

Say you believe in me. Please.

"I have no other choice. We need Brianna to go in there and give it her best shot," Chris admits, shrugging.

Well, I'll take what I can get.

"It's settled. Chris, work with Brianna and make sure she's up to speed to close that deal tomorrow." Jerry scratches the back of his neck—a nervous tic Chris has mentioned.

The call ends. Frustration spreads across my face and my eyes burn. I'm pissed that I wasn't Chris's first choice. He would've called every junior sales guy in our company before me. It's insulting.

Chris and I spend the whole day on video conference reviewing documentation, presentation slides, and talking points.

I eventually move to my room since Javier is nowhere to be found. I share the additional information Javier left on my bed, and we strategize how to integrate it into my talking points.

"You think you're ready?" Chris asks.

I take a deep breath, my voice unsteady. "Yes. I can do this."

I leave the Chremsoft building and breathe easily for the first time in ninety minutes. I haven't heard from Chris since his plane took off, but he's probably going crazy up there. Knowing Chris, he paid extra for Wi-Fi. I probably have several emails demanding a play-by-play. But I want to process the last ninety minutes quietly before he attacks me with five hundred questions about what I said, what I didn't say, what they said, and how they meant it.

The information Javier gave me was really helpful, and gave us the leg up we needed. The Chremsoft team seemed happy when the meeting ended. I should thank Javier, if he'll let me near him. He's obviously avoiding me.

The ride share drops me off and I hustle into the lobby, scanning for him. Javier's desk comes into view—empty chair, but a small crowd gathered next to it. I slow when I spot him standing with the group, his smile wide as he explains something. He looks happy. He shakes one guy's hand and they all head toward the elevator.

Javier doesn't see me as he returns to his desk. He can't cause a scene in the lobby, so I might get in a few words before he bolts.

"Javier." I approach the desk like he's a sleeping dragon.

He drops his pen and closes his eyes for a long moment. But he hasn't run yet, so I'll keep talking until he does.

"I wanted to thank you for the Chremsoft folder. I appreciate you did that for me—for Chris."

Javier barely looks up and nods, his lips a thin line. He stands. "Glad you found it helpful. If you'll excuse me." He walks away, leaving me staring at his empty chair.

Chris and I brave the line at the original Starbucks after our flight from San Antonio. We've got a few hours before our meeting with Linadin Corporation, and Chris insisted we couldn't come to Seattle without stopping here first. My Texas winter coat is no match for the morning chill as we wait in line.

My phone buzzes with an incoming text. *Preston.*

I should just block his ass.

> Marina Man Preston: This will be my last text. If you're willing to hear me out, let me know.

Hear him out. What a lunatic.

After grabbing our coffee, we head to the Linadin Corporation building. I'm grateful the parking garage isn't far since I chose stylish heels over comfortable ones. The lobby is bright and airy, suits hurrying in every direction. Chris checks the directory for Linadin's floor while I head toward the elevators.

I'm still mad about Preston's text. The nerve he has, thinking I'm stupid enough to entertain whatever that is. I may be a fool for not seeing it initially, but I'll be damned if I don't learn after getting smacked in the face with reality.

"Place your bets," Chris says, joining me by the elevators.

I snap out of my thoughts. "Huh?"

He extends his arms toward the six elevator bays. "We're on the third floor. I guess bay three."

I smile, realizing what he's doing. After the horrible Mercury meeting where the data was wrong, Chris refused to play because he was so angry with me. I appreciate this peace offering.

"Four." I point to the closest bay.

He presses the touch screen and we wait.

Elevator two. Such is my luck recently.

As the elevator doors creak to a close, the memory of the utility elevator in The Elysian plays in my mind. That was seriously one of the hottest moments in history for me. Silly and sexy, and I'm sad I took it for granted. That I took Javier for granted. I treated him like he'd always be there while I galivanted on dates completing this challenge. He was the only one who never let me down. I'm such an idiot.

"Hey," Chris says, looking up from his phone.

I peer up at him, but he doesn't seem to notice the emptiness in my eyes.

"I just wanted to thank you for everything you did for the finalist meeting. I've never been..." He exhales, looking up before continuing. "I've never been good at relying on people, especially when it comes to my career." He stands facing forward, only his neck twisted toward me. "I needed you to come through for me, and you did. You saved that meeting, and most likely my sale."

I'm in shock. Chris and I have a close relationship, but it's always been about him. I've always known this. I accept it because I know him deep down. He's not the typical asshole sales executive, although he has asshole tendencies. For him to thank me for saving his ass? I am not expecting it. But it's really nice to hear.

I stay quiet, my face neutral as he continues.

"I know I don't give you enough credit. You certainly proved yourself and I appreciate everything you did to save the sale. Even Javier. Please thank him for me, too. The info on philanthropy and all that additional stuff he gave you—it gave us a leg up on the competition. We might have to take *him* out to dinner if we land this sale."

Yeah, that's not happening.

A half smile grows on my face as the doors open. "Thank you. It's nice to be appreciated." I push off the back wall and Chris follows me out.

My pattern is undeniable. I've been working with Chris for several years and only now does he realize what I bring to the table. What I contribute to his sales. Maybe he's always been the typical asshole sales executive and I never noticed because I only gravitate to the assholes.

I shuffle through the San Antonio terminal looking for coffee. The Starbucks line is way too long, and I forgot to order ahead on the app. I open my airport maps and search for coffee nearby. The only other option is in Terminal A, which I don't feel like walking to.

I stroll around the food court looking for a coffee vending machine. Nothing as cool as Salt Lake's robot barista, but anything will do.

Off to the left is a display of photographs and paintings with large lettering above them—*Local Love*.

My blood turns cold. Isn't that the contest that photographer was talking about? There's no way the photo of Javier and me made it onto this display. *Please tell me it's not here.* I inch along the display, barely breathing as my eyes dart over each photo.

I stop, and my heart falls to the floor.

There it is.

I move closer before I can talk myself out of it. Sadness wraps around me, squeezing the air from my lungs. I finally see what the photographer captured. The way Javier is looking at me—like I'm the only person in the world. His body angles toward mine as he leans against the stone, chest resting on his forearms. His eyes hold this sparkle that has nothing to do with the lights reflecting off the water.

I lean closer, studying his face. It's like he's looking into my soul, and I can't believe a camera captured that—but I see it. I *feel* it every time he looks at me.

Anyone looking at this photo would assume we're a couple completely in love with each other. But it's me. And Javier. And we aren't in love. Right now, he feels the exact opposite.

I take a picture of the framed photo and send it to Sara with the caption, "I screwed up."

I toss my phone in my purse, hike my laptop bag up my shoulder, and head toward baggage claim. I can't think about this right now.

It's been a week and a half since I've seen Javier. I cancelled my upcoming stay at The Elysian and rebooked a hotel several blocks away. Entering the new hotel is disappointing. Check-in is quick. Grace isn't here to welcome me or tease me about my pastry addiction. Javier isn't here laughing with guests, looking all sexy in his three-piece suits. It even smells different.

I ride the elevator up alone, drop my purse on the bed, and head to the window.

"Of course."

Instead of the setting sun shining off buildings and the La Panadería sign, I'm staring at a roof with six air conditioning units and a McDonald's bag that looks like it's been there for months.

My phone starts ringing and I fall onto the bed, reaching for my purse.

"Hello?"

"That boy is in love with you, B. You need to fix this." I roll my eyes as Sara delivers her demands from the other side of the phone. "That photo says it all. And you know you like him. Stop denying it and go fix it."

I sigh into the phone, annoyed.

"He hates me. You should've seen him. He didn't give a shit about me or what I had to say. He wouldn't hear me out. Honestly, if he can so easily cut me off, maybe it's better we don't speak again."

"Stop."

"What?"

"Stop making excuses to keep your heart safe."

"That's not what this is. Maybe I'm dodging a bullet here. You see how amazing I am at picking guys. It's just a matter of time before Javier turns crazy, or decides he doesn't want to work and I have to support him."

"Where the hell did that come from?"

"What?"

"The part about him not wanting to work and you supporting him. Is it because he can't take you sailing? Or buy a second home somewhere with four seasons? Is that why you're not giving him a chance? Because he's *just* a concierge?"

"Ew, no. That has nothing to do with it. We would never work."

"Why?"

"We wouldn't work because . . . "

I prepare to rattle off the many reasons why we wouldn't work. Except only one glaring reason comes to mind—the one that's been haunting me for years.

"I'm waiting," Sara interjects.

"He wants kids." It hurts saying it. Maybe he could be a knight in shining armor. Maybe he could end up being *the one*. But it doesn't matter because I can't give him what he wants.

"Now, give me a real reason."

"That *is* a real reason. It's very real to me."

"B, there are other ways to build a family without a baby coming out of your hoo-haw."

I'm so sick of everyone saying that.

"That's not the point. I don't want to build a family any other way. I want to push a baby out of my hoo-haw. Just like everyone else."

She doesn't understand. She doesn't understand what it feels like when your body can't do the one thing it was born to do. She doesn't understand the devastation that comes with not being able to protect your baby from your own damn body. I want to feel a baby kick. I want to take monthly profile photos showing my growing stomach. I want to smile at my husband as we hear its heartbeat for the first time. I want all of that. And my body basically denies me all of it.

"I think I need to give you some tough love, B."

"Here we go."

"I understand that I don't know what it's like. I also understand it might be hard for you to listen to me because of that. I'll never pretend to understand. I'll never know. And I'm sorry I can't share that pain with you. It kills me every day that I can't relate to what you went through. I hate that you have to carry that alone. I feel like the shittiest friend sometimes because I'll just never get it. And I can't be who you need me to be. I'm so sorry for that."

I wipe the tears pooling at the corner of my eye.

"But I am your best motherfucking friend, and I care more about you than most of my family. And I need to be the one to tell you this because I love you so damn much, but you're focusing on the wrong thing. And because of that, you're stuck. You've been stuck for years. And you'll stay stuck if you don't cut your shit out. Stop feeling sorry for yourself."

I flinch, and my tears spill down my cheeks to the pillow.

She continues, "Your ability to have a baby is a small sliver of who the fuck you are. And I know who you are. You're a rock star. You're incredible, whether you can pop a baby out of your hoo-haw or not. And that's what you need to focus on. You're kind and funny. You're an incredible, supportive, trustworthy friend. You're fun, and have layers and dimensions that shine and impress everyone who meets you. Any guy worthy enough will be lucky to have you. Just as you are. Right now."

She pauses when she hears me sniffling. My tears are flowing again, but this time I'm crying for something different.

She repeats it to drive home her point. . . or because she likes to hear me cry.

"You are good enough, as you are. Right now."

I try to speak but my throat is nearly closed up. I take a breath and manage, "I don't know how to believe that."

"I know." Her voice softens. "But maybe you can start by stopping the spiral. Every time you catch yourself thinking you're not enough, remember what I said. Remember that *I* see you. The whole you. Not just the parts you think are broken."

More tears spill over, but these feel different. Cleaner, maybe.

"Thanks, Sara." My voice cracks. " Thank you for that truth bomb. I guess I needed it."

"I'm just glad you didn't tell me to go fuck myself and hang up."

"It could've gone either way," I say, and we both laugh. I wipe the tears from my cheeks. "How were you able to break away from Grady?"

"I made a deal with Evan. If he took the baby now so I could call you, I'll take bath duty tonight and tomorrow."

I roll to my side. "You're the best. Thank you."

"You're welcome. And when you get back to Dallas, you can thank me by babysitting."

"Gladly."

My phone call with Sara was heavy. I've been so focused on my inability to have kids and how that defines me as a woman—on being defective. I've worn that trauma like a badge of honor for years. Unopen to any other options. Focused only on my inability and what that means.

I don't know if she changed my perspective on Javier, but I'm less likely to sabotage the next guy.

Chapter 41

San Antonio

I'm excited to head back to Dallas today, which is unusual for me. It's not that I don't like Dallas—I love it. My friends and family are there. But I've grown to love my life and routines in San Antonio too.

Late afternoon traffic crawls as I head to La Panadería before my flight. The familiar sight of the bakery makes me nostalgic. I've missed being close to my beloved pastries, missed peeking out my window at midnight to watch the bakers working away.

My hand is halfway to the radio when the car jolts and then dies. Every icon on the dash lights up like a Christmas tree. Oh, no.

I try to start the car. Nothing.

I press the brake, hit the ignition button. Nothing.

A car honks behind me. I ignore it while I reach for my purse and fumble through it for the key fob. I press the key fob to the ignition button. Nothing.

More honking.

Shit.

Panic sets in. The rental car sits dead halfway down the city block, parked cars along the passenger side preventing anyone from squeezing past.

I reach into the glove box for the manual when I hear knocking on my driver window.

Manual in hand, I whip around toward the window, ready to unleash on whoever's bothering me. They think *their* day is inconvenienced? My flight leaves in only hours, and I'm stuck with a dead car in downtown rush hour traffic.

The words are already forming on my tongue when I freeze. My eyes take in the familiar sight—the vest, sleeves rolled up, that wave of dark brown hair.

Javier seems just as shocked to see me. He pushes back from the car, rolling his eyes as he presses his palm against his forehead.

Yeah, I'm not particularly happy about seeing you, either. I've got enough to deal with without your icy vibes.

He points down, mouthing, "Window." I fumble for the button and press it, but nothing happens. Fuck. This stopped working too?

"The other window," he says, and I realize I put down the back window.

Oh, hell.

"Will it start?" he asks, his voice dripping with annoyance.

"Sure, I just felt like stopping in the middle of the street, downtown, at the beginning of rush hour, because, why not?"

I raise my hands, flipping them out abruptly to the sides like the stupid shrug emoji I send to Sara when she asks me something I don't know.

Javier looks up the street, his hand resting on the window ledge. I find myself studying his hands—the way his fingers wrap around the frame, knuckles slightly tensed.

"Put your car in neutral. I'm going to push you into that bus lane over there." He points at a bus stop about fifteen feet away. "You're going to have to turn the wheel hard. Okay?"

I nod, unable to speak. Here he is, helping me again. Saving the day, like he's done over and over.

I tug hard at the wheel as my car inches forward. I look in the rearview mirror and see Javier pushing, the muscles in his shoulders straining. A stranger jogs from the sidewalk to help.

Once I'm safely in the bus stop, I put the car in park and hear Javier thanking whoever helped push. I get out to thank him too, but he's already walking back to his car.

I grab my phone to figure out next steps when Javier pulls up behind me, his car's back end sticking out into traffic, forcing other cars to swerve around.

I join him at the back of my dead rental.

"Do you need a ride somewhere?" His voice is monotone, his face absent of the smile I've grown to love.

"I was on my way to the airport."

He nods, not saying anything for a few moments.

"Okay, grab your stuff. I'll take you."

"Wait—what about my rental?"

"Hand them the keys when you get there. They can come get it."

Before grabbing my suitcase, I glance at his car's front grille. The emblem catches my eye—a circle with a cross and snake inside.

Is that an Alfa Romeo?

I remember a sales exec at a conference mentioning the eighty-thousand-dollar price tag after a profitable year. Javier said the hotel had three guest vehicles, but I thought they were all Cadillac SUVs.

Javier opens the trunk as I approach with my suitcase, feeling humble and vulnerable. He says nothing as he loads it, and I slip into the passenger seat.

I feel like a teenager caught driving past curfew, having my father pick me up.

Silence fills the car as I settle into my seat, purse on my lap. Javier gets in, and the scent of cool water hits me like a slap to the face. He says nothing as he pulls into traffic.

This car looks lived in. There are crumpled gum wrappers in the cup holder, a charging cable draped on the console, and it's dusty. The Cadillac SUV was spotless.

"I need to hop on a call. Here, lift your arm." He pulls out wireless headphones from the middle console.

I don't say a word. Instead, I look out the window, wishing I wasn't confined in this space with him. It's too awkward and I hate it.

"Hey, it's Javier. I'm in the car so I don't have the visuals in front of me."

Another thing for him to hate me for. He would've been back at The Elysian in time for this meeting if I hadn't derailed his afternoon.

He sits in silence for several minutes before speaking.

"I looked at the profitability analysis from last quarter. Utilization is inconsistent quarter over quarter. Do we know the driving factors?"

My brows furrow. *Profitability analysis?*

"That's a good approach. We could probably boost profitability by thirty-five percent. What about the restaurant?"

He pauses. I can't understand why a concierge would be so engrained in the hotel's financials. I also hate how his voice affects me, and how his calm authority makes my body betray me. It's very inconvenient.

"Good to hear we have a cushion, but I'd like us to take a proactive approach. Mark, what operational risks do you see over the next three quarters?"

This guy is talking about stuff Sara used to discuss when

she was director of finance. I pull out my phone and open a new browser.

I search "Chief Financial Officer, The Elysian hotel." I need to start somewhere. I scroll, looking for anything that will confirm my suspicion.

"Excellent. Mark, circling back to room revenue—how are the new pricing strategies working?"

I click on an article mentioning CFO and Elysian hotel. I read as quickly as I can. It's about one of the charity events Chremsoft hosted last year and how much money they raised. I skim until I see Elysian mentioned. Then the words hit me like a sledgehammer.

"Holy shit," I whisper.

Javier glances over at me, his jaw tight.

I stare at him with raw fury burning in my eyes. Javier isn't the concierge at The Elysian. He's the fucking *owner*.

I scoff, throwing my phone into my purse and hurling everything to the floor.

Motherfucker.

No longer do I feel awkward. No longer do I feel vulnerable. I'm *furious*. I lift my arm, pressing my elbow against the window ledge, my head leaning against my fist—the same fist I want to slam into his face.

He keeps glancing my way, as if sensing the indignation radiating off me.

He lied to me. This whole time he played the role of concierge while he's the damn owner of the entire hotel. *The owner*.

Do I have *sucker* tattooed on my forehead? I replay our interactions—the bartender calling him sir, Diane hustling him to meetings, him glad-handing suits in the lobby, what Tobias said about women being fortune hunters. They all knew. They all knew, and made me look like a fool.

And this must be *his* Alfa Romeo. Because of course the *owner* of a boutique hotel downtown could afford one.

Why am I fooled over and over again? Why am I continuously let down by every man I meet?

My eyes sting as I listen to him discuss financial projections.

How does he even have time to play concierge when there are owner decisions to make? Sara was only a director of finance, and she lived in meetings.

I stew in silence as we approach the airport, simmering in my own anger. My eyes begin to sting as rage builds inside me. It sounds like his meeting is ending. I want to scream at him.

"I should be back at the office in forty minutes. Talk soon."

Not if I kill him first.

He takes his headphones out, saying nothing to me.

Energy crackles under my skin, my pulse pounding. I'm a pressure cooker about to blow.

In three ... two ... one ...

"Why would a concierge be on a call talking about profitability analysis and financial risks?" I turn my body to face him fully. Javier stares ahead, briefly glancing at me before looking forward again.

He says nothing. I don't have much time as we approach the airport.

"Unless you aren't actually the concierge and you've been lying to my face for months." I lean over the console. "Months." I let that sink in before continuing. "But noooooo, you wouldn't lie. Because you hate liars. You would never put yourself in a position that would make you a hypocrite." Venom drips through my words.

Javier sighs, dipping his head toward me, his face unreadable.

"I am the concierge," is all he says as he weaves between lanes approaching the terminal.

"I can't believe this." I let out a bitter laugh. "You. Are. The. Owner!" His eyes wince at my volume. "You own The Elysian. This is your Alfa Romeo. You lied to me the whole time. You kept me in the dark while your staff kept up the charade, making me look like a damn fool."

His shoulders sink into the seat, but he continues staring forward.

Fine. If he's not going to talk, I have plenty to say.

"I never lied to you about who I am. I'm Brianna, the implementation manager. You waltzed around convincing me you're just the concierge when you're the *owner*."

Javier whips his head toward me.

"*Just* a concierge? Is that not prestigious enough for you?"

"It was a game to you. At the hotel, when we met Stefan, I said I'd never met a hotel owner before and you said something like, 'Maybe they're right under your nose.'" I blow out a heavy breath as realization hits me. "You had so many opportunities to tell me the truth, especially when you were several inches deep inside me."

That gets him.

He jerks the wheel to the departures curb outside my airline and throws the car into park.

"You also had several opportunities to tell me that you weren't single, especially when I was *several* inches inside you."

I think he really enjoys focusing on the number of inches. Let's not exaggerate any more than we have to.

"I am single. I've been single for as long as I've known you. Maybe it's true what they said about you. You run from commitment. A forever bachelor."

Javier's torso jerks back from the verbal slap I just delivered, and I can tell he's fishing through his brain to figure out who said that about him.

The airport worker patrolling the sidewalk glances our way. Our time is limited before he moves us along.

"I'd like to return the words you left me with in the printer room. I thought you were different. But you're just like the rest of them. You're all the same."

I reach for the door handle. "Trunk," I demand.

The moment it pops, I'm out of the car, yanking my suitcase free and slamming it shut hard enough to rattle the back end. I storm down the sidewalk, my suitcase wobbling unsteadily behind me. I slow my pace because Lord knows I cannot give Javier the satisfaction of watching me face-plant again.

My rage is easier than the hurt, so I cling to it. I can't stop thinking about all the opportunities he had to tell me the truth. I'm sad we ended shouting at each other, hate that I can't erase this week like it never happened. The deception shreds through me like barbed wire, worse than it ever was with Griffin or Preston.

I barely remember getting through security, my mind replaying conversations from the last several weeks.

As I approach the food court near Terminal A, I try not to look at the "Local Love" exhibit, but the only piece that stands out is the photo of Javier and me on that damn bridge. I continue staring at it as I shuffle through the crowd, intentionally inflicting more pain on myself.

I. Am. Done.

Dozen Dates

The bells chime overhead as I push through the door of our favorite brunch spot.

As much as I'm excited to see Beck and Sara at brunch, I know they'll want every agonizing detail about what happened with Javier. Five days since the airport drop-off, and the pain remains fresh.

I shove my cell phone into the pocket of my wide-leg pants. The drawstring waistband will adjust to however many waffles I eat today.

Beck is seated at a table near the Bloody Mary bar. Of course she requested that table. This girl pounds Bloody Marys like water. The thought alone gives me heartburn.

"Hey, nice Chucks." Beck nods down at my feet as she lifts her leg from under the table.

"You too," I say, admiring our matching green and white sneakers. We bought them on one of our shopping trips last September. Sara bought a pair too, but chose the red and white version.

"I see you're close to the Bloody Mary bar. You don't even have to get out of your seat, just reach behind you," I tease, settling into the seat against the wall.

Beck stretches behind her to test the theory. "If only the bacon strips were on this side." She sighs, her face turning serious. "How are you doing?"

I stare back at her.

"Never mind. Your face says everything." Beck drinks her water.

Beck avoids feelings, which usually frustrates me, but today feels like relief. At least until Sara arrives. Sara dissects every emotion while offering validation and perspectives.

One time at happy hour, Sara tried prying breakup details out of Beck. Beck put down her nearly full drink, hopped off her stool, and left. Gone. Sara had to pay for the abandoned vodka-soda, which she couldn't even drink since she's allergic to vodka.

"I hope you didn't start without me," Sara says, taking the seat across from Beck. She picks up the menu and hums over the brunch options.

Sara treats brunch like a sacred ritual—already planning next month's before we've ordered. I could take it or leave it. Breakfast isn't really my thing, though I'll demolish a basket of croissants.

Sara leans toward me, elbows on the table, menu in hand. "How are you?"

Beck chimes in. "No therapy sessions until after we order and I have a Bloody Mary in my hand."

Sara scoffs as I chuckle.

"Fine." Sara returns to her menu.

We order our usual. Beck gets chicken and waffles with the Bloody Mary bar, Sara chooses the Santa Fe omelet and pancakes, and I go with brioche French toast, eggs, and crispy bacon.

The server hasn't even retrieved our menus before Beck stands and heads to the Bloody Mary bar. The thought of an endless Bloody Marys makes my stomach turn. Well, they call it endless, but it's five max. Beck discovered that the morning we bought our Chucks. The sodium hit her so hard that afternoon, her feet swelled and she spent the rest of the day praying her new Converse would fit.

We watch Beck assemble her Bloody Mary like it's dinner theater. The glass bursts with tiny beef sausage skewers, cheese, pickled peppers, blackened shrimp, and bacon.

"Do you think she'll stray from her usual?" Sara asks as we watch Beck reach for another bacon skewer.

"She's a creature of habit. She won't stray or even change the order."

Beck is meticulous about her Bloody Mary. The tomato juice gets poured to an exact level, hot sauce and Worcestershire added in precise squirts. The garnishes come in order: cheese and tomato skewer first, then sausage, then two strips of bacon.

"Do you remember when they were out of Tabasco and Beck left, walked to the grocery store, and bought her own?" Sara giggles as the server pours coffee into her cup.

"She's ridiculous. And she left it at the restaurant so no one else would go without."

Beck sits down, taking her first sip, eyes closing as a groan vibrates in her chest.

"Julie might get jealous if she saw this." Sara sips her coffee, smiling.

"My girlfriend knows she sits below most Bloody Mary bars. It was a relationship stipulation." Beck grabs her second shrimp as it tilts from the glass.

"Speaking of relationships." Sara turns my way.

"That was about as smooth as sandpaper." Beck raises her glass to nibble a sausage skewered between red pepper slices.

Sara rolls her eyes. "Our girl has been through the wringer these last few weeks. We need to know how she's doing."

"And who put her through the wringer?" Beck's eyes bulge at Sara while she chomps on bacon.

"As much as I'd love to blame Sara for all this, it's not on her. It's on me. I accepted the challenge, I chose the jerks. Javier was a bonus asshole who wasn't even part of it."

Beck bursts out laughing. "Bonus asshole. That's great."

"It's not great, Beck." Sara scolds.

Beck throws her hands out and mouths "What?"

"Have you heard from him? From any of them?" Sara asks, crossing her arms.

I stare down at my coffee cup, tracing the handle with my finger.

"No. Nothing."

"Wait, I'm confused. Why do you look like your goldfish died?" Beck questions, a square of orange cheese between her finger and thumb. This girl will be full before her actual food arrives.

"Because Brianna actually likes Javier, though she'd prefer to deny it."

Beck nods, tossing the cheese up and catching it in her mouth. I could take a page from her book on emotions. I'm overwhelmed with mine while questioning if she has any.

I sit in silence. A few days ago, I would've rattled off every reason Javier's an asshole who belongs in my rearview mirror. But I've had time to cool off. When I replay our moments together—how he treats his staff, how he lights up around Angelina and Dominic, how he showed up for me when I needed someone—all I see is the good. He's caring, generous, sexy as hell.

But none of that matters. Even if we could fix this, I can't give him kids. And he wants them.

The server delivers our food, placing a tower of brioche French toast in front of me, topped with whipped cream and berries.

The Javier conversation pauses as we devour our food. Beck works through her second Bloody Mary while I slowly drive my fork around my plate, soaking up syrup and powdered sugar.

"So, when are you back in San Antonio?" Beck asks.

"Not for at least another two weeks. Mercury is wrapped up, Delefont needs more time before implementation, and Chremsoft is reviewing their contract. Until they sign, I won't be back."

Sara and Beck eye each other before turning back to me.

"Do you like this guy?" Beck asks, matter-of-factly.

"I... Well, if—"

"It's a yes or no, Bri. Do you like this guy?"

I huff into my coffee mug, liquid pushing over the rim and burning my finger. Shit.

Sara tosses her napkin at me but they both stay quiet.

"Yes."

"Okay. Then, Operation Win-Javier-Back is officially in motion." Beck chomps on a seven-inch stalk of crimson-stained celery.

"You look like Bugs Bunny chewing a carrot," Sara says.

I laugh-snort into my coffee cup, liquid shooting across the table.

"Oh, for God's sake." Sara pushes back in her chair, arms tight against her sides.

Beck pushes her napkin around the table, sopping up my coffee. "I think you even nailed that person walking by."

"I did not!" I shout-whisper, wiping coffee from my nose.

"I think we're done with coffee, B." Sara pulls the mug toward her.

"Or get her a sippy cup," Beck adds, still wiping the other side of the table.

I start laughing and can't stop. Beck and Sara shake their heads, laughing with me. It feels good to laugh with the two people who have my back, who are only assholes some of the time, like when they suggest sippy cups.

"I need to go blow coffee out of my nose. I'll be back."

When I return, Sara and Beck are deep in conversation.

"I was just saying I'll be in San Antonio for the volleyball tournament and I'm bummed you won't be there. I won't have an excuse for avoiding dinner with the assistant coach."

"Since when do you coach volleyball?" I question.

"Since the head coach went on maternity leave." Beck raises her eyebrow. The words hang in the air. "Oh. Bri, I'm—"

This is why I don't talk about my miscarriages. People either pretend they never happened, or walk on eggshells the moment babies or pregnancy come up. It's not that I hate every woman who can have a baby. Not all the time . . .

"Good for her," I say, trying to convince them I'm not bothered. And I'm not. I'm more bothered by Beck feeling she has to tip toe around the topic.

"So, are you going to reach out to Javier?" Sara asks, squeezing lavender lotion onto her hand before offering it to me.

I shake my head. "No. He wants kids. He's so good with them. I don't want to have that conversation and get my heart broken again."

"That's a bit selfish, don't you think? You're not even giving him the choice. You're making it for him," Beck adds.

Sara nods in agreement, adding a follow-up question.

"If he said his niece and nephew were enough, that he didn't need kids of his own, would you want to pursue the relationship?"

I stare at Sara, contemplating how to respond. I know the answer, I'm just too afraid to say it out loud. Of course I would. In a heartbeat. I'd probably already be planning our future together. But saying it out loud puts me in a place where I can get hurt again. Where I can hope again. And hope is dangerous when you've already lost so much.

"Yes."

Chapter 42

Dallas

I've spent the last week and a half at home in Dallas, enjoying my condo more than I have in years. It's nice not living out of a suitcase, and having a closet full of clothes to choose from. I've cooked nearly every night, making elaborate dishes just to use every square inch of my kitchen. Beck's spice blends have become essential—I can't make pasta without Oregano Trail or fish without her Sage Against the Machine.

But more than that, I've come to accept what this space used to be. There used to be a nursery in the second bedroom. The kitchen is where Dirtbag and I opened a bottle of wine every Friday night before I got pregnant. This condo has been a place I ran from, haunted by what I almost had. But maybe I'm ready to stop running. Ready to build something new here, create different memories.

Work has slowed as we wait on clients. I'm working on presentation decks for Chris and about to log off for the day when my phone starts buzzing.

"Hello, Miss Sara."

"So, we're all dressing up tonight because I haven't worn a

nice dress since before Grady was born. Evan's wearing a suit. Even Beck is dressing up. I told her absolutely no Chucks. You're also required to dress up so I feel like more than just a mama. I need to feel like a woman, B."

"It's Tuesday. Why are we dressing up on a Tuesday?"

"Did you not just hear what I said? I need to feel like a wooooooooman and not a milk producer. So. Please send me photos and I'll select your outfit to make sure you match the rest of us."

I roll my eyes as I hang up.

I lay out three dresses on my bed, snap a photo, and send it to Sara. The first is plum with a lace bodice and half sleeves. The second is soft blue satin A-line with a high neckline. The third is a sparkling black sleeveless A-line with a plunging neckline.

> Sara: I'm showing off my boobies tonight, so you must show off yours. Black dress. Non negotiable. See you at 6:30pm!

I'm quite comfortable in my black leggings and oversized Care Bear T-shirt, also a gift from Sara, but if spending time with my favorite people means dressing up, it's a compromise I'm willing to make.

I put the dresses back, noticing my foot no longer knocks the cardboard box. I glance at the empty floor space, my chest tightening with fear that I'm erasing the only proof they existed.

The box sits at my bed's edge like a sacred relic I've protected for years. My hands hover above it, trembling, before my fingertips graze the worn cardboard. I curl my fingers around the edges, feeling how the corners have softened from desperate, middle-of-the-night touches.

I lift the top off and my breath catches. My whole world,

my stolen future, my love that never breathed—all in this box that's become both shrine and tomb.

My hands shake as I reach for the tiny baseball onesie, so small it could fit a doll. The one my baby was supposed to wear home from the hospital. The one Dirtbag brought home with pure joy, his eyes bright as he talked about T-ball games and teaching our son to catch a fly ball. *Our son.*

I reach for the tiny socks next, my vision blurring. These were meant to warm the feet I created from love and hope and dreams.

Light catches something metallic beneath swaddle blankets that smell of lavender sachets. I hook my finger through the delicate string and lift it to catch the afternoon sun. "Baby's First Christmas," I whisper, my voice breaking as tears spill down my cheeks.

Mom and I searched four stores that day for this ornament. I can still feel her hand on my back as we stood in that Christmas shop, both glowing with anticipation.

When I found out I was pregnant, my stomach twisted with worry. We hadn't planned it. But when I held up that curved white stick in our kitchen, his face transformed.

He ran toward me like I was holding the world's most precious treasure, lifting me in an embrace that felt like flying. He spun me around our tiny kitchen until I was dizzy with laughter and love. When he set me down, his hands went to my still-flat stomach, his eyes shining with tears he didn't try to hide.

After that, every time I came home from a work trip, our kitchen counter had transformed into a shrine to our unborn child. A Texas Rangers onesie spread out like he'd been admiring it. Football booties that fit in my palm. Enough baseball bibs to last several months.

His excitement became my oxygen. I'd never felt so cherished, so perfect in my purpose.

A few weeks later, something felt off. I couldn't explain it, but I felt different. Sara kept reassuring me I was fine. Then I started spotting and panic set in. At the doctor, we received the blow we feared. The ultrasound screen that should have shown a flickering heartbeat showed only darkness. Static. Nothing.

"I'm sorry," the doctor said, and those two words detonated every dream we'd built in eight weeks.

The light drained from my husband-to-be's body like someone had opened a valve.

Losing our baby didn't directly send him running to other beds. We initially grieved together, held each other through those brutal nights.

But his family wouldn't let us grieve. They circled like vultures with their expectations and legacy talks, their pointed questions about "trying again" delivered over Sunday dinner like casual conversation.

I wanted to make him happy, to restore that light I stole from him, so we tried again. And my body betrayed us again.

I felt the weight of his disappointment in every room, suffocating me. It was my responsibility to keep our babies safe. That's what mothers do, what our bodies are supposed to do. I was failing at the most fundamental level.

That's when he retreated completely, not just from our bed but from our life. He moved through our days with mechanical precision while I scrambled to fix something irreparably broken—not just my body, but us.

He stopped consoling me, stopped pretending this wasn't my fault. The terrible truth was, I understood why.

He started staying out late, manufacturing excuses that grew more elaborate and less believable. Each lie felt like another nail in our coffin, but I was desperate to believe we could get through it, together.

I took an early flight home from a work trip and fumbled with my keys at our front door, hoping despite everything that I could salvage something from our wreckage.

The sound hit me first—low moaning that wasn't the TV. Then I saw them in our bed, the bed where we'd planned our future and grieved our losses. Her red hair spread across *my* pillow like spilled wine. His hands—the same hands that had cradled my face when I cried—traced her body like she was precious cargo.

I shattered into pieces so small I'm still finding fragments of myself in unexpected places.

He walked away unscathed, shedding our life like a snake sheds skin.

The doorbell cuts through my thoughts like a blade. I wipe my eyes quickly, replace the lid, and carry the box to the living room.

I rehearse what I'll say as I walk to the door.

"Hi," I say, tears welling up. A lump grows in my throat as I stare at him. Everything I rehearsed goes out the window as my mind goes blank.

I wanted to make this easy. For me. For him. The golf ball in my throat is preventing me from forming a simple sentence.

He stands there, patiently, with a half smile, as if he might have expected this.

I hold up a finger—*one moment please*—and turn away before he can witness me completely fall apart.

I walk to the couch, grab the box, and clutch it tightly as I return to the door.

I take a deep breath and hand him the box.

"Thank you for your donation, ma'am. This will be of great

use at the women's shelter." He cradles the box, as if he senses its importance.

Then he leaves with my fallen dreams in his hands.

A gallon of concealer couldn't hide these puffy eyes. I can only hope the restaurant has dim lighting.

> Sara: Just pulled up. If you're not wearing that black dress, do not come out here until you are.

I reach for the Coach heels Javier gave me, my fingers brushing over the soft leather. The memory stings, but I slip them on anyway. My small black clutch barely fits my cell phone, a card case, and a lip gloss.

Sara rolls down the window as I approach the car. "Damn, you look sexy! This is going to be an epic night!"

I twirl, my dress fanning out at the knees. The movement feels foreign, freeing, like my body is no longer tethered, restricted. A warmth spreads through me, different from the hollow ache I've been carrying—like sunlight breaking through storm clouds. My step quickens as I move toward the car and slide into the back seat. "Let's get this party started!"

My words surprise me with their lightness. I think I need this almost as much as Sara does.

"Looking good back there," Evan says, twisting his neck from the driver's seat.

"Right back at you, handsome. I haven't seen you in a suit since your wedding."

"And even that isn't long enough for me." Evan stares down his nose toward the passenger seat.

We spend the next five minutes talking about what we're going to eat. Sara's already studied the menu online, and she probably has it memorized by now. The second we sit down, she'll start rattling off recommendations like she's our personal food consultant.

Sara shakes her finger in the air.

"I need this, guys. I can't tell you how good it felt to put this dress on." Her earrings sparkle from the front seat as we drive under the streetlights.

"I thought you would want some alone time with Evan. I feel bad Beck and I are crashing your romantic date."

I fiddle with my clutch's clasp, the metal warm under my fingertips.

"No way. We get plenty of alone time. We need to feel like we're twenty-four again, without a care in the world."

The phrase echoes in my chest. Without a care in the world. I can't remember the last time that felt possible. But there's a lightness in my spirit now, something I didn't anticipate. The weight of the past has lifted just enough that I breathe a little easier. My sadness lingers like smoke, but it no longer threatens to suffocate me.

Evan turns into the parking lot, and I lean forward to get my first glimpse of the restaurant. The building sits back from the street, hidden behind a charming brick patio that spreads wide like welcoming arms.

"This place is gorgeous," Sara breathes, already unbuckling her seat belt before we've even stopped.

Soft yellow lights zigzag over the patio, casting everything in a warm, honeyed glow. Large whiskey barrels line the walkway, each one topped with succulents and tea lights that flicker in the evening breeze. The romantic atmosphere hits me unexpectedly, and for a moment, my throat tightens.

I stroll down the patio's brick walkway toward the front door, more tea lights flickering on each empty table. The evening air carries the scent of rosemary and grilled onions from the kitchen. My mouth waters at the scent, and I can't remember the last time food called to me this way.

The front door swings open. The handle catches the light first, then a shoulder—dark fabric against the warm glow spilling from inside. A familiar male silhouette fills the archway, and my world tilts sideways.

That dark wave of hair. The way his shoulders fill out his dress shirt, deep purple, the color I told him looked incredible on him. His tailored vest sculpts the body I know by touch.

Holy shit.

Chapter 43

Dallas

My feet root to the ground beneath me. My lungs forget their purpose.

Javier descends the two steps onto the patio, and every molecule in my body screams contradiction—run toward him, run away from him, I can't tell which. He's here, looking like he stepped from my dreams into this impossible moment.

Behind me, Sara's heels fall silent against the brick.

Why is he here? My brain scrambles for an explanation. Coincidence? Business trip? But the way he's looking at me, the purposeful way he strides across the patio—this isn't chance.

He stops three feet away, close enough that I catch his cologne—that cool water scent that lingered on my pillowcase from our night together. In his hands, a pink bakery box tied with white ribbon.

"Hi, Brianna." His voice is softer than I remember, uncertain.

My knees threaten to give out. Two weeks. Two weeks of missing that voice, that face, the way he says my name like it means something.

"Hi." The word barely makes it past my lips.

Sara and Evan slip around us like ghosts, and I catch Sara's quick nod of encouragement before they disappear into the restaurant. The patio suddenly feels enormous and impossibly intimate all at once.

Javier sets the pink box on a nearby whiskey barrel, and the simple gesture, so deliberate, so him, makes my chest ache.

"I need to apologize," he says.

"Javier—"

His hand raises, palm out. That commanding gesture that still feels gentle. "Please. I need to say this."

I nod, throat too tight to speak.

"I kept a huge piece of myself from you." He presses his palm against his forehead, that familiar stress gesture. "I had so many chances to tell you who I really am. Every morning at breakfast. Every time you mentioned the hotel owner." His hand drops. "I chose not to tell you. Every single time."

The admission hangs between us. A couple walks past toward the restaurant, and he waits until they're gone before continuing.

"At first, it was just fun. Harmless flirting with a beautiful woman who made me laugh." Something flutters in my chest when I hear him call me beautiful. "But then I got to know you. Really know you."

He takes a half-step closer.

"I know you choose Room 1010 so you can watch the bakers across the street in the middle of the night. I know you rub your wine glass stem when you're anxious, that you order caramel lattes when you're stressed, that you eat conchas in bed without shame."

A small laugh escapes me through the tears threatening to spill.

"I know you work as hard as I do, late into the night,

making sure everyone has what they need. That you're kind when things go wrong, always fair. That I can read your entire day on your face before you say a single word."

His thumb brushes my cheek.

"I know you're stronger than you realize. That when life knocks you down—literally and figuratively—you get back up. Every time."

I smirk at the last comment.

"Your happiness became the best part of my day. All I wanted was to be the reason you smiled."

Tears start before I can stop them.

"And when I saw those flowers—" He stops, jaw clenching. "When I thought someone else was making you happy, it destroyed me. Because I want to be the one. The one making you smile, sending you bouquets, being the reason your face lights up every morning."

My breath catches. He'd been watching. All those mornings, he'd been watching.

"When I thought someone else was doing all of that"—his shoulders collapse inward—"I completely lost it. And I had no right." His hands find my elbows, tentative, testing. "I should have talked to you. Asked you directly instead of making assumptions."

His thumb traces a small circle against my skin.

"My only excuse—and it's a terrible excuse—is that I was falling for you. Hard. And the thought of losing you made me crazy."

The words echo through me like a heartbeat.

I need to breathe, but my lungs won't cooperate. He's saying everything I've wanted to hear, but there's still so much unsaid between us.

"When Beck came to see me—"

"Beck?" My eyebrows snap together.

"She showed up at the hotel a few days ago." His mouth quirks up. "Told me about Sara's dare. How much you hated every minute of it."

Heat floods my face. Beck actually did it.

"I felt like such an ass. Here I was, thinking you were happily dating other guys when really—"

"Stop." The word bursts out. "Stop taking all the blame."

He blinks, startled.

"I should have told you about the challenge from the beginning." I can't look at his face. "But I took you for granted. Your kindness, the way you always made time for me. You were always there, and I just . . . expected you to be." My voice drops to a whisper. "I was an asshole, too."

The silence stretches. Then his hand rises to cup my cheek, and I lean into the warmth without thinking.

"Well, then, we can be assholes together."

Despite everything, I laugh. And his whole face transforms.

"There she is," he murmurs. "I missed that laugh."

My relief is overwhelming, and more tears threaten.

"Why didn't you tell me?" The question comes out barely audible. "About owning the hotel?"

His hand drops from my face. The pain that crosses his features is so raw it makes my chest hurt.

"Because I'm an idiot." He runs a hand through his hair, messing up that perfect wave. "Because I've learned the hard way that being a hotel owner is a lot more attractive than who I actually am."

I open my mouth to protest, but he holds up a finger—gentle, not commanding.

"I'm not talking about you"—his smile is sad—"But before you? I dated women who were more interested in the hotel owner who gets invited to red carpet events than the guy who grew up sharing a bedroom with his two older brothers."

His face changes, the confident businessman dissolving into someone younger, more vulnerable.

"We each got one Christmas present a year. My mom worked three jobs just to keep us fed." His voice softens. "That kid—the one who wore the same jeans to school every day because they were his only pair—that's who I really am."

My heart cracks open.

"The women I dated? They didn't want to hear about that kid. They wanted the successful businessman who could buy them designer bags." His jaw tightens. "When they looked at me, they saw dollar signs. Not the person underneath."

"Javier—" My voice breaks.

"That's partly why I work the desk, for self-protection. People see me for me when I'm the concierge. But also. . ." He glances toward the restaurant. "I watched owners who never talked to guests, who knew their customers as numbers on a spreadsheet. When I took over The Elysian, I decided I'd never be that disconnected. I want to understand what people need. That's how my hotel thrives."

The pieces click into place. Every conversation, every recommendation, every meeting, every time Diane came hovering.

His hand settles on my shoulder. "I'm sorry you felt like the staff were lying to you. They have strict instructions never to mention I'm the owner. Please don't be angry with them."

"I'm not mad. Not anymore." The truth surprises me. "I understand why you do it."

I study his face in the soft glow of the tea lights. The urge to touch him is overwhelming. To smooth down that piece of hair still sticking up. To kiss him until we're breathless.

But there's still a weight in my chest. One truth that could shatter everything we're rebuilding.

"Brianna." His voice draws me back. "The last two weeks

have been hell. I've missed you so much I could barely function."

My throat tightens.

"I want you back. Not just as a guest—though you'll always have a room at The Elysian." That devastating smile appears. "I want you back. In every way."

He glances at the pink box. "I brought a peace offering. I'm hoping we can pick up where we left off. Specifically, where we left off on a particular night when I was a very happy man in Room 1010."

Despite everything, I smile.

"If I recall correctly, you snuck out in the middle of the night like I was some kind of one-night stand."

His confident expression falters.

"God, I'm sorry about that. It killed me to leave you. I had a stakeholders' meeting at eight, and I was supposed to spend that evening preparing instead of . . ."

"Instead of?"

"Instead of lying in your bed thinking how I could spend the rest of my life waking up next to you."

The words hit like lightning.

My heart soars and plummets simultaneously. Because now I have to tell him. I have to risk losing it all. I just want to savor this moment a little longer before I lose him again.

"Javier . . ." My voice comes out small.

His expression immediately shifts to concern.

"What's wrong?"

"There's something else." I wrap my arms around myself. "Something important."

The happiness in his eyes dims, replaced by wariness.

"Okay."

"Can we sit?"

He nods, retrieving the pink box and following me to a

small table tucked into the corner of the patio. The fairy lights strung overhead cast everything in a soft, romantic glow, which makes what I'm about to do feel even more cruel.

We settle into chairs across from each other. He places the box between us like hope made tangible. I take a shaky breath, fingers tracing the ribbon.

"I love watching you with Angelina and Dominic." The words come out steady, but my heart hammers. "You're incredible with them. So patient and playful." Javier's face shifts to confusion, probably wondering why I'm bringing up his niece and nephew.

His thumb strokes across my knuckles, and I have to force myself to continue.

"And I remember you said you couldn't wait to have kids of your own someday."

The air between us grows heavy.

"I hate that this one thing about me could change everything." My voice cracks. "I hate that it doesn't matter how much we care about each other, how perfect this feels. There's something about me that could end it all."

"Hey." His other hand reaches across to cup my face. "Nothing about you could end this."

But he doesn't know yet.

"I can't have children, Javier." The words tear out of me. "My body can't . . . It's not possible. Medically, physically—it will never happen."

His thumb stops moving. The silence stretches, filled only by distant conversation from inside the restaurant.

I search his face for the moment understanding hits. When he realizes what this means.

"I know how much you love Angelina and Dominic. You light up when you talk about them, when you're planning their visits." Tears stream down my face. "I know you want that for yourself—your own children, your own family. And I can't give that to you."

My voice drops to a whisper. "I don't want you to waste your time with someone who can't give you what you really want."

The words hang between us like a death sentence.

I've had this conversation before. I know how it goes. The gentle letdown. The "You're amazing, but . . ."

He's quiet. Not just a moment—a full, weighted silence. A variety of emotions flicker across his face. Surprise. Understanding. Something else I can't describe.

Then he shifts his chair around the table until he's right beside me.

"Brianna." His voice is thick. "Look at me."

I force myself to meet his gaze, bracing for disappointment.

What I find isn't pity. It's something that looks almost like . . . tenderness?

"You beautiful, incredible woman." His hands frame my face, thumbs brushing away tears. "Is that what you think would make me walk away?"

My confusion must show, because his expression grows even more gentle.

"Brianna, listen to me." His voice is steady. Certain. "You will never be a waste of time. Not to me. Not ever."

I try to shake my head, to argue, but he continues.

"I'm sorry your body isn't cooperating with what you might have wanted." His thumb traces my cheekbone. "But this doesn't change how I feel about you. Not even a little."

His words don't compute.

"You don't understand." I try to pull back but his palms hold me firm. "I can't have children. And if you want—"

"Brianna." He doesn't let me retreat. "I'm forty years old.

My lifestyle—the hotel, the long hours, the travel—it's not exactly family-friendly."

"But you said—"

"I said I thought about it. The way people think about winning the lottery." His smile is soft. "But what I actually want? What I've been dreaming about for months?"

He pauses, making sure I'm listening.

"I want to wake up next to you. I want to share my favorite spots in San Antonio. I want to watch terrible movies together and argue about whether pineapple belongs on pizza—"

"It doesn't. Ever."

He laughs, and the sound breaks something open in my chest.

"I want lazy Sunday mornings and late-night conversations. I want to see your face every night when I come home." His voice drops lower. "I want you in my bed and in my life and in my future. Kids or no kids. You are everything I want."

I stare at him, waiting for the *but*. For the caveat. For him to realize what he's saying. For the finality of it all to sink in. It always comes.

It doesn't come.

"You mean that," I whisper. It's not a question. I can see it in his eyes.

"With everything I am."

"You're not going to change your mind? Six months from now, a year from now, when you—"

"Brianna." He leans closer, forehead nearly touching mine. "I don't need you to give me children. I want all of you. Just as you are. Right now."

Before I can second-guess, before fear can talk me out of it, I lean forward and kiss him.

It's soft at first, tentative, like I'm still testing whether this is real. But then his hands slide into my hair, and he kisses me back with an intensity that erases every doubt, every fear, every moment I thought I wasn't enough.

When we break apart, we're both breathing hard.

"I want all of you, Brianna. Just as you are." He kisses me again, deeper, and I lose myself in the warmth of his mouth, the solid reality of his hands, the impossible truth that I'm enough.

When we finally separate, he rests his forehead against mine.

"I have one question."

"What?"

"Are you ready to see who we really are together? When we're not hiding anything?"

Something inside me trembles—not from fear, but with the overwhelming possibility of everything I've been afraid to want.

"Yes."

"Good." He pulls me closer. "Because if you'd said no, I was going to have to dramatically throw myself into the San Antonio River."

I arch an eyebrow, fighting a laugh. "You know it's only three feet deep, right?"

"That's why it would be dramatic." He grins, then his expression softens. "Ready?"

I take a breath, squeezing his hand. "Ready."

My heart hammers as we walk toward the entrance. Javier holds the door open, and I hesitate for just a second, the weight of what we just promised each other settles in. This is real now. No more hiding. Then I step inside, his hand warm and steady in mine.

We scan the restaurant for Sara, Evan, and Beck. Sara's arm shoots up from a corner booth, waving us over with theatrical enthusiasm.

I glance at Javier as we weave between tables. His familiar

cologne brings back a flood of memories, both good and devastating. My stomach tightens. Are we really doing this?

"They're holding hands!" Sara whispers not-so-silently as we approach the table.

Heat crawls up my neck. Of course Sara would announce it to the whole restaurant. Javier squeezes my hand.

We slide into the booth across from Evan. Beck immediately reaches over to pat Javier's shoulder.

"Glad you made it," Sara says, raising her wine glass.

"Thanks for setting this up." Javier's thumb traces across my knuckles under the table. The small gesture sends warmth up my arm, but my chest still feels tight with unspoken questions.

"I have to say it . . . Brianna's right about those vests." Sara grins.

My eyes widen into what I hope is a threatening stare. If I could shoot laser beams at her right now, I would.

"Oh, and what does she say about my vests?" Javier turns to me, eyebrow raised.

My head drops. Javier nudges my shoulder with his.

"Just don't ever open any of her delivery packages. You'll be scarred for life," Evan jumps in.

Beck leans forward, pointing toward Evan, "Oh, it leaves no scars, I can assure you that."

I shoot Sara my most desperate *help me* look.

"Let's order," Sara laughs out. "I'm starving."

As Sara flags down our server, reality creeps in. I turn to Javier as the practical side of my brain kicks in.

"Wait, are you staying in Dallas tonight?"

His smile fades. "No. I have a ten p.m. flight."

I pause, processing. "You flew here for just a few hours to fly back?"

Sara jumps in, "Of course he did. You're a gem. And he knows it."

Javier nods. "I have a meeting tomorrow morning, but I couldn't wait until next weekend to see you."

I drop my head back. "Diane is going to kill me."

"You leave Diane to me. She won't be an issue anymore."

I'll believe it when I see it.

The next hour passes in a blur of shared appetizers and gentle teasing from my friends. Javier fits in easily, laughing at Beck's stories and asking Evan about his projects around the house. For brief moments, I forget about the ticking clock and enjoy him here, in my world, with the people I care about.

But Sara keeps checking her phone, and I know she's watching the time as closely as I am.

"We should probably head out soon," she finally says, glancing between Javier and me. "Beck's driving us home," she adds. "You two take Evan's car to the airport."

Our drive to DFW passes too quickly. For once, a Dallas traffic jam would be a blessing.

I keep stealing glances at Javier, memorizing this moment. But I can't shake the memory of our last airport drive—him gripping the steering wheel, fury and hurt radiating through me, convinced I'd never see him again. The contrast between then and now overwhelms me.

We pull up to the departures curb. I put the car in park, my hands still gripping the wheel.

"Thank you for tonight," Javier says.

I want to say something profound, something that captures

how grateful I am that he came, how terrified I am that this still might not work, how there's still a sliver of doubt that he'll change his mind.

Instead, I manage, "Thank you for the conchas."

He laughs—the sound I've missed most.

"That's really your takeaway from tonight? Good to know."

For a second it's like before, easy and natural. But then reality settles back in. Four hours apart. His demanding job. My travel. All the things we haven't talked about yet.

"So, what happens now?" My question slips out before I can stop it.

His expression grows serious. "Now, we figure it out. Day by day."

I walk around the car and step into his arms. He holds me close as I press my face against his chest, breathing him in. I want to memorize this—the steady rhythm of his heartbeat, the way his hand cups the back of my head.

When he pulls back, I look up into those dark eyes that have haunted my dreams for weeks.

He kisses my forehead, soft and lingering.

"I'm going to call you tomorrow. And the day after that."

"And the day after that." My voice comes out smaller than I intend.

One quick kiss on my lips—gentle, promising—and then he steps back.

He walks through the sliding doors, his figure growing smaller until the crowd swallows him up.

I stand there for another moment, car keys cutting into my palm, before finally getting back behind the wheel. The drive home stretches ahead of me, but for the first time in weeks, I don't dread being alone with my thoughts.

Epilogue

I study the painting in front of me. Nearly as wide as a king-size bed, everything in it seems larger than life. The ornate gold frame with carved ribbons and curls serves as a statement piece, and the brush strokes reveal blended colors I didn't know existed.

I step back, eyebrows drawn together, scrutinizing the woman in the painting. The artist made her nose a little too large, and a brush stroke makes her cheek look dirty. Her arms look larger, thicker, than the rest of her body.

But the man in the painting? Stunning. The way he looks at her radiates wonder, desire, longing. Love.

A smile grows on my face. Does she know? In that moment? How much he cares for her?

"It's beautiful, isn't it?" Grace says, joining my side. I don't look at her. My eyes stay fixed on the monstrosity in front of us.

From an outsider's perspective, it absolutely is beautiful—the love between two people captured in an intimate moment. But I see it differently. I see confusion. A woman afraid, not of him, but of what he represents. A woman who doesn't realize this moment is her turning point, that the man beside her will change her life because he'll accept her completely, protect her, become her missing piece.

"Do my arms really look that large in person?" I ask Grace.

She glances at my arm, contemplating.

"No. I think it's the lights casting a shadow."

I mull over her answer as I take in the rest of the painting. The stone bridge, the twinkle lights draped across the river, the classic pink tour boat drifting on the water. I remember how excited the photographer was when he ran up to Javier and me that night. He claimed he'd win the Local Love contest. He mentioned our "long stare," and I thought he was being dramatic. But I see it. The way Javier looks at me, like I'm the only thing in the world worth holding.

The intimacy of the scene feels revealing, like a paparazzi capturing a celebrity at their home. It feels exposing, intrusive, like this moment should be private, just for Javier and me. But instead, it's a moment shared with every single guest of The Elysian.

"Did we really need it in the lobby?" I ask, scrunching my nose as Tobias approaches.

"Absolutely. Because nothing says 'back off, fortune hunters' quite like going full Renaissance and immortalizing yourselves in oil paint the size of a city bus. Very subtle, Javier. Very subtle."

I can't help but smirk at his response.

"That has nothing to do with it, Tobias," Grace chastises. "This painting represents all that San Antonio is. The culture, the history, the love Javier has for the city."

"Is that why the city dropped off ten boxes of flyers for the boat tours?" Tobias quirks an eyebrow.

I take one last look at the painting. I can't believe my life is real. Javier is real. The way he looks at me in that painting is real.

When Javier said he was commissioning a local artist to paint the photo from the Local Love contest, I didn't expect the painting would show so much emotion. The artist captured what I tried to hide that night—how badly I wanted it to be real.

Grace heads back to the check-in desk while Tobias follows me to the bar where my laptop awaits, an instant message from Chris flashing on the screen.

"Which venue are you touring today?" Tobias asks, settling onto the bar stool.

"The Chateau del Rio. Have you heard of it?" I click on the IM—Chris needs help locating client data for the San Antonio hospital system he's been chasing.

"No, I'm not privy to the exclusive invites that Javier gets." He sighs. "Someday, though."

Tobias waves his hand in my periphery.

"Geez, Brianna. Could you stop typing for one second? I'm getting a migraine from the light show. Did Javier just hand you a small chandelier and call it a ring or what?" he says, and I glance down at my left hand, the square diamond heavy as it leans to the right.

I smile, captured in memory. Javier took me to dinner on the Riverwalk, then we listened to a band play at the amphitheater we'd been to St. Patrick's Day weekend. And as we walked over the stone bridge, the same one from the painting, he paused. I was looking down the river, a lime green tour boat casually floating our way.

When I turned, Javier was down on one knee, a small red jeweler's box in his hand. I'll never forget his gaze—hope, excitement, and anticipation wrapped into one love-filled expression. He said, "From the moment you walked into my hotel, I knew you were something special. I knew I was in trouble." Then he chuckled. "You came out of left field and I found myself always waiting for your arrival, waiting for Room 1010 to show occupied in our system, waiting to see you in the lobby, waiting to catch a glimpse of your smile." Here he paused before adding, "Even waiting for you to trip on anything so I could come to your rescue." He may have smirked here, but my vision was hazy.

"I want to be your knight in shining armor," he said. "I want to protect you from anything that will steal that smile, that spirit of yours that has become my drug of choice. But I also want to be your partner, your equal, to celebrate your strength, and support your career."

Javier became blurry from the tears filling my eyes. I was so frustrated; I wanted to memorize every word, every detail of how he looked saying them.

"When you came into my life, you turned it upside down, in the best way. You made it easy for me to be myself. You reminded me what it's like to have fun and be silly, hiding between linen carts and getting caught by Diane in the servant's hallway."

I roll my eyes because my memory of that moment includes Diane's heavy stare of discontent and disgust—not exactly blissful.

"You showed me a life so wonderful, I didn't even know could exist."

I breathe heavily as I know what's coming. His hand trembled slightly as he held the box.

"Brianna, I've built an empire. I've won awards, earned respect, created something from nothing. But none of it—not one single thing I've accomplished—matters as much as this moment right here."

His voice broke and he paused, swallowing hard.

"You walk into a room and my whole world shifts. You smile at me and I forget what I'm worried about. You trust me with your heart and I feel like I could move mountains. Every day with you is a gift I don't deserve but will spend my lifetime earning."

Emotion built behind his eyes.

"I love you more today than yesterday, and I'll love you more tomorrow than today." He lifted his other hand, clasping the top of the red box and slowly opening it. Light danced off the diamond.

"Brianna Whitmore, there is no future without you. Will you marry me?"

I grin as I remember that moment—the one I wasn't sure would ever happen for me. The one I almost didn't let myself have.

I had to go through the grieving, the anger, the closing off. It was part of the process. But had I not found the courage to open myself up again, to risk heartache, to trust myself—the thought of what I'd be missing makes me sad.

For years, I blamed Dirtbag for robbing me of my future, my joy, my belief in happily-ever-after. It took me years to realize I had the choice. Had I remained closed off and bitter, assigning that name to every man I met, I would've robbed myself of this. Of the unconditional love I craved but refused to let in, waiting for someone to prove my worth without giving them access to my heart.

Giving Javier my trust was one of the hardest things I did. Even after he flew to Dallas, I didn't believe he'd still want me months later. That he truly accepted all of me. That he was okay not having his own children. But I wanted the happily-ever-after bad enough to keep taking one step forward, each day, with him.

"Miss Whitmore." Her voice comes out cold, breaking me from my memory. "Javier wanted me to let you know his meeting is running over and he should be down shortly."

Tobias, unaware of my history with Diane jumps in with, "Don't come too close unless you have sunglasses, Diane. Brianna's engagement ring is even blinding the guests that walk by."

I side eye Tobias.

Something shifts on Diane's face—something I've never seen directed at me. Is that a smile?

"Don't you have a front desk to run, Tobias?" The smile fades as she scolds him. He says nothing and slides off the stool.

My body stiffens as Diane takes his place, settling onto the stool with ease—something I've never managed to do.

"I hear you're checking out a wedding venue this evening." Her voice is careful, like she wants to say more.

"We are. The Chateau del Rio. Have you been?"

She shakes her head. "No, but I hear it's exquisite."

Her gaze holds mine and I shift in my seat. For a moment, she says nothing, and I brace myself for more criticism. But her expression is different—uncertain, almost.

"I wasn't always a fan of you, Brianna." She says it carefully, like she's trying to be honest rather than cruel. "When you were in this hotel, everything changed."

I look up at her, confused. "Changed how?"

She speaks with conviction, but there's something vulnerable underneath.

"Javier had my staff running out to buy you shoes and pastries instead of turning down rooms. He was late to budget meetings because he was helping you prepare for sales presentations. He stayed here until midnight worried about you when he should've been home resting."

She pauses, and I see it now—not anger, but exhaustion. Fear, even.

"This hotel has been his entire life for years. He built it from nothing, poured everything into it. And then you arrived, and suddenly, he wanted more. He wanted a life outside these walls."

"You thought my presence would hurt the hotel," I say quietly.

"I thought you'd distract him until you got bored and left." She meets my eyes. "I've seen guests who flirt, who see the owner of a luxury hotel and think they've hit the jackpot. They take and take, then disappear. And Javier is left to pick up the pieces and run a hotel that suffered while he was distracted."

"I'm not those women, Diane."

"I know that now." Her shoulders drop slightly. "I've watched you these past months. The way you light up when you walk through those doors. The way you know everyone's names—not just the front desk staff, but housekeeping, maintenance, the night crew. The way you ask Grace about her kids and remember to follow up." She glances toward the painting in the lobby. "And the way he looks at you. I've never seen Javier this happy. This alive."

My throat tightens. I glance down at my ring, then back at her.

"I'm not going anywhere, Diane. So, we can either keep doing this dance, or we can figure out how to coexist. I'd prefer the latter."

She lets out a slow exhale, studying my face.

"I suppose you're right," she says, sliding off the stool. She pauses, then rests her chilly hand on my arm. "He's one of a kind. Don't ever forget that."

She walks away and my shoulders sink. I barely have time to recover when my phone buzzes.

Sara's face fills my screen.

"Hello, Miss Sara," I say, placing the phone to my ear.

"Well, hello! Are you ready for this weekend?"

"Am I ready to start the next chapter of my life? Yes. Am I ready to spend four hours in a moving truck with Evan complaining about traffic and bathroom breaks? No."

She laughs. "Well, it's either he stops or we pee our pants. Lord knows he avoids Grady's wet diapers. So, Evan will pick up the moving truck Thursday night, and Friday we'll head to your condo . . . for the last time. Beck wrangled some of her basketball players to help—something about alternative strength and conditioning—so we should have you packed and ready to head south within a few hours."

The irony hits me—I avoided my condo for years, running from the memories and "what could've beens." But now that I've sold it, I'm mourning it. I'm mourning the time I wasted being angry and feeling sorry for myself instead of moving on.

"Are you excited to move into Javier's house?"

"So excited. He has this gigantic walk-in closet with a fancy dresser island in the middle. We could perform a dance routine in there."

"I can't wait. This is what you've always wanted. I'm so glad you didn't give up." She pauses. "And you're welcome for that dating challenge, by the way."

I roll my eyes. My dating challenge was a disaster—but the worst moments brought Javier and me together.

Two strong hands squeeze my shoulders, lips pressing against my cheek.

"Sara, I gotta go. Javier and I are checking out a wedding venue tonight."

"Oh! I can't wait to hear about it. Take pictures! I'll see you at home in a couple of days."

I hang up, closing my laptop and stumble off the bar stool like I always do.

"Everything good with Sara?" Javier asks, weaving his fingers with mine. We head for the printer room.

"Yes. Just finalizing plans for this weekend."

I look at him and we both grin, knowing the significance of what this weekend means to both of us.

As soon as the door shuts behind us and any pretense of patience disappears. Javier grips my waist, turning me, guiding me until the counter hits my back. His lips crash into mine. His hands slide down to my thighs, gripping and lifting me onto the counter in one smooth motion.

"I missed you more than I can explain." His mouth finds my neck and I lean back into the cabinets, a soft groan escaping.

"It's only been a few hours," I say, breathless, heat flooding through me.

"Still too long." He smiles against my cheek before kissing me again. Our mouths find their familiar rhythm, desperate at first, then softening to something slower, more intentional. His forehead rests against mine.

His expression turns thoughtful, reflective.

"I thought I knew what love was supposed to look like. And then you crashed into everything with your stubborn independence and that smile that undoes me every single time. And somewhere between you tripping over your suitcase and me staring up at the ceiling in Room 1010, I realized—this is what I've been waiting for. You're not my missing piece. You're my whole damn puzzle remade. I can't wait to open my eyes and find you there—every morning, for the rest of our lives."

My throat tightens, emotions swelling in my chest.

Six months ago, if someone told me I'd be making out with

the owner of a boutique hotel, an engagement ring the size of Texas on my finger, and happier than I've ever been, I would've said they were crazy. That version of me allowed no room for possibility, for love. I had to change how I viewed the world, how I viewed myself.

And thank God I did.

Because this? This is just the beginning.

THE END

Acknowledgments

I have to start with Paige. You are the bestest friend I could ever ask for. Thank you for letting me talk your ear off about this book for the last two years. You cheered me on through every draft, every doubt, and every victory. You're a gem with your sticky notes and markers, and I love you to pieces. I'm so grateful for you.

Sitting in that writing class was hands down the best decision I made. J.J.M. Czep, this book is so much better because of your instruction. And yes, because of you, there are minimal adverbs! (Even my editor was impressed!) Thank you for sharing your expertise and for being such an incredible guide and friend.

One coffee meeting changed my life. Ginger Scott, your time is priceless, and I still can't believe you said yes when I asked you out for coffee way back when. You've been a cherished friend and mentor, and this book straight up wouldn't exist without you. Thank you for believing in me.

Working with my cover artist was a dream. My Lan (@laolanart), you're professional, talented, and you made the whole process so easy. I was impressed at every single step, and I'm obsessed with what we created together.

My editor deserves a standing ovation. Brenda, this book is the best it could be because of you. When you first opened my manuscript, you had a *lot* of work ahead of you (sorry about that). Your expert eye caught everything (and I mean everything). Thank you for making this story shine.

My parents are the real MVPs. Mom and Dad, you've been there for all the highs and lows of this journey (okay, mostly highs). You drop everything to listen to me ramble about what I learned, who I met, what I figured out. I couldn't have done this without your support. Love you both so much. And sorry about the spicy scenes.

My beta readers gave me the gift of their time and honest feedback. Emma, Paige, Alexis, Jengles, Dawn, and Yanela—you're trusted partners in this wild process, and I'm so lucky to have you in my corner.

My sensitivity reader helped me tell this story with care. Tricia, thank you for helping me represent women who've experienced miscarriages with the honesty they deserve. Your thoughtfulness and willingness to share your insight meant everything. You helped me tell this story with authenticity, and I'm so grateful.

To my bootcamp crew—Kerri, Sydney, Colleen, Laura, Melinda, Debbie, LarEssa, Angie, Grace, Sherri, and Heather—you are the best hype squad a girl could ask for. Thank you for making me feel like I'd already hit the bestsellers list. I'm so incredibly lucky.

To Kelly, my proofreader, friend and soul sister—you've known me through many chapters of my life, not just the chapters in this book. You've looked after my wellbeing in every sense of the word. Your intelligence, resilience and the way you truly see me means more than I can express. Thank you for bringing your sharp eye and caring heart to both my health and my book.

And to you, the reader—thank you for taking a chance on me, a debut author who's just trying to tell a good love story. I hope these characters stick with you the way they've stuck with me. I hope you laughed, maybe cried a little, and closed this book with a happy sigh. Here's to happily ever afters—on the page and in real life.

About the Author

With a full career in corporate learning, Megan traded spreadsheets for slow burns, witty banter, and characters who feel like your best friends.

Megan's heroines are over 30, smart, capable, and a little quirky—the kinds of women who know what they want in life... except when it comes to romance. She specializes in warm, character-driven stories where sparks unfold slowly, emotions run deep, and joy is always on the horizon.

When she's not writing, Megan leads workshops that help writers grow their confidence, build meaningful connections, and the mindset needed to pursue their dreams. Her favorite part? Watching writers realize they don't have to do this alone.

She lives on coffee, New York–style pizza, and the chaotic love of her pet birds.

Find Megan online www.megancrawfordwrites.com.

- instagram.com/megancrawfordwrites
- facebook.com/megancrawfordwrites
- tiktok.com/@megancrawfordwrites

www.ingramcontent.com/pod-product-compliance
Lightning Source LLC
LaVergne TN
LVHW030332070526
838199LV00067B/6245